A BEAUTIFUL SUMMER DAY IN THE HAMPTONS AND THEN A SUDDEN DISASTER . . .

ZOE CARTER—The rising young star. Her bitter past only fed her brilliant promise until the shattering accident threatened to end all her dreams.

WILLIE CULPEPPER—The important playwright. Only Zoe could give his new work meaning. He would do anything to speed her recovery—or recoup her terrible loss.

MAXIMILIAN WARD—The malpractice lawyer. He rode the crest of disaster. Zoe's tragic misfortune could make him a wealthy man.

BARNEY LUKACS—The brilliant neurosurgeon. He had grown to love Zoe. He was sure his lightning-quick decision had saved her future . . . until the healing stopped and his season in hell began. . . .

HAD IT REALLY CALLED FOR . . .

Extreme Remedies

Extreme Remedies

ELLEN HOPE MEYER

A DELL BOOK

Published by
Dell Publishing Co., Inc.
1 Dag Hammarskjold Plaza
New York, New York 10017

ISBN: 0-440-12428-X

Printed in the United States of America

First printing—March 1982

To Bob DeMaria, who contributed
largely to the making of this book,
with love and admiration

"Extreme remedies are very appropriate for extreme diseases."

—Hipprocrates

AUTHOR'S NOTE

I owe a lot to people who, in their various fields, were generous with their knowledge and time. My thanks to Dr. Lawrence Kaplan, Dr. Jan Mashman, Dr. Sanford Scheman, Dr. Jean Valiquette, and particularly to Dr. William Bloom, who has been extraordinarily helpful. Dr. Bloom's intelligence and enthusiasm, his willingness to introduce me to many aspects of surgical practice, and his detailed research into medical malpractice have all made it possible for me to write this book. My thanks also to John Lyddane, Bruce Habian, and Terry Lasky, all of whom were patient with my ignorance and instructive in the intricacies of the law.

PART I

....

1

Somebody asked Zoe if she'd like to go next. There was a little stir of excitement in the boat, because she was attractive, and no one knew her very well, and then Krupp asked Zoe if she knew how to do it. Even when she said she did, he went on to explain how. "Just make sure you've got your arms straight out," he said, "and don't try any fancy stuff. Let the boat do the work."

Zoe nodded. Her green eyes shone. She paused a moment on the edge of the coaming. "What is that song from the play?" she asked Freddy. "You know— the one about the watery grave?"

Freddy, who was driving the boat, said, "Oh, yes." He was smoking a joint. He had a long thin face, thick steel-rimmed spectacles, and a cloud of fuzzy gray-blond hair. He stood up, keeping one hand on the wheel, and cast his eyes to heaven. "I'm looking for Jordan, Lord," he shouted ecstatically.

> I'm looking for a watery grave.
> I want to leave below this sinful soul
> I'm looking to be born again.

Zoe turned her face up, too, while he was singing. She raised her arms and turned her hands, with a little flutter, palms upward in a gesture of devotion.

Her head was quite round, as though she were only fifteen, and poised on her slim neck like the bud on a windflower. She stood there for a moment, fixed in the crystal of a clear noon, and then she grinned.

"I'm going to be baptized, chaps. G'bye." She flapped her hand and dove in. The water was green and clear, with a slight swell, and they could see her pale figure underwater as she swam away.

Culpepper was sitting up front next to Freddy. It was his play they were talking about; Zoe was his discovery. She was perfect, he thought, for the lead. One of those translucent green lunar moths who flew in his window on summer nights, splendid and infinitely vulnerable. He moved a little so that he could see her between the others, where they were sitting in the stern. His glasses were speckled with salt, so he took them off to wipe them. By the time he got them back on he could feel the first surge of power in the boat and then, between Krupp's bony shoulders and McGregor's great dark furry chest, he saw her catch the surge and rise up over the green swell like a flapper's Venus, skinny and triumphant. Then McGregor stood up, spilling his martini and shouting in his actor's voice, "Gad, she can do it," and Culpepper lost sight of her.

As Zoe began to feel her balance, she saw McGregor over the white stern of the *Ariadne*, his plastic glass toasting her. She laughed: what an *actor*. He yelled something at her, but she couldn't hear it. She waved and began to lean out. The long trough opened out in front of her, covered with its intricate maps of foam. She went for the wave on the side and hit it just right, and jumped, and headed back across the trough. The speed picked up. She curled over the other wave, catching a wing-splash of water, and back again. She began to feel the rhythm, the surge, the power, the slap of wind against her frame, the whole orchestration of birds and boat and sky and cutting water. There she was, coursing freely over the wild and pitted surface of the globe, and only one tight cord connected her to the tangle back there, the nitty gossip and feuds and the terrible personal crosscurrents and everybody swelling themselves up. How glorious to cut the cord and inhabit only, forever, these pure realms of wind and speed, of coolness.

Culpepper watched her for a while. She looked enchanting. Then he turned his attention to his other guests. They were practically family, in the odd way that people from theatrical companies draw together. Culpepper, in that sense, was Big Daddy. He was not just a playwright, but one whose plays had been translated into ten languages, produced in Paris and London and Rome and in smaller cities all over the globe. In theatrical circles he was a powerful man, though there was nothing in his looks to show his talent and intelligence or his overwhelming success. He was a plump short man with a sensitive face. He wore a tropical shirt and a battered felt hat that came down around his ears.

Culpepper's most recent play was *Sister Glory*. It was a religious play, almost a musical, about a decadent woman who falls in love with a Pentecostal preacher and gets born again. Zoe was cast as Sister Glory, the reborn heroine, and Kevin McGregor as the preacher. Freddy Troy was the composer. He was still rewriting some of the songs, although the play was about to go into rehearsal. Culpepper had invited them out to his house in Easthampton for the weekend along with Lester Jones—the director—and his wife, Mimi. A last fling before the hard work began. They were working already, though; that was clear. They were half into their parts, singing the songs and quoting the Bible and trying devotional attitudes. Laughing at themselves, but getting into it.

Culpepper looked at them with satisfaction, even tenderness. This party was his production, just like the play. The lovely white boat, the flat spread of bay ringed by islands, the gulls, the cast. Even the weather was perfect, he thought. Nature: the ultimate stage designer. After the waterskiing he planned a luxurious picnic on Cedar Beach, near the lighthouse.

McGregor wanted another drink, so Culpepper opened the picnic basket. It was fitted with brass and leather, thermos jugs and cut-glass containers, glass plates, brass knives and forks with polished black handles. He wondered what there was for lunch. He'd asked for smoked oysters and pressed duck, but he'd left the rest up to his cook. It was almost lunchtime.

"Hungry?" he asked Freddy. "We ought to stop soon."

Freddy was fooling around, putting the boat through some rather close curves. He turned toward Culpepper, his pale eyes swimming behind his spectacles.

"Wherefore should I hunger," Freddy asked, with a distant childish smile, "when I am filled with the Spirit?"

"You great oaf, you're stoned out of your mind." Culpepper put his pudgy hand on Freddy's forehead. The skin felt windblown, but hot underneath. It was damp.

"You'll have to cool out, my darling, or we'll terminate your command."

Freddy giggled and peered through the spray-covered windshield. Culpepper took the thermos of martinis. He closed the basket and slid along the seat toward the stern. Zoe was coursing along behind them, leaning back with one foot in the ski and the other pushing against the rope. She looked slender and vibrant, and she was laughing. Even from that distance her orange lipstick showed up against the pearly colors of the shore. What an actress she'll make, Culpepper thought. She was stiff, right now, reserved. But he would shape her. He would release her terrific talent, and after a few weeks' rehearsal she would rocket right out of herself.

Everyone was watching her, but McGregor turned and held out his glass for a refill. "I'll have some more of that," he said. "How about you, P. J.?"

Krupp turned and shook his head. The P. J. stood for Philip James, harmless names in themselves, but Krupp was a journalist and he liked the tough sound of his initials. They worked for his byline; they worked in real life. He was a square Teutonic character with one glass eye and a blunt corny way with words, and it was that talent which appealed to Culpepper. Krupp, who longed to break out of the Long Island scene, was writing a journalistic biography of Culpepper. "Don't get stuffy, dear," Culpepper had said. "I don't want anything scholarly. Just hang around, when you're free. Do something impressionistic and colorful. If the scholars like it, I'll sue you for libel." Krupp worked for the *Island News*, Long Island's largest daily.

"I've had enough," Krupp said. "How about some grub, Willie?"

"Soon. Soon. When Zoe's finished out there."

"I don't know why you serve this poison," Mimi Jones said. She adjusted a ragged silk fringed rose-printed shawl around her bathing suit, a tarnished black affair which hung loosely over her spreading flesh. "Martinis are dated, Willie. Never mind, I'll have a beer."

Lester went to get the beer. He didn't drink, but he was a little high on grass. The boat took a sudden turn as he brought the bottle. He slid across the cockpit into Krupp, who said "Watch it, chum," and put out a hand to steady him. The beer shot out and fell over McGregor like a fountain.

"Damn it, Lester," McGregor said, his deep musical voice rising above the sound of the motor. "Just look what you've done." He took a towel and started to mop his eyes and his curly beard, and then his minimal blue bikini. He had a jackknife, which hung down between his legs, tied to the drawstring at the waist. He wiped it carefully.

Mimi was watching Zoe, who seemed to be taking a break, skiing along straight and easy, looking around her. The *Ariadne* came out of its turn. The rope tightened. Zoe jerked backward; one arm shot up in the air, and she caught her balance.

"Y'know, Willie," said Mimi, "I think we ought to relieve Freddy. He's wilting."

"*Wilt*ing," said Krupp. "Man, he is gone. Bombed. Wasted. Ripped. Spent. Zonked. Inoculated."

Lester laughed. "Fried. Burnt. What else? Wiped out. Fucked up."

"Hey, Freddy," roared McGregor. "Move over. I'm going to drive this tub."

Freddy held on to the wheel and ignored him. "Willie, listen to this," he called. "Everybody listen. Here's your missing music, your lost chord. It just came to me." He began to hum in his terrible stoned composer's voice. "Here it is with words:

> This lady came to the . . . temple
> from the palaces of Mammon
> her throat was hung with diamonds
> rubies in her ears . . .

* * *

That's how our Sister Glory
came to the knowledge of Jesus' love
and in that knowledge she was born again.

How's that for music?" Freddy swung the wheel and the boat took a wide turn.

"Hallelujah," said Lester. "I like it."

"Let's take it from the top," Culpepper said, waving his finger. "All sing. One, two, three."

They all sang, even Krupp. They raised their arms, palms upwards, and threw back their heads. *"Glo-ry. Glo-ry. And in that knowledge she was born again."* They smiled at each other. Laughed. McGregor hugged Mimi. Mimi wiped her eyes.

"It's a great number," said Lester.

"Hey, look at Zoe," said Krupp. "She is really tripping." And indeed, Zoe was doing an angel. One leg straight behind her, one arm stretched out to the tow rope, one flung wide: her head was thrown back and her perfectly modeled child's face, with its wide mouth and deeply rounded eyelids, caught the sunlight through a storm of brilliant droplets.

"Troy, you asshole, turn, *turn*."

Heads whipped around from Zoe to Freddy. *Christ,* thought Culpepper. Freddy was still conducting with two fingers, speeding through the blue haze toward the long black dock that stuck out into the bay between two beaches. McGregor and Krupp jumped for the wheel at the same time, wrestled for an endless moment, pulling it in opposite directions. Freddy gazed at them. Then McGregor wrenched it to the left and the boat swerved violently. There was an instant when the pilings seemed to loom, and then they pulled away. Culpepper was trying to shout in his breathy treble, "Zoe, let go. Zoe, let go."

Then McGregor yelled too. Zoe's eyes opened, flashed green with surprise. She let go the rope.

She saw the *Ariadne* veering off. Culpepper yelling soundlessly. Mimi beside him. The sandy strand, marsh grasses stiff and precise. The dock right beside her as she skidded: each board wonderfully clear. The high pilings, scored with ropes and cuts and pricked with nails, reared erect and blackened as she tried to wipe out in the kindly water, loomed rigid as she turned her face away, crying, "Father, father, *don't*." There was a tremendous blow, and the water received her.

2

Not very far away, a sandy spit reached for perhaps a mile into the bay, white in the heat of noon. A sailboat coasted along its shore, carried by the current. The sailor, a man in his early forties, fooled around with the trim, but it was no good. The wind had died. The sails flapped with the motion of the boat.

He smiled. He'd come out here to think about something, and now there was nothing else to do but think. Too bad. He settled back against the stern and put his feet up. The sun was directly overhead, dimming the sky around it. Toward the horizon the air got thick and hazy and violet blue. From where he lay, he could see Gardiner's Island floating like a pond lily.

He unzipped a black portfolio that lay on the seat beside him and took out a letter, but since he'd read it several times already, he waited, thinking. He did not look altogether relaxed. He looked like a man of vivid intelligence, in whom thought only just controlled the habitual desire to act. His body was tanned and vigorous, his eyes reflected the blue around him. His curved mouth, neck, the way he carried his head: all had the same quality of sensuality and control.

The letter was from the University of Kansas Medical Center. He read it again.

* * *

Dear Barney,

It's been a while, but I have finally gotten my-self into a position where I can offer you a job. I've been working steadily on the cobalt insertion project that we started at Hopkins (we have a topnotch radiologist), and I'm beginning to have some success with it. I'd like to have you with me. You'll receive a formal letter from the Medi-cal Center. They'll offer a full professorship—starting salary in the seventies—with teaching responsibilities, clinic, and so forth. But this place is research-oriented, and we'll have plenty of time for that project, as well as other lines of exploration.

You're wasting yourself in practice, as you well know. I'll bet you're opening them up like frogs to see what makes them tick. Why don't you get off the pot, Starsky, and join

yours, faithfully, in detective-land,
Hutch

Barney folded the letter and sighed again. He didn't know which way to go. He was successful here. He hadn't liked it at first; he was unhappy, the hospi-tal was small, the other doctors dull. He'd kept his nose to the grindstone, made friends, gotten refer-ences, gotten himself established at St. Mark's. Served on committees. Put in extra time in the emergency room. Forged for himself, in fact, a lucrative practice in neurosurgery in an area where the population was small and the referrals few. After the divorce he'd been glad to do it; it was a form of oblivion. He'd played the horses too. Jogged, drank: anything.

But the practice didn't satisfy him. He loved

research. He liked to use his mind rather than his hands. For years he had been absorbed by the geography of that giant cauliflower, the human brain. No organ in the body was so complex, so enigmatic, or presented so many areas for original exploration. No other research was so technically fascinating, either, crying for the development of devices and tools for approaching disease and malfunction. He loved the field. He had given it up for his wife, who wanted something she wasn't getting out of life and who even then had divorced him, after he had gone into private practice, and moved, and was making a hundred and fifty thousand a year. She had taken the girls and left him up the creek *sans* paddle, working his ass off to make the alimony payments.

There's the rub: the alimony. How could he pay the alimony if he took this appointment? What did you do? Did you go back to court and face the angry woman, describe your new circumstances, and ask them to reduce the payments? Would they do it? When clearly you could make more?

After taxes and his malpractice insurance he'd have maybe fifty thousand a year. Less. Could Connie and the girls make out on half of that? They'd survive, he thought, but it would be rough on Piri. *Piri.* He smiled. She was his favorite daughter. Remote, grave, beautiful Piri, deaf and dumb since birth. He wished she were with him now, brown and composed, lying on the deck in the sun, communicating soundlessly. She went to a special school in Illinois, an expensive special school. On a reduced salary that would have to stop.

Barney read the letter again. He wasn't so sure about Kansas. He had a bad feeling about it: cornfields, tornados, Aunty Em and the hired hands, the years ticking by while everyone sat with folded hands and watched the clock. What to do? Which way to go?

He lay back again, and let the sun pour through him. There were advantages here. His practice was hardly boring. It was full of incidents, life-and-death decisions. There were always interesting dilemmas, how to approach some awfulness in the head—a subdural, an aneurysm, a deep tumor. But in the end, it was just maintenance. Basically, he didn't want to patch up old tires; he wanted to figure out *how* to patch them up. So he saved a person's life: what was a life in the parade of lives that marched across the continents and across the centuries? But to make a discovery about how to save lives, that was universal, redeeming. What to do? How should he be spending his life?

He was forty-two, and time was slipping away. He wanted to do something meaningful. Still, it was only August, and he had a month to think about it. His ship-to-shore sounded. Its buzz was distant. He was so deep in his thoughts that he barely heard it. They say that a dream, which seems as long as a movie, actually takes place in a split second before you wake up, set off by a noise or smell, or by a psychic event. In the same way Barney's conflict was polarized by the bleeper. There was the effect of a flash bulb. On one side, lit up by a negative flash, lay Kansas and salvation; on the other, the joys and seductions of his present life.

Two years ago, having established himself at St. Mark's, he had moved to East Hampton. He rented a remodeled carriage house on the estate of J. Willard (Willie) Culpepper, the distinguished Southern playwright. He acquired a Porsche and a stainless steel tennis racket, a bunch of smart, articulate friends, a nifty girl friend, and the gift of gab. He'd taken up

the piano again—at one time he had trained for it—
and now he played music hall songs ("Put on Your
Ta-ta, Little Girlie"), and he found that he was actually in demand around the Hamptons. Most of the
people he knew wrote or acted or painted or else
managed the work of people who wrote or acted or
painted. They talked a lot; they liked him and he
liked them. It was fun, and it had opened up ideas
and areas of speculation that had never before been
part of his life.

The bleeper sounded again, and Barney opened his
eyes. The bay looked like the aftereffect of the flash
bulb. It was white. The sand spit and beaches were
glaring white, but drenched in blue, as though the
lower part of the sky had run down on to them. He
realized that what he wanted was the Kansas job, but
in Easthampton. It was impossible. He got up—what
to do?—and moved automatically to answer the
bleeper.

It was his answering service. "Dr. Lukacs. You are
supposed to call this number right away. They said it
was life or death."

Barney said okay and got the number. He didn't
recognize it. It didn't even ring once before Culpepper was on the phone.

"Barney? My God, Barney, my God. I can't believe
it. It's Zoe. She's paralyzed. It's unbelievable. One
minute we're . . . Where are you?"

"All right, Willie. I'll come. Tell me what it's all
about." He had assumed his professional voice.

Culpepper explained. ". . . So we circled back
and Krupp dove over and dragged her into shore. He
used a life-saving hold. She was flat on her back, on
the beach . . . unconscious, I think, and then she
began gasping. She motioned toward her back with
one arm."

"Did she say anything?"

"No. And she's dead white. Her legs don't move. What should we do? We called the police."

"Wait a minute, Willie. Let me think. Exactly where are you?"

"Perrson's dock. You know, Bait and Tackle?"

"I know it."

His auxiliary motor wasn't all that strong. It would take him about forty-five minutes to get in to shore, maybe less. The girl had a spinal cord injury of some kind below the neck. Bone spicule perhaps, penetrating her cord. It could well be a situation where every minute would count. His mind was racing; he could see several configurations, each worse than the one before. Perhaps the cord was concussed or contused. Perhaps it was compressed. If so, could it be decompressed? He gazed back toward the shore from the cabin.

He could get the ambulance on its way: from St. Mark's to Perrson's would be a good half hour. Some time spent moving her. Probably an hour and a half altogether. If only he could freeze the situation . . . his mind caught on the word, and he remembered some hypothermia experiments he'd done on cats. He'd been following research that had been done in Minnesota. Cats which had injuries that should have paralyzed them would recover—some of them—if you froze the spinal cord. He didn't know, with humans. Perhaps the cord was too deep. It was certainly worth a try.

"Listen, Willie. I'll get an ambulance under way from the hospital. Meantime, don't move her. And for Christ's sake, don't let anyone else touch her. Keep her flat on her back. Yes, on the beach. Get ice. *Ice*. Get all the ice you can get hold of, right off. Make a bed of ice all around her. Dig into the sand

underneath her back and shove the ice in. Keep
bringing more ice—Perrson's will have it—keep packing it. Mountains of it. I want her half-frozen by the
time I get there. Don't worry if she passes out. Now,
hang up and go to it; I'll get there as fast as I can."

He thought again quickly, then called the hospital.
He alerted radiology and cleared the operating room.
Then he instructed the ambulance orderly.

"I want oxygen, cooling blankets, ice packs. When
you get there, give her twenty-five milligrams of
chlorpromazine. What? Yes. Lower body temperature.
And fifty of the Decadron. And hop on it, Joe. I
think time is important for this one. I'll be there, I
hope, before you get her loaded."

As it happened, he beat the hospital ambulance by
about five minutes. The fire department was parked
up on the beach road; he could see the red lights
flashing. He looked at his watch. It had taken him
thirty-five minutes to get here. He wished he had his
stuff with him. Culpepper was standing on the beach,
a childish figure wearing a black turtleneck shirt and
pants. He waved Barney in with his short arms, but
the beach was pebbly and Barney steered for the
floating dock near the shore. Four figures stood helplessly by a pale body. Ridges of seaweed and straw
made a pattern around them. A fifth was collapsed
on the beach. Another, a fireman, made for the dock
and caught the rope which Barney threw him. He
made a quick hitch with it and gave Barney a hand
on to the dock.

The girl was beautiful. Her long body was tumbled
on the beach debris at an odd angle, and in her oyster bikini she looked elegant and strange, something
else that had come in with the tide. Her astonishing
green eyes were wide open, looking straight up at the
sky. Her mouth, which still carried traces of orange

lipstick, was softly opened. She breathed gently, all on the surface, as though trying not to disturb anything inside. Cracked ice, the kind they use to keep fish cool, was heaped and melting all around her.

Barney kneeled beside her. "Zoe, can you hear me? Zoe?"

She didn't answer. He put his hand on her shoulder. Consciousness appeared slowly in her eyes, and pain, and slowly she focused on him. She was clearly afraid to move a muscle, even her mouth.

"Zoe. My name is Barney Lukacs. I'm a doctor and I have to examine you. You are going to be all right." *God help me, I hope so,* he thought, and then controlled the thought in case she felt it.

"Let me see you move your hand. That's good. Now the other one. Now your leg. No? The other one. Okay, don't worry about it."

He reached his hand in through the ice to feel her back. Slowly, from the cervical to the dorsal, down the familiar spinal bumps. Ah, there it was. She winced. D-8 or D-9, he thought. His hand was numb by the time he brought it out. "Has anyone got a safety pin?" he asked.

There was a pause, some shuffling. A hand reached out. Barney took the pin and began to test the right leg for sensation. There was no response to the pinprick all the way to above the belly button. Then he pinched her firmly on the lower calf, catching the Achilles tendon, and she gasped. *Thank God,* he thought, *there's still some action there.* On the left side there was a faint response to the pin.

"Now, Zoe," he said, "I honestly think you can move the leg on this side." He touched her right hand. "Try it." He put his hand under her knee. He could feel the muscles move, and the knee pulled itself a couple of inches off the sand.

"Fantastic," he said. "You can't feel it, but you did move it."

They could hear the siren in the distance.

"Okay, pal. Let's try the other side again." No movement. "The foot." Nothing. He tried the pin. She winced. He pricked the big toe and said, "Move that." She winced; it moved ever so slightly. The hospital ambulance pulled up over the crest of the beach and the noise died away. Two men jumped out with a stretcher.

"When you get there," said Barney, "take her straight into X ray. They're waiting for her. Get an a-p and lateral of the dorsal spine. Alert Dr. Foote for a consultation."

Culpepper was silent. Ahead of them the ambulance flashed and screamed, en route to St. Mark's. Following it, Barney drove automatically, thinking how to conserve time once they got to the hospital, and what he might find if he opened up that back.

When they hit Sunrise, the ambulance began to pull away. Barney looked at Culpepper. "I know you love this bomb, Willie, but it belongs in a museum." It was a 1929 Packard, big and ponderous. There was a sliding glass door that closed behind the front seat, and a speaking tube to communicate with the back. The dashboard was dazzling. The car ran sedately down the highway. The ambulance had disappeared.

"It doesn't matter, they'll get her into X ray without me."

"What do you think?" asked Culpepper.

Barney didn't answer.

"Is it a broken back?"

"I suppose that's what you'd call it. But what kind of broken back? She may have some fractured vertebrae. What have they done to the spinal cord? Is it

compressed? Penetrated? Will surgery help? The
spinal cord is the lifeline from the brain to the body,
and it is one of the organs which cannot repair itself.
Can't tell until we've seen the X ray." They were
silent for a moment. Then he said, "She's quite beautiful. Who is she, anyway?"

"Zoe Carter. The lead in my play, *Sister Glory*. I
had some of the cast out for the weekend. She's new;
you won't have heard of her. One of a million hard-
working actresses who come to New York from Talla-
hassee or Topeka. They live in rooms and do bit
parts or commercials, night clubs, whatever they can
get, and nobody ever heard of them."

Culpepper fluttered his fat hands. His Southern
voice fell into a kind of rhythmic chant. "They con-
sume, during this period, a mountain of hamburgers,
oceans of that cheap brownish coleslaw that comes in
little—*pleated*—paper cups. They work in Broadway
eateries when they have to, scummy fly-brown places
full of other actors and actresses who are out of work
and who are eating hamburgers and coleslaw, and
they try to work the graveyard shift so they'll have
the daytime free for auditions. There are those who
spend their whole lives that way, and those who
don't, who slip away, go home, or take to drink or
find jobs as secretaries in some towering—*alumi-
nium*—advertising agency."

"Where's Zoe from?" asked Barney.

"Atlanta," said Culpepper. "She is different . . .
special. She's one of those rare ones, who pound and
hammer at themselves until they're truly tempered in
the fire. Who kill themselves, becoming what they
have to be. They kill their personal selves to become
their artistic selves. She's the real thing—an actress! If
she doesn't come out of this . . ."

"That would be rough," said Barney. "But we can't

tell yet, Willie. The spinal cord is irreplaceable. It runs through the spinal canal. The spinal canal is a hole in the center of the vertebrae, and the vertebrae make those bumps on your back. The cord is damaged in some way. She seems to be suffering from what's called a partial Brown-Sequard syndrome. On the right side below the waist there's motion but no feeling; on the left there's feeling but no motion. It's a semiparalysis, to oversimplify."

Culpepper hunched himself up against the door and stared out the window at the passing cars.

The Packard was even slower than Barney expected. By the time he arrived at the hospital the X rays were already posted in the viewing box. Dr. Austin Foote, the neurologist at St. Mark's, had seen them and had seen Zoe.

He was a big man with a barrel chest and a limp. He carried an ebony walking stick with a silver knob which he swung in a military style when he walked. He tended to poke at things with the stick, or hit his leg with it to make a point. In the back rooms of the hospital they called him, without affection, the Colonel. He had a short fuse.

He met Barney in Radiology and they looked at the X rays. The films were poor. She must have coughed at the wrong moment, and the technician hadn't given it enough juice in the lateral view. In spite of the blurring the fracture was visible, a definite crack on D-10 and several vague small lines on D-9. There was a small dislocation, quite clear, of about three millimeters.

"Substandard pictures," said the radiologist. "Poor quality. Let's get her back for another. I can do a tomogram if you want."

"No, thanks," Barney said. "I think it's clear enough. I can see the fracture, but it's not enough to account for the symptoms. There's a bony fragment in there somewhere." He turned to Dr. Foote. "Let's get her down to the OR. Are they ready?"

Foote looked at him. "OR?" he said. "Aren't you sort of rushing things? It's not so clear as all that. Maybe it's just a fracture with swelling. Decadron would reduce the swelling and decompress the cord. That may be all she needs. Get another X ray. Aren't you going to do a myelogram?"

"I don't think so. Look here. Here's the dislocation. Here's the fracture. It's not up here or down there. Of course, I can't be sure what will have to be done until I get in there, but you can *see* where the trouble is."

"But I'm not at all sure you have to go in, Barney. You need more information. A complete study. With the legal climate as it is, you're risking a malpractice suit."

"I've gone to a lot of trouble," Barney said, "to get this patient from the beach to the operating room in the shortest possible time because I believe this is a case where every minute counts. I don't care about all your damn routine. The X ray shows clearly the location of the bone injury. It's slight. It may not tell the whole story. Remember, Austin, she has a partial Brown-Sequard; there's got to be some little spicule sticking in there, and the longer it stays the more chance there is that it will damage vital tissues. I want to get it out, and I'm sorry, but I'm taking her down to the operating room. This isn't a teaching hospital, it's a practical place for saving life and limb, and that's what I mean to do."

"Barney, you're a fool. Good medicine requires certain simple objective routines. You rely too much on your judgment, which can't always be accurate, and on your goddamn knife. One of these days you'll be up shit's creek, and you'll deserve it. They'll sue the pants off you." He took a silver pen from his breast pocket and wrote firmly on the clipboard. "Decadron. Consider decompression." He handed it to Barney. "There's my consult. I haven't written decompression indicated, because I'm not at all sure that an operation is called for. The rest is up to you." He turned and walked stiffly out of the room, putting his stick down firmly with each step and then releasing it with a little angry flourish.

Barney stared after him, his heart sinking. Austin was a dogmatic old fusspot, but he was good. Principled. Pompous. Infuriating. Was he right in this case? No, Barney thought. I'm doing the right thing. You can kill a patient trying to avoid a lawsuit. Foote and he had equal rank at the hospital, but in some areas their functions overlapped. It made for some friction. He could refer the matter to the Chief of Surgery, but that would take time too. Zoe was his patient, not Foote's. His mind was made up. He would operate.

Lizzie Auerbach poked her head in the door. "All set, Dr. Lukacs," she said.

It was cold in the operating room. The walls were covered with white tile. The patient was already unconscious, on her belly with bolsters under her chest and pelvis. She was swathed in pale green cloth, except for the place on her back which was prepared for the incision. Translucent plastic surrounded that area, wrinkled like old skin. In the middle a slit exposed a long thin island of flesh, bright and innocent under the lights.

The tables stretched across her shoulders, spread with green cloth and covered with steel instruments. Lizzie, the head nurse, rearranged them, explaining what she was doing to her assistant, Gloria, who was learning the ropes. The circulating nurse spread a green cloth on the floor to receive the sponges for counting. The anesthesiologist checked his arrangements, the screen which described the patient's heart, the automatic breathing which went *shush, shush, shush.* Plastic tubes hung from above the patient's legs and disappeared under the cloth, feeding the body and removing its urine. The orderly brought in a suction pump.

Assisting was Gerry Rubin, orthopedic surgeon at St. Mark's, in a green robe. He beamed the lights where he wanted them, chatting with Raines, the anesthesiologist, about a friend of his. It seemed that there was a spot in Southampton for a practicing orthopod. His friend was qualified. *Shush, shush,* the automatic breather. *Shush-shush,* the plastic slippers that everyone wore over their shoes. Gloria made a joke, and Lizzie giggled. It was about her boyfriend. Barney took a last look at the X ray in the view box, and then he felt the vertebrae on the patient's body, counting up to the one which showed the fracture on the X ray.

The first cut: blood leaped from the white skin. Retractors. Subcutaneous tissue. Now he could feel the spinous processes, those flanges on the vertebrae which make the bumps on the backbone.

The second cut: electrocut, through the fascia. The periosteal elevator pushed the muscles away. Gerry pulled back the musculature with an army-navy retractor. The field was open. The suction pump buzzed and snuffled. Hemostats hung on the edges of the wound like piglets suckling at a sow.

"More saline," said Barney. "Irrigate."

Now he could see the spinous process, and the lamina which projected like wings of bone on each side. There was the obvious fracture, at D-10, just as it appeared on the X ray. Now he knew where he was. The one above it would be the delicate one.

"Where's my Leksell?"

Lizzie put it in his hand. He bit the bone with it. He took off the processes and lamina above and below the fracture.

"More of the bone wax, please. Get it soft."

Blood was oozing from the bones into the field.

"It's too stiff. Get it soft."

"We have been," said Lizzie, rolling the stuff between her fingers.

"Suction," he said to Gerry. "Irrigate. Suction. Oh golly, sponge. Touch me. No. This is no good, Lizzie."

She handed him the bayonet forceps, so he could see over his fingers.

"There. Now touch me." Gerry touched the forceps with the electric cautery. The current snapped as it ran down the forceps and cauterized a blood vessel.

"Again." The field was clearing. At D-9 there were fragments of bone that didn't show on the X ray. Cautiously Barney removed some splinters of bone. Then he approached the broken vertebra. He wiggled it gently, took off the spinous process, what was left of it, and bit off the lamina. He didn't want to push any bone fragment farther in, so he was abnormally precise and slow. He pulled out another splinter. He could see the epidural fat. It lay grossly on the dura, the thick leathery coating that protects the spinal cord inside its bony canal. The blood welled again, overrunning the fat and finding its way over the edges of the wound. It ran slowly into the wrinkled plastic, following the ridges.

"Suction. More wax. How's she doing?"

"Okay," said Raines.

The sponges, pieces of gauze with tails of green rib-

bon, soaked up the blood. The tails hung down between the gleaming retractors. As the sponges
saturated, Gerry took them out with forceps and
threw them away. Jean circled around and retrieved
them with a large forceps, and laid them out in rows
on the cloth. Occasionally, she counted them.

There was lots of blood: too much. They sucked
and sponged it away. When he could see the fat
again, he began to dissect it, and for a few moments
he could see the dura itself, pinkish-gray and shinier
than anything else around. Inside it would be the
spinal cord: contused? Irremediably compressed? He
hoped, actually, that it was merely punctured. It
would simplify everything if he could find a bone
fragment in the dura, and remove it, and let the
wound heal. Then the patient might recover without
too much loss of function. If the cord had been bent
and severely pinched, rather than punctured, it
would likely never recover, like a garden hose that's
been compressed and the kink never comes out. Austin Foote came in to watch, walking slowly—*tap, tap,
shush-shush*—across the floor.

Barney couldn't see much wrong with the dura, except that there ought to be more pulsation. It must
be terribly swollen. He felt gently with his finger, lifting the fat with his forceps: nothing. Nothing. What
was he doing in there, if there was nothing the matter
with the cord? The blood started to flow again, and
the field filled rapidly. Why so much blood? Bone
oozing, blood welling from somewhere.

"Suction," he said quietly, so as not to show his
sudden self-doubt. He looked at Austin Foote; maybe
the old man was right. *Have I made a mistake?* he
thought. *Have I rushed in too soon? Damn it, maybe
she didn't need surgery, after all.* There was a ner-

vous vibration in his hands, but it didn't show. He kept his voice steady and conversational.

"Suction, please. These fresh trauma cases are bloody as hell. How is she, Bob?"

"Pressure's dropping a bit," Raines said. "We'll need more blood."

"Get it," said Barney. Gerry pulled the green tails and got rid of the ones that were full. The new ones filled with blood immediately. The plastic was beginning to look like a vast natural crater, running off in thick waterfalls.

"Sponges," said Barney. "Not enough sponges. Get a whole box of them and lay them out up here where I can reach them. Clear a space on the table." He thought of Zoe's elegance as she lay tumbled on the beach. "Patties. Where's the patties?" He stuffed the small sponges into the opening. "Where is it all coming from?"

Gerry shrugged. "It's those dural veins, Barney. Hell to control. Better you than me."

It was mindless ad lib. Barney always talked while he worked. "I hope it's not the Adamkewicz," he said. He was trying to find blood vessels in the wound, so that he could cauterize them, but because of all the blood he was working blind. He picked up one with his forceps and said, "Touch me, Gerry."

Gerry buzzed the forceps. Snap.

Barney found another one. Gerry was changing sponges.

"Touch me. Here. No. Is the juice on?"

"To thirty."

"I can't hear it. It's not working." Blood welled, up and out and onto the plastic sheet and down. It dripped steadily into a pan on the floor.

"Thirty-five. Forty."

"It's not on. I can't hear it."

"Forty-five." Snap.

"There we go."

Barney picked up an epidural vein. "Touch me, Gerry. Ah. That should do it. No. Damn it all, let's get some more of those vessels." He was cauterizing blindly to stop the flow. It seemed endless. There was an awful silence in the room, except for the mechanical noises.

"Where's that blood?" Barney asked. Raines spoke on the intercom again.

"It's coming."

"Let's check those bolsters," Barney said. "Maybe they've slid together." If they had slipped under the belly, the transmitted pressure might be causing the flow of blood. Or perhaps it was just pressure from the swollen cord.

"Here we go, Gerry." Snap.

"And again."

The blood arrived, and Raines's assistant hung it up. The field was clearing a little.

"Gerry." Snap.

"Oof," said Barney. "That's better. Irrigate."

As the blood cleared, the dura came into view again. He thought he could see a depression in its surface, way over to the left.

"Sponges. More saline."

Was there something there? He reached with the forceps, felt the contact, though he couldn't really see too well. There was something. He closed with the forceps and pulled; there was a spicule of bone, wedged-shaped, perhaps half an inch long.

"Christ," he said. "There's the bastard." He laid it fondly on the green tablecloth. The tension went out of him. "Oh, you beautiful baby, we've got you now. Send this down as a specimen, Lizzie." He looked at

Gerry in pure delight, and Gerry smiled back at him. The bleeding had subsided.

Barney cauterized a little more and cleaned out around the dura. There was a longitudinal slit in the pinkish membrane, emanating watery spinal fluid.

"Four-oh silk," Barney said.

He put two stitches in it and began to clean up before closing. The operation was justified. The patient had a good chance.

"We were lucky," he said. "It perforated the dura longitudinally. You remember that guy, Di Napoli?" Gerry nodded.

"He came in with a bread knife in his back," Barney said to the others. "His wife put it there. It went right through the cord and into the vertebral body. But it went in straight up and down, not across the cord. It spread the fibers, but it didn't sever anything. He walked out as good as new. Went home, killed his wife, and now he's in Sing Sing. If this spicule had gone in sideways, we'd be rained out."

He didn't look at Austin Foote, but went straight out and changed. He was supposed to find Culpepper in the coffee shop and let him know how it went.

3

It was a quarter to seven. Maximilian Ward opened his eyes. Sun was coming through the venetian blinds in heavy golden stripes. It fell across the turquoise bedspread and picked out the orange lights in Carole's hair. She was pretty, but some of the excitement had gone out of their affair—at least for him it had. He didn't love her, but she was useful and reliable. An ordinary woman with an ordinary job. She was an accountant at the hospital. She was divorced, and she had two children, and Max was aware that she had great hopes of him.

He nudged her. She woke up, her face puffy in the dimness. She smiled and rolled toward him, interlacing her legs with his. He pushed her gently away and kissed her on the cheek.

"I've got things to do this morning, Carole. Be a good girl and get the paper. And don't get mad. It's nothing personal."

Carole got out of bed. Her short slip fell flat across her breast and belly, and her nipples stood up under it. For a moment he had regrets. She put on a skirt and blouse and went out without saying anything.

Max put her pillow on top of his and lay back. He hoped she'd bring some coffee too. He looked around the room. It wasn't where he'd meant to be when he decided to move out to this neck of the woods. Aside from the bed and the dresser, there was a dinette table with a plaid formica top and four wrought-iron chairs, another formica table which he used as a desk, and beyond them a kitchen niche with cupboards and a stove-sink-refrigerator unit littered with last night's dishes.

It wasn't Watch Hill, not by a long shot: lazy summer days in the old beach house, with his mother and sisters, tea and decorum and tennis, and the sound of piano lessons from another room.

His father had been Judge Theophilus Ward. He was always closeted in his study off the hall; bookshelves filled with heavy volumes; green glass-shaded lamp; beveled glass set into the study doors; little Maximilian looking in. He would never *measure up,* little Max, with his toads and his tantrums.

He never did. He failed at Columbia, failed at Brown. Failed at everything. It was better after his father died. Relieved from the pressure, he found he could actually accomplish things. He got through N.Y.U. and law school. But still the pained and grating thing inside of him pushed and pushed, and still he managed to do everything wrong. Attorney for Lamonte and Rainer on Wall Street, and married to Nina Lamonte, he failed to keep his hands out of the till and failed in discretion and failed eventually to keep his license.

It had taken him seven years to get back to square one: reinstated in the bar. He never got Nina back. By then he had been a legal clerk in Providence (where his father had been on the Supreme Court), a driller on an oil rig off Galveston, a real estate salesman on Greater Exuma. He'd learned a lot. He learned that it wasn't worth the effort of failing because nobody noticed. He learned that he wanted profoundly to be established. He wanted to hang out his shingle in a beautiful place, and to find a specialty that would bring him gorgeous financial rewards: he wanted success most desperately. One big case would do it. The right case.

The door opened, releasing a blast of early sunshine. Out there, beyond the porch, was the beach and the flat blue of the Atlantic. Children were hustling around already, playing frisbee. Carole came in and closed the door. She could barely see after the brightness outside.

"No, I didn't bring coffee," she said, "but I'll make some."

He put on his bathing suit and opened the venetian blind. As usual, it went higher on one side than the other. The newspaper was on the formica table, so he sat there. Carole brought the coffee over.

"No cream?" he asked.

"There's only milk."

He unfolded the paper. Occupying a large part of the front page was a photograph: a wonderful pure face with a remote look and a wide thin mouth. The headline under the picture read: SKI ACCIDENT FELLS ACTRESS, PACKED IN ICE. The article was by P. J. Krupp.

A promising young actress was seriously injured in a waterskiing accident in the Hamptons yesterday. Zoe Carter, twenty-nine, who was recently cast as the lead in Willie Culpepper's new play *Sister Glory*, was said to be in guarded condition at St. Mark's Hospital. A weekend outing that included many members of the production ended in disaster as the young actress crashed into the pilings of Perrson's dock while skiing. The cause of the accident remains unknown.

By coincidence Dr. Barney Lukacs, the neuro-surgeon from St. Mark's Hospital, was sailing nearby and was reached by ship-to-shore. Before starting for the scene of the accident Dr. Lukacs directed that Miss Carter be packed in ice, a technique known as hypothermia, in order to freeze the site of trauma before the patient's condition began to deteriorate.

Lester Jones, who directs all of Culpepper's plays, and the well-known actor Kevin McGregor obtained the ice from Perrson's Bait and Tackle Shop, and carried it down to the beach where Miss Carter was lying on the sand. . . .

The patient was taken by ambulance to St. Mark's in Waterville, where Dr. Lukacs operated on two broken vertebrae in her back and removed a fragment of bone from her spinal cord. In spite of a general optimism at the hospital, the future for the young actress is still in doubt. Dr. Lukacs could not be reached for comment. . . .

There was a row of smaller pictures below, showing Culpepper, McGregor, and Lester Jones.

"Hey, you didn't tell me about this," Max said. He spread the paper in front of Carole.

"No. The operation is a big success. Or everybody thinks so. Barney found a piece of bone sticking into the spinal cord, and he pulled it out. She's in Intensive Care."

"But for Christ's sake, Carole. This is the kind of thing I have to know about. When was the accident?"

"Around twelve thirty. Yesterday."

"What was all the ice for, anyway?"

"Barney's brainstorm. If you can operate quickly

you may be able to save an organ. If you have to wait for hours, freezing can keep everything, well—frozen—until you get to it."

"Was the operation smooth?"

"No. I heard it was difficult. Dr. Foote had an argument with Barney. Really chewed him out."

"Why?"

"Didn't want him to operate yet. Also Foote wanted a myelogram. Another diagnostic test."

"Carole, keep me posted. Get a look at her chart, everyday if you can. And get me Xerox copies of her file. Can you do that?"

"I don't know if I can. It would look funny, me hanging around the ICU. I'm an accountant, not a nurse."

"Well, forget the chart. Can you get hold of the file?"

"Honestly, Max, it wouldn't be easy." She leaned back in her chair and crossed her legs. "I'd have to get around Lizzie somehow."

"But you can do it? You did it with that laminectomy."

"Yes, but that was ordinary. This Zoe's a celebrity."

He studied her as she hesitated. It was a kind of silent bargaining in which she seemed to be weighing the risks and rewards, and in which he seemed to be considering the right strategy.

"I could lose my job," she said. "What would my kids do then?"

"Carole, I need you. There may be something really worthwhile in this. And if there is—" He moved closer to her. She pouted. He put his arm around her waist. "If I can just get hold of something big, you may not need a job." His features became ambiguously gentle.

"What do you mean?" she asked.

"Who knows? We might even get married." He tightened his grip, pressing her against him. He was tall and muscular. She had to look up to him. She held back, caught between suspicion and desire. "I don't know, Max. You get me all confused."

He smiled. "Well, let me clarify things for you." He kissed her, once, twice, at first gently, then more passionately, trying to conceal his insincerity and apparently succeeding. She melted. She agreed. They went back to bed.

They made love in the tangled sheets, a fragrance of coffee in the air. He kept his full weight from her body. She rose to him, her eyes closed. It was good—almost domestic. And afterward she said, "Did you mean it, Max?"

"Did I mean what?"

"About getting married?"

"Why not? All we need is a real break—something like this actress case maybe. Do you know what kind of money is involved—"

She cut him short. "All right, Max. I'll try. I promise. But if I get caught—"

He stopped her with a kiss.

Zoe lay motionless on her bed. Everything around her was simple. There was no light there, but the chrome pipes which formed her cubicle gleamed in the dimness, and the white curtains which hung from them forced a cube of reflected light. The fourth wall was open. Zoe could see other cubicles, and the nurse's station in the center of the floor: shaded lights and starched white figures moving without sound.

She was not herself. Something abominable had happened to her, but she couldn't remember what it was. The whole middle of her being was filled with pain and her mind with confusion. She didn't understand why she wasn't home with her father and her little brother. Instead she was in a hospital. She tried to remember what had happened. It seemed to her that she was being punished for something. Yes, that was it. She remembered Mr. Emmett, very red in the face, marching her into the principal's office. She couldn't remember what she'd done. Something.

The school must have notified her father, because there he was the next day in the darkening kitchen, peeling the last bits of bark off a willow switch, and saying coldly, "I told you, Zoe, I told you a hunnert times. I just won't have it." He was a big man, thick, with a greasy windbreaker and a red plaid shirt under that. Some people thought he was good-natured; he was always joking and he had a great time out with the boys. In fact, it seemed to her that he'd just come in from one of those expeditions—out in the woods somewhere, drinking and hunting. "Well, I'm going to learn you this time. It ain't easy for me, girl, trying to bring you up without no mother."

She couldn't speak. The radio was on, a yellow dial on the shelf over the stove, and she could hear her brother Buddy crying from his little room off the kitchen. "Lemme out," he called, all choked up. He was frightened. She wanted to go to him, but she didn't dare. Her father whistled the willow branch through the air, and it hit the kitchen light, which started to swing in a crazy way, lighting up the old refrigerator and her father's face, distorted by the sudden shadows.

She panicked. She ran for the door, but the stick whacked down on her shoulder. She threw an arm up to protect her face, and the next blow caught her in the middle of the back. The radio was playing *Gonna rock, rock, rock,* and Buddy started screaming. Her father bent her over the table and pulled down her panties, and she felt the stick on her buttocks, and then she too started to cry in utter confusion and pain and humiliation and then—what? She couldn't remember. Her mind clouded with nausea, and she was filled with an unreasonable sense of alarm.

There was a tiny red point of light: the nurse's station. She fixed her mind on it. The pain was bad, but she could contain it as long as she didn't move and didn't let herself think about it. He must have beaten her, and then taken her to the hospital. Was that possible? She was uneasy. It seemed to her that something was wrong with her comprehension.

A door opened and white light fell across the floor. A tall figure in a jacket walked over to the nurse's station. There was a stir of excitement, low voices in the gloom. The tall one looked over to her cubicle and spoke to the others. One of the smaller figures detached itself from the group, became larger, entered her place. A light came on. A hand on her forehead suddenly, horribly, made the connection between flesh and thought, and as quickly she was in chaos. Pain invaded her and she opened her lips and moaned.

The tall one arrived at her bedside.

"Temperature?" he asked.

"It's 101.5," said the nurse.

"Okay. Give her a sponge bath, Mary. Aspirin. We'll need a CBC, and get another one in the morning, please."

His hand came down toward her eyes and rested on her forehead. Zoe gave herself up to it, and to the sense conveyed by the hand, that things were under control. He nodded at her.

"Some temperature. It's par for the course. How are you feeling?"

She didn't want to speak or to move. It might confuse her again.

"I know," he said. "Terrible. You'll go back to sleep now. Just let me try one or two tests first." He pulled the sheet back and took something out of his pocket.

"Do you feel that?" he asked cheerfully.

A tiny pain crystallized on her left leg. She nodded reluctantly.

"That?" She nodded.

"That?" She nodded again. His face lit up.

"That was your right leg, my dear girl. You had no feeling there before. That shows real improvement." He pulled up the sheet.

"The nurse will give you something for the pain. See you in the morning." He nodded at her and walked away, stopping briefly at the nurse's station. He spoke there in a low voice and moved on, until he got lost in the square of light where the door was open. His footsteps squeaked as he went down the hall.

In the morning Barney examined her again, methodically testing every group of muscles in the lower limbs. The left leg, which had been immobile on the beach, now gave evidence of a small but definite increase in capability. Her response to the pin was more pronounced. On the right side, where there had been no feeling, there was now a faint reaction.

Barney was pleased. He went down to the coffee shop to meet Culpepper, who was waiting to hear the results. Culpepper was sitting at a table in the corner, next to a group of doctors. He had his eyes fixed on *The New York Times,* but Barney could see that he was listening to the doctors' dialogue.

"Someday I'll go to the theater and hear about that

fractured kneecap," said Barney, laughing. He sat down. The waitress arrived and he ordered coffee.

"How is she?" asked Culpepper.

"She's better," Barney said. "There's marked improvement in some areas. In fact, it looks good. But we won't know for a while how it will turn out. The back has sustained two massive traumas, the accident and the operation itself. There's a lot of swelling, but she's on steroids, which should reduce it. In a few days I'll have more news for you."

"I guess what I have to know," said Culpepper, "is whether or not there is some hope that she'll be able to act in my play. Rehearsals are suspended—the whole production is suspended. Everybody's on my back. There's money involved—the lot of them are still on the payroll."

"Yes. Well, there's nothing I can say. Today, that is."

"I want Zoe, nobody else. The producer wants to get another lead."

"Tell him to wait a week."

"A week. That's thousands of dollars you're talking about."

"I'm a doctor, not a businessman, Willie. Ask me again in a week. Even then it may be only a guess."

Barney became aware that someone was hovering by his shoulder. He looked up. It was Austin Foote. He introduced him to Culpepper and Foote sat down, leaning his stick against the back of his chair.

"I expect you're here about Zoe Carter?" he asked Culpepper. He automatically started to rearrange the table, wiping off the surface in front of him. His hands were heavy, and he wore a gold ring with five small diamonds set into it. He put the salt next to the pepper and moved them both so that they stood in a pair next to the sugar bowl. He collected the empty sugar wrappers and started to fold them into thin rectangles.

"Yes," said Culpepper.

"Austin is a neurologist," said Barney. "He can probably tell you more about Zoe than I can."

"I can't tell you anything," said Foote. "Let's just hope the damn operation was justified."

Barney was embarrassed and angry. "We removed a spicule which had penetrated the dura. What more do you want?"

"Did you now?" asked Foote. "That spicule could have come from anywhere. Too much blood to see."

"Exactly what are you saying, Austin? That I lied? That there was no spicule?"

"Of course you found a spicule," Foote said ironically. "If you hadn't there wouldn't have been any reason to operate."

Barney controlled his anger. "He doesn't like being upstaged," he said to Culpepper. Then he stood up suddenly. "C'mon Willie, let's get out of here."

Foote stared after them, his face flushed. "Did you want to order, sir?" asked the waitress.

"No," he growled. He picked up his stick and walked stiffly out.

"What's his problem?" said Culpepper.

"He's Mount Sinai trained: the neurologist does the thinking, according to them. The neurosurgeon's only a technician, like a high-class carpenter. Besides, Austin likes to be in charge," Barney said, sitting down again.

"Obviously," said Culpepper.

"He and his friends have a tight hold on the local medical community. None of them like the fact that I've moved out to East Hampton. I'm outside the group. They're ingrown. They live in hundred and fifty thousand dollar homes and only see each other, and only talk about medicine, golf, and how the liberals will ruin the country."

Culpepper smiled.

Barney looked at his watch. "Listen, Willie, I've got another patient to see here. I'll see you later."

"Come up for a drink. Bring Maggie if you want."

"Good. Ciao."

Culpepper always enjoyed the approach to his house. Lawns lapped the road on either side, broken by handsome elms and long curving driveways. Enormous houses, high hedges.

The Packard purred along in the sunshine, and then turned into his driveway. On the right was the Gatehouse cottage, which he rented now to Barney, rising from a soft blur of rose bushes. Its gabled windows reflected the sun, and it was topped by an improbable turret that overlooked the drive.

The tennis court was beyond. After that the carriage house, where horses and chauffeurs had formerly lived. It now housed the Packard, and Culpepper had his studio upstairs. The main house was a large shingled structure with white trim, a mansard roof, and many deep porches. It faced inland, but in back it gave on to the dunes and the great Atlantic.

Culpepper parked and walked up the steps to the front porch. Ngiep opened the door. He was a Vietnamese refugee who had gotten out early, and then worked in a dreary restaurant in the city until Culpepper "discovered" him. Slight and clean-looking, he was now the chief steward of Culpepper's principality. His name was anglicized as Yip.

"Mr. Hunt on the phone, sir. Two, three time. Most compelling."

"Urgent."

"Yes, sir. Urgent."

"Thank you, Yip. I'll call him."

Culpepper paused at the opening to the living room.

"Yip, the *dahlias*," he said in tones of awe and pleasure. And indeed, in the midst of the huge white, light room burned a heap of purple and crimson blooms, massed gloriously in a deep copper kettle.

"Thank you, dear boy," he said. "Thank you." He kissed Ngiep gently on the lips.

Culpepper went to the telephone.

"Billy King Hunt? This is Culpepper speaking . . . Yes. Yes, we are all deeply concerned about Sister Glory. About Zoe . . . No. He can't or won't give us a prognosis at present. However, he is hopeful. He'll have news for us in a week . . . Yes. Yes, I know . . . Billy, I know all that. There *is* no one else—absolutely and most finally not anyone else . . . Calm down. *Du calme, mon cher.* Listen: here is our plan. We suspend everything for a month. Hold up production. Discharge the cast. Most of them will wait. Zoe will recover. The doctor seems very optimistic, but he doesn't want to say so yet . . . Yes, of course I know him. He's my tenant . . . No. Of course we'll have to finish the sets . . . Yes, and stored. We'll store them and wait . . . No. Stave them off. Tell them she's recuperating. Anything . . . I have to tell you, Billy, there is no question of alternative. If we don't wait for Zoe, I withdraw the play . . . Yes, you're right. I am a fool. Good-bye."

Zoe was still in Intensive Care. She wasn't sure how long she'd been there. Three days? Four? It was always so dark, her memory was uncertain, and time was unimportant. She lay like a hurt animal, acquiescent.

She wondered again why she was lying here. What was the matter with her legs? She felt obscurely guilty, sinful. Odd scenes from her life flickered in her memory. Singing a solo in the dark little church. Her mother's death—that was *very* long ago. The senior play, when she'd gotten sick on opening night and they'd had to cancel. She remembered a boy she'd known that she'd been mean to and Radio City Music Hall, big and showy. She'd been an usher there for a while. She realized that she was much older than she had thought at first.

She remembered now what she had done wrong, that day her father had beaten her so hard. She'd been around thirteen. She'd been caught in the utility room at school with Evan Worth, the little rich kid. They were hiding there because Evan had pinched a cigarette from his mother's purse, and they wanted to try smoking it. They were both coughing and dizzy when the door opened and the janitor caught them.

"Fooling around with boys, huh?" That's what her father had said, and then he'd gotten out the stick. She remembered that she had left her father almost a year later, on a heavy brilliant day in late summer. She stood in the front yard wearing her mother's hat and waiting for him to drive her to the station. She was going to Atlanta to stay with her grandmother. The land around their place hadn't been farmed, and it lay parched and eroded under the hot sun. She hated her father, but she didn't want to leave him. It was like leaving her life's work, which was to make him love her. She was frightened.

Her father came out on the porch and stood there next to the old freezer where he kept the game he shot. He looked at her coldly. "Son of a bitch," he said. "So the little lady's going to Atlanta. Dressed up fit to kill. You ain't goin' to like it there, Zoe." She looked down then, at the hard reddish ground, ants crawling around. She felt as though she were dying. The future had suddenly disappeared as though it had been snipped away by a giant pair of scissors.

A patient moaned and Zoe, forgetting herself, had a quick impulse to go to him. Her left big toe moved. She was sure of it. She tried it again. The whole foot moved. She caught her breath, and suddenly, in her excitement, she saw herself flying across the sparkling water. She saw the white boat ahead of her, and the water curling out behind it, McGregor holding up his plastic glass. Everything came back to her, New York, the audition, *Sister Glory,* the accident. It was an accident, not a punishment. Relief flooded her.

After a few minutes she tried the foot again. Then the knee. She put her hand on it to check. It came up off the bed. It was alive. *Oh, my God and Father,* thought Zoe, *I believe in you and your sweet son Jesus, and all your flaming angels, and I promise on my soul I'll never leave you again, or forget, or cease to praise you and thank you.*

She could move. Could she walk? Today she would ask the doctor. They had both avoided the subject up to now. She'd been preoccupied with remembering who she was, and besides, she had been afraid of what the answer would be. *Well, Doctor,* she tried it out in her mind. *Will I walk again?* She wasn't sure that she had the courage, but when he arrived, she found she was eager to put the question. She waited while he examined her.

He touched her arm lightly with the pin.

"That's how it feels," he said. "Now how does it feel here?"

The pin traveled quickly—peck, peck, peck—up her left leg. She could feel it clearly, much more than before.

"Ouch," she said. She smiled at him.

"As clear as that?"

"Almost."

"Now here?" He vibrated the pin on her right leg.

"Hey," she said. She couldn't help herself. She was grinning widely. "That almost hurts."

His response leapt into his eyes. "My dear girl," he said. "I think you're going to make it. Let's try for movement. Wiggle this foot."

She wiggled it.

"The toe. Good. Now let's try that knee."

"Now let's see if you can sustain it. No, not for long. That's all right: it will come. Position." He pushed her big toe down. "Is that up or down?"

"Down."

"Now? Don't look."

"Down again."

"Good for you. Now?"

"Up."

"Good." He went on to the left side.

"Did I pass?"

"You get an A plus. How do you feel, weak? Would you like to sit up?" He wound the bed up. "Too much?"

"No. I feel better. How do you mean?"

"A little dizzy?"

"A little. Right now, from sitting up. But stronger in general." The moment had come. She contracted with tension.

"I wanted to ask you, Doctor—" Silence. Her mouth simply didn't say anything more.

"You wanted to ask me . . ." he prompted, gravely. Silence.

"Well, I'll tell you anyway. It's still early. I can't be absolutely sure. Nevertheless, I think you'll be walking out of here."

"I'm an actress," she said.

"I know. You're famous. You've been in all the papers."

"I mean, that's my work. Will I walk on crutches? Limp? There aren't a lot of parts for women on crutches."

"No," he said. There was a pause. "I can say this. I'm pretty sure you'll be walking—with some support—in a couple of months. I believe there'll be a complete recovery. It partly depends on you. You'll be out of Intensive Care tomorrow. You'll start physiotherapy. Work at it. Don't push yourself, but work at it."

He bent closer to her. He was wearing an old corduroy jacket, and he smelled of salt air and sweat. He put his hand on her cheek and said in a whisper, "From what I see of you, I think you'll do it."

Then he was gone, and Zoe was left with a sudden sense of loss and excitement. He was wonderful. He was going to heal her. She took a deep breath and held it for a moment before releasing it in a sigh.

Max Ward, the disbarred, reinstated lawyer son of the late Judge Theophilus Ward, had not been idle since his promise to Carole that he would get hold of something big and settle down. Among his connections was the journalist, P. J. Krupp. He pinned him down to drinks at Van's and pumped him for information. "You're on to a good story. Beautiful young actress and all that. I like your coverage. And now maybe a touch of scandal."

"What do you mean?" said Krupp.

"Wasn't there some question about whether or not to operate?"

"Forget it, Max. The operation was a success. Go chase some other ambulance."

"Yeah, but this Lukacs character is an oddball. Wasn't he involved in a malpractice suit recently? Somebody named Vail?"

"Oh, yeah, some alcoholic with a disc and a limp. It was settled out of court for about ten grand. Lukacs could have fought it, but he wanted the guy off his back."

"That was dumb."

"Maybe," said Krupp. "Some doctors just don't like to go to court."

"Some doctors ought to be in jail," said Max and nodded to the waitress for another round of drinks.

Krupp smiled, but he looked momentarily lost in thought. Then he looked at Max. "So what do you know that I don't know about Lukacs?"

Max suddenly looked smug. "I'm working on it."

"Okay, when you get something I can print, let me know. I'll make it worth your while. I need the copy and you can use the publicity. One hand washes the other, right?"

"Right."

Zoe was improving. A week after the operation she was transferred from the ICU to a private room. Technically speaking, Barney had done his job. The operation was over and the patient was well cared for. In an ordinary case he might have left her to physiotherapy at this point, with an occasional check. But he stopped in to see her the day she was moved.

She was glad to see him. Peck, peck, peck. The pin felt like a toy woodpecker traveling up her leg. Peck, peck.

"Hey, whaddaya think I am, a pincushion?" she said.

He laughed and caught himself staring at her. Her beauty was heightened by her smile. He went back to his needlework. "Honey," he said, "the more it hurts, the healthier you are."

A shadow crossed her smile.

"What about the therapist?" he asked. "Did he come today?"

"Yes. He *kneaded* me."

"Well, everyone needs to be kneaded. Raise your knee."

Zoe raised it.

"See how good I can do?"

"Not bad." He stood up. "How do you like your room?" The window by the bed looked over a marina.

"It's nice," she said.

He lingered as if he had something else to say and then left abruptly. "See you tomorrow."

Barney had a craniotomy scheduled. He went down to the coffee shop to take a break. Connolly, Chief of Medicine at the hospital, was there. He was an energetic, small man in his fifties.

"Hello, Barney," he said. "Beautiful job you did on the berry aneurysm."

"Thanks, Dan."

"Brilliant. I didn't think he had a hope."

"It was touch and go. And for a while there it seemed more like go."

"I can imagine. How's our princess?"

"Coming along. Really coming along."

"Did you see the interview in the paper?"

"I did indeed. That bastard Krupp is milking this case."

"Well, it's news. I see you have Malkin scheduled for this morning. Have you talked to Austin? Uh-oh. Here he is now."

Foote was bearing down on them, chest thrown out, stick swinging. Black pinstripes again. He skirted a table full of nurses and thrust himself into a chair. Barney was suddenly conscious of his clothes. He'd been in a hurry that morning and had come as he was: patched blue jeans and sweat shirt.

"Good morning, Daniel. Barney. May I join you?"

"Sure thing," said Connolly. "Coffee?"

"No, thanks. Barney, you went ahead and scheduled that craniotomy?"

Barney squared his jaw. "Did you see the CAT scans?"

"See them? I ordered them. Why haven't you done an angiogram?"

"We don't need it. I know where the tumor is. Austin, we've played this scene before."

"Yes. But you want to know what kind of tumor. Its vascularity. Meningioma? Glioma? Then if there's any trouble afterward, you've done your homework."

"I will adapt to the situation either way, Austin, once I see it."

"You may have to adapt to a malpractice suit."

"Oh, God," said Connolly. "Here we go again. Clinical judgment versus paperwork. Why don't you guys knock it off?"

"I've already scheduled it," said Barney. "I'm due up there in half an hour."

"Unschedule it," said Foote. "I want a complete study. And I think you might do something about the way you dress."

Barney felt a wave of anger rising in him. His words came out like ice. "I'll notify the OR staff," he said. "We'll do your angio. But what I wear is my own goddamn business." He stalked out, cursing in his mind that rigid, pompous, self-important character.

*   *   *

He was still angry when he left for the day in his yellow Porsche. It was early evening and the sun was going down behind him. He had a date with Maggie.

Her house was up one of those little alleys in East Hampton, between two shops: slate path, white walls, espaliered fruit trees, lantern. At the end, a two-story shingled building, a lot higher than it was wide and listing to one side.

There was a shop on the ground floor, and then a doorway. A card pinned to the door frame said, Maddalena Galleani. Maggie came from solid Italian stock. Barney went in. An exceedingly tall narrow flight of wooden steps ran up between slanted walls of matchboarding. Everything was painted white. A notice painted on the wall inside the door said LEAVE YOUR SHOES HERE.

Barney grinned. He took off his running shoes and went up the creaking stairs. A large rubber plant stood at the top of the stairs, and a black arrow pointed where to go.

The upstairs was all one room. Even the floor was painted white. There were a lot of plants and hardly any furniture. There was a mattress on the floor in one corner, covered with natural canvas. Some pillows. A bureau.

Maggie stood, typing, at a shelf that ran between two upright beams. She was six feet tall, barefoot, and she wore a plain long linen shift fastened at the shoulders. She was built to a magnificent Italian design, the cinquecento kind that they had more or less stopped producing.

"Hi," said Barney.

She turned in mid typewriter flight.

"Barney," she said. "What's up?" Her steel-rimmed glasses flashed as she took them off. Her pudding face, when she smiled, became both challenging and winsome. She walked easily over to Barney, her bare toes curling on the white floor, and matched her long body up against his. They were the same height. She kissed him. Verdi's *Requiem* swelled in the background.

"How's life at the orifice?" she asked.

"Dreary. And you?"

"I finished the poem. The one about the California Condor." She had a warm throaty laugh. "It's the best. The damn bird has a wingspread of nine feet, so I rewrote it in nine stanzas of three lines each. A triolet, sort of."

"Let's hear it." Barney sat down on a giant pillow on the floor, and she passed him a tray with some prunes and peanuts on it.

"Campari?" He nodded. After she got the drinks she found the poem and read it, holding it out in front of her, and pacing the floor under some large asparagus fern that hung from hooks. Light from a bare bulb in the ceiling filtered through the fern. Maggie paced in and out of its shadows, reading the lines in a talking/singing voice that rose at the end of each line.

"I like the setting. The feeling of space," he said. "It's good."

"I know," said Maggie.

Maggie emanated an extraordinary freedom. She lived like a bird, pecking at oats and groats and drinking herbal concoctions.

The earliest light would find her pacing the beaches, her full length cape dampening behind her, and with the beginning of darkness she would get ready to go to bed. Winters she went on tours, reading her work at colleges; summers she wrote and "humanized." But only to a point: she didn't want anyone invading her life. No strings attached, that was Maggie.

She was standing, breaking some dry bits off the fern. Was she wearing anything under that virgin shift? He doubted it. One hip bone stuck out, creating a hollow that curved toward her belly. The material clung there, making a triangular shape.

He reached up from the giant pillow and caught her by the hand. He dragged her down. She allowed herself to fall, but only satirically. "I thought we were going to the Patersons'," she said.

"I'd rather go to bed."

"You doctors are so down to earth."

"And you poets can't keep both feet on the ground."

"The air is purer up here."

"Yeah, but there's a lot more heavy breathing down here."

She pulled away from him and laughed. "Come on, we're going to the Pattersons'. I promised." Barney wasn't listening. He touched the hollow inside her hip bone, stroking the rough material of her dress and feeling her soften. She touched his thigh. Everything changed. There was a hush, soft as bird's feathers, expectant. The sweetness caught in Barney's throat. Maggie laid her head back on the pillow and she undid some buttons at the side of her dress. "I didn't promise to be on time," she said, joking.

Barney lifted the fabric of her shift and paused. He didn't want to hurry, and besides, he wanted to look at the perfection of her body. He studied it, first with his eyes and then with his hands, molding her deep breasts and small waist and, worshipfully, the softness between her legs. The asparagus fern cast a speckled shadow over her flesh. Maggie watched him and then suddenly she wasn't watching him anymore, her eyes gone golden and inward and her hands undoing his belt. He took his trousers off. He was hard with desire, but still he didn't want to rush. He wanted to prolong the moment, and he knelt over her and cupped her breast and took the nipple in his mouth and played with it, tongued it, nipped at it, feeling the currents that ran through her body, the rise and thrust of her breasts and the rhythmic thrusts below, and all at once, the whole movement become one terrific swell, he entered her fiercely and together they rode the course, cresting and falling away and cresting again and finally crashing in mindless splendor on the shabby strand, the huge pillow, the hard white-painted floor.

After a while he opened his eyes. The light bulb glinted through the fern. He looked at Maggie. She turned her head, still lost, but then she smiled.

"Comrade," she said.

Barney laughed happily. "Yes. Sometimes I wish— But it's not that way, is it?"

"What way? Oh, the heavy breathing. Personal passion. Love. No, it's not that way."

"Well, I love you anyway. Like a brother."

They both laughed. Then they scrambled up off the floor and went to pay their visit to the Pattersons'.

Peck, peck, peck. Barney was at it again. Zoe was restless. She was suddenly conscious of her thin legs spread out there, of the catheter which was doing her peeing for her, of her dirty hair.

"When do you think I might get in a wheelchair?"

"When you feel like it. You ready today?"

She nodded. "Could I take one of those wheelchair showers?" she asked.

"What'samatter, you don't like the services here?

Sponging, bedbaths, massage, and she wants a shower." He shrugged. "Women."

"Don't talk to me like a child. I want to wash my hair."

Barney spread the sheet over her again.

"Not yet, Zoe. I'll take your stitches out today, but you'll have to wait for them to heal. Press your button, please. I need the nurse."

The nurse came, wheeling her trolley table. They rolled Zoe on her side and pulled off the dressing. She gazed out the window while he scratched around at her backbone. She was depressed. It didn't seem possible that she would ever really get better. She remembered an old lady in Atlanta progressing at a snail's pace across the sidewalk to the door of a department store, holding on to a bright chrome walker which looked something like a kitchen step stool. Each step took a couple of minutes. The careful, shaky placement of the foot. The lifting and placing of the walker. The absolute concentration.

"There. And the catheter too. From now on, you're on your own." The nurse left. There was an awkward silence. Zoe looked distracted. He went to her, but he didn't know quite what to do. "What's wrong?" he said.

She shrugged and looked away. "I don't know. I feel—ugly."

He smiled. "Well, you're a minority of one. Everybody else thinks you're beautiful."

"I don't feel beautiful. I feel crippled."

"A bird with a broken wing?"

"Yes. Hideous." She made a face.

He took her hand. "Doctors aren't supposed to talk to their patients this way, but you're something special, Zoe. Not just beautiful. That wing will heal.

You'll fly again. People get depressed when they're sick. It's only natural."

Her hand was pale and fragile in his. He suddenly felt self-conscious. Her eyes had drifted to his and seemed to be looking for something inside of him. It was a silent, searching question that he did not quite understand. He drew away.

And then there was a clatter at the door and an aide wheeled in with Zoe's lunch. "Here we go, duchess," she said. "Hungry?"

Barney looked at his watch and stood up. He was behind schedule anyway.

The next day Zoe was able to sit on the edge of her bed, and on the following day she graduated to the wheelchair. Barney's job was over, but he made time for her every day, usually at the end of his hospital rounds when he could spend a comfortable half hour. He helped her the first time she tried to stand, supported her when her knees buckled, stood her up again. On the fifteenth day she took one fumbling step, and Barney applauded. "Baby's first step," Zoe said, laughing and clinging to him, tears springing to her eyes. He put her gently back in her chair.

"You're doing very well," he said. "You'll be out of here in no time."

"What's no time?"

"You should be ready to go by the end of September."

But when he saw her again, on the morning after, she was subdued. Her robe, a silky thing the color of sand that Culpepper had brought for her, hung loosely from her thin shoulders and her hair, newly washed, swung as she turned to greet him. She was sitting by the window, looking pale and clean and rather sad.

"What's the matter, Zoe?" he asked.

"Oh, nothing," she answered, in that way that says *oh, everything*.

"Good. Shall we see how you're doing?" He helped her up, and she took the step again—took three, in fact, with his arm firmly supporting her, before she leaned heavily against him.

"That's fantastic," Barney said when she was back in the chair. "Why aren't we celebrating?"

For an answer she passed him a letter that lay open on her hospital table. It was written on a piece of lined school paper, in a bold round script. It read:

> Dear Zoe, I heard about your troubles from Mister Culpepper. What kind of people you hanging out with anyhow He wrote on pink paper. You didn't write and I ain't seen you in ten years and now I have to hear from strangers that your sick. Whose paying for the doctors and the hospital I want you home and I want it now I'll be up to get you as soon as Buddy takes over here. That wont be for a Month anyway he's doing a job for Floyds. When do you get out of this Hospital? I want them to keep you till I get there answer me Zoe right away I won't have you beholden to strangers Dad.

Barney read it twice. The first time for a general sense of the writer, who seemed to be unpleasant, and the second time for the meaning.

"Well, Zoe," he said finally, "I see that your father is an agreeable soul. His heart's in the right place, though. It's nice that he wants to take care of you."

She flashed him a scornful look, but her mouth trembled. Barney touched her on the shoulder. "Tell me," he said. "If there's anything I can do, I'll do it."

"I can't talk about him," Zoe said. "I'm scared to death of him. He'll come up and get me—now, while I'm an invalid and I can't do anything about it. Barney, it would kill me to go back there."

Her eyes had filled with tears and he could see that she was making an effort to hold them back. He bent down and hugged her, though it was awkward with her in the wheelchair, and his ordinary sympathy seemed to be the last straw. She put her arms around his waist and sobbed childishly against him, and he let her, feeling her shaking shoulders and her fine straight hair under his hands. His heart ached. The room was dim and sterile. Outside the open window the marina, half-obscured by a morning mist, was full of half-masts and unfinished rigging. From somewhere came the sound of dripping. He stroked Zoe's hair and gradually she stopped crying and just clung to him, her face buried in his belly. Her shoulders under his hands were firm and delicate. He was full of peculiar feelings himself—vague longings, a sense of her fragility, an enchantment, a possibility, a warmth. What a detached character he had become, he thought, with no ties except for his daughter, no real commitments. There was Maggie, of course. They were buddies and he loved her, in a way, but there was a whole range of feelings that simply wasn't called on between them.

Zoe leaned back in the chair and smoothed some of the hair back off her face. Her eyes were swollen and her cheeks were pink and wet, but she smiled at him. He couldn't take his eyes off her mouth, smiling still, quivering a little, and before he knew what he was doing he'd leaned down to touch it with his own. It was warm and salty, sweet, and he'd have liked to stay like that, not kissing exactly, but touching mouths. He couldn't, though. The familiar alarm had gone off in his mind. She was a patient. *A patient.* Not a woman, but someone who is essentially weakened and in shock. He pulled back, and sat in the other chair.

There was an embarrassed pause and then Zoe said, "Thank you, Barney. Sorry I'm such a crybaby."

"That's all right. You don't realize it, but you're still weak. It makes everything affect you more."

"What a comforting person you are."

Barney thought for a moment, then he said, "Okay, let's get back to the problem. You know Willie is underwriting your bills here?"

"I know. I don't know why he's doing it."

"He admires you. He thinks you're a great actress. He announced that he'd withdraw his play unless you're in it. Also I think he feels responsible. And so he should. It was his party and his boat, and he should have been more careful. Don't worry about it, Zoe, he's got enough money. Now, have you anywhere to go when you get out of here?"

"Only my apartment. Two and a half with wall-to-wall and H and C. That means one room with bath and an alcove that barely holds a chair and a book." She smiled. "The book is Shakespeare, of course."

"Of course," he said. "Is that where you want to go?"

"Doesn't that make sense?"

"In the normal course of events you'd be out of here in about a month on crutches. I can extend that somewhat. But you know, Zoe, you might be better off if you went home for a few weeks."

Zoe didn't say anything, but her expression was pained and stubborn.

"Go on—say it, whatever it is," Barney said. "Don't clam up. It can't be that unspeakable."

"To me it is."

"Why?"

She thought for a while, frowning. Barney could see that she was sifting pictures in her mind. Then she shook her head and said, "You know, I can't remember. I've buried it for too many years. I left there when I was fourteen."

"Where did you go?"

"To Atlanta, to live with my grandmother."

"Tell me about that."

"I don't want to, Barney. I spent ten years forgetting everything I could about growing up. You know? I worked hard. I read everything I could get my hands on. I saved pennies and nickels and I hung out in elegant places to listen to people and hear how they talked and what they talked about. I was teaching myself to act, and also I took a lot of classes in the evening. I must have had twenty different jobs before *Sister Glory* came along. Dumb jobs, I mean, ushering or waiting table. Occasionally I landed a bit part, or a commercial, and a couple of years ago I had a six-week engagement at the Down Under, singing. I committed myself—totally—to acting, and I managed to forget almost everything about the rest of my life. Let's keep it that way."

"You didn't like your grandmother?"

"I don't think she liked me all that much. She sort of took me on, because it was her duty. She was my mother's mother. She hated my father."

"And you too? Did you hate him?"

"No. Yes. Barney, please." She held her hands out in a beautiful gesture. Her voice was low, like an oboe, bittersweet, emotional. "Don't let's talk about it. Let's just assume that I can't go home. Is there anywhere else?"

"Let me think about it. There are places—nursing homes, that sort of thing. It doesn't matter too much, does it, as long as it's definite?"

"Really. Just as long as it's not home."

He raised his eyebrows, but he didn't say anything more about it. Instead he asked, "What does your father do?"

"He's a butcher. And he's a guide. He takes parties of people out hunting."

"And your mother?"

"She died."

Barney got up and put his hand on her head. "Poor Zoe, you weren't very lucky, were you?"

"Luckier than most," she said. "I have my work."

"Yes." It was time to go, but he didn't want to. He stood for a minute, not knowing what to do. He mustn't get too close to her, but he wanted to help. She sat there trustfully, her face turned up to his, her eyes wide and green and clear. He shrugged. "We'll figure something out," he said, and left.

The next few days were all surgery. Barney's life was like that, suddenly filling up with emergencies after a period of routine. Something woke him early one morning, tense and exhausted, in the middle of a dream in which he relived step by step the operation he had performed the night before. It was still almost dark. He squinted at the clock. It took him a moment to remember that he was supposed to meet Maggie.

He climbed out of bed and went to the window. She was down there. Her eyes caught the early light, and she was laughing to herself. As he watched she stooped to gather another clod of soft turf and heaved it at the window.

"Hey," he said. "I'm here." But earth spattered against the edge of the casement.

"Slug-a-bed," she called. "Get up."

He spit out some bits of loam, told her to wait, and

pulled on some sweat pants. It was lighter when he got outdoors.

They ambled up the lane. Culpepper's house was silhouetted against the sky, a great heap of sloping eaves and windows that glittered faintly. They skirted the lawn and went around to the dunes. "Race you," said Maggie, and Barney sprinted down the sharp slope to the beach, and on down to the hard sand at the edge of the waves.

Maggie pulled up beside him. "Glorious, isn't it?"

He nodded, and they turned to walk east. The sun was just coming up, pale silver behind a dense radiant haze. The beach stretched out beyond the limit of vision.

"I should do this every day," said Barney.

"Why don't you?"

"Too busy. Too lazy. I was in the emergency room until midnight." He grimaced. "Life seems laborious. I don't know why I can't make it simple. *You* do."

"You don't want to. You like excitement."

"Don't you?"

"No. And I don't like families. I don't want baby eyes peering up at me and saying Mommy. I want exactly what I've got: work, solitude, friends. You, for example."

"Don't you get lonesome?"

"Yes," she said.

"I wouldn't want not to have had Piri."

"How old is she now?"

"Seventeen. We're very close. It's partly because she's mute, I guess. We worked together from the time she was two. I learned sign language, taught her, trained her to speak, even though she doesn't use it much. She was a joy, wonderfully intelligent. She communicates in ways that aren't open to people who merely talk."

"I remember her from last Christmas. I liked her. She's earthy and she's wise. Is she coming again?"

"Yes, for her vacation. Mary, my other daughter, doesn't see me. She's taken sides, but she'll get over it."

"Did you decide about Kansas?"

"No. Well, I've shelved it. I'll be going out there in October to look the place over and work out the grant proposals. I'll give them my answer then. I want to get Zoe over the hump first."

"Isn't she over it? How long is it now since the operation?"

"Three weeks. She's doing very well. She started with the walker."

"Barney, you don't usually spend so much time with your patients. What's going on?"

"Jealous?" he asked. Maggie snorted, and he laughed. "I know, I know—you're above all that petty human stuff." Then he spoke seriously: "You really are. I admire you."

"Thank you. So what *is* going on? Is it Piri all over again? Teaching, molding? You love to put people back together again."

"I don't know. I can't think ahead. She depends on me. She's making good progress, and I don't want to rock the boat. She's all heart, you know, full of feeling, breakable. Something about her worries me."

"When would you go to Kansas, if you go?"

"End of January: second semester. I won't decide until I see the place, anyway. There's a lot against it, mostly financial. Piri needs special education. Mary's in college. Connie—my ex-wife—just wrote. She wants to stop work and get her Ph.D. in sociology." He made a face. "Geriatrics. I'd like to help her there, but I won't be able to if I take the research job. *She* helped *me,* when I was in training."

"That's a consideration. But let's look at the other side. What's in favor of the job?"

"The work. I love the work. And I'd like to get away from Foote, here, with his defensive medicine, his neurotic terror of legal action. We clash constantly. I'd like to get out of the marketplace and into pure science."

"And how about your love affair with East Hampton? Do you still yearn to stay here?"

"I'm not sure. Willie's party Saturday was almost enough to turn me off. The one you wouldn't go to. It was one of those parties that's all ego—literary and social greats, and a whole lot of smartass people trying to climb on each other's shoulders, show off, make contacts, get ahead. Talking away like a monkey house."

"I told you."

"I know you did. And Freddy Troy—you know, Willie's composer, the one who was driving the boat when Zoe crashed? He was there. Fuzzy hair, steel spectacles, wandering around like a ghost. Withdrawal symptoms, Willie told me. Said he'd lost his cocaine. But Willie had it. He showed me the bottle."

"What was he trying to do, reform Freddy?"

"I guess so. If so, it was a flop. Along about two in the morning, Freddy walked into the Atlantic and damn near drowned himself."

"Guilt?"

"Nerves, I'd say. Honestly, Maggie, I'm a simple man. I don't like these games. I'm beginning to see Willie as a puppeteer. He manipulates people, and stands there watching to see what they'll do. Is that what writers are like? And you know, Zoe's going there to stay with him while she recuperates. I arranged it." He banged his head with his fist. "Idiot."

"It seems like a natural solution."

"It did," Barney said gloomily. "Before the party. He's delighted, of course. He's having her room redone. He's bought a Jacuzzi and found a physiotherapist. He showed me a dress that he'd bought for her; a sick sort of maroon thing with diamond buttons and puffy sleeves. She's going to be his dress-up doll. I hope you'll visit her, Maggie. She'll need a breath of fresh air from time to time."

"That's your thing, Barney, not mine. I'm not a fixer-upper. I spend time with people because I like them, not because they need me." They had reached a long broken jetty of rocks, and Maggie paused before turning back. "Maybe we should have our swim now." She gave him a severe look, but when she spoke her tone was kindly. "Are you falling in love with your patient, Barney?"

His cheeks reddened. Was he? He was attracted to her. He cared about her. But basically, he thought, he just wanted to mend her wing and set her free. "I don't think so," he said.

Maggie stepped out of her cape and left it in a heap on the beach.

"Have you had your nuts and berries yet?" asked Barney curiously.

"No. First the walk, then the swim, *then* the nuts and berries. Do things right. Be orderly. Keep it simple." She unfastened her shift and left it with the cape. "Coming?"

She was naked. Barney looked around, involuntarily. There was still no one on the beach, although the sun was burning red through the top layers of mist. Maggie raised her arms and jogged a few steps in place, laughing, teasing him. Her breasts jiggled; her long legs went up and down.

Barney reached for her. He seized her hips and brought them in to him and held her there until he felt her soften. He kissed her mouth, with his lips and his tongue, but as he relaxed, she broke away and flashed a challenge at him, and plunged whooping through the breakers. She dove into the ragged swell beyond and swam away.

Barney followed. The water was so cold that he came up quickly, gasping. He caught a glimpse of Maggie ahead of him, thrashing out to sea. With a bellow, and the thrill of pleasure deferred, he settled into a crawl and swam swiftly after the splashes ahead of him.

That same afternoon, Culpepper paid Zoe a visit at the hospital. She was in her usual spot by the window, and she was gently, abstractedly, stroking her arm, as though the touch of flesh was a new and pleasurable experience. Culpepper had never seen her look so open, so purely feminine. Her face lit up when she saw him.

"Willie, hello!" She had never called him anything before but Mr. Culpepper. As an actress she was confident and warm, but as a woman she had been self-conscious. "Come and sit with me. How are you?"

Culpepper walked to the window. He took the hand she held out, bowed over it, kissed it, and held it while he looked at her curiously.

"What's happened to you, my darling? You look so different."

Zoe laughed. It was a bubble of a laugh, floating out, an escapee from some ecstatic reservoir inside of her. "I'm going to recover," she said.

"Of course you're going to recover. We've held up the whole production for you. Ah, here's the nurse."

Abigail had come in, bearing a tray. Red roses waved above it. She put it in on a small table by the window. There was a bottle of champagne in a silver bucket, caviar, sour cream, two iced glasses. Culpepper popped the champagne and poured it.

"Here's to your recovery, dear, and to your very great success."

She raised her glass, half-smiling to control a surge of emotion, and nodded at him. "Thank you, Willie. I have so much to thank you for, it's getting embarrassing."

"Don't think about it, dear. In loco parentis, perhaps. I'm looking forward to our little vacation, and so is Yip. Your room is ready, everything is ready. Of course, there'll be talk . . ." He winked at her, a bulbous distorted wink from behind his glasses.

She giggled and toasted him. Culpepper spread some caviar with a silver fruit knife and handed it to her.

"You can come next week, Barney says. On October first. By then you'll be on crutches. Yip will take care of you, and we'll research your part as Sister Glory. I have a preacher who will be coming to see you; a deliciously fat man named Brother Luke, who says 'Thank you, Jesus' in every sentence. We'll get your ridiculous limbs back in order and then we can start rehearsals. That's how it is."

Zoe smiled. "It sounds great," she said. "Tell me, Willie, why are you doing all this for me? I'm only an actress in your play."

Culpepper selected a rose from the vase. He held it up against the light. "I could say that I feel responsible for you. It was my boat, my crew—my fault, maybe." He turned the rose. "But it wouldn't be true. You satisfy me." He looked at her suddenly and said without any defenses, "You're beautiful. I want you with me."

Zoe frowned.

"Not that way. Just with me." He inserted the rose

carefully, and when he spoke again, it was in his usual manner. "My dear, I am a greedy old man, surrounded by shadows. Nothing lasts, expect that in my work I've been honest. You're so young. Stay with me; it would give me such pleasure."

Zoe raised her glass. "Thank you," she said. "I'd love to. Can Barney visit me there?"

"Of course." He looked at her closely, and then he sighed. "Ah, I see. You have come out of your shell. You're not falling in love with your doctor, are you?" Zoe didn't answer, except that her face seemed to become more luminous. "But of course you are. How ordinary." Culpepper sat down again.

"You're not normal right now, Zoe. Don't forget that. You're an invalid, and like any invalid you're weak. Susceptible. Things that mean something now don't count in the long run. In the long run you're an artist. You have unusual talent. Don't neglect it. You have to be ruthless."

"Are you? Ruthless?"

"Entirely. I'm a writer. That's my religion."

It was the last day of September, crisp and bright. It was Barney's last day of work. He'd be leaving for his initial conference in Kansas the next day. It was also Zoe's last day in the hospital, and Barney was vaguely conscious of that throughout a complex piece of surgery that took most of the morning. At last it was done—it was a glioma, a poor outlook—and Barney sighed and flexed his fingers. He asked Gerry Rubin to close up for him. Methodically he checked out his other patients, and then he hurried down the hall to Zoe's room. He didn't know why he hurried, but he was excited and he couldn't wait to see her.

Her door was open, sunlight falling through it, and as he got closer he could hear the great hollow bells of Berlioz's *Symphonie Fantastique* on the radio. A nurse stopped him to ask a question, looking at him anxiously, but he didn't understand her because his mind was on the bells, and on Zoe, and he had to ask her to repeat it. He listened this time and okayed some medication, and then he went on down to Zoe's room.

She was flushed and excited, holding on to the bottom rail of her bed. As Barney entered she let go and staggered across the floor. He saw her crutches lying on the bed. She was walking unassisted—it was too soon—and he held out his arms as he ran forward to meet her. She fell against him and hugged him and laughed and put up her lovely face. He kissed her, full of adoration, forgetting that she was a patient, an actress, an invalid, an unknown quantity, forgetting everything except her frailty, her beauty, her courage. Afterward she kept touching him, while she talked about going to Culpepper's, about her favorite nurse, the one on night duty, and about another letter she'd gotten from her father. Barney said that yes, he had thought her father would be here by now, and Zoe passed him the letter.

> . . . And Buddy had to go so I'm stuck here for awhile Zoe I don't like your going to that man's house What's he to you? I raised you up right and don't forget it. I'll be coming up there in November I'll make arrangements with him then Tell him he'll get every penny back Dad

Zoe said, "Isn't it wonderful? He's not coming for weeks," and she touched his arm. They were sitting by the window now, and some of the magic was passing. Barney thought that lots of people fall in love with their doctors—*temporarily*, and then he thought he'd have to tell her about Kansas, which was still only a possibility. Then he thought again, that he'd better not, because she was on the verge of leaving the hospital and taking up a new and less protected life, and it might throw her. Zoe thought that perhaps he was still only being her doctor, being encouraging, and that what had seemed so right, so perfect a few minutes before was now perhaps only ordinary. The patient had walked, and the doctor had kissed her. It meant congratulations. But still she felt ecstatic, because whatever he meant there had been the flash of revelation for her, the sense of reality, the sureness of love. She thought, *I'll have to be content with that for now*, and she touched him again, on his thigh, as though to reassure herself that he was there.

Barney smiled and then he got up to go, jostling the long-stemmed roses on the table. They swayed and nodded, back and forth, and Zoe was reminded suddenly of the kitchen light swinging wildly back there in Georgia, in her other life, and of her father's face alternately distorted with brilliance and then plunged into darkness. She heard the stick slash down on the table and she shivered, but then she thought, What was so terrible about that? She looked at Barney again for reassurance, standing there clean and comfortable in his old corduroy jacket and looking at her questioningly.

"What did you say?" she asked.

He said, "Weren't you listening? I'm going away for a few days. Will you be all right?"

She looked at him, startled. "Where are you going?"

"A conference in the Midwest. It's something doctors do. They read papers on medical subjects—things they've discovered or new techniques. It's an exchange of information." He put his hand under her chin and tilted it up. "I want you to take very good care of yourself, lovey. Enjoy yourself with Willie, but don't let him get to you. He's a peculiar character. Work hard at the therapy. By the time I come back I expect to find a lot of improvement."

"Yes, *sir*," she said, but she thought, *I love you,* and she put up her mouth. Barney kissed it chastely, thinking, *is it real?* but all he said was, "Take care."

4

Zoe made the move to Culpepper's without mishap. Her room was light and airy. Casement windows looked out on the lawn and the enormous timbered garage where Culpepper had his studio. She could almost see Barney's cottage through the trees, and as time went by she watched the leaves turn from that heavy end-of-summer green to pale yellow and rose and then to brown. It seemed to her that Barney was gone a long time. She got a postcard from him with a picture of cornfields on it. "Held up here," it said, "but I'll be back in a couple of weeks. It's a great place, the Heartland, not what I expected at all. Are you standing on your own two feet (ha-ha)? Love, Barney." Zoe laughed, but it was only a casual greeting, and she felt edgy and disappointed.

She worked hard at her exercises. She asked Culpepper to get her an anatomy book, and she learned by heart every branching nerve and muscle from the waist down. After a while she could call up any one of them, like a yoga artist. She put her crutches in the closet after two weeks and disciplined herself to a cane.

Culpepper spent the days in his studio, but they met every evening for cocktails. He bought her some extraordinary clothes: meager silky dresses which fell over her thin chest and shoulders and emphasized her pallor, long crystal eardrops, a stringy orange boa to match her lipstick, a golden snake ring with a ruby eye which hung loosely on her long hand. He bought her a lot of sheet music as well, country music, and asked her to learn it. He said it was atmosphere for his play. "Country music created Sister Glory," he told her. "It made her think that love was salvation. When she couldn't find human love, she tried the divine variety."

Sister Glory was a poetic drama, not a musical, but the music was essential to it. It was the story of Amanda Jordan, the unhappy wife of an Atlanta executive. The opening scene took place in Amanda's expensive kitchen, late at night. She is drinking by herself and singing—along with the radio—a heartbreak tune called "Lonesome Lady."

Amanda yearns for salvation. By the end of Act I she has renounced her shallow life in order to join a Pentecostal group ("I'm Lookin' for You, Lord"). She gets a divorce, leaves her children. In Act II she falls in love with the preacher, Brother Gabriel. They are united in Christ, and together they set out to carry Him to the unredeemed. She becomes famous for her singing and for her healing hands and is widely known as Sister Glory. In the end, however, she finds out that Gabe has a clandestine bank account in seven figures and a lot of clandestine credit with the young women of his flock. In their empty mission, plastered with written symbols of joy and Christian love, Sister Glory draws a tiny silver pistol and shoots Brother Gabe in the mouth.

Zoe threw herself into studying the play. She read it and reread it, practiced the songs, sang the music that Culpepper had brought her. She thought about her part. What inner disturbance had turned

Amanda Jordan, a hard and frivolous woman, into the divinely tender Sister Glory, and finally into a murderer? It was something she would have to understand before she could act the part.

Zoe had been a Baptist when she was very young and had gone to church with her mother. But then her mother had died, and nobody else in the family was religious, so she had little feeling for the born-again scene. She read the Bible, and she read charismatic literature, the books and gospel tracts and periodicals that Amanda Jordan would have read. Culpepper collected them for her in supermarkets and from the florist, who had a whole rack of such things. He made a trip to Riverhead one day to the Living Waters Christian Bookstore and came back with a lot of books in a white paper bag printed with a fish symbol and JESUS CHRIST GOD'S SON SAVIOR. Zoe read them all, *A Walk with God, The Next Step, Forerunner, Messianic Truth,* and *A Thief in the Night.* She read comic books on recycled paper, which showed how bad guys, murderers and prostitutes and scientists, came to renounce Satan. On the last page there was always a form which told you what to do and how to pray. "Dear Father, I know that I am a sinner and need forgiveness. I am willing to turn from sin. I now invite Jesus Christ to come into my heart and life as my personal savior. By God's grace I will obey Christ as the Lord of my life." Underneath there was a box that said, DID YOU ACCEPT JESUS CHRIST AS YOUR OWN PERSONAL SAVIOR? YES ☐ No ☐ DATE _____.

Zoe remembered a song that they used to sing when she was young, called Great Speckled Bird. It used to make her laugh, but now she tried to remember it.

* * *

A beautiful thought I am thinking
Concerning the Great Speckled Bird ...

Tum tum te tum tum te tum tum. She couldn't
remember the rest of that verse, but the next one
came to her whole.

With all the other birds walking around
She's so despised by this world
The great Speckled Bird is the Bible
Representing the great Church of God.

It still made her laugh; it was blasphemous. You'd
think somebody would sue. She wished Barney were
back; she wanted to sing it to him.

Barney spent three weeks in Kansas. After a re-
warding discussion about the forthcoming research
project, he signed his contract with the University
Medical Center. He was pleased, excited even, by the
prospect of the job, and he liked the town. It was neither the loamy fields and yellow sky of his imagination, nor the dreaded flatness of Aunty Em's Kansas;
it was a pleasant easygoing place, lively, and he met
people he liked while he was there.

In the back of his mind there was his unresolved
personal life. It seemed to him that he had fallen in
love with Zoe, but he shied away from it. There was
an undeniable attraction; nevertheless, the whole situation had been unreal, and it would stay that way until she was back to normal. Until then she couldn't
know what she felt. She wasn't technically his patient
anymore, of course; he'd signed her over to rehabilitation. But she was his patient in fact, and there was
a whole web of restrictions around her. Patients were
notoriously unstable in their emotions. Doctors always

made sure there was a nurse around when examining female patients, so they wouldn't get sued for rape. Barney had been informal about this, but the years of training created a psychological barrier, a little switch in his mind that went *click,* and made women patients unapproachable as women.

There were other practical difficulties. Zoe was an actress, almost a star. She wouldn't want to go to Kansas and be a housewife. New York was the place for stars, or possibly the Coast. Someone was covering for him at St. Mark's, so he had stretched out his visit, thinking that it would give Zoe more time to recuperate before they met again. Thinking also that it would be better if he simply got over her; it would be better not to love her; it would be better to finish up at St. Mark's and move west in an uncomplicated way, footloose and fancy free, and start his new job. That would demand a clear mind. He longed to see Zoe; yet he was reluctant to see her. There was a feeling of pressure with Zoe. One felt the unspoken needs of her whole submerged self, the part she never talked about or let anybody into.

When Barney came back, he talked to the administrator at St. Mark's. He wanted to take a year's leave of absence. The new job looked good, but if he didn't like it, he'd come back here. They worked it out that way.

Later that day, he walked up the drive to see Zoe, wondering how she was coming along. Should he tell her, yet, about his new situation? It wouldn't be surprising if in her new life at Willie's house she'd forgotten all about him. He felt calm, but underneath he was alert, stirred. He broke into a jog.

Willie was at work in his studio. Ngiep showed Barney upstairs. He knocked, and the actress voice rang out, "Do come in, darling." She thought he was

Willie. When he opened the door, she was standing in the middle of the room, rehearsing a scene.

"Barney! You're back." She flushed. There was such unmistakable delight in her voice that Barney's cheeks reddened. She waited for him to kiss her, and when he didn't there was an uncomfortable moment. Then he said, "How are you doing?"

"Marvelous. Look." She swung across the room, using her cane, and came to a stop in front of him. "Did you have a good time?"

"Yes," he said. "Great." He wouldn't tell her about it now. He'd wait first and feel out the situation. There was that hidden quality about Zoe. She was unpredictable. He avoided the subject of where he'd been, and instead they talked about *Sister Glory*.

"Look at this stuff," said Zoe, showing him the comic books. "Isn't it incredible? It's hard to imagine anyone falling for it. But I put myself in that frame of mind for the play. I'm getting born again, for Amanda's sake. There's a preacher coming to see me too."

"Just don't fall in," Barney said. She looked splendid. Whatever was going on, it was doing her good.

"You look great," he said.

"You do too. How was the conference?"

"Informative. Boring."

"Did you miss—let me see—being here?"

He laughed and put a hand on her shoulder. "Not at all," he said mockingly, and then he caught his breath. She was lovely. She looked at him very directly.

"*I* missed *you*. I'm glad you're back." A vacuum cleaner started up somewhere downstairs. He hesitated, held back. Sorrow crossed her face like a squall on the water. All his elaborate thoughts fell away, and he did the simple thing. He stepped forward and put his arms around her—it felt absolutely right—and kissed her, formally at first, and then, as he felt her slender body come in against his, with warmth. Still, he was controlled, delicate. He had a sudden vision of belonging, as though after great wanderings in barren territory he was enclosed in a domestic place, a cottage perhaps, with a stone floor, and straw on top of it, and copper things winking on the sideboard, and the kettle hissing, everything orderly, seemly, and a great lumpy wooden bed covered with a quilt that you had to climb to get into. But he only rumpled Zoe's hair affectionately. "I missed you too," he said.

Barney visited at Culpepper's after that, but not as often as Zoe would have liked. He kept their meetings affectionate, pleasant. It seemed artificial. It was as though they were singing some trivial tune, but there was a whole orchestration going on elsewhere, sweet and full, and just out of earshot. He seemed evasive.

It was true. He was uneasy. Everything had developed so quickly between himself and Zoe, and now it was stalled. He didn't know why it was stalled. He didn't quite trust her. He didn't tell her about his impending move, but he felt like a liar when he was with her. He was in love, and trying not to be, but it became a persistent distraction, a constant companion, intervening in his work, spoiling his pleasure.

He worked hard through the end of October and most of November, seeing Zoe occasionally and Maggie, after his first visit, not at all. At the hospital he went doggedly about his business, avoiding Austin Foote as much as possible. He did a lot of surgery, on cases that would be terminal anyway after another six months. It seemed an exercise in futility. A patient came in: Joe Giordano, hunchbacked and hydrocephalic. Barney had seen him often enough. He lived in Hampton Bays, where he rolled around town in a motorized wheelchair, selling little packets in urethane bags to the kids on their way to school. He'd been hit by a car.

The CAT scan was awful; the man's whole head was an ocean inside. The liquid which filled the interior had pushed his brain up against the back rim of his skull. He was in the ICU. A nurse switched on the light in his cubicle, and for a moment Barney was blinded by the white bed. The huge head hung there, turned sideways on the pillow like a grotesque madonna, inert, breathing. Joe's legs had been paralyzed, and Barney pulled back the sheet to see if there was any improvement. He thought of Zoe as she had lain tumbled on the beach, and he was suddenly moved by these little curled up bird bones. They were unbelievably fragile. He ran his warm hands over them, stroking them, cupping the tiny bony knee cap. Nothing happened, of course. They were immobile. He must tell Zoe that he was leaving.

Another time a young man arrived in emergency, shattered in a motorcycle accident. He was only nineteen. His brain was edematous with massive contusions and there was brain stem injury. Barney couldn't bear to look at the father. It would be a long time: months in the hospital and afterward, if the boy was lucky, months or even years in a rehabilitation center, with God knows what deficit. It was not unusual—there had been plenty of such cases in Barney's life—but it hurt him in a new and unusual way. His sense of humanity was extended. He felt everyone's pain, and the more he felt it the more he was hampered in his work.

He didn't make mistakes; it was rather that he took fewer risks. Austin Foote was pleased with him, even

complimenting him one day when he closed early on
a meningioma, a benign tumor of the brain. He'd
gotten half of it out and decided against crossing to
the other side of the brain for fear of running into
the superior sagittal sinus; the results then could be
worse than the effects of the tumor. So he said, "We'll
just count our blessings; we've taken out the equiva-
lent of a large tangerine." Everybody nodded, and
he'd closed the wound, but he came away furious
with himself. He'd relieved a lot of the pressure and
the patient would be okay, but it would have been
better to get more of it out. Dangerous, but better.
That Foote approved only made it worse. That was
the tip-off, Barney thought; he must be losing his
touch.

It was a long month. He was increasingly impatient
and abstracted. He was just marking time really, at
St. Mark's, until his replacement took over in January. He must tell Zoe that he would be moving.

Zoe was a lot stronger by the end of November. She
still needed the cane a lot of the time, and she tired
easily, but the forecast was good. Barney said the
limp would improve until it was barely noticeable, if
at all. She was restless. Culpepper was keeping the
producers of *Sister Glory* at arm's length until her
recovery, but she felt ready. She wanted to get to
work. She wanted something to happen with Barney.
She felt pinned down by Culpepper, claustrophobic
in his beautiful house, full of precious objects—of
which, occasionally, she thought she was one. And she
noticed that whenever Barney came over to see her,
Culpepper became more acid. He never mentioned
Barney now, except in tones of sarcasm. He called
Barney "the good doctor," or "the boyfriend," and
once when he tried to talk to her seriously, he said,

"Barney's only a man, you know. Angry and needy and childish, like all men, and looking to gobble you up. He wants food, babies, clean undies, and when things have gone wrong at the hospital, he wants someone waiting for him in his bed. He could have been a concert pianist, you know. He trained for it for a while, and he's good. But he chose . . . life. You can't do both. You're an artist, Zoe, one of us. You're royalty." He told her Barney was sleeping with Maggie anyway. "Did you think he was just a teeny bit *amoureuse*, of you? I did too, for a while. But it would hardly be suitable."

In the evenings, if they were free, Culpepper worked with her on the script, shaping her interpretation of the part. And he set a date for the local born again preacher to see her, so that she'd have some direct experience with the Pentecostal movement.

Brother Luke was large. He wore a business suit, navy blue, the jacket flapping open over a white shirt that strained across his belly. Zoe received him in the living room.

"How do you do, Father."

"There is only one Father," he said, shaking hands with her. "I am Brother Luke."

He was a wholehearted man, a Greek. He had once been wholehearted as a hard liver, a drinker, a confirmed and successful gambler; he was now equally impassioned about his mission. He walked on his toes like an athlete and, like many big men, moved with massive delicacy.

"Now you just sit right down, Brother Luke, and make yourself at home."

He didn't sit. He walked up and down for a minute, and then he faced her.

"I'm not interested in your researches, Zoe, and I'm not interested in this play you're working on." He spoke quietly, in a deep voice. "I'm interested in your whole self. I don't want to see you leave this—" he looked around "—rich man's home. I don't even want to see you get healed. I want you should love God. I want you should love his only son *Jee*sus (he crooned the word Jesus, lingering tenderly on the first syllable), "who is the word made flesh. Who took our sins to Himself. Who paid for those sins in his flesh."

Zoe asked him a lot of questions, and gradually, without quite being aware of it, she slipped into her role as Amanda Jordan. She flirted with him and acted as though she really wanted to be saved. Brother Luke paced vigorously, waving his short arms. His eyes were large and sweet, and seemed to focus abruptly on Zoe from time to time, drawing, drinking her in, shining with excitement.

"God loves you, Zoe. His love is there for everybody. All you have to do is accept it and you will see. Joy pours from heaven as light flows from the sun. He is reaching out to you; reach out your hand. Repent. Believe! Believe, Zoe, that Jesus Christ died for you, rose from the dead for you, and that He went to sit at the right hand of His Father to intercede for you. You. You personally. Love *Him,* Zoe. Invite Him into your heart and mind. Receive Him as Savior and Lord. Lo-o-ove Him. Lo-o-ove Him."

Zoe felt herself drawn in. She didn't know whether she was Amelia or herself. Her body seemed to grow large with an inner commotion, and she felt a hunger to join, and to share, and to be part of whatever it was. She leaned toward him unconsciously, but when he invited her to Bible Study (Thursday evenings) and Fellowship (Friday evenings) and the Sunday meeting and the Sunday potluck and the Christian movie (Mondays), she drew back. "I'm a little busy

right now," she said. "Rehearsals will be starting
soon."

"Too busy for God?" he asked intensely, taking off
his thick glasses.

She was embarrassed. "Well, I'd like to come on
Sunday. Will—" she didn't know how to put it. "Do
people get saved at church?"

"People get saved anywhere," Brother Luke said.
"What do you mean?"

"I mean, do they—you know, go into a trance and
speak in tongues?"

"Come and see," he said. Then he peered at her
nearsightedly. "Have you been *pretending*?"

"A little," she said, blushing.

"Well, you're not fooling anybody but yourself.
And you can't fool God. He gave you that limp for a
reason, child. Just think about it."

"It was an accident."

"Nothing is an accident," he said, with his hand on
her shoulder. "I won't come again, but you'll be coming to see me. Even when you're well again, you'll be
a cripple without the love of Jesus in your heart."

It was the last Tuesday of November, and Barney's
day off—the day he usually came to see her. Zoe had
hoped he'd come for lunch, but he hadn't, and she
pottered restlessly around the living room, listening
to records. She gazed at a Picasso—Blue period, sensitive youth, clown clothes—and then she started to
look through a copy of *Interiors,* which was lying on
the coffee table. She put it back. She couldn't concen-
trate. She thought, for the thousandth time, about
Amanda Jordan and why she'd been born again and
turned, like worm to butterfly, into Sister Glory.

Brother Luke had been impressive, Zoe thought,
rather than comical. She could see that Amanda

would go for the simplicity and love that he talked
about. It would be nice to forget oneself in that way.
Let Jesus do the worrying.

Still, she went on, gnawing away at the problem, it
had to be deeper than that. Religion wasn't just a pill
you took when the chips were down. It was a philoso-
phy as well, an understanding of the universe. Zoe
stared at Culpepper's harmonious *salon*, the muted
colors, the paintings, the wicker and glass, the extrav-
agant plants. It was just a collection of objects, after
all, nothing special, nothing you could offer up for as-
sets at the final Bar, nothing that would do for Judgment Day. No different—the image flashed into her
mind—than the orderly carcasses that hung on racks
in her father's refrigerator room, swaying and mag-
got-white except where the blood had congealed. It
was all just life, no matter how well organized it was.
It didn't mean a damn thing.

And Amanda Jordan's life wasn't even orderly. It
was decadent, stupid—frightening. Amanda had been
terrified, that was her story. A journey. A road that
led nowhere through a meaningless landscape, and
Amanda traveling along it and seeing herself from
above, her whole life merely spread out in space from
beginning to end—psychic terror. And then joy. That
same landscape illuminated, all its elements related
one to the other in an ecstatic confluence of parts,
meaningful because divine.

Satisfied at last, Zoe limped to the glass wall and—
still seeing with Amanda's eyes—examined the nifty
workings of God's world, the wintry dunes, brilliant
sun, bitter wind that clattered among the marsh
grasses spewing sand and spray against the glass.
What wholeness, what clarity!

She felt redeemed but tiny, a part of the whole and
then, slipping from Amanda into herself again, she

was aware of a similar harmony in her own life. It
was Barney, of course. She looked around the room
again. In the dreamlike atmosphere here, Barney appeared like the sun itself, vigorous and direct. Warm.
I'm heliotropic, she thought, the word exploding in
her mind from some distant course in biology. She
got out the dictionary and looked it up. "Heliotropic,
adj. Bot. turning or growing toward the light."

She paused in front of the mirror, studying herself.
It didn't show that she was heliotropic. She made an
ogre face and moved away. Outwardly, she hadn't
changed all that much. Even Willie, observant as he
was, was unaware of how profoundly she was involved. She had maintained her general style, aloof,
radiant, bitter. She still hunched her shoulders and
swung her loose light hair and released occasionally
that one-way high-voltage smile that thrilled but did
not invite: star quality. But she was filled with inward excitement. It was with her most of the time,
secretly thrumming through her blood system. She
woke up in the morning aware of it; exercised, ate,
studied, aware of it. She chatted flippantly with
Culpepper, or rehearsed, sang, entertained his friends,
watched the tube, always aware of the something that
was happening inside of her: the thrumming, the hic-
cup of pure joy. Sometimes, seeing Willie's frog eyes
fixed on herself, ancient, retracted, curious, she would
think triumphantly, *He doesn't know, he can't understand,* but at other times she would look at him with
pity. He was outside of it, not quite human. She
wasn't royalty anymore, *one of us,* dedicated, solitary.
All those years of discipline in the city, the distrust
that had seemed basic to her character, had dropped
away. After twenty-nine years in the gum machine,
she had dropped her defenses, and it seemed to her
that there was an exquisite bond between herself and

every other creature with two legs and a head. She was in love.

Is it all right? she asked herself, with pleasure and a panicky sliding. The wind rattled at the glass doors in a sudden rage, and there was a knocking behind her at the front door. Barney? She looked at her watch—three o'clock—and turned. The door burst open as soon as Ngiep touched the knob, on a gust of wind, and sunlight spilled in. It *was* Barney. His cheeks were vivid, and he was cold. He flung his arms around himself.

"Brrr," he said. "Sorry I'm so late today." He kissed her cheerfully. She was suddenly angry. It was always like this now. Cheerful and polite and friendly. The pull of mutual attraction, the drag of his resistance. There was something insincere, something stifled, about their meetings. Perhaps she shouldn't be impatient, she thought. She should be different, a comfortable fat earthwoman who simply nourished and waited. But she wasn't like that. She determined that today, somehow, she would break through.

"Come and sit down," she said. Ngiep brought coffee and cake on a tray, and they sat decorously on Culpepper's elaborate sofa. She passed him a cup. The spoon rattled loudly and fell on the table. Barney picked it up, spilling some coffee on the down pillow with its white velour cover.

"Oh, God," he said. "I've despoiled the virgin pillow."

"It's all right. It'll wash." She raised her eyes. "You've been staying away."

"Not really. I'm here, aren't I?"

"It's all so polite."

"You want me to be rude?" he asked, laughing. He settled back and put his feet, shod in Alpine hiking boots, on the glass coffee table.

"Barney, be honest. You've been staying away."

He met her eyes. "Yes. I've stayed away. I don't know what to do."

"It seems simple enough to me."

"Yes. Well, clearly there's a lot of feeling, isn't there? I've been falling in love with you, but I don't think it's the right time or the right place. I—" He stopped.

"You?"

He didn't say that he was going to Kansas in two months, but afterward he would wish that he had. He didn't say it because he didn't know whether or not to ask her to go with him. It would be a kind of rejection, he thought, just to say that he was going out of her life. On the other hand, he wasn't ready to ask her. It was unreal here, like a classroom where he was cast as the professor and she the brightest and prettiest of his students. Would it mean anything once they got outside? Once she was well?

"I'm not ready," he said.

"What do you mean?"

"Neither one of us is quite ready for a serious involvement. I was knocked out by my divorce. You've been knocked out by a traumatic experience and how you feel about me comes from that. Partly, anyhow. Don't you see? You need me now. I need you now. But—"

"But what? Willie told me about Maggie. Is it her?"

"No, it's not Maggie. We're good friends, and we were lovers too. In that order. But I haven't seen her for a month because my thoughts are full of you."

"Me too. I think about you all the time."

"Is that true, Zoe? Or is it only true now, while you're in limbo? It's like one of those summer affairs. In the fall we all go home again."

"Home? Home to what? You are home to me."

"Am I? What about your work? Our lives may not always lie in the same place."

She paused, remembering everything that Culpepper had said. "That's true. It might not work that way. I can't really think about the future yet; it's too scary."

"That's what I meant. But you will." Barney sat up and reached out to her with both hands. "Shortly you'll be back to normal. You'll be in the theater again, and then you'll know better what you're doing. What you want. And we'll see if it's only summer, baby, or if it's—" He wiggled his eyebrows suggestively and Zoe laughed, and he laughed too. He pulled her closer. "Now that we're on the level, I can kiss you again," he said, and he embraced her with a roughness and passion which had not yet been part of their exchanges. They were both breathless. Barney grinned at her. "There's something to be said for that, all right," he said, and they kissed again.

Maggie said, "Well you didn't have to ignore me for a month, did you now? For a mere emotional upheaval. We're friends, aren't we?" It was the next day. She sat cross-legged on a pillow, her face shining with affection, while Barney tried to get things straight with her.

"No, but I didn't feel like talking."

"And do you now?"

He shook his head. "Not really. It will all come out in the wash, one way or another."

"Time wounds all heels?"

Barney laughed. "I'm not being a heel. I'm trying to be good—not giving way to impulse. I don't want to take advantage of an emotional situation."

"One thing is obvious, Barney. You have to be

straight with Zoe about the fact that you're leaving. It's causing confusion."

"I know. I've been a coward. It's just that she depends on me. I was waiting, till she was stronger." Maggie regarded him without comment.

"I have the feeling that she's horribly delicate, inside, and I don't want to make a false step. I want to see her—I don't know."

"Flower?" Maggie suggested. She sighed. "That's how it always is. It's these girls who have to *flower* that get the good guys. Why the hell don't you just take her with you?"

"How can I?" She's just about to achieve everything she's always wanted. Here, not there. She needs her work."

"She's grown up. Why don't you give her the choice?"

"I will, when she's back to normal. There's something stagey about the whole thing right now."

"The doctor and the actress?"

"No. The doctor and his patient. An old cliché."

"Yes, I see what you mean. It's a gamble. But don't treat her like a baby. At least tell her what your plans are."

Just before dinner that same evening, Zoe's father drove up to the house in a taxi. He hadn't written or phoned, and he arrived in the middle of one of Willie's highly selective little dinner parties.

There were six guests, each of them stylish in his own way, or rich. They were seated around the great glass coffee table having drinks, and they'd requested a song from Zoe, who stood by the doors which gave on to the deck. The winter evening had an exceptional clarity. The sun had just set and the sky shone with deep color, aquamarine and violet and peach; a single star hung there, near the horizon. Zoe leaned on her walking stick, the sequins flickering on her thin dress. She fastened her mind on the sky and casually, without thought or effort, released her reedy contralto.

> *Just because I haunt the same old places*
> *Where the memory lingers everywhere*
> *Just because—*

The door knocker sounded loudly. Zoe turned, and the candles on the coffee table blew low as Ngiep opened the door. Abner Carter walked in, clearing his throat, and stopped in the archway to the living room.

He was a stocky man, about sixty, with an air of good fellowship and cold gray eyes. He wore a sports jacket resplendently checkered in brown and green and a shiny lime-green shirt. He looked at the company, and not seeing his daughter or anyone who might remotely be his daughter, advanced into the room. "I come to see Mr. Culpepper," he said, with natural dignity.

Willie rose and put on the air of affability he extended to everyone who wasn't, as he saw it, quite human—a group which included plumbers and businessmen and housewives, and those millions of souls who don't speak the Queen's English.

"How do you do, sir," he said, holding out his hand. "I'm Willie Culpepper."

Abner ignored the hand. "I come about my daughter."

"Ah," said Culpepper. "The father arrives. The plot thickens." He laughed; he'd had a couple of drinks. "I'm delighted to see you, Mr. Carter." He turned toward Zoe, who stood shocked and immobile by the glass doors, the light fading from the sky behind her. "Zoe!"

She hadn't seen her father for thirteen years, since the time she'd visited home again from her grandmother's house, for the summer vacation, and then she'd spent the whole two months avoiding him. It hadn't been hard. Between his butcher shop and his hunting Abner was rarely home, and when he was there he spent his time reading the paper and drinking, or playing some tapes, like "The Waltz of the Flowers" or *La Bohème*. Then, in the middle stages of inebriation, the tears would come to his eyes, and he would invariably say, "Listen to that, Zoe. That's what I call beautiful," and he would put his arm around her shoulders and look at her with his reddened eyes, and sometimes lurch a little so that she had to support him.

Abner stared at her. "So that's my grown-up daughter! Well, Zoe. How you doin'?" She didn't move, but stayed by the doors leaning on her stick and holding on to the drape with her other hand.

"What kind of a welcome do you call this?" Abner went on, when she didn't answer. "Come here and say hello to your father."

The company was looking at her curiously. Zoe pulled herself together and crossed the floor—it seemed forever until she got there, limping badly—and when she got to him she held out her hand and said very carefully, like Eliza Doolittle in one of her favorite plays, "How are you, Dad? How nice to see you." She spoke in a carrying voice that seemed to echo awkwardly around the room. "Let me introduce you to everybody."

She performed the introductions in the same manner, and there was the long business of everybody getting up and shaking hands. Abner seemed to be at ease. "Glad to meet you," he said with every introduction, flashing his bad teeth. Then he sat down in the chair Culpepper had vacated and apologized, in a roundabout way, for Zoe's lack of warmth in greeting him.

"She ain't seen me in years, not since she was sixteen, and she always was a timid thing. But I brung her up after her poor mother died, and you can't say I did a bad job. Can you now? She could sing all of Boheem by the time she was ten. And she—"

"Dad. I don't think everyone wants to hear all that," Zoe said. Everyone laughed politely, and Culpepper intervened.

"I understand that you're a hunter, Mr. Carter," he said.

Zoe's father took the bait. Perhaps he was more ill at ease than he seemed, because he talked at length. He regaled the company with stories of his hunting parties, and the people he'd taken out. Some of them were quite well-known, corporate types, and a popular journalist. Once he'd even served as guide to the gubernatorial party. He talked only to the men, assuming their interest and their male solidarity. He described the bear and possum and bobcat, and drinking up in the cabin in the foothills after a long day, and running the rapids and then, invited to stay for one of Ngiep's exquisite dinners, he continued to talk all through the meal, not boasting, but telling stories of terrific and dangerous deeds.

Culpepper was delighted with him. After everyone had left (Abner had taken a room in a motel out on the highway), he said, excitedly, "What a brute, dear. What a marvelous creature. I can't believe it. *That's* your father?"

Zoe looked exhausted. Culpepper took her hand. "I know you're not on the best of terms, sweetie, and I

can see why. But your father is quite an original, and
you're grown up now. You mustn't let him bother
you."

"You don't know him. I wish you hadn't written
him, Willie."

"It was natural. You were in critical condition.
Good grief, Zoe, you might have died. One notifies
the parents. Tell me why you're so upset."

Zoe shook her head. "I don't know. I can't stand
his flesh."

"What on earth do you mean?"

"I don't know, Willie. He was vile to my mother
and vile to me. The only one he got along with was
my brother. I hardly even remember him. I buried
him years ago, in my mind. I couldn't even have told
you what he looked like, and then he walked in and
instantly I knew him, through and through, even
though I didn't recognize him. God knows what he
wants, but it's sure to be bad."

"Well, he'll only be here for tomorrow. He'll state
his business, and then he'll go back and you can forget him again. Don't worry, I'll be with you."

Zoe spent a sleepless night. Abner's visit had raised
the lid of her Pandora's box, and out flew a most un-
welcome flurry of memories, beastly winged things
that beat and breathed on her hot face until she
raised her arms and turned her head into the pillow.
Her mother padding around in that awful old
dressing gown, trying to please him. Abner striking
out; her mother cowering. Abner terrifying all three
of them with his shotgun and shouting, "Where can a
man go to be a man?" Abner bloody from his shop;
the kitchen light swinging, swinging. She slept and
woke again, the blood ringing in her ears. She tried
to compose herself, folding her arms on the pillow

under her head and lying very still. She was angry at herself; why was she so obsessed? She was twenty-nine—he couldn't touch her. But still the light swung on his handsome jowls, and the whistle of the willow switch sounded in her ears, and she thought, *There's something more, something I don't understand.* Even as she strained to understand it, her mind performed its familiar trick, and a healing darkness began to obscure her memory. Abner faded, like an old photograph with darkened edges, until nothing was left but his glaring eyes, and Buddy faded, and the little ranch house faded, and finally when dawn began to lighten the sky, all the sticky little beasts were back in the box and the lid was closed, and Zoe slept. Her last thought made her smile: She was going to have dinner with Barney tonight.

When Abner came in the morning, he asked Culpepper for a financial accounting. "I don't aim to be beholden to you, Willie" (they'd gotten on first name terms over dinner), "an' I ain't rich. But I can pay my way. You tell me what Zoe's cost you, an' I'll see that you get it. I aim to take her home with me."

Culpepper looked at Zoe. She said, "No."

Abner got up and stood in front of her. "Nobody says no to me, my girl, not like that. Where's your manners? Besides, it doesn't look good, you staying in Willie's house and eating his food. You come home now like a good girl, an' when you get better, you can come back for the play."

"It's not like that, Abner," Culpepper said. "I feel that I have some responsibility for her: The least I can do is to see her through her recuperation. I assure you that no one thinks badly of Zoe."

"Willie," Abner said, "this is family business. You got no call to intrude. Zoe, I want you home. You're my daughter and you and me ain't seen each other that much. Time we got to know each other. I'm sixty years old an' I want to make peace."

"Peace? What do you mean?" She frowned, looking up at him from the deep armchair.

"You know what I mean."

"You mean, when you beat me up so bad?"

Abner glared at her, his mouth working. "Honey—" he said. And then, with an effort, "Please."

"No, Dad, I can't. I'm sorry. But I'll go back to the city if you want. I'm well enough."

"Please," he said again. It came easier this time.

"No," she said, and burst into tears. "Just go away."

"All *right*, goddamn it," Abner shouted. But then he lowered his voice. "Have it your own way. I'm goin' now."

He turned to leave, stopped, said uncertainly, "I'll be in New York City this week, at Cousin's, if you change . . ."

Zoe didn't show any sign that she heard him. Abner shrugged. He shook hands with Culpepper. "Women," he said. "You send me a bill, Willie, an' I'll send you money." He looked at Zoe, a bleak expression on his face, but then he said softly, "Goodbye, daughter." She didn't look up.

When Barney took her out that night, he noticed that Zoe was in a peculiar mood, both dreamy and tense. She told him about Abner's visit. She made a joke of it, as though it were a scene on stage, and acted out some of the parts. "My father acts as though women don't exist," she said. "He turned Willie's dinner into a stag party." She took on her father's air of sly masculinity and retold part of a story, and then she did the women's reactions, one gone all fluttery and feminine and another contemptuous. "That was Mrs. Francis Dart Montpelier the Third," she said, and Barney laughed. For a moment Zoe had looked like her.

"You're a comedienne too. I didn't know that. So you didn't mind your father too much, after all?"

"Well, let's say I survived him. My father has a certain awful charm. I can see that now. The charm of the male elk, bellowing in the wilderness. Willie adored him."

"I expect he did," Barney said. Over dessert he talked about his dissatisfaction with private practice and his desire to get into research. Maggie was right, of course—Zoe should know what his plans were.

"I can see why you'd prefer that kind of life," Zoe said. "Can't you make a change? What do doctors do, when they're looking for a job—advertise?"

"Not exactly. But they write to places where they'd like to work, or contact people they've worked with before."

"Why not give it a whirl?"

"I already have, Zoe." She became very still. "I've been offered a job, and I've taken it, at the University Medical Center in Kansas. It's exactly what I want—teaching, surgery, and plenty of time for research." He went on to describe the project he had been working on before he'd gone into private practice, and the results he had hoped for. He got out a pencil and, opening up a napkin, he drew the shape of the skull and a potential technique for inserting cobalt into the brain. "The idea is to irradiate the tumor from the inside," he said, and he looked up at her.

A different person looked back at him. Someone in the grand manner. She smiled, showing her perfect teeth, and leaning back in her chair she picked up her wine glass with a gesture that was deliberately elegant and raised it to him. "How perfectly marvelous, darling. I'm so pleased for you. When do you start?"

"At the end of January."

"But that's terrific, isn't it? Have you told anyone? This is a celebration." She took a sip of the wine and toasted him again, but then she put the glass down rather suddenly. She leaned forward and rested her forehead on two fingers and said, "You know, Barney, I believe I'm too tired for the movies. D'you mind? Get the check, darling, would you?" She was pulling on her wrap, smoothing her hair. "Dear me, I'm just not up to everything yet."

Barney looked at her, confused, but suddenly the waiter was hanging over them. "You're wanted on the phone, Dr. Lukacs," he said.

"Damn," said Barney, standing. "They've tracked me down. Get off this act, Zoe. This isn't the Palace. Don't move; I'll be right back."

It was St. Mark's on the phone. He'd told them where he'd be. Another motorcycle accident—urgent, as always—was waiting for him in Emergency. He paid the bill and called a taxi for Zoe. When he came back, she had already started for the door. Even with a stick she moved gracefully, head high, her body swinging lightly forward. People turned to watch her, and Barney could see the recognition in their faces. "That's Zoe Carter," they were saying. "She's in Culpepper's play. She's the one who . . ."

Zoe turned to wait for him at the door. She smiled radiantly. He opened it for her, and they went out.

Zoe fell, going upstairs. There was no reason for it; she'd been going up and downstairs for almost a month. But tonight the cane slipped. She seized the banister and watched the cane slide and clatter down the steps. Culpepper and Ngiep, who were playing chess, came running out to the hall. Ngiep leapt up the curve of the stairs. She swayed, one hand reaching out, and Ngiep reached her as she turned, her skinny dress sparkling, and overbalanced downwards.

He blocked the fall. They collapsed together into the uphill slope of the steps, Ngiep underneath, and nothing happened. They lay there, and Culpepper came up, and then the two of them helped Zoe down to a couch in the living room, where Culpepper fussed with the pillows and a throw, patting Zoe with quick fluttering pats, and getting her a brandy. The ivory chess men gleamed on the black-and-white squares of the board, and the fire hissed.

Ngiep put some things on a tea tray and started to go out. Zoe thanked him in an excited way, speaking breathlessly and playing with the fringe on the blanket. Culpepper got his glass of wine and sat beside her.

"Can I get you anything else?" he asked.

"No, thank you. I can't think what happened there, all of a sudden."

Culpepper brushed at his suede jacket with his fat hands. His eyes were calm. "What's the matter, Zoe? Why didn't Barney bring you home?"

"He had an emergency. I'm all right, really. Don't fuss."

"I don't think you are. You're splendidly capable with that stick of yours—but not so capable with your emotions. Something has happened."

"Barney's going away."

"I know."

"You know? But he just decided—"

"He's been considering it for some time."

"But apparently nobody thought of informing me!"

"Barney said he'd tell you himself." Culpepper sat

quietly for a few minutes, watching the flames, and Zoe, watching him, tried to absorb a little of his serenity. She was hurt and angry. Apparently everybody had known but her. Apparently she had overestimated her importance in Barney's life. Apparently he was just going about his business, getting a job, leaving town, not even thinking it was worth telling her about. Or worse, he was treating her with kid gloves, like an infatuated schoolgirl, jollying her along until she got over it. Or like an excited female patient, hanging onto her doctor and imagining that he was in love with her in that self-important way that women can have. She flushed painfully.

"When did he tell you?"

"A couple of weeks ago. Somebody wants the cottage, so I asked him if he'd be staying or not."

It was all so ordinary. There was nothing of any significance between her and Barney. She was just another piece of business in his life, a loose end to be tied up before he left. He'd been kind to her, and she'd made a fool of herself. Another wave of scarlet flushed across her face and neck.

Culpepper took her hand and began to stroke it in a dreamy way. His voice was dreamy too, and he didn't look at her. "I can see where you'd like him, Zoe. He's a likable fellow. And he may have had some romantic feelings. But it's all wrong for you, sweetie, he wants a *Frau*. A nice girl who'll follow him anywhere and do what he says and play domestic games. Is that you, with your beautiful talent? You will fly, Zoe, while Barney still putters around in the garbage of ordinary life. Besides," he said charmingly, "you are mine." He shifted his enormous eyes to hers. "I found you. We could even get married, if that's what you would like."

Zoe looked away.

"You care too much about love," he went on, still stroking her hand. "Hold tight to what you do. Your work is everything. Your salvation, and ours too. You'll be a very great actress, one of the best." The fire sputtered. Something popped in a shower of sparks, little incendiaries which blazed for a second and then went into darkness, and Zoe shivered. Willie was right, perhaps; but it seemed very cold.

"I don't see why I have to be a nun to be an actress. It's not a religion, after all."

"All art is a religion. It's a matter of priorities. In *your* life, art comes first."

She was calmer now, hypnotized by Culpepper's quiet voice and the transient flames. She had a purpose in her life—the same purpose that had sustained her since she was tiny. She wasn't a fool; she was a hard-working, disciplined actress. That's what she was good at, and that's what she would do.

Barney walked into emergency at St. Mark's fourteen minutes after he left the restaurant. The boy was comatose, almost cyanotic. He was choking on his own secretions. They couldn't get the suction tube in, so Barney did a hasty tracheotomy. He made a quick slash in the neck, snapped hemostats on the bleeders and cut into the tracheal cartilage. An enormous blast of air and mucous was expelled, spraying him and the nurse and the resident.

"Thank God," Barney said, and inserted the tube. In a matter of seconds the patient regained a normal color, and Barney went on to examine the head and neck injuries. They were bad, and Barney took great care. Zoe's changed face hovered in the back of his mind, hurt and defensive, her eyes two green points and her mouth talking away like an actress. He had a panicky feeling that he'd done something irrevocable.

His uneasiness grew while he finished the examining, arranged for medication, talked to the mother who was waiting outside. Finally he was outside in the starry night and climbing into his car and driving home, and the whole source of his anxiety burst in on him. Zoe had thought she didn't matter to him. What else should she think, after all? He'd done it all wrong.

He drove swiftly, angry with himself and angry with her. Why couldn't she have more faith in him? The answer came easily enough: She didn't have that much faith in herself. She lacked confidence. Offstage, that is. Onstage she was just fine. That irritated him, and he sped along the highway in an unhappy daze. His personal life, like the dark spaces unfolding around him, seemed too muddy to resolve.

When he got home, he didn't go in right away. He went up the outside steps and stopped on the balcony outside his door. It was cold. He shivered and looked up toward Culpepper's house. There were lights in Zoe's windows. Perhaps she was in there watching the cottage. Perhaps she had seen his headlights when he drove up, and her heart had leapt into her eyes as he had seen it do.

He wanted suddenly to run up the hill and tell her. Tell her what? She thought he was leaving without her. He must tell her quickly. It was all utterly clear to him, suddenly and without preamble. He loved her. He couldn't leave her. He wanted to tell her. He wanted the ceremony, the acknowledgment, the recognition of love. He looked at his watch. Eleven thirty. He couldn't go up there, this late. But it didn't matter. It would all work out. Maybe there were some theaters in Kansas. They could get married; he would ask her tomorrow.

*   *   *

Zoe stayed in her room all day, resting up from her fall. Ngiep brought things to eat, and she immersed herself in a book that Brother Luke had left for her. It was a paperback with a purple cover. Under the title, which was *Jesus,* a passage from the Bible was printed in large white type.

It was about twelve o'clock when the sun stopped shining and darkness covered the whole country until three o'clock; and the curtain hanging in the temple was torn in two. Jesus cried out in a loud voice, "Father! In your hands I place my spirit!" He said this and died.

God, how beautiful. So utterly simple: *In Your hands I place my spirit.* No problems; no unknowns. I'm hopeless at human relations, Zoe thought. I don't trust anyone. Last night in the restaurant, for instance, when Barney had told her about his job. She'd been so wounded; she'd ruffled her feathers like a goddamn turkey. What a fool I am, she thought.

Suddenly she remembered a time, she must have been very little, when her father had come home from work and collapsed into an armchair. She had run to him and clasped his knees, and when he didn't look at her, she had climbed up to his lap. His face was yellowish—perhaps he'd been sick—and he didn't even open his eyes. She had reached up and pushed his eyelid open, and his bloodshot eye had stared at her without any pupil showing. She didn't remember any more, just that awful eye where she had looked for the eye of love.

Jesus wouldn't do that, she thought, and then she laughed at herself: *I must be losing my marbles.* No, she wouldn't go that route. She had her work, and as Willie said, it was better for her to be single-minded about it. She saw herself in the future, moving in and out of lights, a white figure sternly dedicated to the art. Willie was right. It felt right. She needed it. She had to be involved in something big and impersonal, where her miserable little ego didn't keep poking and scratching at her.

It was a relief to arrive at a decision. They had probably all been right, after all. She had been ill and susceptible and she'd done the storybook thing: she'd fallen in love with her doctor. Now she was stronger, thank God. She could remain aloof.

She was still in bed, studying, when there was a knock at the door and Barney came in. He looked magnificent. He was rosy and joyful. He came toward her with quick vigorous steps.

Zoe looked up. She was still in her dressing gown. There was fluffy white fox fur around her neck and shoulders, and she wore a pair of half glasses for reading. She pushed them down on her nose and peered at him over the top.

"Oh, good morning, Barney. How are you?" She held out her hand.

He paused, surprised, and then shook it.

"Do sit down. I'm pleased that you came by. How soon do you think I can get back to work? Willie thinks it wouldn't hurt if Amanda has a limp."

"No, I don't suppose it would. Do you feel ready?"

"More than ready. I'm dying to start." Zoe took off her glasses. Her head fell back on the pillow; her eyes closed and she passed her hand over them, rubbing her lids.

"Barney, *would* you pull the blind? The light . . ."

The light? Barney thought. It was snowing outside. He turned at the window.

"Yip tells me that you fell last night," he said.

"Wasn't he marvelous?" she said. "He simply

sprang up the staircase to rescue me. He has more bruises than I do."

"Nevertheless, I'll have to examine you."

"Thank you, but it's not necessary. There's nothing."

Barney pulled back the covers, and did a methodical examination. Her delicate milky skin stirred him, but she was remote, a patient. She had a bruise on her elbow. She got up and walked for him, with and without her cane.

"You see?" she said, sitting in a chair. "My fall was a reminder, Barney. It's time for me to get back to work."

"Of course, you have to get back to work; it's important to you. But work isn't everything. You have a personal life too."

"Maybe I don't. Maybe all I need is my work." She sounded offended.

"Look, I'm sorry about the way I broke the news to you. I've been thinking about it. I've been thinking about you, I mean us, and . . ."

"I've been thinking about it too, and you don't have to worry about me. I'm fine. I've come through everything now, and I'm all together. Emotionally, physically. I'm standing on my own two feet."

"Yeah, but maybe I'm not."

"Sure you are, Barney. I really don't think you need anybody. People lean on you; you don't lean on people."

"What are you trying to say?"

"Nothing. Nothing at all. You've been incredibly good to me, Barney."

"It's more than that, Zoe . . ."

"I'm sorry. Of course it's more than that," she said warmly but coldly. She reached out to him with one hand. The other pulled the white fur together over her chest. A snake curled around one finger, its ruby eye glinting.

"You've been absolutely marvelous to me." Her voice dropped and took on its ready, deeper tones. "Thank you, Barney. I hope your new job is everything you want it to be."

It sounded like good-bye. Barney hesitated, confused and angry, and then he left. Zoe heard him banging down the stairs. She sobbed miserably, the tears running down her cheeks and on to the fur. She half-hoped he would hear her and come back. But Barney had flung open the door of the closet downstairs in the hall. He was rummaging around looking for his coat. Willie had been listening for him and came out of the living room.

"Is she all right?" he asked.

"She's running on all two cylinders," said Barney, shrugging into a battered down jacket. "Did you put her up to this, Willie?"

"Up to what, my dear fellow? What's the matter? Come in for a moment. What will you have?"

P. J. Krupp and Billy King Hunt were having a drink in front of the fire. Barney took a scotch. Hunt shook his hand and asked him how Zoe was doing.

"Fabulous," said Barney bitterly.

"Can we set any kind of a schedule? My God, we're into December already."

"No."

"Nothing at all? Two weeks? Two months? No idea at all? We don't want to press her, but I've got a whole production waiting in the wings."

"You mean, she's a valuable property?"

"You're damn tootin'. She's a gold mine."

Barney laughed. Precious Zoe. "Well, Willie," he said, "you know I can't commit myself, but strictly off the record, *and* if you can do with a slight limp, I'd say she'd be ready to go a month from now. That's not for publication. And don't say anything to her yet, for God's sake. Something tells me she's not quite ready for the real world."

Yesterday's snow dusted the ground, but the day was brilliant. Zoe's room was full of light, sharp and clean, defining the gables and the angles of her ceiling, shining on the wheelchair she no longer needed, glimmering on the stainless steel of the breakfast set.

There was a single scarlet rosebud on her tray and the morning paper, neatly folded. The coffee had a rich Byzantine smell. Zoe lifted the cover from her breakfast plate: bacon and chicken livers, scrambled eggs, English muffin. On the radio a light voice was singing "Darling Billy." She sipped some coffee.

She had *cast off*: she was floating in a great bay of light. She wouldn't see Barney again; it was too hard. She was free and unshackled, strong, alone. *Free. Alone.*

She wanted to dissolve into those bright solitary spaces that seemed to be revealing themselves beyond her room. What were they? she wondered. The fabled realms of art, now open to her by virtue of her aloneness? So vast! So cold! She turned away, and as the angles of her vision shifted (she seemed to be looking at the universe through a giant white kaleidoscope) there in the middle was an ivory eye, compelling and implacable, drawing her in. She stared at it, resisting, and then with an effort she pulled herself back to reality, her room, the reds and blues of the oriental carpet on the floor. There was a buzzing in her ears.

Zoe looked at her tray. She had eaten her breakfast. Oh, Barney, she thought, willing him to come. The same voice was singing on the radio, *I've got spurs*

that jingle, jangle, jingle, and she started to laugh,
but her laugh threatened to get out of control and
she clamped her mouth shut. My God, my God, why
have you forsaken me? I am an artist, she thought.
And then, *Who am I?*

She shook her head. Why was everything suddenly
untethered, floating? Her room was full of fragments,
bits of plants and furniture that vibrated and seemed
to move toward her. She clutched the breakfast table
and shook her head again. The room steadied. She
mustn't let things get out of control. She wanted reality, solid objects, hard facts. Her eye fell on the *Island News,* still neatly folded on her tray. She picked
it up and opened it. On the front page, right in the
middle, was a smiling photograph of herself. It gave
her a terrific jolt of pleasure: SISTER GLORY REGAINS
HEALTH. She looked like a good trooper, in a battered
trench coat with the collar up, her short hair swinging over her face, a leather bag and some binoculars
over her shoulder. She remembered the photo; it was a
still left over from a stint she had done as a model for
a magazine story. She read on. The article had
Krupp's byline.

> Zoe Carter, slated for the lead in Willard
> Culpepper's new play, *Sister Glory,* is making a
> remarkable recovery from the waterskiing acci-
> dent that broke her back and delayed production
> of the play for at least four months. Neurosurgeon
> Barney Lukacs, who performed the notable "ice
> pack operation" on Miss Carter, describes her
> condition as "fabulous." She will be functioning
> normally by mid-January, when rehearsals for the
> born again play will commence. Miss Carter, one
> might say, will herself be born again.

* * *

January? So soon. Zoe's heart started to thump heavily. She wasn't ready. She couldn't be ready. Spasms of fright spread out from her belly. She wasn't strong enough. The slope of the ceiling seemed to harden and tremble, the walls to close in. Her chest was tight, as though her lungs were overinflated balloons. There wasn't room for the air she kept breathing. A great bird was growing inside her, or inside her room, spreading its wings from wall to wall. Her mother, lying in a cluttered dark room after Buddy was born, said, "I wish I could die." *What's the matter with me?* Zoe thought, and into her mind came a dark, plush horseshoe of a theater, with dim points of light and red letters saying EXIT, filled with an audience whose faces stare back at her. She is alone on stage. They are beasts. Their long wet tongues hang out of their whitish faces; their eyes are vivid holes. *What if I'm no good?* Her legs seem to have melted. She falls on the boards and looks up into the flies, where sheets of canvas and bare battens hang over her, and the gridiron way way up, and the great bird thrashing and hawking in a panic, and herself struggling to get to her feet.

Her tray had fallen on the floor. The bed felt wet. Zoe carefully folded the newspaper and put it on the bedside table. *I must be very careful,* she thought. *I mustn't babble. I can do that part. I want to do that part.* Acid sweat ran down the sides of her body. She wanted to touch somebody, to be touched, to be warm. The inside of her body felt raw, like a wound.

There was a knock at the door. Willie poked his head in. It looked grotesque.

"Zoe!" he said. Then he saw her face. "My dear, what is it?"

There was for Zoe a terrible silence. A void. A thunderclap. What would she say? She didn't know. She seemed to be sinking. She stared up at him. He put an arm around her shoulders, and the sudden warmth moved her to tears. Her teeth chattered.

"I can't move my legs," she said.

Culpepper waited drearily in the coffee shop. It was almost empty, but there was a clatter of dishes behind the counter. Two residents in green laundered coats hunched over a table. The door opened and some nurses came in, chattering and laughing. Behind them came Austin Foote, clumping briskly, swinging his stick. He stopped and twirled it, while he located Culpepper.

"Mr. Culpepper," he said, holding out his hand. He sat down. "I'm sorry. I haven't got very good news for you."

"Well."

"It's just as I thought. There's too much scar tissue in there. We shouldn't have operated."

"Scar tissue?"

"Scar tissue can form from any wound. Fibroblasts come into the remnants of the blood clot and form tissue. In this case, there was simply too much bleeding. A postoperative hematoma. In other words, there's a clot in there and tissue forms from it, in the sheath which contains the spinal cord. It grows, hardens, presses on the cord itself." Foote spread his heavy hands. "And there you are."

He spoke in a heavy, compassionate voice, but there was an air of triumph lurking there, suitably damped.

"What does that all mean?" asked Culpepper. "Will you have to operate again to remove the scar tissue?"

"It's too late for that. Perhaps, if it had been done postoperatively. Now it would only compound the problem. In these areas surgery frequently creates more problems than it solves. As I said . . . er."

"Well, then?"

"Miss Carter is suffering from chronic adhesive arachnoiditis. Her condition is roughly the same as it was after the accident. It's best to face these things. She has minimum function from D-9 on down. From the point of trauma, that is."

"I can't believe it. D-9?"

"The waist."

"You mean there's no remedy? No surgery? A nerve transplant?"

"I am so sorry, Mr. Culpepper. Nerves do not regenerate. Once damaged, they cannot be rejoined. I could pretend to offer you some hope, but I don't believe it. Further surgery will induce an added growth of scar tissue, and she runs the risk of even further deficit."

"Deficit?"

"Lack of function. Paraplegia, perhaps. Total paralysis. You must realize, Mr. Culpepper, that life is not over for her. She's not that badly off. There are many things she can do."

"I'll have to get another opinion, Dr. Foote."

"Of course. I can suggest an eminent neurologist, if you like. But perhaps you have someone in mind. I'd like to emphasize that this is a problem in neurology, rather than neurosurgery." He looked at Culpepper.

"You don't think Barney should see her?"

"I didn't say that."

Barney had been off duty when Zoe was brought in, and anyway she had refused to see him. She appeared to be afraid of him, but Culpepper didn't say anything to Foote. "What happens now?" he asked.

"She can go home, if you want. She'll need extensive therapy, of course, to learn how to manage herself. There are rehabilitation centers. She'll have to face some difficult realities."

"So will I," Culpepper said.

PART II

It was only the fourth of December—the day of Zoe's relapse—but there were Christmas lights already. Max Ward grimaced. *Jingle bells, jingle bells.* His life seemed to have ground to a standstill, mired in tacky little divorce cases, collections, closings. "You call that a law practice?" his father would have said with a sneer. "I call it garbage."

Max turned south off Montauk onto one of those long streets which lead down to the sea. In East Hampton and Bridgehampton and Southampton they are lined with trees that meet gracefully overhead; in Hampton Bays they are lined with little ranch houses. He swore under his breath at his Toyota, which was underpowered, and then apologized to the car out loud, in case it decided to take offense and die on him.

Doorways and porches shone with colored lights. A life-sized creche—stable, sheep, Mary, Wise Men, star—was set up on a trim lawn, illuminated by spotlights, and on the low pitch of the roof behind it was a full sleigh with Santa Claus driving, and all eight of his Donners and Blitzens landing near the ridgepole.

His family had always spent Christmas at his grandmother's farm when Max was young. They'd go out into the woods and cut hemlock boughs and saplings to cover the walls in the pine room; they made stained glass out of brown paper rolls and cellophane to cover the long windows; and they lit a big fire. He could smell, in retrospect, the resinous evergreen and woodsmoke, and the wax on Christmas Eve after they put the candles out. Self-pity and rage attacked him: What was he doing on Long Island? He didn't belong here.

But soon the houses were behind him and there were fields and the smell of the sea, and then he turned into a road devoted to old summer cabins. Each group was clustered around a central office, where a peeling sign carried a message like "The Roses . . . Cottages" or "The Smiling Dolphin." His own group was called "The Windmill." The office was shaped like a miniature windmill, white and blue where the paint was still on it. Max rented a cottage year round. Since nobody else was there in the winter, it was very cheap.

There was a light on, which was nice. Carole was there already. His headlights swept the dock at the end of the road as he turned in. Carole heard the car door. She came out on the porch, smiling and hugging her arms and shivering. She kissed him.

The cottage was warm and steamy. Max had installed a gas heater with its own bulk tank. The table was laid for dinner. There was a bunch of flowers and two candles. Carole had drinks ready: hot buttered rum. She wore lots of eye make-up and an ultra-suede pants suit.

"I didn't expect you so soon," he said. "What about the kids?"

"They're with their father. He took them a day early. How's every little thing?"

"Fine. You?"

"Okay. You notice anything different?"

Max looked around.

"Wine on the table?"

"Um-hmm."

"Flowers? What's up?"

"Oh, nothing. Anything else?"

"Smells good in here."

"Umm." She sat down on the arm of his chair and looked at him pointedly. He laughed, in an embarrassed way, and shrugged. She turned her head, putting a hand to her hair.

"Aha. You've got a new hairdo. It's very nice."

Why did women have to be *loved*? Carole was all right—a good girl friend, useful and obliging. But he'd like her better if he wasn't supposed to love her. He put his hand to her head and smoothed it. "You look wonderful," he said.

"I am wonderful. You just wait." Her eyes, with the messy lavender around them, shot messages of pleasure and affection.

"What's for dinner?" he asked.

Carole served up a steak. Max opened the wine, and he said the right things, and she was once again reassured.

"What's all this in aid of, Carole? Are we celebrating something?"

"Not really. I'm just feeling good about my—research."

He frowned. "What are you talking about?"

"I'm talking about Zoe Carter and Dr. Barney Lukacs."

"What about them?"

"The poor thing's had a relapse. It may be the kind of thing you've been waiting for."

Max sat back in his chair. His stomach felt suddenly warm and sweet—the rum?—and the untuned fragments of himself, which had seemed to be all over the place, were called home.

"What exactly happened?"

Carole gave him the details.

"And Foote is her doctor. Not Barney?"

"She won't even see him. I don't know what happened. It was the great romance of the year. I feel kind of sorry for them, but as you say, it's the insurance company that pays."

Max was suddenly all business. "Get me the dates, will you? Admission and discharge; you'll have them in your bookkeeping files. I'll get the records. I want them before the hospital's alerted. I've got to get this case. It's going to be a case where we sue the pants off everyone—the surgeon, the assisting surgeon, the hospital, the lot. Too bad we can't get the police department in there. Wait till the jury sees this plaintiff: beautiful, talented Zoe Carter, destroyed by that knife-happy son of a bitch. Trapped forever in her silver wheelchair. I'll dress her in white. And what a witness she'll make—an actress! Poised, restrained, hesitant to make any charges. I'll take the same attitude, right down to the wire. Then I'll let 'em have it."

"Hey, Max, take it easy. You don't even know if she'll sue. Barney and her were, you know—" She held up two fingers close together.

"Yeah, well why isn't he seeing her then? Why didn't she call him in?"

"I don't know. He was off duty. Or maybe they had a fight."

"That would be even better. She might be glad to sue. Let me think. I'll make a call on Mr. J. Willard Culpepper first, feel out the ground."

"Zoe's father's around somewhere."

"Is he? Good. Perhaps he'll have some business sense. He'll want his daughter properly represented—God knows what these theater people think about. I don't know if I can get this case, but the more it's in the news, the better. I'll have to see Krupp. I want to make sure the papers are full of it. Carole, you're wonderful." He kissed her and said suggestively: "This may be the beginning of something big."

There was a casement window on the east wall of Barney's bedroom. As the sun rose it reflected off a mirror on the far wall and, this morning, because of the wind blowing the trees outside, it made a morning tattoo in bright flashes.

Barney groaned and turned his head into the pillow. He was in the middle of a dream. His wife Connie, larger than life, was wheeling him along a country road toward a hospital, a shining tower that rose among the hills ahead of him. There had been a lot of political maneuvers, and papers signed by Connie, and now she was taking him in for a therapeutic operation in which he would be cut in half at the waist. Piri, about six years old in the dream, was dancing around the wheelchair, silent and powerless and terribly distressed, trying to stop her mother. Barney groaned again and turned over. He opened his eyes and shut them quickly against the glare. But he preferred to wake up, so he turned away from the mirror and opened his eyes again.

He thought it was a stupid dream. His marriage was over. It had been his fault as much as hers. They'd loved each other, and then they'd gone in different directions. The gap had widened, painfully, and they'd both become bitter. He hadn't taken the trouble to understand what she wanted. He'd thought that in marriage the man was more important than the woman. He'd been afraid of her female power.

He was different now. Ready for a real marriage, a partnership. He thought sadly about his last encounter with Zoe: another example of human confusion. She had gotten defensive after he told her he was going to Kansas. When he had gone to her to offer himself, he had been hurt by her coldness. Then yesterday, his day off, he had deliberately stayed away from her. Now there was all that confusion between them to be ironed out.

But it was not irreversible. He would see her again, today, and explain himself with absolute clarity and gentleness, even if she was holding him at arm's length. He knew in some ultimate, irrational way that she loved him. All he had to do was make it clear that it was mutual.

He felt suddenly joyful, optimistic. He leapt out of bed and dressed. He would see her today. Take her down to Van's for lunch, away from Culpepper's. First, rounds at the hospital. Call her from there. He was only taking a leave of absence next year. If Kansas didn't work for her, they'd come back here. The dream had been sent as a reminder: The enemy of love is fear.

Early that same morning Max went to a surgical supply store in Bay Shore. He bought a white cotton jacket and a stethoscope. Then he called the Mersey Rehabilitation Center. He asked the receptionist to recommend a doctor to consult about his recuperation from a bad back injury.

"Dr. Thompson is the man you want, sir. Dr. Bailey Thompson."

Later that day he walked into the medical librarian's office at St. Mark's. He was wearing the white jacket, and the stethoscope bounced against his breast. Her name was on the door.

"Hello, Mrs. Ardsley. I'm Dr. Thompson from Mersey. I need more information on Zoe Carter." He looked at her gravely. I'd like some precise data on her mobility immediately before and after the original operation, which was on . . ." he fished a note pad out of his pocket, "August thirteenth."

"Such a shame, isn't it, Dr. Thompson? Hold on, I'll get her file."

When she came back, Max took the file and sat down. He flipped through it, concentrating on three or four detailed sheets. He went back to the desk.

"Give me a Xerox copy of these, will you? And, I think this one, and this. I've already talked to Dr. Morton, but I'll take a couple of his reports on re-hab."

"Sure thing. I won't be a minute."

Max sat down again, while she went over to the copier. His heart was beating fast. The phone rang, and Mrs. Ardsley answered it. It was obviously a friend. They were talking about somebody's wedding. Max squirmed. Hurry, hurry, he thought. Finally she hung up, and went on with the Xerox.

Austin Foote put his head in the door. He was rushed.

"Get out Zoe Carter's records again, will you, Mrs. Ardsley?"

She looked up. "I've got them right here, Dr. Foote, if you'll wait a minute. Dr. Thompson—"

Max froze, but Foote said, "Good. I'll be right back to pick them up." He pushed off down the hall. Mrs. Ardsley finished up. She put the sheets in a new file folder, labeled it, and handed it to Max.

"There you are, Dr. Thompson. And good luck. Do you think her chances are—"

"Thanks so much. Sorry, I have to run. But yes, I think her chances are excellent, for a long and comfortable life." He smiled at her and skipped out the door. Down the stairs he went, clutching the file, and

back into his Toyota. He pulled up at the first bar he
came to, buttoned his overcoat over his medical identity, and downed the most refreshing beer he'd ever
had. Then he went to the phone to make an appointment with Culpepper.

Wisps and streamers of cloud were blowing in from
the east, obscuring the early brightness. Barney
pulled in at the stationery shop to pick up the *Times*.
He was on his way to the hospital for morning
rounds. He would call Zoe when he got there, make
a date for lunch, and at lunch everything would come
clear. He jumped out of the car and walked buoyantly into the shop.

"Morning," he said to Mr. Osborne.

"Morning, Barney, how are you? Sorry to hear
about your star patient."

"What star patient?" asked Barney, feeling a preliminary tremor in the solid earth.

"Why, Miss Carter." Mr. Osborne waved his hand
at the *Island News*. Barney saw Zoe's name in a headline. He paid for the paper and took it out to the
Porsche. ZOE CARTER RELAPSE. Krupp again. Barney
read through the piece: paralysis, Foote, chronic adhesive arachnoiditis. *Arachnoiditis!* He's out of his
mind. Why hadn't Zoe called him? The paper said
she was at St. Mark's.

When he got there, he went straight to radiology.

"Sorry about Miss Carter, Doctor," the radiologist
said, not quite looking at Barney. A week ago everybody had referred to her as Zoe. Now it was Miss Carter: she must be in bad shape.

Barney put the original X rays up in the view box,
and yesterday's next to them. They'd done a myelogram too. He put that up. There was scar tissue, but
that was to be assumed after such an operation. It

was definite but not massive. The myelogram was unclear: a fair amount of the contrast had gotten past the point of operation. There was some obstruction, but it was not a blockage. The pictures did not differ enormously from what Barney would have expected if she were still making progress. Nevertheless, it was possible that the scar tissue was more extensive than appeared, tethering the spinal cord, that it was worst at the point where he had removed the spicule, that it was reproducing the conditions for the Brown-Sequard symptomology.

As he went upstairs, he reviewed the operation in his mind. He was sure it had been clean. Once the spicule had been removed, there was no reason that the fibers of the cord should not have closed again around the vertical slit that it had made. There had been a lot of blood. Had he cauterized insufficiently? Perhaps there was another bone fragment. Even the first one, the one that he'd removed, had not shown up in the original X rays. But if there was another, why had her recovery been so perfect?

The light was dim in the stairway, absorbed by cement block walls and shining dully on the green-tiled steps. Only the staff used it. As Barney climbed toward the hollow steel door that gave on the third floor, it opened and Austin Foote emerged hurriedly, squat and powerful in his black suit. The light in the ceiling, right over his head, picked up the iron-gray spikes of his hair and cast his long shadow down on Barney. He waited.

"Good morning, Barney."

"Hello, Austin. I've just seen Zoe's X rays. Where is she?"

"Room 356. What did you think of them?"

"I don't know. They're not conclusive. However, I

see from the paper that you have drawn your conclusions."

"Indeed I have. You know how much blood there was. Capillary oozing. Obviously there's been a massive formation of scar tissue, and just what you'd expect, a compromise of the local blood supply."

"That's absurd," Barney said. "Your description of a five-millimeter scar as massive is absurd. Furthermore, there's nothing unusual about scar forming at the site of bony penetration."

"Barney, you haven't seen her. There's no doubt that clinically and radiographically, she has chronic adhesive arachnoiditis. Her motor signs have deteriorated. She has a Babinski sign. The blood supply is clearly impaired. But we don't have to carry this any further at this point."

"Right," said Barney. "I'll go have a look at her."

"I'm sorry," Foote said. "I have to inform you that she is my patient now. There is no call here for neurosurgery: additional surgery, as you know, can only compound the problem. I was called on the case; it is now my case. Miss Carter has informed me that she would prefer not to see you. Given her emotional state, I think I must ask you to respect her wishes."

Barney looked at him. It was as though he had received a powerful blow in the middle of his back. He could think of nothing to say. Foote glared back at him. The silence, and the bleakness of the stairway, were incredibly personal. Barney pushed past Foote on the narrow landing, pulled open the heavy door, and found himself under the bright flat lights of the corridor. He went straight to Zoe's room.

Her bed had been wound up so that she was halfsitting. There were dark moist shadows under her eyes, as though they had been done in watercolor on a wet day, but her face was resigned and passive, her mouth soft. Oh, my dear, thought Barney. He went straight to her and gently gripped her shoulders.

"Zoe, what happened?" he asked in a low voice.

She didn't answer. She seemed to be looking out at him from an impossible distance. He tightened his grip.

"Zoe?"

After a while, he said, "You must speak to me. Let me help you."

Her mouth opened, and closed, and in a voice full of grief and surprise she said, "I can't."

It was an awkward situation. He really shouldn't be here at all, and certainly he should not examine her. It was unethical, under the circumstances, and it seemed to be giving her pain.

He looked over his shoulder. There was no one in sight. He pulled down the covers. Her hospital gown was rucked up, and he tugged it down over her thighs. He pinched the Achilles tendon of her weak leg. There was no response. He didn't have a pin on him, or anything sharp, so he tickled the sole of her left foot. The big toe lifted sharply. The Babinski sign. It was all in keeping with the Brown-Sequard.

He looked over his shoulder again. What swift examination would give him the information he wanted in the most immediate way? Position sense, perhaps. He put his thumb under her big toe and pushed it up.

"Where's your big toe, Zoe? Is it up or down?"

"Down," she said, without any hesitation.

"Now where is it?"

"Up."

"Now?"

"Up."

"And now?"

"Down."

She answered rapidly. Sometimes she made mistakes, but she never hesitated. Barney heaved a sigh of relief.

"Not bad," he said.

A patient with an impaired position sense doesn't answer so quickly. She doesn't know where the toe is. She would be sweating it out, feeling for answers, saying, "Try it again; try it just once more." Barney was pretty sure the machinery was all there. The nervous system was in order; the *mind* was telling Zoe how to answer. He smiled at her. She wouldn't even understand that if he told her, but at least he knew. She was not paralyzed; she was hysterical.

"Listen to me. You can get over this. Don't worry about anything. Rest. Take it easy. Nobody can make you do anything you don't want to do. When you're ready, call me. I can't even recommend a consultation, unless you ask for me. But you must see another neurologist." Did that sound like pressure to her, he wondered? "*When* you're ready," he repeated.

God, what drivel, he thought. He was running off at the mouth. He couldn't seem to stop talking, but he couldn't reach her either.

He covered her up again and turned her head gently, so she was looking at him. "Get well, Zoe. You have a life to live. And we have a whole life to share, if you want it. I love you."

She didn't answer. There was nothing else he could do. He wished he could call a psychiatrist for a consultation. He felt stunned, empty.

There were rounds to make. The motorcycle case, Martinson, was still in a coma. Rain was streaking down the windows. The sorrowful faces of patients followed his progress down the hall. He was trying to remember Freud's analysis of the hysterical conversion reaction, but his memory was imprecise. There

was that one case, a woman named Anna O., where
the reasons for paralysis had been entirely psychic.
He had no surgery today, thank God, but he had to
give testimony in a compensation case at Riverhead.
The library there was decent. Once he'd finished his
rounds, he would do some research.

There were vast puddles on both sides of Lily Pond
Lane, so Max drove straight down the middle. As he
turned into Culpepper's driveway he shifted down to
second. The Toyota coughed and stalled out. Max
looked around. Barney's cottage on the right, the tennis court, the eaves and timbers of the enormous garage, the rhododendra. He got the Toyota going
again, and it coughed along the driveway and around
the circular sweep to the front porch. Ngiep showed
him into the living room and then disappeared to
bring in a tray of coffee.

Culpepper called after him. "Make it Irish coffee,
Yip."

Max had invested in a glorious Harris tweed jacket
for this occasion, and he wore his old good whipcord
pants and a black turtleneck. When the coffee came,
heaped with fresh whipped cream, he hunched forward in his chair and applied himself to reducing the
mound to a drinkable level. The sharp mellow taste
of the whiskey made him lick his lips. Then he said
abruptly, "Let me get right to the point, Mr. Culpepper. I want Zoe Carter to sue Lukacs, Rubin, and St.
Mark's Hospital. She'll sue for malfeasance, misfeasance, and malpractice, and I want to handle it for
her."

Culpepper was astonished. "But my dear fellow,"
he said, "What an extraordinary idea. What possible
basis do you find for such a thing?"

"What basis?" asked Max indignantly. "A young

woman, like Zoe, with her life destroyed by an arrogant and incompetent surgeon? A star? A lifelong
career in the theater and perhaps in the movies?
Doomed to spend the rest of her life as a cripple?"
He leaned back in his chair, and placed the tips of
his fingers and thumbs together as though his hands
contained some delicate abstraction. It was a gesture
his father had been in the habit of making.

"Do go on," said Culpepper, appreciating the performance.

"There is an injustice to consider. Are doctors ac-
countable to no one? They collect intolerable fees,
and they can do it because they have the power of
life and death. They speak a special language, and if
anyone questions their special knowledge, they are
beside themselves with rage. Do you tell your doctor
off when he charges you three hundred dollars to
treat a broken toe? You wouldn't dare. You're afraid
he'll let you die at some moment when the chips are
down."

"You've got a way with words," said Culpepper.

Max ignored him. "But do they care for their
flocks, these technological shepherds? Do they make
house calls? Do they give you real attention in their
honeycomb offices? Nonsense. You're lucky if you get
five minutes of their time. You go in there with
twenty other patients. You finally get to go into your
cubicle. You wait there, undressed, shivering, afraid,
while he sees five other patients in five other cubicles,
wondering whether or not you're going to die. Then
he makes his entrance. Busy. Distracted. Trying to
remember which one you are. You don't talk it over
with him: there are too many others waiting. He ex-
amines you and disappears. You wait half an hour in
his office until, somewhere between x, y, and z he gets
a moment to come in and hand down his judgment.

Clutching your prescriptions, for God knows what mysterious potions, each one worth its weight in plutonium, you go and pay your bill to the lady at the outside shrine. Thirty dollars, if you're lucky. Come back in three weeks. Another thirty dollars. For eight minutes. And who are you? Nobody he knows, but he has fulfilled his obligation. And it's worse, if you have the bad luck to penetrate the hospital. A production line, costing your whole life. A marketplace: we sell health. It appalls me.

"Lukacs is one of the worst. He digs into people's brains. Half the time there's no hope anyway, but he gets a charming fee for trying. He's arrogant, bull-headed and optimistic. Foote told him not to operate. But he wasn't about to give up that fee. He'll do anything. He's been sued twice already.

"Think a little further. How is Miss Carter going to live now? Who is going to support her? Do you think Lukacs is going to make it up to her, for taking her means of livelihood? No. He has insurance. But the only way she can tap that insurance is to take legal action."

Willie was silent for a moment. A series of expressions passed through his round eyes, made bigger by his glasses. Surprise, interest, greed, excitement, suspicion.

"You feel strongly about this," he said.

"Very," said Max.

"And what is your fee for representing Zoe in a lawsuit?"

"The law has wisely provided for that. The attorney is permitted to pursue the case on the basis of a contingency fee. He charges nothing until the verdict is rendered, but by preliminary agreement with the plaintiff—the person who sues—he will take a certain percentage of the amount awarded to the plaintiff by the jury. Naturally, he does not undertake such a case unless he is pretty sure that a wrong has been done."

"Naturally," said Culpepper, a little ironically. "You mean to say, unless he thinks he can win."

Max nodded.

"Actually, Barney wouldn't have to pay a cent. His insurance company would pay it, and Zoe would be provided for?"

Max nodded again.

"What are the actual facts that would form the basis of the case?"

"In a case like this you hardly need them. All you'd have to do is show Zoe to the jury in her wheelchair. However, the case would turn on the medical facts: An unnecessary operation resulted in a massive growth of scar tissue that exerts pressure on the spinal cord. There would be expert witnesses arguing the point on both sides. Charts and diagrams to explain the physiology to the jury. A blowup of the X rays before and after and the myelogram. For a myelogram, fluid is injected into the spine which shows up in a photograph. If the course of the fluid is obstructed, the contrast color will not show beyond that point. In other words, if the scar tissue at the point of operation in Zoe's back is compressing the cord, the fluid won't get past it, or rather only some of it will."

"Let me ask you this," said Culpepper. "Do you really think that Barney was at fault?"

Max returned his gaze. "Yes. I don't believe he should have operated, at least not immediately. And I don't think he got all the bleeders. In short, it is my opinion that he was rash and incompetent."

"I'm not altogether convinced. I'm not even sure— forgive me, Max—how much I trust you. But let me talk it over with some people. I'll get back to you."

"Okay. I think it should be soon, rather than late.

Did you see Krupp's article in *Island News*? There's a lot of public feeling about Zoe, right now, and that can't help but improve her chances."

"I'll call you," said Culpepper, without any particular inflection.

Three days later, in her room at the Mersey Rehabilitation Center, Zoe was visited by Culpepper, Abner Carter, her agent Sidney Greene, and a tall tough-looking man who was unknown to her. He was introduced as Maximilian Ward, and Culpepper said, "Honey baby, Max is going to take care of you."

Max blushed, much to his own surprise. It was the face—the same face he'd admired so much in the *Island News*. It was an innocent face and it made him feel incredibly corrupt.

Culpepper was explaining the situation. "It is a matter of form, Zoe, a game one plays, a sort of ritual. It's something that everyone understands. In other words, unless we take legal action there is no way we can tap the insurance money that you have coming to you. Barney himself will understand that."

Zoe was tired. Her life at present was devoted to therapies. She was learning to live with her disability, and the narrowness of the life she faced. She existed entirely on the surface; she did the exercises, followed the routines, practiced the range of things she could do in a state of permanent semiparalysis. Inside, at the center of her being, was a great blank. It reminded her of Barney's description of the CAT scans of Joe Giordano's hydrocephalic head: an inland sea surrounded by a rim of vital tissue and hard thin skull. The image stayed with her, but in some way did not daunt her. She didn't want to probe the watery space in there. It was a Mediterranean, full of storms and sudden rages, monsters of the imagination, terrible mythic journeys.

The four men were looking at her. She was supposed to respond.

"You mean it doesn't matter?" she asked Willie. "It's just a legality?"

"That's how I see it. I've talked it over with my lawyer. He says that *au fond,* you have no choice. It's a matter of course."

"You know, Willie, that I have no desire to sue Barney."

"Of course not."

"I don't wish to hurt him," said Zoe.

Culpepper suggested that Max explain it to her, and Max said: "I don't see why it should, Miss Carter. Dr. Lukacs will expect to be sued, in such a case. It's not personal; it's a matter of law. You may not realize it, but Dr. Lukacs won't have to pay a red cent. His insurance company will pay whatever the jury sees fit to award you. I expect, actually, that he would want you to have it."

"What's all these tender feelings for the doctor?" Abner broke in. "He's still walking around healthy and here's Zoe, all broken up." Abner had read about Zoe's relapse in the papers, and had returned to keep an eye on her situation.

"I'm not broken up, Dad. I'm doing very well. And Barney is a good doctor. No. Whatever the forms are, there's something wrong about all this. I don't want to do it."

It made her tired. She closed her eyes. There was a whispered consultation among the men, and then a scraping of chairs. When she opened her eyes, only Max Ward was there.

He sat serenely for a while, looking out the window. Zoe rested. Eventually he spoke: "Miss Carter,

I've admired you from a distance. Now that I've met you, I feel it even more. I want to be of service to you."

She didn't answer, and he looked out the window again.

"I have nothing against Dr. Lukacs, although I think this is a clear case of bad judgment and/or negligence," he began. "Either way, the doctor must be held responsible, and the hospital as well. Have you considered how you are going to be able to live?" He looked at her. "Naturally, you'll be eligible for some social services, but the amount of help you'll receive there is hardly appropriate to your needs. I don't suppose you'll want to return to your father's house." He looked away delicately.

"Nor do I suppose that you'll be satisfied to let Mr. Culpepper support you as an invalid."

Now Max turned his gaze fully on hers. "You are entitled in the law to certain benefits, benefits which will make you independent of both your father and Mr. Culpepper. I believe that you should take the formal steps required to obtain proper legal compensation for your disability."

He spoke quietly, and then he got up and stood with his back to her, his arms folded. A couple of children were throwing small stones at a dog in the street. Above them a runaway orange balloon had caught in a TV aerial. Max turned. There was a faint tinge in Zoe's cheeks.

"Thank you, Mr. Ward. I'll go along with whatever you say."

2

"Hello, Culpepper speaking." It was Friday of the following week.

"Hello, Willie. It's Barney Lukacs." Culpepper cleared his throat. There was a pause. "I hear Zoe's back from Mersey. How's she doing?"

"Adapting, I guess. She's either adapting or suffocating. It's strange. Nothing seems to matter much to her. Even being an invalid. She doesn't mind it. Barney . . ."

"I take it she doesn't want to talk to me yet."

"No."

"Willie, I have to see you. When can we get together?"

"I don't know. This week's fantastically busy."

"Come on, Willie. I'm not the big bad wolf; I'm a competent surgeon. Zoe's relapse is a freakish occurrence. It's being mishandled by Foote, who, as you know, is bull-headed, and dislikes me. Dangerously mishandled. I must talk to you before it goes any further."

"I don't see that it will do any good to talk to me. I don't know anything about medicine. I can't handle more than one point of view at a time."

"You can listen to what I have to say, and then call in a purely objective opinion."

"I've already had a second opinion."

"Whose?"

"Evans's."

"From Islip? He's a friend of Foote's. I can't buy it, Willie. We have to talk. Privately."

"Why privately?"

"I don't want Zoe to hear the conversation."

"All right."

"Today? Now? I'll meet you at O'Malleys in half an hour."

Barney hung up. He didn't like Culpepper's tone, and when they met at the restaurant, it was worse. Culpepper managed to greet him without looking at him. He held out his pudgy hand and fixed his eyes on Barney's right cheekbone. Culpepper was embarrassed. He thought perhaps that Barney had heard about the lawsuit, but he hoped not. He didn't want to talk about it, and certainly he didn't want to be the one to tell Barney about it. The whole situation aroused in him a fastidious distaste.

Barney sat down. "Listen, Willie," he said. "Let's put our cards on the table. We've been friends, and it seems we aren't anymore. But that's not important right now. This is a medical matter. Your feelings about me don't count any more than mine about you."

"My dear boy," said Culpepper.

"No. Let's be blunt. I've had only a few minutes with Zoe, but even in that time I was satisfied that her relapse is not organic."

Culpepper looked blank.

"*Organic*: having a physical basis. The opposite is *functional*. That means psychogenic. Zoe's relapse originates in her mind, not her body. It's what they used to call a hysterical illness."

A round blond waitress came over.

"What can I do for you fellows today?" she asked, beaming at them. They ordered drinks.

"But she's not hysterical at all," Culpepper said, relieved to find that they were going to talk medicine, not law. "She is calm, blank, quiet, and conscientious. She's lost all sensation in one leg, and the other is paralyzed. She has been through extensive examinations with both Foote and Evans, and a lot of therapy with Dr. Bailey Thompson at Mersey. None of them has suggested anything but that Zoe has succumbed to scar tissue, following on your operation."

"I've seen the X rays. They can be read either way. There is always scar tissue following on a bony penetration like that. I've tested her, briefly, and I am convinced that the relapse is psychological."

"But the symptoms are real."

"The illness is real. But what is its cause? The mind or the body? Hysteria is a medical term, Willie. Not to be confused with the word people use. It doesn't mean that she's obsessed and frantic. It means that under extreme stress she has been able to convert a psychological conflict into a physical disability. It's even called a *conversion* reaction. It's often symbolic. For instance, a woman can't get along with her husband but can't face leaving him, develops rheumatoid arthritis which begins in the third finger, left hand— under her wedding band. She can't stand the stress; she has converted her emotional conflict into an illness. That's the hysterical conversion reaction.

"From that come what are called primary and secondary gains. The primary gain, for this woman, would be that since she is ill she doesn't have to make a decision that she is incapable of making. And she can take off her wedding ring. The secondary gain usually lies in all the attention she gets as an invalid, the pampering and the fuss and the fact that she doesn't have to do things she doesn't want to do, like making love."

"All right, Barney. You want bluntness. I think Zoe is eminently sane. You did an operation and now you've come up with egg on your face." Culpepper sat back and looked at Barney. It seemed to him now that Barney must know about the lawsuit. Must be trying to wiggle out of it. "Your hypothesis doesn't make sense," he continued. "For instance, what kind of conflict was Zoe suffering from when she had her relapse? She had everything going for her. What primary gains did she stand to make? Being an invalid instead of a famous actress?"

"We don't—" Barney started, but Culpepper swept on.

"Or secondary gains?" he asked sarcastically. "She was the center of attention to begin with, and was indulged in the fondest way. And furthermore, she couldn't make up this whole thing—you can't pretend you don't feel a pin stuck into your leg."

"She's not 'making it up.' It's not conscious. It all takes place deep in the levels of consciousness. I deal with this stuff often, Willie. There are a hundred diagnostic tests I could make, if only I could get to her. And particularly in a case like this. Hysteria is often based on some minor physical reality. In Zoe's case there is still a fair amount of residual deficit left over from the accident and the operation. Her mind builds on this, in order to avoid some conflict that you and I don't understand—yet. Possibly I enter into that conflict, which is why I'm the last person in the world to treat her, right now. I want to recommend a neurologist, and if it's the way I think it is, I want her to see a psychiatrist."

Culpepper bulged his face in mock horror. "A headbender?" he asked. "You're asking me to have one of those oafs trample around in Zoe's psyche? She's an artist; I won't have her made over into a normal human being."

"Why not?" asked Barney mildly. "Human beings aren't so bad. Besides, a lot of artists get analyzed."

"I don't believe in it. The psychiatrist's job is to make people normal. But it's precisely because Zoe's character and talent are special that she's a great actress. You want to change her from a suffering, sentient creature to a narcissistic plodder, a mote on the beach, a nothing. I won't have it."

"You seem to think of psychiatry as some sort of old-fashioned electric shock treatment."

"I do. They come out bland and unenergetic, and they talk about themselves all the time."

"Zoe doesn't have to spend ten years being brain-washed, you know. A few months should do the trick. It wouldn't turn her into a cretin; it would deal with her fears and help her walk again. There's nothing so unusual about hysteria, Willie. It happens. A patient may lose his memory. Develop paralysis. Have fits. Go blind, or deaf. I've seen a guy, for instance, with a bent back. He walked around my office looking like a shelf bracket. In medical school I saw a man with his legs stuck full of pins. He had no feeling at all. Both of them were psychological cases."

"How can you tell?" asked Culpepper, getting interested in spite of himself.

"There are signs. And besides, the treatment worked."

The waitress came over. Barney ordered a hamburger. The place had filled up, he noticed. It was full of lunchtime buzz and clatter.

"Here's what I want to say, Willie. There's nothing the matter with Foote. He's a good man. So's Evans, for that matter. But they're not looking for this. Zoe has a lot of leftover damage in her back. It shows up on the X rays. So they do the normal neurological exam, and they find what they expect: Brown-Sequard. Meanwhile Zoe, backing away from we don't know what extreme of mental stress, has seized on the whole Brown-Sequard syndrome in her mind. She's very familiar with it, after all, and she's recreated the whole symptomology. They don't expect that. They're not looking for it: why should they? But here's the bad part. Their diagnosis has confirmed her own conviction that she's ill. They have perpetuated the illness in her mind and therefore in her body. It's as though, by accepting her diagnosis of herself, so to speak, they have helped her to create the condition. It is truly dangerous, Willie. It may have irreversible effects."

Be calm, he told himself. Keep it low-key, or he won't believe you. "I really think she should be seen by a top neurologist. Somebody quite outside the whole situation. I can give you names in the city, for instance, if you'd like. People I don't know. Or you could ask the head of Neurology at the State University."

Culpepper was regarding him with a caustic eye. "You're an intelligent fellow, Barney. You've given me a lot of background, but you haven't really related it to Zoe. What motivation would she have for this complicated maneuver? Tell me why you think that Zoe in particular would choose the life of an invalid over the life of an actress?"

"I can only guess at that. I don't know her well enough. But, good grief, Willie, she hated her childhood so much that she's half-forgotten it. It's a functional amnesia. And you can see that her illness might at least postpone any conflict she might have about me, for instance. Or fears she might have about her role in your play." Barney's cool deserted him. He felt bitter and childish. "I told you not to tell her the rehearsal schedule was set. I told you she wasn't ready. Damn it, how dare Krupp write that story?"

Culpepper didn't answer.

"My own fault. I could kick myself. I shouldn't have said anything. But that's water over the dam; it's the present we have to deal with. Will you take her for another opinion?"

"I'll think about it," said Culpepper. "I'll talk to Dr. Foote." He didn't believe Barney. He was sure by now that Barney was running scared, making a case for himself, afraid of the trial. He didn't like the thought of putting Zoe through another battery of examinations, just for that. And somewhere, deep in his unexamined self, the present situation did not displease him. Zoe depended on him. They were closer than ever before, and Abner Carter, who was by now aware of his, Willie's, importance and reputation, accepted his word on anything touching Zoe's well-being. Abner was staying for a few weeks, and Zoe seemed now to accept his presence. And there was his play. Culpepper smiled, the way people smile when they think of an inner pleasure. "I've started another play for her, you know. A wheelchair play." He laughed, without being aware of it. "It's called—so far—*Winter Soulstice*. A pun."

"Willie, you're talking about the girl's whole life."

"Yes, yes, yes. All right. Give me a reference. Perhaps I will take her to someone else."

Barney couldn't get a firmer commitment from him. He knew nothing about the legal action, and it seemed to him that Willie could hardly ignore the things he'd said. He gave Willie the name of a top-notch neurologist in the city and sat back, satisfied. They talked about Barney's daughter, Piri, for a while. Willie had met her on her last visit, and Barney was looking forward to her arrival for Christmas, only ten days away.

A muddle of enterprise clotted the sides of the highway, mostly well-advertised car emporia: Ford, Chrysler, Volkswagen. Gas stations, Two Brothers, Carmine's Carpet; Zoe kept the directions in her hand.

"There's Nathan's," she said. "Turn left, Yip. Wait a minute. There it is."

It was nearly two weeks after Zoe's relapse, two weeks of curious, drifting blankness. She hadn't felt unhappy; she hadn't felt anything at all. It was as though she had expected it all along. All of a sudden this morning, she had thought how bored she was, how unimportant everything appeared to be, and the idea had come into her head that she'd like to go to one of Brother Luke's Christian gatherings. There was no point, really; it was just curiosity.

Ngiep turned the Packard into a dirt parking space between the back of Nathan's and the Good Steer. There was a large white wooden sign hanging between two wooden posts which said IOOF, and behind it a foolish white clapboard structure with Victorian fretwork. It looked like a cross between a chapel and a schoolhouse.

"Eye-oof," said Ngiep.

"International Order of Odd Fellows," Zoe translated. "I suppose they rent it."

There were other cars parked there, a van with a full-length spread of Western sunset painted on it, a dirty Honda, and a blue 1959 Chrysler complete with wings and fins and one hammered-out brown fender. Ngiep parked and got out. He took Zoe's wheelchair out of the back, where it leaned against the two jump seats, and carried it up the wooden steps. The white doors were closed; he looked at Zoe. She gestured at him to go on in, so he opened the door and put his head through. Then he came back to get her.

As he carried her through the doors, she could see the plain interior of the hall: double-hung windows and a big clear space. About thirty old oak kitchen chairs were set up in rows. Zoe's heart began to pound with excitement. Simplicity! Nothing graceful, or even particularly comfortable, nothing distracting, nothing civilized. Mere reality waited here, humble and unabashed.

A woman with two remarkably quiet young boys sat in a chair at the end of a row, crocheting an afghan square in ugly colors, scarlet and yellow and nile green. She turned and smiled at Zoe, and Zoe smiled back. She nodded at Ngiep, who left, and then wheeled herself to a spot near the window, out of the way.

A bunch of young people came in from the other end, carrying guitars and laughing over something. The girls were dressed in long cotton skirts with flounces, and the young men were wearing jeans. One of them had on a leather western hat with brass studs and an emblazoned leather vest. He sported a bushy handlebar mustache. They set themselves up on the platform at the end of the hall, checking the speakers. It had cleared up outside, and sunlight now angled through the windows, striking the tow heads of the boys and the bright colors of wool, and the shiny bits on the musical equipment.

More people came in and moved to fill the rows. A large honey-colored man with a lilting walk shepherded his family down the aisle, shy brownish girls and boys and a plump wife. He was humming, but he broke off to kiss first one person and then another who turned to meet him. The air was filled with his low intermittent hum, and voices greeting and murmuring, "Hallelujah, thank you, Jesus, thank you, Lord." A lovely tall woman in a long bright green print skirt sashayed up to him, her arms out, palms up. She kissed him ("Praise the Lord") and kissed the wife and kissed one of his daughters, keeping her hands on the girl's skinny shoulders.

"So the Lord is sending you to Bible College," she said. "Hallelujah."

The girl blushed.

Brother Luke came in from the back, with another man. They talked for a moment, and then dispersed among the group, kissing or shaking hands. When Luke saw Zoe, he recognized her with a look, over someone's shoulder, and a little later he came over to shake her hand.

"You've come," he said. "I thought you might."

He looked at her lovingly and Zoe, returning his gaze, felt her self flying out to meet him. She had been numbed, and now, face to face with Brother Luke, she felt alive again. She felt that she had come home, that she was acceptable—no matter what her character might be. That here, in this warm cheerful atmosphere, there was a place for her. Tears came to her eyes, and she became self-absorbed. Then the tall woman went up to the platform and began to speak.

"I have a little miracle to share with you today— Praise God—for all of us that are still thinking that miracles were only for back then, in the time of the Apostles. Dead now, not for us. I mean, I *know* that miracles are still alive, and when you're spirit-filled, they're all around you, small and big, and they're showing that God answers our prayers."

People stood and held out their arms and one woman cried, "Thank you, thank you, Jesus," and

Zoe became aware of a chorus of hallelujahs and a babble of low voices chanting in an African-sounding language. "That must be tongues," she thought, and though the tall woman went on talking, she couldn't hear her anymore, and could only catch a glimpse of her now and then, through the swaying bodies. It seemed that the various noises rose in a rhythmic crescendo, and then she heard the tuning of guitars. Someone handed her some dittoed pages, stapled together, and pointed to the right page, and then the guitars were playing and everyone began to sing. Zoe scanned the sheet, and joined in. Her voice was low at first, as she felt out the song. But it was of the simplest order, and her rushing, flowing feeling became the song itself, lifting and roaring through the channels, strengthening as it went:

> *Oh I'm so happy, so very happy,*
> *I've got the love of Jesus in my heart.*
> *And I'm so happy . . .*

People around her turned and looked. Their voices faded away as her fluid contralto reached its full strength.

> *I've got that joy, joy, joy, joy*
> *Down in my heart, down in my heart.*
> *I've got that joy, joy, joy, joy*
> *Down in my heart, down in my heart to stay.*

After the meeting the tall pretty woman, whose name was Claudia, told everyone that it was like the voice of Jesus was singing through the crippled woman. "I never heard a voice like that," she said. "Like a hot-line opened up and there ain't nothing there but pure love." She smiled, and shook her pretty curls in admiration, and raised her arms, "Thank you, thank you, Jesus." And everybody standing around her raised their arms and said, "Thank you, thank you, Jesus." And Brother Luke was overheard telling Brother Abe, "She's a natural. An absolute natural," but his eyes had been wet, and anybody could see that Brother Luke felt that a miracle had been given to them and was still there, in their midst, in crippled flesh. Zoe herself felt like a miracle: she carried her wounded legs like stigmata, and the gesture of spreading her arms seemed in some way to link her in a common bondage with all of them. Tears streamed down her face. She was incredibly happy.

"Send the kids out, would you, Carole? I've got to talk to you."

"Sure, honey," she said. "But it'll have to be fast. I've got to be back at work at two o'clock."

The children looked so sweet, playing jacks on the floor; she hated to send them out. She liked Max to see them like that, happy and affectionate with each other, and the kettle whistling on the stove. But even as she thought that, Cathy said, "You moved," and Eric said, "I did not," and Cathy began to get that victimized look. She bundled them up and sent them outdoors, and then she came back to the dining room.

Carole brought a tray in with her, with coffee and a half-eaten chocolate cake, but Max waved it aside.

"Listen, Carole, which of Barney's operations in the past couple of years might be considered questionable?"

"What d'you mean, questionable?"

"I mean, which ones did anyone argue about? Was there ever any question about whether he should or should not operate? Any complaints? Did he and Foote quarrel? Anything controversial?"

"Well, let me think." She poured herself some coffee. "Sure you won't have any?"

"No."

Carole was reluctant to give him confidential information, but all the same, he was being so nice. It would be bliss, she thought, if they could get married. He was waiting for an answer. And it wasn't really all that confidential. Anybody at the hospital would know it.

"There was that case of the child's concussion," she finally said. "Williams, their name was. Her parents brought her in, about three years old and cute as the devil. She fell off a jungle gym. Let's see. Barney saw her. No obvious damage—probable slight concussion."

"Did Foote see her?"

"I don't know. Barney told the parents to bring her back if there was any change at all. They brought her back the next day. She was in a coma three hours before they brought her in. She died, and then they complained that it was the hospital's fault for sending her home. It was a subdural."

"Good. That's the kind of thing. Williams? He wrote it down. What else?"

"Well, there's lots of, you know, iffy things. Some laminectomies. Yeah, guy named Allbright. Said he'd been ripped off. He didn't get the kind of relief he expected. There were others. I can look them up. A meningioma. A boy who broke his neck in the swimming pool. He died on the table. I'll go through the records."

"Good," said Max, getting up. Go through your records, get the names and dates, and then see Mrs. Ardsley and get a look at their files. Copies, if you can. I have to see Foote this afternoon, but I'll meet you for dinner."

When he got to Foote's office he had to wait for quite a while. There were about eight patients. He looked at them with some awe. He didn't know what he expected, but everybody looked terribly normal. He thought about the kind of diseases that neurologists treated, and decided that there ought to be at least somebody there who was trembling or comatose or disabled, or maybe having a seizure. But they were well-dressed and quiet, reading magazines or talking to whoever was with them. One woman walked with a kind of delayed shuffle, he noticed, when she was called in. He shuddered. He was glad he was here on business.

Foote greeted him at the door of his office. "What can I do for you, Mr. Ward?"

"Well, I'm not sick, if that's what you mean. Knock wood." He sat down in a big leather chair studded with brass upholstery tacks. "I'm here on a legal matter."

"Oh?"

"I've been retained to represent Zoe Carter in a malpractice action."

"Uh-oh. What exactly do you propose?"

"Miss Carter, strictly between us, is entering a complaint against Lukacs, Rubin, and St. Mark's Hospital. I guess I don't have to tell you why. I'd be very interested, Dr. Foote, if you could give me your view of the case."

"Clearly you already know it."

"Well, yes. I've read the paper, and I've talked to Mr. Krupp—the guy who interviewed you."

"You mean, you got him to write the damn article."

Max ignored that. "I understand that your diagnosis is chronic adhesive arachnoiditis, caused by post-operative bleeding. Would you care to tell me how that came about? Is it a normal development?"

"Not necessarily."

"Was it normal in this particular case?"

"No," said Foote, and he clamped his mouth shut. His cheeks were a deep brick red.

"Can you give me some particulars?"

Foote didn't answer. Obviously he was undecided as to what course he should take. He glared at Max. His breathing deepened. Finally, he said, "Mr. Ward, I have done nothing but make a straightforward diagnosis of this case. I don't want to be any further involved."

"You are involved already, whether you like it or not," said Max. "You wrote the consulting opinion. You watched the operation. I can call you as a witness. Look, Dr. Foote. I'd really like to have you on our side. You know very well it was badly handled: a genine case of medical negligence. If the doctor is at fault, the public must be protected. There's got to be some accountability."

Foote nodded.

"Besides, Miss Carter is now an invalid. How is she going to survive? The insurance money is there; she should have it."

"You won't get any agreement from me on that point. Every time insurance money is paid out, the insurance premiums go up. The patients' fees go up. The public pays for it. Can you really think of any reason why my other patients should support Zoe to the tune of a couple of million dollars?"

Max retrenched. He'd pushed the wrong button.

"Is it your opinion that Lukacs is a responsible and competent doctor?" he asked.

Foote opened his mouth and closed it again.

"I don't think it is," said Max gently. "Would you consider, for once, testifying for the plaintiff, for Miss Carter, in this action?"

"I'm not sure it would do you that much good," said Foote. "In the context of medicine I can make this or that statement, but in a legal action my opinion wouldn't have that much weight. Besides, there's been some bad feeling between Barney and myself before. Someone would testify to that."

"That doesn't matter."

"Leads to very bad relations in the medical field. A fellow doctor, Mr. Ward. A member of the team. No, I don't think I can do it."

"You mean, really, that you have your convictions about his incompetence, but you won't help me nail him? I don't believe it, Dr. Foote. The integrity of the profession should be preserved. In Lukacs you have someone who is undermining the professional reputation of all of you."

Foote nodded. He thought it over, his mouth bleak and his eyes hostile. Max thought, *I haven't handled him well. He feels cornered.*

"It's a very complicated situation, Mr. Ward. I don't believe I can take part in it. Everybody wants to sue. It's a rainbow with a pot of gold at the end. As somebody said, we are a litigious society. When I gave that interview to Krupp, it never occurred to me . . . I don't like it. I didn't think Zoe was that kind of person. That she'd sue, I mean. I suppose you talked her into it. No! There are a lot of disasters in medicine—but there would be more without it. Why don't you people just sue God and be done with it? Half the time you're suing because you're ill, not for the way the doctor deals with your illness. I won't have any part of it."

Max stood up. "Well, I'm sorry. The fact is, you

can't help yourself. If you can't play ball with us, I'll have to name you along with the others as a defendant in this suit. I need you on the stand. Think about it."

Carole had lunch with Betty Ardsley, the medical librarian. They talked about schools and *Kramer* v. *Kramer*. They were both divorced. Afterward they walked back to the hospital, hugging their coats around them.

"Gloria's getting married next week," Betty said. "You going?"

"I always go to weddings. It gives me a laugh. Oh, listen, Betty, I have to check the date on a couple of lab billings. I'll just get my files, and then I'll be up."

When she got there, Carole started a conversation about Zoe Carter. It was still a subject you could count on around the hospital.

"I've got a friend who's born again," she said. "My kids play with hers. Zoe went to their church, or whatever you call it, last week. My friend, Claudia, was ecstatic about her. Zoe sang, and the way I heard it, everybody there thought it was the Rapture."

"What's the Rapture?"

Carole ran some of the records Max wanted through the copier. Yes. Here was little Karen Williams. Poor thing.

"The Rapture's when the good guys, the ones who are saved, go to heaven. It's in the Bible. Thessalonians, I think. Jesus comes like a thief in the night and takes everyone who's born again up to heaven with him. The rest of us get left behind."

"That's not so bad," Betty said. "I think I'd rather be here." She made a satisfied tour of her office with her eyes. She came from a German family, and everything was clean and efficient. There were potted plants in the window, and a blue and white ceramic plaque on the wall that said, in German lettering, *Gib uns heute unser tagliches brot.* Give us today our daily bread.

"Me too," said Carole. "I'd rather be alive than happy. I think." She gave a weak laugh and tucked the files under her arm. "See you later."

The Williams's place wasn't far from his own. Max found Bay Avenue and drove south. East on Sands Road and right into Driftwood Court. Number seven was a yellow house with globular yew around the foundation.

Mrs. Williams was a harried-looking woman with black hair, a swollen belly, and two kids. As she opened the door, there was a blast of music. Things were slovenly inside, dark and unwashed-looking.

"My husband will be home any minute," said Mrs. Williams. She showed Max into the dining room, which was comparatively peaceful. "Do you want a drink? TANYA, TURN THAT MUSIC DOWN."

"Thank you," said Max. "Scotch and soda?"

Mr. Williams came in. He looked detached and peaceful and young. He'd be good on the stand, Max decided. They shook hands and sat down. Without asking, Mrs. Williams brought her husband a beer. He looked as though he wanted to read the paper.

Max explained that he was representing Zoe Carter in a suit against Dr. Lukacs. "In the course of my research certain other things have come to my attention."

Mrs. Williams's eyes flashed. "I should hope so. The guy's a public disgrace. I can tell you about him all right. Our little girl—"

Her husband looked at Max and gave him a singularly pleasant smile. "I guess you know about it, or you wouldn't be here, right?" he said.

"Yes," Max said. "But I'd like to know more. Would you mind? It was a terrible tragedy."

"What do you want to know?"

"I'd like to go through the whole thing, if it's not too painful for you."

"I don't mind," said Mrs. Williams with some satisfaction, Max noticed. She must play this over and over again. "I took the kids down to the playground, see? It was summer, and I never liked taking the baby to the beach."

Max consulted his notes. "This was in June. A year ago June?"

"Yeah. Tanya, that's my oldest, was climbing on the jungle gym and Karen was pulling her little wagon next to it. She was three, almost four. The baby was in the carriage, and I was rocking it and talking to my girl friend, who was upset because her husband just left her. Then the baby started crying, and I could hear someone calling me, and all of a sudden I hear a yell from Tanya, and there's Karen lying on the ground. I'll never forget it, you know. Everything seemed to like, stop."

"It wasn't Arlene's fault," said Mr. Williams.

"It wasn't my fault," Mrs. Williams said. "I can't take care of everybody at once." She gestured to her husband.

"Karen had started to climb on the gym," he said. "Tanya knew she wasn't allowed and called her mother. When Arlene didn't answer, Tanya just sort of . . . pushed . . . Karen—to help her mother, you know? It wasn't her fault. She was only six. Anyway, Karen's head hit the edge of the concrete."

"I took her straight to St. Mark's," Mrs. Williams continued. "The emergency room. Karen was unconscious, but she came to. Lukacs examined her. Rest, he said. *Rest.* Like hell. He sent us home. A concussion, he said. The next morning she was knocked out, white-looking, you know what I mean? So I pulled down the shades so the light wouldn't bother her, and fixed her up nice in her bed with the TV in her room. I was busy with the baby, and that day the plumber came. But the next time I looked in she was unconscious."

"How long do you suppose that was?" asked Max.

"Oh, not very long. Maybe a couple of hours. I thought she was asleep."

"Actually, it was at lunchtime when I came home," said Mr. Williams.

"Well, I had a lot to do," she flashed.

"Never mind," said Max. "What happened next?"

"I took her to the hospital," Mr. Williams said. "But she never came out of it. She was in a coma. They oughtn't to have sent her home. That's what I think."

"I agree with you, Mr. Williams," Max said. "In my opinion it constitutes gross negligence on the part of the hospital."

"It wasn't the hospital; it was that doctor. He was the one that saw her."

"And the cause of death?" asked Max.

"He should of known. It wasn't a concussion at all; it was something called a subdural hematoma. How am I supposed to take care of something like that?"

"Exactly," said Max. "Now I'd like you to answer this as precisely as you can. Aside from rest, what other instructions did you have from Dr. Lukacs?"

Mrs. Williams thought about it. "Rest, plenty of fluids, no food. He gave me some medication for her."

"Nothing else? Any instructions in case she passed out again?"

"N-no. Just to bring her in right away, if there was any change. What do they mean, change? I thought she was asleep. How am I supposed to know if there's any change? *They* sent her home."

"That's just the point," said Max. "They behaved irresponsibly." He put his notes away. "I think you have a case."

They both looked blank.

"You should sue. Both the doctor and the hospital. Didn't you ever think of that?"

Both of them answered at once, and from the living room came a swell of music that could only be the Beatles. Mr. Williams went out, and when he came back it was quiet.

"We can't afford a lawsuit," he said.

"I will undertake the lawsuit. If you win it, you can pay me a certain percentage of the award. If not," Max spread his hands, "you pay me nothing."

"By God," said Mrs. Williams. "I'd love to sue them bastards."

Mr. Williams was reluctant, but Max talked to him. They would be performing a public service. By the time he left they had agreed to initiate an action. Max felt he'd learned something: one of the great satisfactions of a malpractice suit lies in fixing the blame on someone else. The stupid woman hadn't even noticed when her concussed child went into a coma. He chugged northwards. His next appointment was with the failed laminectomy in Riverhead.

A week had gone by, and Barney was still waiting to hear from Culpepper. He told himself that he did not feel any great suspense, and actually he was convinced that any objective neurological exam would confirm his own diagnosis. Nevertheless, he was on edge. Zoe should have seen a psychiatrist weeks ago, before she got rigid in her beliefs, and before her body began to degenerate.

Piri was arriving today for a week of her Christmas vacation. That was pure pleasure. He peered at himself in the mirror and shaved carefully around a pimple on his upper lip. His hair, still damp from the shower, clung in curls around his forehead and neck. He was still young. But there were a lot of little lines sweeping out from his eyes and curving over his cheekbones toward his ears. He could see the old man's skull lurking behind his flesh. Zoe was only twenty-nine.

He checked through the cottage to make sure it was clean and welcoming. He'd bought some roses. They hung like drops of fire above the coffee table. The doorbell rang.

The postman handed him a familiar envelope and presented a clipboard for his signature. His heart sank. "Supreme Court of Suffolk County, Riverhead, N.Y." Not again.

He put it down on the table and got himself a late breakfast. Another damn summons. Somehow he felt he could afford to wait before he read the thing. When he'd eaten, he poured himself a cup of coffee and gazed out the leaded window. The envelope lay in the corner of his vision, large and white. He'd have to leave soon for the airport. He'd set Piri's arrival for an off-duty day. While he thought about seeing her, his hands reached for the letter and opened it.

ZOE CARTER! The words leapt at him. He understood it all in a flash, her silence, Willie's reticence. *How could she? How could she do this?*

Church bells rang. Noon already. He had to go to

the airport. He read quickly through the complaint.
He felt quieter now. He noted that Foote was named
among the defendants. That was a relief. The rest
was familiar stuff, but painful all the same, as it always was. He was being horsewhipped through the
streets for following his best judgment. He reminded
himself that it wasn't like that—he wasn't really being
charged with incompetence in his work; he was being
used by someone who wanted to make money. Zoe.
No, Max Ward. That parasite. That jackal. The last
time he'd tangled with Max was over a small but ludi-
crous claim. Barney had decided not to bother with it
and had settled out of court for three thousand.

Barney read on.

. . . That on the 13th day of August, 1979,
the defendant Dr. Lukacs did in fact perform a
certain surgical procedure upon the Plaintiff, Zoe
Carter, described as a laminectomy.

That at all times hereinafter mentioned, each
and every defendant, their agents, servants,
and/or employees so negligently, carelessly, and
recklessly treated, advised, consulted, and tested
the Plaintiff, Zoe Carter, so as to constitute her
care and treatment by the Defendants named
herein . . . as malpractice, malfeasance, misfeasance, and neglect.

Neglect!
Barney reddened. It was easy to forget that this was
a form—especially because he had expended so much
extra devotion on Zoe's case. And the endless repeti-
tion made it seem more savage.

That the negligence, carelessness, recklessness,
malfeasance, misfeasance, and malpractice of the

Defendants named herein, their agents, servants, and/or employees consisted in failing to treat the Plaintiff, Zoe Carter, in accordance with the approved medical practices and standards as practiced and established by the medical community; in maintaining St. Mark's Hospital in a careless, reckless, and dangerous manner; in hiring incompetent, inept, and inexperienced physicians to administer to and treat their patients; in performing a certain surgical procedure upon the Plaintiff described as a laminectomy in a manner not consistent with good surgical practice; in performing the aforesaid procedure in a negligent and careless manner . . . in causing, allowing, and permitting this Plaintiff to languish without adequate and proper treatment; in prematurely abandoning and discharging this Plaintiff . . . in failing and omitting to exercise and take proper care and caution in the conduct, care, and treatment rendered to this Plaintiff so as to prevent unfavorable medical complications and personal injuries to follow . . .

And on, and on, and on. *Allowing this plaintiff to languish* . . . It was just ordinary legal garbage. Barney knew that. It was the usual form for a general complaint, and there would be a lot of legal jockeying before they got down to particular charges. Still, it was embittering. Zoe, languishing! Damn it, he'd been sued twice before. Both cases had been small, opportunistic, and without a legitimate basis in medicine; neither had been worth the time he would have had to spend in court. He'd settled each time, but he hadn't liked doing it. This time he would fight. He'd fight it all the way down to the wire. But he knew it wasn't like Zoe. It was Abner and Culpepper and

Max Ward using Zoe, he'd bet his bottom dollar on it, and he was damned if he'd let them get away with it.

Piri's plane came in at MacArthur. Flags were flying; the air was keen. Barney waited in the wind, his mackintosh flapping around his knees, and watched her come down the aluminum steps.

She was growing up. It was the first time in years that he'd seen her out of blue jeans. She was a big girl, in a suede coat with dark kinky flyaway fur around her neck, and her voluminous brown hair was done up in a bun. Her face was almost womanly, but the eyes were the same. Shining. She was going to be handsome, Barney thought, and a good thing too. She had enough on her plate, being deaf. She saw him and waved, and when she got to the concrete, she ran across, looking like an adolescent again.

He felt a rush of warmth, protective and admiring. For all her handicaps, she was strong and she was loving. He took her to O'Malley's for lunch. Christmas was in the air; the place was festive. He talked for a while in signs, just for the pleasure of using the language again, though he knew she could read his lips without much trouble. They had learned sign language together. Piri had been trained to talk, but her speech was clumsy and forced, and hard to understand. She only used it when she had to.

Maggie came into the restaurant. She recognized Piri and came over to say hello, and then she stayed while they had dessert. She said she was sorry to hear about Zoe's relapse.

"What happened?" she asked. "Everything was going along so well."

"I don't know. She's incommunicado as far as I'm

concerned. She won't see me. The X rays aren't clear." He explained who Zoe was to Piri.

"Is she difficult?" asked Piri. "Complicated?"

Barney translated for Maggie. She laughed.

"My dear, Zoe is a walking neural syndrome, all by herself."

Barney grinned at Piri. "Maggie doesn't like her," he said. "But she doesn't know the half of it. Zoe is suing me for malpractice."

"That's a bummer," said Maggie. "What a charming woman. Does she have anything on you, really?"

"I don't think so. I was a little rash, perhaps, about the doctor-patient relationship. I dealt with her as a human being, not a patient. Our medical community wouldn't look kindly on that."

"No, I don't suppose they would. But that wouldn't come up in court."

"Anything can come up in court. Then it gets stricken from the record. Meanwhile, it's there, in everybody's mind."

"What are the charges?"

"So far, the same as always. Misfeasance, malfeasance, negligence, malpractice—it's poetry, Maggie. You have to see it. But it's just the opening volley. The next round comes in the Bill of Particulars. My lawyer has to ask for that."

"Have you got a lawyer?"

"I'll be assigned one by the insurance company."

"How long will it take?"

"A couple of years, five years, maybe ten. It depends how eager everybody is. If they really hustle, they can get it on the agenda within a year. And from what I've seen, they'll hustle."

"It's a rotten situation."

"It is, indeed. It's not that I think we're above the law. Peer review should be strengthened. Doctors themselves should get together, through their contracts with their hospitals, and act to root out incompetence and stupidity within their own ranks. It does exist. But that's quite different from the whole malpractice situation. We are all—patients included—victims of an absurd, clumsy, and opportunistic legal setup."

"In what way?"

"The whole thing: tort law. The legal machinery which assigns fault. The contingency fee. They've got us by the short hairs."

Barney was signing to Piri at the same time as he talked.

"If you slip on a banana peel, you find out whose sidewalk it was on which the banana peel reposed. Of course it belongs to the town. You find out whose house is behind the town's sidewalk, and you sue the pants off the owner of the house. You can always afford to, because lawyers are allowed to be business partners with their clients. They can gamble on a business potential. That's because they can operate on a contingency basis. If they win, they get a giant cut. If they lose, they lose. All they've lost is their own time. It takes things right out of the area of right and wrong, good or bad practice. All that counts is winning, and the reward is money.

"Can you imagine doctors working on that basis? If I save your life, you pay me. Otherwise you can keep your money."

Maggie laughed.

"We are concerned with the purity of our profession. Our oath, our duty, is to work for the better health of the patient. We may make mistakes, but we don't gamble on good medicine. We are simply required to practice it."

"You do all right anyway."

"Yes, we do. But also we work hard, and we take an awesome responsibility. We should do all right. I think my basic point is this: We live in a society which believes that the good life should be the birthright of everyone. If it doesn't happen, someone must be to blame—your mother, your father, society, the neighbor's sidewalk. Or your doctor. There's no room in our thinking for the whole random awfulness and richness of life, the good and the bad all mixed up. If something is bad, we think, someone's got to be to blame. If things go wrong, they've got to be fixed up. Well, there isn't always someone to blame, except oneself perhaps, and there isn't always a way to fix things up. It's in the lap of the gods."

He grinned at Piri. "You should know that. You're deaf because your mother had German measles when she was carrying you. You want to sue her? And Maggie, you could sue somebody, the government maybe, because nobody pays a poet. Zoe knows all this. We've talked about it. She's in a psychological funk, and she doesn't know what she's doing."

"Damn kind of you," Maggie said. "Seems to me she knows very well what she's doing. How much is she suing for?"

"I don't know yet. That doesn't come out till later. Millions, I suppose. They all are. A little girl just won a million dollars. Some of her shoulder nerves were damaged at birth, and she didn't have full use of her right arm. She—or her mother really, or, really, the lawyer who dug them both up—anyway, they sued the obstetrician. The fetus's shoulder was impacted during delivery. She was a large baby, eleven pounds. It was shoved up against the pubic bone. They couldn't get the baby out, and they couldn't operate because the mother had had a stroke during pregnancy. The plaintiff's attorney explained it to the jury this way, in his summing up: The obstetrician had interfered with nature's plans by rotating the baby, had exerted pressure to get it out, brutally wrenching and lacerating the nerves in the shoulder. Good grief! If nature had her way, they'd both be dead."

"And Zoe? Would she be dead?"

Barney shrugged. "I doubt it. But it's controversial in an accident of that nature, whether to operate immediately or not. In her case I was sure that there was bone penetration, and, therefore, the bone fragment should be removed. There are other ways of dealing with it. I did what I thought was best. All I have to rely on, finally, is my judgment. They'll say I should have relied more on diagnostic tests. I think I can show they are wrong. But, it's going to take a good half of my time and attention for quite a while." It had gotten late. The restaurant was empty. Barney leaned back, spread his hands.

"So there it is. You've arrived in a crisis, Piroshka."

"When isn't?" Piri said, with her elegant signs.

"And it's Christmas. We'll go get a tree, and you can do your stuff on it. It's better than a million jelly doughnuts to have you here right now." It was a family joke.

"Maggie? You want to help decorate the tree? We'll roast chestnuts. Gerry Rubin's coming over with his family. How's it going with the odes and epics?"

"Okay. Okay to both questions. I start my tour in February, but really, I've got enough new stuff for a couple of tours. You know, Barney, I'm surprised you haven't tried your hand at writing, after all this time in the Hamptons. It seems like everybody who comes here ends up writing, and God knows, you can express yourself."

"I have," said Barney. "Though it's not maybe

what you'd call inspired. Would you like a list of my publications?"

"You've published?"

"And how. Maybe a hundred and fifty times." He laughed at her. "How's this for starters: Autotransplantation of anaplastic astrocytoma into the subcutaneous tissue of man? Or here's something more in my line now. Deep cobalt insertion in therapy of gliomas. When I get to Kansas, I'll be working in that area."

"When do you go? February?"

"The last week in January. I've taken a leave of absence here. If I don't like it there, I'll be back. If I do, I expect to hear you at the Poetry Center. If there is one."

"Where will you be, Piri?" asked Maggie. "You must be almost through school."

"University of Kansas," Piri said with her hands. "I'm going to work with children like myself."

"Do you write? I should think you would."

"Reams."

"She's good," said Barney.

"I'd like to see some of your work."

"Yes," gestured Piri.

"Listen, folks. This place is deserted," said Barney. "Our waitress is standing over there, shifting from one foot to the other." He paid the bill. When they went out a Christmas carol was chiming in the streets, and the wind was wild.

LUKACS SUED AGAIN: WAS IT NEGLIGENCE? (Story on p. 3)

Bull's eye, Max thought. Got it in, made the front page. Good for P. J. They'd met the night before for a drink.

Edward Williams of Driftwood Court, Hampton Bays, initiated another action against Barney Lukacs, the neurosurgeon who performed a recent operation on actress Zoe Carter's broken back.

Little Karen Williams, age three, and suffering from a subdural hematoma (bleeding inside the skull), entered the emergency room at St. Mark's on a busy day in June 1979, where she was examined by Dr. Lukacs. Diagnosed as a "probable concussion," she was sent home, where she lapsed into a coma. She died the following day.

The hospital could not be reached for comment, but Arlene Williams, Karen's mother, was interviewed at her home. Overcome by her grief she said, "It was a terrible tragedy. It's terrible having it all reopened again."

The Williamses will be represented by Maximilian Ward, who is also handling Miss Carter's case against Dr. Lukacs. Mr. Ward, in a telephone interview, was reluctant to comment on the case. "I will only say that one begins to entertain grave doubts as to the way the emergency room is handled at our local hospital."

The phone rang, and Max picked it up.
"Yes. P. J. here."
"Hello P. J. What's up?" Max said.
"Well, we're keeping you up front," P. J. said. "Did you read it?"
"I'm right in the middle of it. It's good, P. J. Dynamite."
"It fills the bill," P. J. said modestly. "I've got a

deal for you. You know Celia Brophus? That friend of Willie's who runs *Forum*?"

"Of course."

"She was looking for a malpractice lawyer to appear on her program. I fixed it up for you."

"Sounds good. What, specifically, does she want?"

"You know her style. Investigative reporting. She's doing a spot on the malpractice situation, wants to present both sides of the issue. I gave you a terrific buildup. Any developments?"

"No. The case is pulling together smoothly. I've got Dr. John Herman Randolph to testify for us. You know him? The guy who wrote *The Risks of Surgery*?

"Great."

"I'll keep you clued in, don't worry. Thanks a lot, P. J."

"That's all right. Brophus will call you."

"Good."

Max went back to the *Island News*. Over the story there was a picture of Karen, a chubby, round-faced little girl with angel lashes and brown curls. Max smiled: a ringer, if ever he saw one. At the back of his mind he heard Arlene Williams's shrieking voice. "TANYA, TURN THAT MUSIC DOWN!"

The mail was heart-warming. Every morning brought new offers of help, even money, and letters from people all over America who had suffered terrible injuries. It was extraordinary. She had been so solitary all her life, and suddenly the world was her community.

Zoe always read the mail with her breakfast in the same sunny room at Culpepper's that had been hers before, and which seemed, by some firm but unspoken agreement, to have become her home. Dear

Willie, she thought. He's so good to me. And everyone else; so many letters.

"Dear Zoe," this one began, in a childish, rounded hand. "I have suffered too, the way you're suffering. You're not alone. Your trouble is a sign. God loves you and because he loves you he is punishing you. If he didn't, he wouldn't bother. 'For whom the Lord loveth he chasteneth!' "

The letter was from Red Cloud, Nebraska. Nebraska . . . Kansas. Zoe blotted out Kansas, she didn't know why, and reached for her Bible Concordance. She looked the passage up in the Bible and drew a line through it with a clear yellow marker, as she was learning to do.

The passage gave her a feeling of warmth. It said she was one of God's children. And if she was crippled, it was only his rebuke. Indeed, it was a reward in that sense, not a punishment.

She had been a Baptist when she was young, but the words in church had sounded like the quarrels between her parents, hurtful and full of threat. All the time she could remember, though it seemed to her that her memory was patchy, her aim had been to escape, to leave behind father, mother, church, house, even the red-loamed countryside and the keewits calling. Even herself.

And now, she thought, she'd come home. Willie, the letters, Ngiep, Brother Luke. Even her father had suffered, was one of God's children. Even Mr. Ward. She must pray for him. Each of these persons was a vessel, awkward, even deformed, but each one of them carried the seed of his self, his perfect self, that is, and it illuminated and shone through them and around them, and waited, waited for each of them to unite himself with Christ, in cleanliness and love, to become whole.

Zoe flipped through her Bible again. Most of it was unmarked. The yellow passages leapt to the eye, and she easily found the one she was looking for. "That if thou shalt confess with thy mouth the Lord Jesus, and shalt believe in thine heart that God hath raised him from the dead, thou shalt be saved."

With thy mouth. To confess with thy mouth. A ripple of excitement ran through her. She raised her hands, as the others did, palms upwards and fluttering, and thought again. *With thy mouth.* It seemed rash, personal. But she thought of her mouth and her uplifted arms and her immense desire, and she said out loud, "Jesus I believe in you. I love you, Jesus."

Zoe went to Bible Study that evening. It was just after Christmas. She had been to church again, at IOOF, and had experienced again the harmonious swelling pleasure that it had given her the first time. She didn't *think* about religion; she seemed to be drawn blindly toward it, a moth to the candle.

Bible Study was at Claudia's house—the tall pretty woman from Brother Luke's ministry. None of the born again people seemed to use their last names, and Zoe didn't know Claudia's. The house was simple and homey. Folding chairs had been set up on the glassed-in porch, and three card tables covered with an oil cloth that was patterned with cherries. On the shingled wall she saw an embroidered sampler that read: "And *that* every tongue should confess that Jesus Christ *is* Lord."

Claudia tipped Zoe's wheelchair back and maneuvered her down the step to the porch. Brother Luke was sitting at one of the card tables, but he got up and came over to kiss her. "Praise God," he said. He introduced her to Claudia's husband, Frank, who kissed her also, and to a white-haired woman who looked like a nurse and who seemed to have a permanent smile fixed on her face. Her name was Betty. She spread her arms and did a sort of two-step as she approached Zoe, smiling, and kissed her, and said, "There's room for your chair over here."

Some other people came in. A round middle-aged woman with glasses and sausage curls; a man named James, about forty, with workmanlike hands. His wife, Mildred. They all knew each other and kissed and asked each other questions about their families.

Claudia met each of them with a joyful air and put their coats away. When James and Mildred were seated, she said, "I hear Kimmy is going to sing at the Revival. Hallelujah."

Everybody said, "Praise God."

James said, "Yes, and she's going with Brother Abe too, in the spring to sing in Texas."

"Has he heard from the North?"

"He's invited to Toronto, and I wrote to Buffalo. I think he'll preach there too."

"Praise God. Now," Claudia went on, "I have something I want to share with you all. The Lord will provide."

"Thank you, Jesus."

"Hallelujah."

"Well, you know Frank's been out of work for several months now, and we were low on milk. I prayed, but I didn't worry. And then it was all gone and I said, 'Lord, it's in your hands.' Now, you won't believe this. At eight o'clock in the morning the phone rang, and I said to the children, 'That's the Lord calling.' And it was. At least it was Community Action with ten quarts of leftover milk. Thank you, Jesus. And people say the days of miracles are over."

They all responded, and finally everyone was seated. There were nine in all. Brother Luke opened his Bible, where he had it marked with a list of chapter and verse.

"Since we have a newcomer here tonight," he smiled at Zoe, "I thought we would read from Acts, chapter two." There was a whispering of paper while people turned the pages of their Bibles. Zoe was still looking up Acts in the index when Brother Luke spoke again, but Claudia leaned over and found it for her directly.

"This is the right season for you to come to us," he said to Zoe, "when the little Jesus has just been born and you, perhaps, will be born again. I don't suppose you know about the Pentecost, or why we are called Pentecostals?"

"No."

"Well, in Acts it tells about what happened to the Apostles, after Jesus died and rose again to his heavenly Father. They didn't know what to do, you see, after the Master was gone, and they were sitting around in confusion when suddenly"—Luke began to read, following the sentences with his forefinger— "'there came a sound from heaven as of a rushing mighty wind, and it filled all the house where they were sitting . . .

"'And there appeared unto them cloven tongues like as of fire, and it sat upon each one of them.

"'And they were all filled with the Holy Ghost, and began to speak with other tongues, as the spirit gave them utterance.'"

The biblical language sounded to Zoe like the ringing of bells, sonorous and thrilling. A chorus of hallelujahs rose from around the card tables.

"There is the beginning of Christian life," said Luke. He looked at Zoe, to see if she were following.

"That's the Pentecost?" she asked timidly.

"The Pentecost was the first mass conversion,

described right here in Acts. Jews out of every nation under heaven were drawn there, where the Twelve were sitting, filled with the Holy Ghost."

"Praise the Lord," put in Claudia.

Luke smiled at her. "Why don't you read some more of this chapter for Zoe," he said. "Start with verse thirty-eight."

Claudia obviously enjoyed reading. She said the words in a harsh poetic voice, but her blue eyes were dreamy.

" 'Then Peter said unto them, Repent, and be baptized every one of you in the name of Jesus Christ for the remission of sins, and ye shall receive the gift of the Holy Ghost.

" 'Then they that gladly received his word were baptized: and the same day were added unto them about three thousand souls.' "

"That's how it happened," said Brother Luke. "That's the Pentecost. James, tell Zoe what happened next."

"Well, next they gave everything away that they had, and they went around from house to house praising God. They didn't have nothing, but theirselves an' each other an' the love of Jesus in their hearts."

"Yes," said Brother Luke. "That's how it all started. The apostles and the disciples went out and worked with the people—the simple people."

"Is that what you all are doing?" asked Zoe.

"Yes."

"What does it mean, being born again?"

"Turn to John 3:3. Jesus explains to Nicodemus. 'Except a man be born again, he cannot see the kingdom of God.' So Nicodemus says, 'How can a man be born when he is old? Can he enter the second time into his mother's womb and be born?' "

Zoe was covering all the words with her sharp yellow ink, so that they seemed to spring into the light. She thought they were beautiful.

Brother Luke said, "And here is where Jesus makes it clear, that there are two kinds of birth, two stages, one of the flesh and then the second, of the spirit. 'Except a man be born of water and of the Spirit, he cannot enter into the kingdom of God. Marvel not that I said unto thee, Ye must be born again.'

"You see, Zoe? When you are born the second time, you are born in the spirit, and you can hear the sound of the Spirit which is divine, and which you could not hear before. And, furthermore, you become a vessel of the Spirit, which may blow through you as the wind, and you will open your mouth and the Spirit will speak through you, right through your mouth, as brass speaks in the trumpet when it is blown."

"That's speaking in tongues," said Claudia.

"The joy of the Lord is my strength," said Mildred.

Zoe shivered. The words moved her so. She felt frail, unbelievably frail, a dry transparent husk of something, lying on a dry field somewhere, lifted by the whisper of a breeze. Everybody was smiling at her, as though she were a child, but she seemed to be in some other place, removed, seeing them and seeing her pale golden husk of a body in the room, a vessel, and then she heard Brother Luke speaking, in God's voice, about the ones that refuse Him, the ones that won't be saved. It seemed as though he were speaking to her.

Zoe felt her spirit passing right out of her body. She was desolated. What had she done wrong that she was nothing, nothing, nothing? What had she always done wrong, since she was born that she felt hollow in herself, wanting, pale?

She heard Brother Luke's voice again, full and sweet, saying, *"Come.*

"And the Spirit and the bride say, Come. And let him that heareth say, Come. And let him that is athirst Come. And whosoever will, let him take the water of life freely."

When Zoe came out of her trance, Elsie, the large lady with the sausage curls, was leaning over her, saying, "Ain't she a love, though? She's one of us already."

There were some refreshments on the table and Zoe had a little coffee, but she was tired. She asked Claudia to call Ngiep, who was waiting outside with the car.

Brother Luke said, "I hope you'll come again next week, Zoe. I have a hankering to hear you read."

Zoe said she would, and then Ngiep came in and helped her get the wheelchair out of the porch and through the living room, and down the steps to the sidewalk.

"You okay?" he asked.

"I don't know. Yip, do you believe in anything?"

"The wind blow, and it raise dust on the doorstep," he said. "After a while, dust settle."

3

Barney touched Piri's arm, and she turned to look at him. "We're almost there," he said. "Just wait till you see this."

Piri's vacation was half over—she had only ten days to spend with him—but Barney didn't want to postpone any longer seeing the lawyer assigned to him by his insurance company. They were coming into the city now. The expressway penetrated the flats of Queens, and then it rose. New York was revealed in the distance, its towers rising from pearly smudges into a clear wintry blue.

"See that spire? That's the Chrysler building. There's the Empire State, and down there the new Trade Center. Isn't it fabulous?

"I got an extremely nice letter from your mother," Barney said. "She said she could wait another year before going back to school. Do you think she minds?" It was difficult to drive and communicate at the same time. He turned his head so that she could see his lips moving, and then looked ahead again. But there was hardly any traffic, and he turned again so that he could see her answer.

"Not too much," Piri signed. "She's happy. She has a new boyfriend."

"Oh-ho. You didn't tell me about that. Who is he?"

"Another doctor, believe it or not. A heart specialist."

"Just what she needs," said Barney benignly, and laughed. "Is he nice? Do you like him?"

"He's all right." The subject obviously embarrassed her.

"He's not married, I hope?"

"Divorced. He's quiet. Shy."

"I'm awfully glad," he said, and Piri nodded.

When he'd parked the car he checked to see that she had some money and told her to enjoy herself.

"You've got the address for La Paloma, right? I'll meet you there at one thirty." He kissed her. "Don't be late, sweetheart, or I'll worry about you."

"Good luck," Piri said. She had a long walker's stride. He watched her as she disappeared in the crowd, her round head rising confidently from the brown fur. She's going to make it, Barney thought, and then he turned his mind to the meeting with his lawyer. He'd never met the man. The insurance company had hired him.

The office was in one of those great glass and aluminum towers on Third Avenue, midtown. Barney found the directory. Timmons, Parkhurst and Bell, seventeenth floor. They had a whole floor, he saw, when he emerged from the elevator. There was a low glass table stacked with magazines, three mocha-colored couches covered with Brazilian leather, some Rothko prints on the wall, and a receptionist seated behind an immense burled wood desk. She asked him to wait, but he'd barely picked up a magazine when the sliding glass doors opened and a middle-aged man came over to him, holding out his hand.

"I'm Dave Sperling," he said. "How do you do?"

"Barney Lukacs." They shook hands. Barney liked

the man immediately. Sperling was thin, tall, and slightly stooped. His manner was direct and gentle.

"Come into my office, Dr. Lukacs."

There was a view looking downtown. Barney could see the massed buildings of Wall Street and the Williamsburg bridge.

"Tell me about the case—everything. The operation to begin with. The relapse. Your prognosis. You don't mind if I record it?"

"No." Barney went through the whole thing. He described the initial X rays, the final X rays, Foote, Zoe, and his brief examination of her afterward. He had with him some Xerox copies of technical information on hysteria. He handed it over to Sperling.

"Freud believed that hysteria is entirely sexual in origin," said Barney, "and that it arises from a profound sexual guilt, and that the tendency is established in the early years of childhood. A lot of modern thought confirms his work, but two world wars have given us scads of other material. There was a lot of hysterical illness among soldiers, particularly during the First World War. Extraordinary. Men went blind, literally blind, for instance. And were sent home. Some of them were cured later by psychotherapy. When a conflict becomes intolerable, some personalities are able to convert it into physical symptoms. For them it's a matter of survival, psychic survival."

"You want this to be true, don't you?" asked Sperling, gently.

"You don't believe me?"

"I don't know. I'm just getting into this."

"Okay. Of course I want it to be true. But not because of the lawsuit: I never believed that Zoe's relapse was organic. I did that operation. It was clean. The X rays and myelogram can be read either way. And I had that brief chance to examine her after her relapse. Furthermore," Barney hesitated. "As an individual, she has some characteristics that might indicate . . ."

"That she's a hysterical personality?"

"Not in the popular sense of that word. But there is a certain theatricality, aside from the fact that she's an actress, a versatility, a sort of excitement. She's changeable. She's charged, high-strung, vivid, imaginative, but sad too. She's hung up on something inside."

"You seem to know her very well," said Sperling.

Barney hesitated again. "I might as well level with you. We can't know what will come out at the trial. The fact is," he said, reddening again, "I'm in love with her. I think they're confirming her in a hysterical illness that came out of a temporary panic. If they didn't believe it, she wouldn't, and now she's gone into a complete tailspin. I can't get at her. I've tried to talk them into getting her to someone else, but the ranks have closed. I don't know if I was successful there. I can only hope that she has been seen by someone who isn't involved, someone who isn't predisposed to think that the relapse is physical in its nature."

"Were you lovers, you and Zoe?" asked Sperling.

"Not in the technical sense, but close to it. After she was released from my care, of course."

"Yes," said Sperling, leaning back in his chair. "Well. They may attack you on that basis. Unprofessional conduct."

"I don't think Zoe will say anything about it. Actually, I think that our relationship may have been a factor in what's happened to her. It created conflicts for her. It may have tapped childhood traumas that I can't know about. Then, before she was strong enough, they were pushing her into a production schedule."

"Possibly. But Dr. Lukacs, to tell the truth, we are way off the subject. We're talking about a legal action, not a character analysis." He met Barney's eyes. "I'm pleased that you've been so straightforward with me, but what we need are medical facts, evidence. We can't go to the jury with a hunch. Has she any past medical history that would confirm your analysis?"

"Nothing that was on her chart." Barney thought for a moment. Something was catching at a corner of his mind, a phrase, something suggestive, but it eluded him.

"Well, perhaps it will turn up in her deposition. But if there's nothing there, there's no point in pursuing this line of action. Legally, your feeling that her illness is hysterical means nothing. It's mere fantasy, at this point, and one is tempted to think that you may be covering yourself. The jury would think so."

"What do you mean, covering myself?"

"That you messed up, she had a relapse, and now you're trying to get out of it by saying she's hysterical."

"I'm not trying to cover myself. I made the same diagnosis before there was any question of a lawsuit, right after the relapse. There's no proof of that, because it was no longer my case. I didn't enter it on her chart. But it was a genuine appraisal of her condition, even then. I'd ask you to believe that at least."

"I do, for what that's worth. But since you're personally involved, any conclusions you offer are necessarily seen as biased. She has apparently no significant medical history. Of course, she'll be examined by our own neurologist. A prestigious, practicing neurologist. Probably someone attached to a university. Someone above reproach. Jim Harvey, possibly? What do you think? Of course, then we have to accept what he says. He may not agree with you, you know."

"I think he will."

"Furthermore, he may not agree that the operation should have been performed. So quickly, at least."

Barney laughed. "Any operation like that can be controversial. There was as much indication that it should be done as that it shouldn't. I'm not worried about that. Can we get a psychiatrist to see her?"

"Can't do it. The suit's not based on psychiatric damage; it's based on neurological damage. But I tell you what we can do. A lot of these fellows have dual certification. Neurologists and psychiatrists are certified by the same board. A neurologist can give a lot of psychiatric testimony. Harvey may be both, for all I know. But it wouldn't prove hysteria unless there was other evidence to that effect."

"But it's one way to get her to a psychiatrist," said Barney. "In the long run, it may help."

"That's outside of our subject, I'm afraid. My job is not to cure Zoe, nice as that would be; it's to get you off the hook." He smiled at Barney.

"Let's see how the case shapes up. Basically, what we have to show is this, that you did everything absolutely right, and that you are not responsible for the bad result. That's the law.

"Second, that the neurological tests, the X rays and the myelogram, do not conclusively point to arachnoiditis. That will be up to our expert witnesses. The neurologist, who we will choose carefully. There will actually be several of them. Since the plaintiff has named several defendants—Foote, Rubin, St. Mark's—each one is entitled to have the plaintiff examined. Then, of course, we'll have other expert witnesses."

"Like who?"

"A radiologist, for instance. Then we'll have to find a neurosurgeon who'll back you up. Both on the original decision and on the method of operating."

"That won't be hard," said Barney. "You could say that what I did was controversial, but it was not unusual."

"Right. And you've hit the basic point there. It's up to the plaintiff—Zoe—to prove that you did something that is contrary to standard medical practice—not the best or the most brilliant medical practice—just standard. If this weren't a pity case, they'd find it hard to prove. But a beautiful woman in a wheelchair is bound to be a big factor. The jury will feel for her. Whatever the facts are, they'll figure she might as well have the money, because she'll need it, and because it's money that only comes out of the insurance company's pocket."

"Little do they know," said Barney. "It comes out of their own pockets."

"Okay. You're right, of course. But let's get back to brass tacks."

"Yes," Barney said. "So the burden of proof is on Zoe. She has to prove that I was an incompetent doctor. Evans, the neurologist who examined her aside from Foote, will say that she has scar tissue due to butchery."

"Absolutely. And we'll show that it was a brilliant piece of surgery. As I see it, so far, our case is this: In the opinion of the operating surgeon, yourself, there was a foreign body impinging on the spinal cord. The spicule. You knew that there were certain risks connected with immediate surgery, but you did not believe that she would recover without it.

"Second, once the patient recovered, you were out of the picture. To say that the neurosurgeon has damaged connective tissue is stupid, because in an operation like that there is always damage to the connective tissue.

"Third, it depends on the extent of the damage. And the plaintiff will have to show that there is a hell of a lot of it. The X rays and myelogram do not show this.

"That's our case so far. We'll see how it develops. You acted within the parameters of accepted medical practice; you are not responsible for the damage."

"I suppose you're right," said Barney, "but I don't like it. The burden of proof may be on the plaintiff, but it seems to me that we have to do more than that. I don't want to just fight a lawsuit; I want to get at the truth. The truth is that the relapse is functional. Psychological. Besides, your outline of the case is purely defensive. I think we have to offer some alternative for the jury to consider."

"You're a stubborn man," said Sperling. He smiled. "And maybe you're right. We've got to counteract the potential pity settlement. Perhaps, really, the burden of the proof is on you, and you have to satisfy the jury that there is some possible alternative cause for the injury. The hysteria is tenuous, but if you can come up with anything . . ."

"Why don't we hire somebody?" Barney asked. "You know, a private eye. Someone who'll do some digging, and maybe come up with something." What was it? he wondered, that little clue he was trying to remember. Something Zoe had said.

"If we come up with anything from her past, and it combines with a good neurologist's analysis of her condition, then the jury might consider the case for hysteria," he said.

"How about Zoe?" asked Sperling. "Is she a convincing person? Is the jury liable to believe her?"

Barney thought about it. "Unfortunately for me,"

he said, "she's absolutely convincing. She radiates integrity, and what's more, she actually has it. But she's a peculiar character—I don't know how to put it." He wished that he could remember the little thing he was trying to remember. Perhaps if he went on talking, it would come to him. "You know the myth of Proteus?" Barney asked. "The old man of the sea? He could change himself into any shape he wanted, like an elephant or an octopus, but if you could actually seize him and hold him, he became the soul of truth and a visionary. Well, Zoe's something like that. You think you've got her nailed, and she changes. You touch her, and she becomes something else. But each thing she becomes, she becomes with her whole heart and soul. She's what the textbooks call labile, changeable, and yet she has a radiant integrity."

"She'll have the jury eating out of her hand," said Sperling.

"Yes, unless we can prove what we want to prove. If Zoe could be reached, if she understood what was happening to her, it would all be over."

"Okay, Barney. You win. I've got a private investigator who works for me from time to time—he's a good guy—Ross MacGill. Shall we call him? Do you have time to see him while you're in town?"

Barney nodded. Sperling looked up the number in a rotating file on his desk and dialed it. Then he smiled.

"We've lucked out. He's home . . . Ross?"

Barney listened to the explanation. Sperling said, "Two thirty?" and looked at him for confirmation. Barney nodded. He'd take Piri along.

Sperling wrote the address down and tore it off a pad. He got up and came round in front of the desk, holding out his hand.

"Good luck, Barney. You're going to need it."

* * *

The detective wasn't at all what Barney expected. He had his office in his apartment on Riverside Drive. It was a big carved stone building with a green copper roof. The doorman rang through to the apartment, and they went up. MacGill met them at the door.

"Hello," he said. "Come in."

Barney shook hands. "This is my daughter, Piri," he said. "We're in town together, so I brought her along. I hope you don't mind."

Piri smiled calmly at MacGill and held out her hand.

"Piri is deaf, and she talks mainly by signing," said Barney.

MacGill looked at her with interest. He was young, in his early thirties, a comfortable-looking man with a springy beard. He was wearing a plaid flannel shirt.

"I'm glad to meet you," he said. "Do you understand what I say?"

Piri nodded. She looked lovely, with her hair piled up like that.

MacGill took their coats, and they went into the living room. The plain windows looked out over the river to the Palisades. One wall was filled with books and records and a lot of highly technical stereo equipment. Minute lights went on and off in different parts of the set. There was a throb of electronic music. MacGill turned it off, and they sat at a big round table. He brought in a tray of coffee.

"Dave gave me the broad outlines on the phone," he said. "Suppose you fill me in."

"We want to dig up something in Zoe's past that confirms my diagnosis of hysterical illness. So far there is no evidence of any tendency in that direction, but there was something she said to me. I can't put my finger on it . . ."

"Where is she from?"

"Pittsville, Georgia. She has a father, a hard-nosed character named Abner Carter. A butcher, as I remember. She's afraid of him. Baptist background. Mother dead. Oh, I remember." The scene came back to him, not that it helped much. It was at Culpepper's. He and Zoe had been sitting on the sofa, courting, he supposed, doing the Sunday crossword puzzle and enjoying each other's closeness. The theme of the puzzle had been movie greats and the answer to one of the clues—Zoe had gotten it—was *Gone With the Wind.*

"That's right, Atlanta," Barney had said. He remembered that she had refused to talk earlier about living in Atlanta. "You lived there, didn't you? Tell me about it."

But Zoe had gone into one of her vanishing acts; she became remote. She twirled her long string of beads and said in a challenging way, "D'you know, I can't remember a single damn thing about Atlanta?"

"I know. You told me that before. Not anything?"

"Well, I played Blanche Dubois in the high school play. I was sensational."

"You stayed with your grandmother, right?"

"Yes."

"But I imagine from your father's letters that he didn't let you go too easily?" She hadn't answered him.

"Why did he let you go?" Still no answer. "God, it's like pulling teeth, just trying to find out who you are."

"Honestly, Barney, I don't understand it. I just don't remember."

"Did you have an accident? Amnesia?"

"I don't think so. But the doctor said I was all right."

"What doctor? Were you sick?" She shook her head. "Why did you have a doctor then?"

"I don't know. There was a doctor." Then she'd laughed. "What is this, Barney, an inquisition? I live in the present."

"It wasn't anything I can put my finger on," Barney said to MacGill. "Though she suffered from lapses of memory. But she was vague, defensive about ordinary things. She told me that she moved to Atlanta when she was fourteen. She mentioned a doctor, but she couldn't remember why she saw him. She was upset, talking about it. But it wasn't what she said, it was the atmosphere. There's something guilty and secretive there, something. Perhaps she saw a psychiatrist, either in Pittsville or when she got to Atlanta. At any rate, we want to know who she did see."

MacGill nodded. He was writing everything down. "You don't know the grandmother's name?"

"Carter, I suppose. No, I think it was her mother's mother. I don't know."

"Never mind. I can find out. I'll start with Pittsville and take it from there."

"I guess that's all we can do. It's going to be an exercise in archaeology. Just dig around and see if you can turn anything up." Barney gave MacGill the few facts that he knew, and filled him in on the current situation.

"What we need is a significant piece of medical history."

"Yes, I can see that," MacGill said. "It's all very intangible. No evidence. Well, I love a problem. If you really want me to do it, I'll shake it and shake it, and whatever's in there will come out. Don't expect too much. Meanwhile, I'll learn sign language, so I can talk to your beautiful daughter."

Piri nodded, and her hands flashed into movement. It was elegant. At first it looked like rabbits leaping, and then she made a gesture that included the table and Barney and MacGill's notes.

"She says, Is this the kind of thing you usually do?"

"Yes. I work for lawyers. I started out to be one myself, but I like this better. Usually, though, they give me a real shoe to smell before I start hunting."

Negligence Cases Multiply Against Lukacs
by P. J. Krupp

Dr. Barney Lukacs, the neurosurgeon who has already had charges filed against him by both Zoe Carter and the parents of Karen Williams, is the subject of still another malpractice suit.

Rufus William Lenahan, the contractor who built Quogue's Leisure Dunes, has initiated an action against Dr. Lukacs, and St. Mark's Hospital as well. Mr. Lenahan underwent an operation for severe back pain, a right hand laminectomy, which was followed by intense sciatic pain on the left side.

Asked what the charges consist of, Maximilian Ward, who represents Mr. Lenahan as well as Miss Carter and the Williamses, said briefly, "Dr. Lukacs operated on the wrong interspace."

I'm in trouble, Barney thought. The whole thing is getting out of hand. He wondered whether or not to show the article to Piri. She was wolfing Cheerios across the table from him. He decided against it.

Nothing she could do, except worry, and she was going home today. It was the third of January.

"You all set?" he asked her.

She nodded.

"I'll miss you."

She did an arpeggio with her hands. "I'd like to come to Kansas for spring vacation."

"Okay, good. Ask your mother." He was pleased. The worst part of divorce was missing the kids, particularly now, when they were hatching, flying, almost gone.

"Piroshka," he said, getting up. She stood too, cool and sturdy, and he smoothed the hair back from her face. "Take care of yourself. I have to go now." He had an operation scheduled. "The limousine will be here at ten to pick you up. Study hard. Get ready for the hearing world."

She nodded cheerfully. "Good luck," she signed.

"I'll need it," he answered.

It was a heavy day: two operations scheduled, and no sooner had he gotten through those than a highway accident came into the emergency room with multiple head injuries. He didn't get to patient rounds until midafternoon. Office hours were scheduled from four to seven. At the back of his mind, Barney was turning over the latest malpractice development. Three lawsuits within as many weeks. There was a gross abnormality about the acceleration of events. Lenahan was a rich egotistical fellow who considered himself a favored child of the gods. He had been affronted when the sciatica followed on his operation, and he'd complained loudly about it. It was the doctors' fault. The hospital staff had laughed. Barney had laughed too, but he'd hated the criticism. The sciatica was not his fault.

He gave fleeting consideration to the thought that

a malevolent fate was at work and dismissed it. And it couldn't be coincidence. Either it was Max Ward, drumming up trade, or it was a rash of lawsuits suggested to individuals by the notoriety surrounding Zoe's case. Probably the latter. Maybe both.

"Turn your head to the left," he said to his elderly patient. "Push against my hand. Yes, with your head. Now look up." He noted the corneal reflexes.

If he could scotch Zoe's case, Barney thought, the others would collapse of their own accord. In themselves, each was the kind of case that probably would not even come to trial. Added together they created a moral tornado that would wreck him—even if, legally, each one was supposed to be taken individually.

But I've got work to do, he thought helplessly. "You're improving, Mrs. Bertelson," he said, and she cocked a bright seventy-five-year-old eye at him. When she left, he clicked on his recording apparatus and reported on her progress and treatment. His secretary would type it up and put it in her file.

It would have to be war, he decided. He was the wrong person to see Zoe, perhaps, but somehow he would have to get to her, talk to her, examine her, see if he could break through to her. It was no good waiting for the trial. By then he might have twenty cases out against him. He'd just have to figure out a way to see her.

Later that evening the Packard lurched sedately up the drive, past Barney's window. Culpepper was driving. Barney looked at his watch. He gave Willie fifteen minutes to get home and settle down, and then he picked up the phone.

Ngiep answered. "Who is calling, please?"

"Barney Lukacs."

"Mr. Culpepper not at home."

Later on he called again from the hospital. When Ngiep answered he said, in a mildly British voice, "This is Billy King Hunt's office. Mr. Hunt for Mr. Culpepper, please."

Culpepper answered this time, and Barney said, "Willie, this is Barney Lukacs. Don't hang up, it's important."

There was a short silence, then Willie answered him. "My dear fellow, I can't talk to you. We're in opposing camps. Why don't you recognize that?"

"I do. Did you get an outside opinion?"

"Listen, Barney. When I was a young man, I got into a certain kind of . . . trouble." Culpepper's thin voice fell into a rhythm, as though he were reading a piece of poetry. "There was a scandal. My father took me aside and he said, 'My boy, there comes a time in every young man's life when he has to leave town. That time has come for you.' My father was right; it is perhaps the only thing I was ever grateful to him for. Now I must say the same to you. Pack your suitcase, young fellow, and leave town."

"Don't be silly. I haven't done anything wrong. I only want to get at the truth. I want to see Zoe."

"The subject is closed. You cannot see her." Culpepper hung up.

The *Island News* was a powerful organ. It was distributed from Queens to Montauk Point, with a circulation of roughly 700,000. It had more to report on the following day.

At a Rotary luncheon the mayor, Ralph Tuthill, had made St. Mark's a major subject of his talk. Tuthill had come uncomfortably close to scandal in a recent development scheme involving three hundred and sixty acres and a low-income housing project. Various civic groups opposed the project; Tuthill favored it. After it had been endorsed by the Town Board, a connection had been uncovered between the mayor and the developer, and now Tuthill, hoping to distract the public and demonstrate his probity in one stroke, was launching a campaign to clean up corruption in the hospital.

"If there's one thing that's close to our hearts," Mayor Tuthill said, "it's the integrity and excellence of our hospital. Waterville has always been proud of its medical service. We have all made sacrifices in order to keep our hospital open.

"Bring me your sick and your poor has been our motto, and it is a fact that St. Mark's has served this community unstintingly for eighty years. We cannot afford to let this tradition falter.

"But what do we find? The nurses and technicians, already more highly paid than most people in the area, have asked for a 14 percent across the board raise in salary. Now I hear that they're meeting secretly with high-level union organizers from the city. The new wing, funded in part by village funds, began construction on an estimated budget of one and a quarter million: it has now passed the two-million mark, and it's nowhere near completion. Finally, the competence of the hospital and its staff has recently been called into question, the emergency room in particular, and one surgeon whose name I need not mention. There are four malpractice suits pending against St. Mark's. What is going on here?

"I am deeply concerned. I have requested a meeting with Mr. Vandegrift, the hospital administrator, and when I see him I'll put it to him. Those staff members who put financial gain

above their dedication to public service should
be released from their contract . . ."

The emergency room on Saturday night was only
just behind the front lines. Every young fellow on
Long Island was out popping pills and gunning his
motor and, apparently, aiming his vehicle at whatever immovable obstacle presented itself. Broken
heads and bodies clogged the aisles. Barney felt bad-
tempered and the staff was jumpy. It was three
o'clock in the morning before Barney got to bed.

On Sunday there were two more unscheduled operations. He was exhausted. When a break came, Gerry
Rubin showed him the mayor's speech in yesterday's
Island News. So that's what everybody's been buzzing
about, thought Barney. His first reaction was one of
pure rage, but that was followed by a sense of frustration, and last and worst, by the conviction of his own
impotence. There was nothing he could do about it.
He was going to be the fall guy. The mayor hadn't
even mentioned his name, but every step he had
taken in the last four months had been followed by so
much publicity that everyone would know who the
mayor meant. It made his work here seem meaningless.

A dreary winter evening closed in early. The highway stretched out like an empty wet ribbon. Barney's
eyes felt raw. His eyelids kept falling, closed by their
own weight. When he got home he made a fire and
mixed himself a scotch and soda. *Forum* would be on,
the TV magazine program run by Celia Brophus.
He'd met her several times at Culpepper's, and she'd
even asked him to appear once on her program. That
was after his ice-pack treatment had been in the papers. He had turned her down, and she had been an-

noyed. But the program was always lively, and Barney often watched it.

He switched on the set and Celia appeared, cool and incisive, prepared to turn over a rock and investigate some curious corner of American life.

". . . A civil war," she was saying, "with lawyers across the country ranged on one side, doctors on the other."

Barney's attention sharpened.

"The malpractice crisis surfaced in 1975," Celia went on. "That year, the New York insurance companies refused to carry doctors any longer. There were too many lawsuits and too many losses. Finally, two special insurance companies were formed, with the sole purpose of insuring doctors. Commissions were formed to investigate the crisis.

"In 1971 only three cases in the country were settled for a figure above one hundred thousand. By 1975 the awards were in the millions and snowballing. By now they are multimillion. In California, two cases have been settled for over a billion. Health costs—I don't have to tell you—have skyrocketed.

"In a thirteen-year span, the total amount of money paid by doctors in insurance premiums rose by 4,000 percent.

"Dr. Martin Singer, an orthopedic specialist attached to Columbia Presbyterian, and President of the New York Medical Society, says that the high cost of health these days is a direct result of the malpractice crisis. Dr. Singer?"

An earnest face appeared on the screen, framed by diplomas. "One third of the money spent for health in this country is spent on defensive medicine—things done 'just to be on the safe side' by doctors and hospitals, so they won't be slapped with a malpractice suit.

"What is a malpractice suit about?" he asked, in a

slow, worried manner. "It's about money. It's a way of
getting money for the plaintiff (the patient, that is)
and his business partner, the lawyer."

The camera switched to Celia. "Maximilian Ward,
a malpractice attorney in the Hamptons, sees the issue in a different light. According to him, there is no
crisis."

Max appeared, wearing his glasses and riffling
through some papers at his desk. "Malpractice, actual
malpractice, has been around for years," he said. "It's
only beginning to attract attention because people
have realized that they're not powerless. They can sue.
The contingency fee makes legal help available to everyone. The real and major reason for the rise in
malpractice cases is careless medical treatment by a
small minority of doctors. It's high time they were
brought to account.

"The actual number of medical malpractice lawsuits is declining, although you hear a lot about them,"
Max continued. "An attorney like myself rejects more
malpractice cases than he accepts."

Liar, Barney said to himself. *You're out there
scrounging for cases.* But Max put up a good front.

"Malpractice cases are too much work," he continued, "and the prospects are iffy. Doctors don't cooper-
ate. They are cover-up specialists. They all know
who's incompetent or unscrupulous, but they won't
tell. They should police themselves."

Max hesitated. "I have to admit I'm not overfond
of doctors. They don't want to be questioned; they
don't want to be criticized. So they won't question or
criticize their fellow doctors. Somebody has to do it,
and that's my job. I'm here to keep them honest."

"I suppose you're right, Max," said Celia. "But
who do you see when you're sick?" Max laughed.

Barney was getting sleepy, in spite of himself. He

didn't quite follow Singer. His hands were still cutting and snipping and tying off. His brain longed profoundly for rest. Celia's voice began to throb in his ears. ". . . Indiana . . . pain and suffering . . . India . . . India . . ."

A log fell in the fire, and his eyes opened. On the tube the camera surveyed a room which looked dreadfully familiar. Barney sat up, wide awake. There was Zoe, seated in her wheelchair by the glass doors. A book was open on her lap.

"Zoe Carter's case has not yet come to trial. She is an actress . . ." Celia described the case. "Ms. Carter is suing for an unspecified amount—so far. Tell me, Zoe. What exactly are you suing Dr. Lukacs for?"

"Negligence. At least that is the legal category as I understand it. Apparently the operation was controversial."

"Apparently?"

"My lawyer tells me there is a medical basis for the lawsuit."

"You mean, you don't feel that Dr. Lukacs ruined your life? Why are you suing him, then?"

"My life isn't ruined; it's changed. Things happen to you which make you take a different road, that's all. I was a selfish girl. I wanted to be a star. But God has given me a way to understand that, and I know now that acting doesn't mean anything. We all serve in the ways that are open to us." Zoe fingered her Bible. The cover was a soft black leather, embossed with gold. She spoke like a child, seriously, but her voice was low and sweet. A dreamer's voice, thought Barney, watching Zoe closely.

"If you feel like that, let me ask you again: Why are you suing Dr. Lukacs?"

"I am entitled to some recompense," she said. "It won't be easy for me to earn a living. But beyond

that, the money will help a lot of people." She
paused, and then looked directly at the camera for
the first time. "Have you ever felt—" she leaned forward and made a gesture with her hands "—empty?
As though you'd been promised something, you didn't
know what, and it had never happened? Well, that's
it, that's the state of human quiescence, waiting, waiting . . . for the love of Jesus."

That voice, thought Barney, deeply moved.

"You mean," asked Celia, "you're just going to
make a bundle on the lawsuit, and carry your
message everywhere?"

"God opens the doors," Zoe answered. The camera
pulled away from her until she was a small figure in
the light that came in through the glass.

"That's Zoe Carter," Celia's voice said crisply. "We
would have liked to present both sides here, but Dr.
Lukacs prefers not to appear on our program."

That was a low blow, Barney thought. It made him
sound as though he were afraid to face the charges
against him. Things were building up unmercifully—
Max digging up more cases, the newspapers exploit-
ing them, the mayor, and now *Forum,* a national
program. What could he do against this tide of public
reporting? He was worn out, but not sleepy anymore,
and he found himself pacing up and down his living
room, nervously going over and over the whole order
of events. Was there something he should have done,
but hadn't?

The phone rang, and Maggie's deep voice said,
"Barney! Brophus is a bitch. Are you upset?"

"Very. At this rate they're going to drum me out of
town. Did you see the *Island News?*"

"Yes, just now. It's bad. And what's with Zoe? She's
gone all smarmy and religious."

"I don't know. I can't get through to speak with her. But she seems to have fallen in."

"Maybe she thinks she's Sister Glory. Life imitates art. What do you think?"

"I think she's in a trance and doesn't know what she's doing. How come you saw the program?"

"I'm at the Pattersons'. They knew about it beforehand."

"Nice of them to let me know," said Barney.

"I don't suppose they expected it to be like that. What are you going to do?"

"There's not much I can do. Except to get in and see Zoe by hook or by crook. I may still have some influence over her. If I can wake her up, the other cases will fall like a house of cards. Meanwhile, thank God for the job in Kansas."

"I don't know about Zoe," Maggie said. "She's pretty far gone, but I guess you have to give it a try. Hang in there, Barney. Let me know if there's anything I can do."

Barney felt remarkably cheered. It was nice to know that there was, at least, one solitary comrade-in-arms. Yes, he had to see Zoe. Once, at least, before he went off to Kansas, he had to make a stab at talking to her. Perhaps she was waiting to hear from him, and Culpepper was running interference. Perhaps, if he could reach her, she would flutter her eyelids and wake up, like Sleeping Beauty, and meet his eyes. Perhaps he'd hate her. He didn't know. He felt a strong connection, even now. He decided to go early in the morning, before the household was up. Maybe he could sneak in.

Max and Carole were also watching *Forum*. They lay in Max's bed after a Sunday afternoon snooze, comfortably entwined, resisting the rainy darkness outside.

"She's something else," said Carole. "But you'd think she'd say *something* against Barney. The impression I get is that he didn't do anything wrong."

"It doesn't matter." Max untangled himself from Carole.

"But she doesn't seem to know what it's all about," Carole said.

"It's beneath her," Max said simply.

Carole rolled over and began to stroke him. "When do you come on again?" she asked.

"Soon, I think. Don't do that; the commercial's almost over."

"You looked angelic," Culpepper said. "That white dress was just the thing."

Zoe nodded. "I think I must have gotten through to a few people," she said seriously. "Do you think so?"

"I expect so. Did the program bother you? Did you agree with Max or with Dr. Singer?" He looked at her curiously.

"I didn't pay too much attention," Zoe said. "It's not what is important. God's rules are perfectly clear. They're all set down in the Bible. Love is what counts, and submission to God's will."

"And your legal action," Culpepper asked ironically. "That's love?"

"No, it's God's will."

The alarm went off. It was still dark: 5:00 A.M. Barney dressed quickly. The whole thing was absurd. If he thought about it he'd never go through with it. Barney Lukacs, the darling of the medical societies, speaker at conferences in Rotterdam and Rome and

Tokyo, respected neurosurgeon, cloak-and-daggering around an antique beach house in the empty deep-freeze of the last hours of a January night. Clam shells crackled under his feet, so he moved over onto the grass. He passed the dim gables of the garage and circled around the drive. The front door was locked. Naturally. The side door was locked too, but next to it a window was raised a few inches. It was high off the ground, and underneath the sill was a mass of rhododendron bushes. Barney decided to try on the ocean side first. They might not bother to lock the big glass doors.

A light was on in the living room, falling on a massive curlicued chaise longue, and on a man who was sleeping there. He was snoring. Quivering jowls, glasses, a pale blue-gray uniform with brass buttons and a badge. They'd hired a guard. Barney stood there, wondering if he should give it up. He was in over his head. But then, he thought, *there's no other way*. He moved away. Some folding chairs were stacked against the wall. He took one and went back to the kitchen window.

Parting the branches slightly, he opened the chair and placed it on rough ground between the bush and the wall. He placed one foot on the chair and, grasping a drainpipe that he hadn't been able to see but which came to his hand when he needed it, he shifted his weight and pulled the other foot up. The rhododendron branches whistled back into place. The chair wobbled, but the drainpipe held. He raised the window, slowly, but even so it made a familiar window noise. He waited: nothing.

The sill was low to the floor inside. Barney tried to visualize the kitchen. There was a big wooden table in the middle, as he remembered. He could see the pilot lights on the stove. There must be chairs. He made his way around the central area, feeling the chair backs, and over toward the door which opened into the front hall. The other one went to the dining room, and he would have to pass the guard to get to the stairs.

There was a dim spill of light in the hallway from the living room. He could see the gleam of the newel post, and the polished edges of the steps. Almost there. There were rugs in the hall. Barney crossed them and tested the first step. He went up as close to the wall as he could, thinking that there would be less creaking there. Two, three, four. As his foot left the fifth step, it released a rusty squawk, and he stopped, listening. The snores stopped with a choking sound, and he heard the springs of the chaise. He tried to stop breathing. Steps: heavy steps. A throat clearing. Steps into the hallway.

The heavy man came at him. He pulled Barney from his perch and locked his arms, and marched him down the steps and through the living room. Then he was holding a gun, which pressed into Barney's back.

"Open the door," he whispered.

Barney slid open the door. A blast of cold salt air met him. The guard pushed him out, and followed him through the door. He planted his huge fists on his hips, one still curled around the gun, and looked at Barney. He laughed. "I suppose you're Dr. Lukacs?" he asked. Barney didn't answer, and the man laughed again. "Run along, Doctor. And don't come back."

That day there was an emergency meeting of the board at St. Mark's Hospital. The mahogany conference table, islanded in the center of the room, lit from concealed sources and surrounded by somber men, resembled nothing so much as a giant coffin. Light filtered through the venetian blinds. The Chairman of the Board cleared his throat.

"Gentlemen, I have asked for this meeting for obvious reasons. We're getting a lot of flak from town and from the press. I don't have to tell you how important it is that we maintain good relations there.

"Another suit was filed against Dr. Lukacs yesterday, though not, in this case, against the hospital. The publicity has been unusual. The man is in an unfortunate situation, but the bottom line for us is how all this reflects on St. Mark's. I'll turn this meeting over to the administrator at this point: Mr. Vandegrift?"

Vandegrift, a thin pinched-looking man in his sixties, impeccably dressed, opened his attaché case and placed several files on the table in front of him.

"The mayor is pushing a three-point program," he said. "He wants a 7 percent raise for the staff to forestall their unionizing. He wants Begley—the contractor for the new wing—fired. Finally, he wants us, well, as he put it, to 'get Lukacs.' " He looked around the table.

"Of course," he went on, "Mayor Tuthill's attacks are not the only consideration. We have some very real problems here, and my first concern is the stability of this institution. I believe that we can handle the staff. Everyone here is running scared right now. I think we can throw them a 2 or 3 percent increase, and stop the union talk, if we get rid of Begley and Lukacs. Begley's part of the problem. He's a bottomless well. The more we throw in, the more he needs. The staff feel that they're working their heads off and all the money goes to Begley."

There was a murmur of agreement.

"Dr. Lukacs is a different problem. The publicity.

That medical reporter for *Island News*, for instance—P. J. Krupp."

Vandegrift opened a file and with fastidious fingers
selected some news clippings, glued to sheets of
typewriting paper. "Here's a bunch of interviews he
did with people who went to Southampton's
emergency room instead of ours, although they're
closer to us. They distrust our emergency room service, most of them blaming Dr. Lukacs for their
uneasiness.

"Dr. Lukacs came to us with superb credentials,"
continued Vandegrift. "He had a brilliant record at
Clairmont. Before that he was attached to the University of Pennsylvania, where he was considered one of
the most promising men in his field, with a distinguished performance both clinically and in research.
He is a member of the American Academy of Neurological Surgery, the American Association of Neurological Surgeons, the American Society of Stereotactic
Surgery, the Research Society of Neurological Surgeons, and he served on a study section for the NIH.
He was deeply involved in microsurgical research,
techniques and instruments, and experimental investi-
gations with primary malignant brain tumors. He
published frequently.

"Now, of course, he's been in practice since he
joined St. Mark's, about six years, but even so, I don't
think he's forgotten in those circles. You can see why
we considered ourselves extremely lucky to get him.
Now—"Vandergrift spread his hands—"I don't know.
I've done a personal investigation on him, on my own
and in conjunction with the executive committee of
the hospital, and I'd like to present my findings for
your consideration.

"I should say, first of all, that we can do without
Dr. Lukacs. We have Dr. Edson, the neurosurgeon

from Islip. He's been our back-up here for several years, and he gets along with Austin Foote, something which Lukacs has never been able to do. Then I have a replacement on hand for Dr. Lukacs, since he was about to take a year's leave of absence. I have to tell you that the medical board recommends that Dr. Lukacs be suspended temporarily from the hospital."

He paused. The members of the board shifted uneasily in their chairs, coughed, exclaimed, and started to talk to each other. Mrs. Francis Dart Montpelier, the only woman on the board, spoke across the length of the table.

"But is it fair?" she asked. "I mean, are we . . . 'getting' Dr. Lukacs because he's done something wrong, or because he's recently gotten bad publicity?"

"That's what I've tried to uncover, Mrs. Montpelier. The fact is, opinions have polarized around here. To begin with, he's not popular with the medical community at St. Mark's. His life-style counts against him with many of the doctors. They feel he's more interested in his jet-set life than his work. He lives in East Hampton. In an emergency it takes him a half hour or three quarters of an hour to get here. The doctors feel that he's loose, uncommitted, not substantial. He's not married, for instance. Has girl friends. There've been reports that he mixes with an oddball bunch of people in East Hampton. And again, he's been asked not to be out on his boat when he's on call. He says he's got a bleeper and can get back in time. That seems to be true. Sometimes he's made his rounds at midnight. It's many little things, but it's led to free-floating resentment. Basically, I guess, many of the doctors feel that he's too unconventional. Aggressive too. Overconfident. Thinks he's above the rules and regulations. His first responsibility, they say, should be to serve the community."

"They're right," said a white-haired man. "As a doctor myself, I've always felt that one's character was as important as one's medicine. Hippocrates described the first principles of medical ethics. He said, 'A physician should be an upright man, learned in the art of healing . . . conducting himself with propriety in his profession *and in all the actions of his life.*"

Mrs. Montpelier said, "That's true, Dr. Fagan. But I've met Dr. Lukacs. He's a charming man. He doesn't seem wild at all." And a dark heavy man, Father Lyman, said, "Sounds like personality differences more than anything else."

"Well, it does, Father Lyman," Vandegrift said. "But there are real things involved. Twice Dr. Lukacs signed out to a neurologist. It's his responsibility to see that the emergency room is covered for neurosurgery. One of those times he was at a conference in New York. Dr. Edson, the back-up, was on vacation. The neurologist diagnosed a subdural, a blood clot which was expanding and pressing on the brain. Had to be removed instantly. Bracken—our Chief of Surgery—was frantic. Couldn't get anybody. He had two general surgeons lined up to do the job, but he didn't like it. He put in a last-minute call to Barney's hotel and fortunately found him in. Barney, Dr. Lukacs that is, came back and did the operation. The fact is, a situation like that shouldn't arise. Bracken, however, is one of Barney's strongest supporters. Thinks he's terrific and says he doesn't care how the man lives.

"The trouble really starts with the Zoe Carter case, which sparked a lot of smoldering bad feeling. Dr. Foote says the operation was unnecessary. Decadron— a drug that reduces swelling—would have handled the situation. His consulting opinion, which is on record, was *consider* Decompression.' In other words, *con-*

sider operating. He has elaborated on that." Vandegrift read from his notes. "He says, 'I meant, and I
said at the time, that *if* there was a positive myelogram, surgery might be in order. Dr. Lukacs never
even did a myelogram. He just waded right in there.
I went to the OR to follow through. There was an
awful lot of bleeding. It's my opinion that the famous
spicule was just another small bone fragment in
there. It hadn't really penetrated. It's my opinion
that if we'd relied on Decadron, there'd have been no
operation. If there was no operation, we wouldn't
have all that scar tissue, and we wouldn't have the
paralysis. Finally, it's my opinion that Dr. Lukacs depends too much on the knife.' Dr. Foote has a lot of
support."

"If the man's taking a leave of absence anyway,"
said the priest, "can't we just let it blow over?"

"I don't think that will do the trick," said Vandegrift. "What we need right now is some action on the
part of the hospital. If St. Mark's is endangered by a
situation that is rapidly becoming a public scandal,
then the scandal's got to go. The executive committee
listened to much testimony, and they decided that Dr.
Lukacs should be suspended for six months. I agree
with them, and I'd like to ask for your support."

There was further discussion, but when it came to
a vote there was little opposition: thirteen to two in
favor of suspension.

Mrs. Montpelier said, "I hope we're not doing the
poor man an injury," and later she argued for a more
substantial across-the-board raise for the staff. It
passed muster at 5 percent. The members then voted
to threaten Begley, instead of firing him, and the
meeting broke up in a general atmosphere of self-con-
gratulation. Mrs. Montpelier paused to chat with Fa-

ther Lyman, and then went off to a meeting of the
East Hampton Shakespeare Club. When she thought of
that nice Dr. Lukacs, she shook her head. Such a
handsome man, you wouldn't think he'd be so, *rash*.

4

Barney had nothing to do. It was worse than a divorce. He wandered around East Hampton, looking in shop windows, and tried to think of all the things he always wanted to do that normally he didn't have time for. But he was a man of habit, a working man, someone with appointed rounds. He was used to being inside the general machinery, clicking into place, doing his daily job. He liked it that way.

The empty day loomed ahead of him. He was expected nowhere until his four o'clock office hours. He still had to check out former patients, but he couldn't take on any new ones. He had no place to do surgery. Without a hospital, he was a man without a country. It was bloody cold. Main Street looked wide and uninhabited, and bits of things flew around in the wind.

He stopped in at O'Malley's for a cup of coffee and then decided to make it a beer. Nobody was there, so he talked to the bartender.

"Cold out there," he said, feeling embarrassed. It wasn't quite lunchtime. What would the bartender think of him, hanging around with nothing to do in the middle of the day?

"Colder'n a witch's tit," said the bartender amiably, and Barney brightened. The man was friendly. He tried to think of something to talk about, but he couldn't come up with a topic. He nodded at the man and opened his paper. Even the paper was likely to be full of the subject he'd just as soon avoid. He'd sidestepped the *Island News* and the *Times,* and gotten the *Daily News* instead.

Barney turned to the sports section. It was a couple of years since he'd doped out a race, but some of the field was still familiar. In the fifth race he recognized Coogan's Alley and Sandsprite. Sandsprite used to be a good horse. But, Barney noted, he hadn't been out since May. The handicappers didn't like him. Coogan's Alley was three to one in the morning line, which ruled him out. There was no honor in betting favorites. He cast his eye down the list of entries. Three Onions, Honorable Discharge—ah, there it was: Lukas' Folly, going off at thirty to one. Cordero up, and a good stable. He made a mark beside it. No point, really, trying to figure them. He was out of practice.

Some men came in, noisily, calling out to the bartender.

"Hey, Al, what's up, man?"

"Hi there, Tom."

"Cold enough for you?"

"Michelle in yet?"

Barney looked up. Yellow slickers. Their easy camaraderie made him feel like an outcast. He envied them.

"First round's on me," said one of the men.

"It's only ten of twelve, Tom," said the bartender.

"Oh, well, we'll just hang out for ten minutes, won't we, fellows? Then we'll have it."

Everybody laughed. The bartender brought four beers.

"I won't touch mine," Tom said. "Not until the ding dong." He left it there, in front of him, while the others raised their glasses, admired them, smacked their lips, drank.

"Mm-hmm. That is good," said one. He burped jovially.

"I can wait," said Tom. His voice vibrated, tinkling glasses and raising the hairs on the back of Barney's neck. "I've got discipline. I'll be getting laid while you guys are getting laid out at St. Mark's." There was a lot of laughter. Barney folded his paper and put some change on the bar.

"By Doctor Lucky Ass down there."

God, he thought, in terror. *Do they know it's me?* Then he realized that Tom meant down at the hospital. He put his paper under his arm and left, covered by the sound of their guffaws.

He drove over to Southampton and hung around the OTB parlor for a while, listening in.

"Coogan's Alley's a shoe-in," said an old fellow with military sideburns and workman's clothes.

"Coogan's? Never make it. Can't do the distance. Can't close. I wouldn't put two cents on him." The speaker was a spreading housewife. She had on a huge flowery apron under an ancient overcoat. A weedy character with a fine exhausted face said, "What do you think of Duke MacGregor?"

The minute he mentioned it, Barney was convinced Duke would win the race. He wanted to stay with his own pick, but now he knew it would lose. He wavered for a while, his eyes on the changing odds, and then he studied a *Daily Racing Form* that some-one had left open on the table. Sandsprite had the best overall speed. He wondered why no one was betting her. All the horses suddenly looked very good. When the results from the first race were posted, the housewife nodded seriously and went to cash in her ticket.

Duke MacGregor or Lukas' Folly? Barney's mouth was dry. His heart was racing. As soon as he decided on one, he could see the other one galloping across the finish line. He couldn't decide. Maybe they were both losers. He got in line at the window with the betting form in his hand, and just before it was his turn he decided to bet an exacta coupling both horses, ten and ten reverse. Then he put twenty dollars on Lukas' Folly to win and place. Wotthehell. He winked at the housewife.

"Good luck," she said, smiling, and he was stabbed with relief. She was kind. Her big pearly eyes, surrounded by fat, were filled with innocence and kindness. How could he leave this place? It was dim and busy and small, already drifting with torn-up tickets and bettings forms and people who were familiar with each other shop-talking in accepted ways. He was all right here. But the fifth race was his race, always had been. He didn't want to bet the others. He went out and got into the Porsche.

Now that he didn't have the race to think about, his appalling situation rushed in on him. What should he do now? It was only two hours until four o'clock; he could have lunch. Actually, it was only ten days until he went to Kansas. And he had a lot to do before then. He listed the things he had to do in his mind. He had to clean up his office, finish off patient records, pack. He had to see his lawyer, and he wanted to see the private eye again, find out if he was onto anything. He still hadn't gotten his ticket. He'd better get started. As soon as he thought that, all his energy melted away. He was possessed by an enormous apathy. But he knew that it was worse than that. He felt humiliated, and worse than the press, worse than the hospital board, it was that damned guard with his fists on his hips, laughing at him, that stayed in his mind.

The next day he woke up around eleven, still feeling lethargic. He hadn't gotten anything done, after all. He called in to his office, but nothing special had come up. He didn't know what he'd do if it did. He might as well go book his flight to Kansas.

At the travel bureau he devoted serious attention to the choice between going straight there, or stopping over in Chicago to see Piri, deciding to stop en route. Afterward he toured past the OTB parlor. Yesterday's ticket was in his back pocket. His horse was letter B and Duke MacGregor was C: BC. Magical. It sounded so right. Before Christ. Before Christ, I swear I did nothing wrong. His pocket felt warm, and his face was flushed. BC.

He inched his way through a crowd of bettors who were waiting for the first race to go off, and over to the board where yesterday's results were posted. The place was filthy. Tickets, stale smoke, stepped-on cigarettes. He stopped while the race was called. "C'mon Stepper," someone yelled. Stepper, High Stepper that is, came in. The fat woman from yesterday, her hair pinned around white plastic curlers, stopped by a wastebasket and tore up a stack of tickets. Barney tried not to look at the board, but he'd spotted the sign that said *Yesterday at Aqueduct*. He moved closer to it, but he kept his head turned, and his eyes still on the housewife. His heart was thumping. BC: He could taste it. The housewife had taken a folded page from the newspaper out of her apron pocket. She was doping out the next race. Finally, he was in front of the board. He read the results of the first race, and the second, but then he couldn't keep his eyes any longer away from the fifth. It leapt out at him: BC.

He'd won. Dear marvelous old BC. It paid a lot, too. He looked around: nobody had noticed him. And he was a fantastic winner. Both horses were long shots. Lukas' Folly had finally gone off at thirty-eight to one. He had a ticket on him worth $520, and the exacta had paid $1,801. Barney tried to look unconcerned, but he picked the tickets out of his wallet and edged over to the housewife.

"Well, whaddaya know," he said casually, showing her the ticket.

She looked at it. "Holy shit," she said. "You was on those horses. Hey, Bob, look at this."

There was a flurry, and several people looked at Barney's tickets.

"Beats me," said a watery-eyed gent. "I'm here every day, dawn to dark, 'n you just walk in like that."

"Some people have all the luck," said the housewife.

When he got home the mail had come. There was a letter from Hutch Gordon at University Hospital. "Dear Barney," it read:

> This is bad news. I've just talked to the administrator here. He's very hot under the collar, very apologetic, but he's firm. It's not your malpractice suits per se, it's the national publicity they've gotten. He wants to cancel your contract for next year. In fact, I gather, the Board feels very strongly about it. If they can't get out of the contract, they'll pay you to stay there. They are consulting their lawyers.
> We could fight it, Barney, legally, but I don't think it would do you any good. Private practice

must be shit. Get the trial on the agenda as fast
as you can—as soon as it's over we'll get you here
on the next train. I'm sorrier than I can say, not
just for *your* troubles but because I was looking
forward to our work together.

Let me hear from you, and let me know if I
can help. Character witness? Yours,

Hutch

Barney looked around him in amazement. He was
down and out. His living room looked, suddenly,
small and musty, contemptible. And it was only his
until the end of the month. He was a member of the
great unemployed, shorn right down to his skin. A
bum? Three months ago he'd been a big cheese. It
was amazing.

He made an ineffectual gesture with Hutch's letter,
thinking that he ought to put it somewhere. Then he
laughed. Good grief, where? What for? He didn't
even live here anymore.

Pack. He had to pack and get out of here. The
place was already rented to a new tenant anyway. *Ah,
my boy, there comes a time in every man's life when
he has to leave town*. Did Zoe know what was happening to him? He didn't think so. She was in a
trance. Incredible! Barney laughed out loud.

In some odd way everything was exciting. He
didn't have to watch his step or take part or be responsible and manly and make tough decisions, or,
for that matter, think about anything at all. Even his
wife, Connie, couldn't ask anything of him. Legally,
she had him by the short hairs. Factually, you can't
squeeze blood out of a stone, especially a rolling
stone, or money out of an unemployed man.

Wind whistled in the rigging. He was outside of society; he could do anything. He could drink himself

to death, or take up some other trade. He could be anybody—a journalist, a bartender, a con man. He could take what he had and buy a quarter of land in Colorado and be a hermit. He could take his boat to the Keys and pig out on mangoes. Extraordinary. He felt evil, as though he were sinking his teeth into an unbelievable soft fruit, mushy and fibrous and running with oversweet juices.

I've been good, he thought in surprise. I never even noticed it, but I've been good, and they didn't like it. I've taken out life insurance and voted and minded the traffic lights. I took care of my family, and I gave up the work I liked, and even when Con left me I came through. I've done my human best at surgery. I've filled out forms and forms and forms to justify my place in the world, and the world has found me unacceptable.

He laughed again. He was packing. Rather methodically, he noticed. He didn't have to do that anymore. He could just throw everything in some boxes, if he wanted, and go. Or just leave it all. But he went on folding things and putting them neatly in cases. He found some cartons in the storage room downstairs and marched from room to room filling them. Records, books, kitchen things, boat things, papers, tools. A tennis racket, a bust of Hippocrates. The painting Bill Patterson had given him: a stiff disconsolate woman, sitting vaguely in a chair. He hesitated. It was beautiful. It filled him with longing and, at the same time, satisfaction.

Bums and adventurers, Barney thought, do not haul haunting canvases around the country. He put it aside to sell. It was worth a few thousand, and the Benson Gallery would take it. Adventurers need money.

The pile of boxes grew, neatly corded and labeled

with a black magic marker. Orderly. Satisfying. His
life, stored up in cubes in an empty room, the bronze
bust balanced on top. He was almost done. He'd forgotten the bathroom. He picked up a carton and ran
to the bathroom. His face prickled with sweat. He
emptied the medicine cabinet. He corded the carton
and carried it back to the living room. *Bathroom.* he
wrote on it, in handsome black square letters. How
about Piri, he thought. What will happen to Piri?

Fog rose from the floor of his mind and curled
around the spaces there. obscuring the vividly printed
cubes piled up in the middle. It was hot in the cottage, and he was tired. Nauseated. He sat down on
the bathroom carton and thought, I'd better decide
what I'm going to do.

PART III

1 ⋯⋯⋯

Ross MacGill ambled cheerfully through the little town. They were all the same, north, south, east, west. Different trees and different houses, different voices, but small town life had the same smell anywhere. He came from one himself, in Maine. The big houses, the little ones, the emptiness. It was all familiar.

He stopped at the stationery store—Tappert's—and bought a copy of the *Pittsville Journal*. Post cards, pinwheels, pipes, a magazine stand, a dirty magazine stand, Western Union. An elderly sick-looking gent ran the place. He had a long, curved, balding forehead and a yellowish white mustache.

"Morning," Ross said.

The old man nodded.

"Nice weather," Ross said.

The old man looked at him. He didn't answer. Ross read the paper for a while to give the old fellow a chance to get used to him. A large heavy fly was buzzing around.

"You Mr. Tappert?" asked Ross.

"That's right."

"Got a fly swatter?"

Mr. Tappert handed him a blue plastic fly swatter. Ross stalked the fly, and finally bagged it on the embossed tin over the magazines.

"I see there's a new highway going through," Ross

said, nodding at his paper. "Think it'll change any-thing?"

"Well." Mr. Tappert paused. "Make some differ-ence. There'll be more people coming through."

Ross read the obituaries, lounging against the counter. Then he folded up his paper and stuck it under his arm.

"Know a family named Carter?" he asked Mr. Tappert.

"I reckon. Who wants to know?"

"I'm Ross MacGill," Ross said directly. "Down here trying to trace Zoe Carter. She's come into some money."

"You could ask Buddy Carter, her brother. He's down at the butcher shop. What I hear, she don't need no inheritance. She's suing some doctor for a million dollars."

"She got any other family here?" asked Ross.

"Abner's up north. That's her father. He's helping her sue." Mr. Tappert gave a wheeze, which Ross took to be a laugh.

"Mother?"

"Dead. Put her head in the oven a while back."

Ross's nose sharpened. Don't get excited, he told himself, but he was.

"Uh-huh. Wearing an old green robe with pink circles all over it. An' a hat with pink feathers. I was in the fire department then."

"They called the fire department?"

"Kids called us. Zoe. She was only a little thing, pretty as a picture. Now I can't say as I blame Me-lanie. She had a hard life."

"What happened?"

"Who knows! First she was alive, and then she was dead." Mr. Tappert nodded and picked up a paper from the pile of invoices in front of him.

Ross said, "Thanks, Mr. Tappert. Can you tell me where the school is?"

Mr. Tappert waved a fragile hand. "Two blocks down, take a right. You'll see it."

"Thank you," Ross said.

The school was a comparatively modern building. A sign hung between two posts: PITTSVILLE JUNIOR HIGH SCHOOL. Underneath there were replaceable letters in slots which read: VALE TINE DANC FRI 8. Ross asked in the office if he could see the principal. He was sent straight in. "What's his name?" he asked.

"Mr. Emmett."

Mr. Emmett turned out to be a pudgy man in a blue-striped shirt. As Ross entered, he was putting on a Dacron jacket. There was a gold freemason's button in his tie.

Ross introduced himself and came straight to the point.

"I'd like to find out anything I can about a girl named Zoe Carter. She would have been in school here about fifteen years ago. Were you here then?"

"I was here."

"Do you remember Zoe?"

"This is a small place. Of course I remember her. Zoe was . . . Zoe was not ordinary. You couldn't forget her."

"Tell me about her, would you?"

"I reckon she was the most beautiful thing I ever saw. Not, sir, in the usual way. There was nothing . . . silly, about Zoe. She didn't have, shall I say, curls or eyelashes or—" his hands described an hourglass—"but she was beautiful. She looked like a flower. Fragile. Drooping, if you know what I mean. But the next minute she'd be blazing away at you. She had green eyes."

"How about her grades? Was she a good student?"

"No, I can't say that she was. Not that she didn't have a mind, sir, not at all. Standard testing, Metropolitan, Sanford-Binet, she'd go right off the page. IQ," his hand rose, and kept rising, "very high. Zoe was smart. Street smart, book smart, a whiz. But not a good student. Her mind was elsewhere."

"Where do you suppose it was?"

"I don't know. She was changeable. God knows what she had on her mind. With Zoe, one minute you'd be talking to the Dowager Duchess, and the next minute, maybe, Jezebel. Maybe she read too much. That's a funny thing for an educator to say. Zoe was so full of longing, it made your heart ache. I wonder, we all wondered, if—" He turned his hand, palm up.

"If—?" asked Ross.

"If she was happy, before the accident. If she got what she wanted."

"I haven't met her," said Ross. "Can you tell me what happened here? Why she left school?"

Emmett looked at him. "I talk too much," he said. "Why do you want to know?"

"She's suing my client."

Emmett nodded. "I can't give you what you want, Mr. MacGill. Zoe's school records are confidential."

Ross took an envelope out of his pocket and extracted a document, which he passed to Emmett. It was a subpoena. Ross held his breath, while Emmett scanned it, and then read it more carefully. He had the attorney's authority to draw it up. Emmett couldn't know it wasn't binding.

Apparently he didn't. He handed it back to Ross without a word, and depressed a button on his office intercom.

"Jean, get me a Xerox copy of Zoe Carter's records, will you?"

"Well, Mr. MacGill, here's the picture." His manner had become businesslike. "Zoe came from an unhappy family. Her father was a rough man, hard on his family. Her mother killed herself. Zoe started okay, here, in junior high school. We admired her. Look where she came from. Extraordinary self-possession, president of her class. Always got A's. But she got more and more excitable. I've seen it often enough. Girls hit adolescence like a roller coaster. You get all sorts of funny things. Zoe started going with a rough crowd. She dressed like a tart. Her marks fell off, badly. She daydreamed. She was rebellious, demanding, self-centered. She made trouble out of nothing. I'd call her in—I was Disciplinary Officer then—and there she'd be, forlorn, apologetic, enormously appealing. I knew I was being had, but I'd let her off. She wanted everyone to love her." He made a defeated gesture.

"She started fainting. She'd get excited, her eyes would get big, startled-looking—*inward,* if you follow me, and—"he shrugged"—she'd be gone. Ten minutes, half an hour. Very unsettling.

"I wrote Abner Carter, and asked him to come in. I just wanted to talk the problem over with him. I hadn't met him then. He didn't answer. Then I had to suspend Zoe. She was smoking marijuana, quite openly, on the front steps. She came back to school after three days, covered with bruises. So one day I walked over to Carter's store. He's a butcher." Emmett made a face. "Carter was in back, sawing up a side of beef. He's a big man, you know. Full of pride—macho, I guess you'd say. And proud of it. I made a couple of remarks about business, just to get started. He ignored me. Then I asked him if he knew anything that was troubling Zoe. She was slipping in school so badly. I liked her, you see. I wanted to help.

"Well. Carter just stared at me. He went back to his butchering. I said that I didn't want to intrude, but that I, all of us at the school, were concerned about her. Had she seen a doctor? Did she have any female relatives, perhaps, that she could talk to? Stay with, maybe? She seemed to need direction, I said. I felt like a fool. I kept talking and he didn't respond, or even look at me, except every once in a while this sort of whitish stare, and, finally, well sir, he just ran me out of there. Never said a word, not once. I was interfering in *his* family, you see. He couldn't accept that.

"Then she started dropping things. Chalk, if she was writing on the blackboard. A baseball. She'd drop her notebooks in the hall. She was losing weight, all bones and white skin and blue shadows. She looked to be on the edge of some terrible thing, who knows what?"

The secretary brought in a file. Emmett opened it and flipped through the sheets.

"Yes, tenth grade. God, I remember that. She fainted at the Christmas concert, halfway through 'The Drummer Boy.' It was an emotional rendering, magical. The audience was worked up, half in tears, you know, over this little slip of a thing up there in a ragged boy's jacket and a child's drum slung over her shoulder, and then I could see it coming on and there you are. She stumbled and went down slowly, sideways sort of, and lay there under a six-foot star that the kids had made out of corrugated cardboard and painted bright yellow. The principal then, George Beasley, wrote Carter a letter. He said that Zoe seemed ill and asked him to come in for a talk. I have the copy right here: It's a very inoffensive document.

"Carter came storming in. He was on his way out to the woods—he hunts, you know—red plaid shirt, shotgun. He waved the damn thing around. Said the school's business was education and not medicine, and he'd thank us to leave him and his family alone. Called Beasley a fag. That was it. After that we went through Social Services and Family Court. Zoe was sent to Atlanta to live with her grandmother. Never heard of her again, till this malpractice thing came up. That's not to say I didn't want to."

Emmett took off his gold-rimmed glasses and wiped them. "Funny thing, Mr. MacGill, education. You have them for a few years, and you see it all so clearly. And then they're gone, full of desire and hope, and half the time you never find out. Zoe was vivid. She was an unusual event. A meteor, that sort of thing. But other times she was helpless, some little creature that you wanted to take care of. Well. Anything else?"

Ross thanked him and said he'd been a great help.

"I can give you her grandmother's address. She was a nice woman. Must be quite an old lady by now, if she's still alive."

In Hampton Bays, Claudia wheeled Zoe into the meeting. The hall was crowded, and the rain which beat heavily against the windows emphasized the light and warmth and the great burgeoning of human activity that was taking place inside. The younger Christians were sitting on the floor in the front of the hall and the center aisle, toddlers and six year olds, and baby adolescents. The music was tuning up, a group of friends who had formed a Christian rock band. They called themselves the Hallelujah Chorus. Claudia, dressed in a long soft ruffled dress and scarlet slides, flung up her hands and fluttered them, and danced around Zoe's chair swaying her hips. As she reached the full circle and stood in front of Zoe, she stooped impulsively and grasped her hand.

"I'm tellin' you, Zoe," she said in her honest Plains voice, "there is no love like the love of Jesus, and when you have it, Zoe, you just can't handle the joy. You've held off long enough." She kissed her, her soft curls brushing Zoe's flesh, and drew back, beaming, radiating love. "Join us tonight," she murmured and, collecting two of her children to her, she sat in a metal and plastic folding chair next to Zoe and opened her Bible, page upon flimsy page of close print, scored with clear lines of orange and yellow ink. There was a riffle of orange and yellow pages, like a comic-book movie. She looked up at Zoe and smiled. She started, quoting from memory, but the sounds of the band began to drown her out. The young man with the studded cowboy hat led two girls out to the microphones and began to sing. The girls sang too, and for the next chorus the whole room joined in, standing, dancing where they stood, in a primeval African shuffle. Lights reflected off the blackness of the windows, and outside lightning flared sharply as the song reached its climax and people cried, "Hallelujah, hallelujah," and Brother Luke appeared at the altar, saying, "Glory, glory to God. Glory. Glory." He nodded at the band, who were taking their gear with them off the platform, and he said, "God made the sweet breezes but he also made the thunder." There was a wave of laughter and a chorus of amens, and a lot of people closed their eyes and broke into tongues around the hall as Brother Luke repeated his incantatory opening lines, "Hallelujah, praise God, hallelujah, hallelujah." His voice rose, vibrated, blended with the thunder outside, and became exhortatory— and then he preached for a while, lost, himself, in the words, and his voice became rich and deep.

"The Lord spoke to me, that I am anointed of John today, that I will speak of John the Baptist, of John the friend of the bridegroom, the intermediary of the bridegroom, the chosen one of the bridegroom, and who is the bridegroom?"

"Jesus," roared the crowd. "Jesus is the bridegroom." A lot of people spoke in tongues again.

"Jesus is the bridegroom. And who is the bride?"

The response came like a dull explosion, "We are the bride," and the ululation of more tongues.

"And who is here that is not saved? And who is here that is not clad in wedding dress? One, I see one in the multitude. Come forward, one," and Luke held out his arms in welcome. "And are there others, waiting to be wed? Others here, in bridal finery and empty hearts, waiting here, for the gift, for the blessing, for the blessing of the Holy Spirit, waiting desolate and alone, for the touch of Jesus' hands? Oh, two. Oh, raise your hands. Stand up! Oh, three. Oh, six, oh, seven. Hallelujah. Lord, let me help these children now to know you. Let their hearts become an open vessel, let them be open, Lord, that they may receive the gift of the Spirit."

Arms still outstretched, Luke's enormous head drooped, and he prayed in silence while people came by ones and twos, stepping around the small ones seated on the floor in the aisles to stand in front of him. Then he raised his head in the silence and looked directly at Zoe.

"All you who are not saved come forward," he said in a voice of absolute command.

A flutter of many hands seemed to pass over Zoe. Children rustled out of her way, and she was there in front of him. His eyes beamed softly at her. Music began to throb from the darkness at the sides, and Brother Luke called softly, "Is there no one here to help me? Is Tommy here and Danny Halloran? Let some holy men come up and help me with these children."

Men detached themselves from the meeting and made their way to the front, and stood behind the seekers, touching their hands, their shoulders, sides, heads, transferring the spirit, praying for them, while the seekers raised holy hands and vocalized, *lalalalala-lalala,* and Brother Luke exhorted them to open their hearts and receive the Spirit and gradually, carried away himself, he fell into the Aramaic rhythm of tongues. He passed along the line of seekers, laying his hands to their heads and calling on the Spirit of the Holy Ghost to come and fill their hearts, while the Christians gathered in the hall murmured and chanted, also inviting the Spirit, and Zoe felt its approach, dark and fearsome, inviting, terrible—full, and coming to gather her into its fullness.

"For it says in the Bible that if thou confess with thy mouth the Lord Jesus and shall believe in thy heart that God raised him from the dead, thou shalt be saved. For with his heart man believeth unto righteousness, and with the mouth confession is made unto salvation."

Her mouth was full of blood, and the flesh was saturated. There was nothing left of her but her mouth, reaching, open, appealing to the spirit. All the rest of her fainted away, and there was only her mouth, and she heard, as from some distant bed, strange unholy vibrations and gouts of sound that came out of her mouth like spring water welling up in the sand, murmuring, calling, praising. Praising. Praising. Praising. Her spirit seemed to escape her altogether, issuing from her mouth and hovering above it, a plump whitish bird with a tinsel ribbon in its beak, in a cloud of light, incredibly airborne on its strong white wings.

The grandmother's house was 14 Decatur Street. Ross hoped she was still alive. It was a pleasant red brick half-house with a garden to one side and exceedingly clean white steps.

A young pink-faced woman answered the door, not opening it all the way.

"Mrs. O'Rourke?" she said. "I'm sorry. Mrs. O'Rourke died three years ago. That's when we bought the house." She opened the door all the way. "Would you like to come in?"

"No, thank you," Ross said. "Can you tell me who you bought the house from?"

"It was the executor of the estate. I don't remember his name—Rush, maybe. My husband would know. He'll be home around five."

"Thank you. If I haven't tracked it down by then, I'll call him. Your name is . . . ?"

She told him her name, and Ross scribbled it down along with her phone number. The door closed. He shrugged his shoulders. Simple things were always complicated. There was a public phone booth at the corner of the street. Ross went in and looked up the number for the county clerk's office.

Mr. Bell, the county clerk, said he'd be pleased to look up the deed for 14 Decatur. Yes, he understood. Would Mr. MacGill kindly hold the line? Yes, indeed. Yes, he'd be right back. Ross surveyed the empty street. Zoe had probably walked past here every day, to school. What was she like, this mysterious girl, transplanted from down-at-the-farm to this urban place? He imagined her walking down here, but the figure in his mind merged into someone sturdier than Zoe, calm and ruddy, with shining eyes and hair piled up on her head. A deaf girl. Piri. She haunted him. He had only met her that once, but he couldn't stop thinking about her.

Mr. Bell came on again, saying, "Here we are, Mr. MacGill. The name is Rusk. Brenton K. Rusk. Yes, that's the executor. Lives in Compton, thirty—forty miles from here. No, no address. It's a small place. No trouble at all, sir, no. Glad to be of service."

Ross depressed the hook for the telephone and put another dime in. He got Rusk's number from Information and dialed it.

"Mr. Rusk," he said. "This is Ross MacGill from New York, trying to trace a girl named Zoe Carter. I believe you knew her grandmother, Mary O'Rourke?"

"I did indeed. And Zoe too, for what it's worth. What can I tell you?" He sounded old.

Might as well come out with it, Ross thought. *If it doesn't work, I'll go see him.* "A few facts about the time Zoe spent in Atlanta. How long was she here?"

"She was in tenth grade when she came but, let's see, she lost a year of school. Damn nuisance of a girl. She stayed until she was eighteen, maybe nineteen, when she graduated high school. Then she went North. Came back a few times when Mary sent her the fare, but Zoe had a one-track mind. Stage struck. She wanted to get on stage, and that was all she cared about. Worked hard, I'll say that for her."

"How come she lost that year of school?"

"Well, moving in from Pittsville. She wasn't well. She did the whole of tenth grade over again."

"She was sick?"

"Sick maybe. Confused. Blow hot, blow cold. Girlish fits. Had a doctor who said it was a disease called adolescence." Rusk laughed, a high old man's laugh. "More like spare the rod, spoil the child, if you ask me. Mary worried too much."

"Can you tell me the doctor's name?"

"Maybe. Jewish fellow—hold on, Cohen. That was it, Dr. Cohen. I don't remember his first name, if he ever had one." Rusk laughed again.

"A psychiatrist?"

"I don't know. He called himself a therapist. A lot of high-sounding nonsense, if you ask me. Charged twenty-five dollars an hour—guess that makes him a doctor, right?"

"Thanks, Mr. Rusk. You've been very helpful."

Ngiep brought in the morning mail; it was a hefty packet. Zoe was still getting letters from Oshkosh and Los Angeles and Elizabeth, New Jersey. Even from overseas. She answered quite a few of them.

Culpepper went through the stack of letters; he was in his studio, up over the garage. Outside, birds sang. A mist of green shone round the trees and cirrus cloud streamed across a blue sky. Spring had come.

There was a letter from his producer, asking about the schedule for his new play. It was almost complete, the first draft done, the second in the works. Then the polishing. He had written it especially for Zoe—it *was* Zoe—but she wasn't interested.

For all the pressure of what she owed him, and for all his machinations (reading parts of it aloud, asking her advice, leaving the script around), he was unable to squeeze from her the slightest evidence of interest. Suddenly her whole golden talent was devoted to the Fellowship, her voice to Jesus-Rock, her person to smiling, like all those other devotees, and talking about love, and baking cookies. Culpepper sighed audibly: He'd saved her from Barney only to have her fall into the hands of God.

A letter addressed to Ms. Zoe Carter caught his eye. These people weren't usually *Miz* inscribers. They believed that men were the chosen vessels, closer to God than women can be. The return address was The St. John Chrysostom Mission of Faith, and Culpepper stared at it for a moment, making a face, and listening to signals going off in his head. Then he opened it.

232 Spring Street
New York, N.Y.

Dear Zoe,

You have not answered my letters, so I presume they're not getting through to you. You would have answered, I think.

I don't believe you are aware of what you are doing to me. I have lost both jobs. Your lawyer is employed by four other clients who have filed suit against me, following on the publicity which your case attracts. You know that I am not incompetent. You're allowing yourself to take part in a gross injustice.

Finally, my lawyer informs me that my insurance company has dropped me, since I have become too great a liability. There are only two such companies in this state; the other one is unlikely to take me on at this juncture. I am unable therefore to practice neurosurgery. The world may not be the poorer for it (though I think it is), but I most certainly am. My work is my life.

I want you to reconsider. It can't be Christian to be so opportunistically destructive. God didn't open this door for you; the devil is a more likely candidate.

I don't ask you to consider what we've been to

each other. I ask you only, simply, merely, to admit the possibility that what you are doing is wrong.

Barney

Culpepper pursed his lips, his forefinger absently tapping the surface of his desk. At least she was stable now. She had found her community, the family she must have been looking for all her life. He was closer to her than ever, in spite of her attempts to bring him into the fold. And his attempts to win her back to the Muse.

He considered tearing the letter up, but then he was reluctant to do that, so he slipped it in his pocket, and all day he was conscious of it, of its appeal, of the choice it presented, of the possibilities of change and new development that it suggested. He worked well, in consequence, and made some substantial changes in the second act.

He was still excited when he saw her later before dinner. Zoe didn't drink anymore, but she took a Coca-Cola served in Waterford glass. Culpepper had a martini.

He set it carefully on the Indian tray beside his chair and took a cheroot from his breast pocket.

"My father used to smoke these," he said. "Bitterly, on the back porch. My mother, Miss Elvira, forbade them in the house. He had a secret stash of brandy there as well, from which he filled his flask. He was not by nature a sober man, nor a kind one; nevertheless, I feel for him—in his own house he was an exile."

"Did you love him?" asked Zoe.

"Not then. I had no use for him at all. He venerated the grape. He was coarse. He was an absence more than a presence, and he was, as I said, not kind. But I remember him now with more affection, looking over his shoulder and taking a quick pull at his flask, and rocking out there on the back porch. He had fat hands, like mine. I remember his index finger tapping on the arm of his chair, tapping and tapping the minutes away. The smell of his cigar and the sweet smell of jasmine and wet earth. My poor father. He was a potato distributor. Zoe, do you think about Barney? Don't you wonder why he hasn't called, or written?"

"I don't wonder, Willie," Zoe answered peacefully. "It's the lawsuit. Why should he call on the woman who's suing him? But that's nothing. One day he'll know I love him, with God's love. Everything's different now, Willie. It's like a play, where you suddenly understand that all the things it seems to be about are not what it's about at all. Underneath the words and dialogue something else is happening, and no matter what the characters say or do, things move inevitably toward that thing which is really going to happen. And that thing is one's relationship with God; everything else is trivial. Barney will understand that, when things get bad enough for him. It takes an earthquake to move the solid earth. When Barney comes to disaster, then he'll be here, and he'll be saved. Praise God."

Culpepper looked at her curiously. So much for Barney's letter. Barney's misfortune, apparently, was God's good fortune. He took the letter out of his pocket and looked at it. She wouldn't even understand it. It wouldn't make any difference at all. She was looking out across the room at the darkening sea, full of faith—full, he corrected himself, of a kind of incorruptible self-importance. She was chosen of God. He tore the letter in half and dropped it in the fire.

"Everything is trivial?" he asked, with a stagey laugh. "My work, for instance? My life? Barney's life? Your being a cripple? The lawsuit? The whole works?"

"I don't mean it that way. They're trivial in themselves because they're an isolated fragment of something larger. It's only when they come into relation to God that they take on meaning. If I'm a cripple, for instance. It doesn't matter any more than a bird getting caught by a cat, or a brick falling off a wall, or a noise in the desert. In that way, it's just a fact. But each of these things takes on value, a new level of meaning, when joined with God. If I'm a cripple, it's because it was meant. I'm a piece of the game, an instrument of the Lord. It was meant that I should be struck *down*, in order that I should understand the Word. Halle*lu*jah. That I should spread the Word. Halle*lu*jah. That I should sing the Word.

"Do you see? In that sense, we all count, but in no other sense. Barney was a vehicle for God's intention. The lawsuit is a vehicle. If God means us to win we'll form a mission; we'll campaign across the country. Barney will join us." She leaned forward in the wheelchair, her lace blouse framing her stern face. "You will too," she said.

"God told you, did he, that J. Willard Culpepper, distinguished, mortal, and drunk, would ri-i-ise to heaven at the side of his son Jesus?"

"I already told you, Willie. I pray; I hear Him; I talk to Him. You will too," she said again.

"I don't have to talk to God." Culpepper smiled ironically, his enormous eyes half-lidded, and toasted the air with his glass. "I am God."

"Don't joke, Willie."

"I'm not joking. I am a creator, and I am my own salvation. It's only death that won't go away."

"Well, there you are," she answered seriously. "I'd be pleased to have you come with me tonight. You don't have to do anything, just come. Tonight is the first night of the revival meeting in Sag Harbor. We've been preparing for it. A preacher is coming up from Texas who's a healer."

Culpepper raised his eyebrows. "I wouldn't miss it for the world," he said, lifting the cocktail to his lips.

He could have written the script himself. A field, off Sunrise Highway, behind some development homes, scattered with cedar and clumps of trampled, succulent Long Island cactus. Claudia sitting in a folding deck chair, surrounded by picnic equipment; a carpet bag that contained her crocheting; a beaded bag with nail scissors, lollipops, and other impedimenta for surviving the evening; a white linen laundry bag embroidered PRAISE THE LORD in Persian lettering, containing wraps, shawls, and extra sweaters. Her children running around. A place beside her saved for Zoe.

The three or four hundred people milling around during the break between the afternoon service and the evening, meeting, greeting, wreathed in smiles. The women with babies, families, the men in T-shirts talking solemnly about how to raise children when the devil is all around. The children playing ball, buying T-shirts displayed in small tents. The T-shirts themselves, a pale blue, silk-screened with white clouds, and a red sun like a bleeding heart and JESUS SAVES. The jeans, the billowing skirts, the smell of hot dogs, the Portapotties; the stage, the bands, the glittering paraphernalia, the amplified sounds of tuning and testing; and the amphitheater itself, formed by ranks of folding wooden chairs, untented. *(We are here in this room: what room is that? what house?*

*what building? what temple? Can you tell me what
room we are in?* GOD'S ROOM.) The banner: JESUS
SAVES. The buttons, pale blue with red letters. The
spotlights strung on sweeping wires defining, as evening came on, the space of this community, a circle of
light in the darkness of the field and the blotched
shapes of cedars; the sun dying in the West.

Halle*lu*jah. Praise God. Halle*lu*jah. Halle*lu*jah.
The preacher himself, slight, pale-faced, observant,
wearing jeans and a pale blue knit shirt. (*Hallelujah.
How shall they call on him in whom they have not
believed? And how shall they believe in him of whom
they have not heard? And how shall they hear without a preacher? And how shall they preach, except
they be sent? As it is written. How beautiful are the
feet of they that preach the gospel of peace.*)

The saved returning to their seats. The preacher
listening to the Lord, and describing one who is in
the audience who had abdominal pains and blood in
her stool, and that one, astonished, rising and coming
forward, and the preacher laying hands on her head,
casting out the devil, assuring her that she is healed.
The audience hushed and then, as she is walking
proudly back to her seat, triumphant. Praise God.
Thank you, Jesus. Tongues. Another and another,
the lame, the halt. The miracle of Christ's healing,
the rampaging joy, the sun gone now, the world in
darkness save for this crescent nebula. Zoe described,
and going up to the space in front of the stage, her
hands propelling the silver wheels, the crowd pressing
in, touching her softly, blessing her, calling on God.
The preacher and his holy men closing round her,
hunched and intent and all together, like a broody
chicken, and Zoe disappeared among them, and
sounds of exhortation and exorcism and the sour
chant of tongues from the crowd, and then the

muffled drumroll, and the huddle breaking and a silver wheelchair hurtling out, empty, and falling over on its side as the crowd roars and the music swells, "Victory shall be ours," they cry, and all raise hands and sing and praise God and sway, and the huddle of holy men breaking again and Zoe bursting forth and falling on the ground, and the crowd by deep instinct beginning to dance as they praise, glory, *glory*, and the preacher and another raising Zoe to her feet and walking her to a seat, a miracle, and she raising her head in ecstasy, and saying thank you, thank you, Jesus, and everybody singing with joy.

And the group, the Sunrise Psalmists, playing again, and spontaneous fragments of people joining hands and dancing—the Jericho March—into the lighted place before the stage, into the mystery and the joy, and falling back among the saved and being replaced by another wave. And the voice on the loudspeaker crying, And who is the saved? and the crowd, better than a thousand now, We are the saved. And who is our Lord? and the answer, Jesus, and the voice saying, And how shall we be saved? and, like the full voice of a single entity, Saved by the Word. And the young people in jeans leaping up and down in the center of the pink and blue lights, their arms in the air, and a little boy saying, "Sheesh, you should see the bucket they've got going around. It's like a tub, this big, and it's full of ten-dollar bills."

Later the people were packing up and leaving, and most of the lights had gone off. Zoe clung to the folding chair where they'd put her, but when Culpepper came up with the wheelchair and leaned over to help her up, she said, "No, I'll do it myself."

She put her weight on her feet and pushed herself up with her hands. She looked exhausted. Culpepper could see, in her reasoned movements, that her faith was far from absolute, and when she fell over onto the ground again, he tapped a man who was passing on the shoulder, and together they lifted her into the wheelchair. Again she spread arms and said, "Thank you, Jesus."

"What for?" asked Culpepper.

"For reminding me. It's not time yet for healing. The Lord will let me know. Meantime, he has work for me to do."

Zoe's father had taken to flying up for a monthly visit. He enjoyed it. He'd gotten friendly with Culpepper, who had never lost his enthusiasm for Abner's storytelling abilities and his originality of character. Abner would stay at a motel and come over for a couple of meals, and as he felt himself accepted by the famous man, he expanded. They became cronies. Culpepper listened to him, studied him—had taken him as a model for a character in his play.

Zoe strove mightily with herself. She felt she must forgive Abner, must love him, as the Bible commanded, must see him as one of God's numberless children. She felt strengthened in her religion as she brought herself to accept him. She didn't look into herself to ask why she had such strong feelings against him. It was easier to know what was right and to do it.

Abner himself was pleased with his own virtuous feelings. He was looking after his daughter's interests. The lawsuit excited him, and he thought of himself as Zoe's business manager. He was visiting on the weekend of the revival meeting, and he came over for Sunday dinner on the following day.

Zoe was thoughtful. Culpepper, thinking that possibly Zoe would be more interested in his play now that her God had failed to heal her, began to describe a scene from it. He could see it in his mind, already on stage with lights and costumes, and he became quite carried away as he talked.

"Willie," said Zoe, interrupting him. "You know that I'm grateful to you, and I'd like to do your play for that reason. But I'm not an actress anymore. I have other business here and the fact is I'm not doing enough."

"Business?" asked Abner with sudden interest.

"Yes, Dad. Not in the sense you mean. I've talked to Brother Luke about this. I'm going on the road with him in his next campaign." Zoe spoke with the incandescent serenity of the prophets themselves. "It will be very simple. We don't have much money. Yet. But we can't wait. Brother Luke is going across the country this summer and into the fall, carrying God's word."

"That's what you call a campaign?" said Abner.

"Yes. A campaign to save souls. I've made up my mind. If God doesn't want me healed, it's for a reason. And the reason is that I can do more as I am now. Willie, will you forgive me? Later, after I've given some time to God, I'll give some to you."

"I don't mind, but I wish you wouldn't be so damned serious about it. Besides, I'm not sure I like your priorities. Why don't you do the play first and collect some money? Your salary will be high. Then the trial, and then you can do the campaign properly. Maybe that's what God wants you to do."

"No, I talked it over with Him. This morning."

"Yeah? And how does He expect you to get along?" asked Abner. "Where you gonna sleep? Eat? Does Luke have funds for this thing?"

"Not much, I guess. But he has it all set up. He says the people everywhere we go will take care of us, Christian communities all over the country. I'll be all

right. I have to do this, Willie. Do you know, they
call me Sister Glory now at the ministry? That's
funny, isn't it?"

"Funny? It's plagiarism."

Abner offered to go with her, for part of the time
anyway. Zoe was surprised. "What would you want to
do that for? Are you beginning to believe?"

"Hell no, Zoe. I just— Buddy's taking over more of
the business now, an' I wouldn't mind seeing some of
the country. You got no head for business. I'm gonna
come along and take care of you."

Zoe's spirit rebelled, but as usual she controlled it.
It was proper that she should have her father with
her. It would help her get over what she thought of
as her own evil tendencies.

Atlanta again: a Holiday Inn. Two vast double
beds at sea in a navy blue room. Ross MacGill could
see himself in the mirrored wall over the dressing
table, a bearded man seated in an armchair under a
light, smoking a pipe. The buzz of the air conditioner
set up an additional barrier between him and the
world-at-large, a world apparently no longer occupied
by Dr. Cohen.

What had happened to Cohen? He was not in the
phone book, not registered with a medical society.
Ross had talked on the phone to several psychiatrists.
One of them remembered Cohen, but that was about
all. Yes, Cohen was a psychiatrist. Possibly he'd retired; he'd be in his sixties by now. His interests?
Fishing and Zionism. The post office recorded no for-
warding address. Ross had found a blank, nothing
where something had been, a missing but very necessary link in the chain. Where then? Not licensed in
Georgia to drive, not registered to vote, not practicing, not, thank God, in the Registry of Deaths.

The school confirmed Cohen's existence; he was listed in Zoe's records there. But the principal didn't know where he was, or even that he was gone.

Zoe had been a model student. She'd done well. She'd acted the lead in *A Streetcar Named Desire* and most people remembered her vividly. Class Valedictorian too. But withdrawn—no friends, kept her nose to the grindstone. A public figure at the school, strange and attractive, but unknown. She'd pulled away from other people.

So far, but no farther, Ross thought, shrugging. He went through his notes. Everything he needed was in there—everything but the proof. Signs of hysteria marked every page. He felt more like a bloodhound than ever. The smells were everywhere; the victim was near; he could taste it—but the actual proof was locked up in Dr. Cohen's head. The elusive Dr. Cohen.

It was a familiar sensation, being so close to his goal, and with it came, as it always did, a feeling of intense hunger. His stomach rumbled, though he'd eaten downstairs in the carpeted and mirrored dining room. He put his pipe on the ashtray, nodded good night to himself in the vast mirror, and went to bed, reviewing various ways of locating a retired psychiatrist. Memberships first, professional associations; the Zionists and various subdivisions thereof. Ross turned restlessly. He thought about a former girl friend for a while, dark and demanding, very sexy. But Piri's beautiful strong rounded shoulders intruded, her calm, opulent body. Crazy. What was he, a cradle snatcher? He turned on the television and watched a war movie. Five men crouched flickering in a rain forest, fighting off a battalion of small yellow men, and plowing through swamps and wet plastic foliage to reach base HQ. Ross could predict every scene before it developed, but he fell asleep while they were running zigzag across an open savannah, dodging bullets and, some of them, throwing up their arms and tumbling into the deep grass. He knew which one would get there anyway.

In the morning he looked up *Physicians* in the yellow pages and found himself a cover. Then he called Information. He got the number, in Washington, of the American Association of Psychiatrists, and then, when he had gotten through, he asked the secretary if they had a service.

"I'm looking for a psychiatrist who seems to have retired. He's left no address behind him."

"May I ask who's calling?"

"Yes, indeed. This is Dr. Benjamin Riley, neurologist at the Washington Irving Hospital in Philadelphia. I need to know my patient's psychiatric history. She was Dr. Cohen's patient some years ago. It's very important, I might say urgent."

"Yes, Dr. Riley. We have a computerized service which normally carries the name of every licensed psychiatrist in the country."

"Is it current?"

"It's updated automatically every three months. We send out computer cards. I'll connect you."

The service came up with an address, a post office box in Gloucester, Massachusetts. No phone number. Not retired. There was that sensation of hunger again. He was almost there.

The phone number was unlisted. Ross wrote out a subpoena and took it downtown to the Bell Telephone offices. There was a lot of red tape, a hierarchy of persons to be consulted and pressured. Eventually he reached the top of a small pyramid, a florid fellow who pushed back in his office swivel chair and yelled for his secretary.

"Mr. MacGill is here on an urgent legal matter, Rita," he said importantly. "Kindly give him whatever he needs."

Rita was sharp. She clicked off on her high-heeled shoes and returned a few minutes later with the number typed on a Bell memo pad.

Ross called Cohen from the public phones downstairs in the lobby. A female voice answered. She was sorry but the doctor was not in the office. When would he be in? The doctor was away at present, but if he would give his name . . . When would the doctor be back? He was away in Israel, visiting members of his family. Yes. Yes, of course he'd be back. But in the meantime . . . What? Oh, August. Would Dr. Riley like his address?

Exhausted, as though he'd been running, Ross wrote down the address.

2

"Will somebody answer that damned phone?" Barney said.

Nobody answered it, and it went on ringing. He finished tying off a suture.

"Okay, old man," he said to the boy. "You'll be batting three hundred in a couple of weeks." He dried his hands. A woman was wiping blood off the floor, and a neat old colonel-type was running the floorbrushes, which hummed electrically. Someone was groaning. There was a clash of steel instruments. The phone rang and rang and finally Barney went to answer it himself. The nurse at the station was taking notes from the loudspeaker, which was reporting with a lot of static: ". . . Female, age sixty-five, Spanish-speaking. The woman is a diabetic . . ."

"Mustard and warm water," Barney shouted into the phone, "until he vomits. Can you bring him in?"

"Dr. Lukacs, call 3582."

He was tired. A teen-ager, flushed and drowsy, came in with a friend, both wearing purple football jerseys. The boys stood around, looking foolish, then a nurse took them into a cubicle. It was the Fourth of July. Barney suppressed a quick dreamy vision of a family picnic in a meadow. His mother had been there, talking about the paintings she'd seen in a palace in Vienna, and Connie and the two girls—tiny then—romping after butterflies. He fastened his eyes on an indigo sweater one of the nurses had hung on the back of a chair. Behind it the counter was littered with papers and bottles, and beyond that was one of the square masonry pillars supporting the roof on this ancient building. A poster was tacked onto the white brick: AN APPROACH TO THE EMERGENCY MANAGEMENT OF POISONINGS.

It had taken Barney months to find a job while the case was pending. Without malpractice insurance neurosurgery was no longer possible for him, but in May he had found a position as an staff emergency room doctor. He was employed by the Williamsburg Hospital, an overworked institution in the toe of Manhattan. The hospital was glad to get him, with or without that insurance. It was legal—it was called "going bare"—as long as the hospital permitted it, but it was personally risky for the doctor.

"Dr. Webb, call 441."

"Dr. Lukacs, we've got a concussion here. Peter Di Silva, age fifteen. He got pushed off a second floor fire escape, only about ten feet. He banged his head."

"How long ago?"

"About an hour. Left side."

Barney looked at the boy and questioned his friend.

"Keep him here for a while," he said to the nurse. "Check him every fifteen—no, ten—minutes. Check the eyes."

The friend went into the waiting room.

"Barney, come look at this guy, will you? I can't tell if he's drunk or ill." It was one of the residents, in a white jacket. They were all young, just starting, but they relied on him. It was something of a joke. In order to practice this kind of routine medicine, Barney had had to bone up on a lot of basic procedures that he hadn't touched since medical school: How to handle a simple fracture, how to diagnose a myocardial infarction, ulcers, poison, OD's, the lot. In some ways, for all his sophisticated training, he was a child compared to the residents. And his own specialized ability was a constant ache. Would it atrophy—dry up, wither, like an unused limb? He was tense with the desire to act, frustrated by his inability to do what he did best. He was uninsured. He was very careful. Another malpractice suit, and he was dead.

The nurse tapped him on the arm.

"Dr. Lukacs, the Di Silva boy, the left pupil's enlarged."

"Pulse?"

"Sixty."

"Ouch," Barney said.

The pulse, when he took it, was fifty-two. Left pupil dilated. "Pressure on the third nerve," he said. The nurse nodded.

"Right arm paretic. Patient semicomatose. Call Dr. Erskine, will you?" Erskine was the Chief of Surgery. "It's urgent, an epidural hematoma. Tell him that."

Barney watched the patient slide deeper into coma. The eyes were shadowed and the lashes lay darkly on flushed cheeks, still rounded with baby flesh.

When Erskine came, Barney nodded at the boy.

"An epidural," he said.

"We'll get him down for an angiogram," said Erskine. "Only way to be sure."

"I wouldn't wait for that," Barney said, with some hesitation. "That would take forty minutes at least—though I suppose we ought to be covered."

Erskine looked at him. He knew Barney's history. There was a pause, then something shifted in Erskine's eyes.

"Whatever you say, Barney. I'll get on to Dr. Kramer." He strode over to the nurse's station and picked up the phone. Kramer was the neurosurgeon. Barney watched Erskine. He was cool. He hung up, and got the operator back, waited, fingering his chin, talked some more. Barney checked the patient again. Rigidity on the right side. Pulse fifty. He could see, as clearly as if there were a diagram superimposed on that charming boyish head, what was happening inside it. The temporal bone cracked, the main temporal artery, running in its groove inside the skull, broken; blood spurting inside the limited space in there and collecting where there wasn't any room for it, more and more of it, pushing the brain to the other side, pressuring it. Within an hour the boy would be brain dead. Barney's fingers ached. So easy, just to bore a hole. Get in there, let the blood out.

Erskine tapped him on the shoulder.

"Kramer's in surgery. Platt's out of town. We're stuck with it." He looked at Barney questioningly.

"Not me," said Barney slowly. "I'm sorry, John. You're stuck with it."

"I wouldn't really know what I was doing, Barney. I'm not qualified."

Barney was silent. He couldn't afford to do it. It was out of the question. The hospital itself wouldn't allow him to operate, unless he were covered by insurance. If it weren't successful, Christ—he was in enough trouble.

"You mean, in all of greater New York, you can't dig up a neurosurgeon?"

"Sure. I could spend half an hour on the phone, trying to locate someone. Another half hour to get him here. Meanwhile . . ."

They both looked at the patient.

"Tell you what," Barney said. "I'll stand by, talk you through it. Assist, if you want."

"No," said Erskine. "You'll do it. I'll assist. That's an order."

Barney thought about it. If Erskine ordered him to do it, it was all right with the hospital. Legally, it wasn't a problem. But personally, if the results of the operation were bad, he could be sued again. He wanted to do it, but it scared him. Everything scared him these days, Things seemed fragile, heads, systems, lives. The boy's blood was spurting, collecting, pressing. What kind of character was he turning into? He nodded at Erskine.

"Okay, let's take him in. You got a room cleared? Nurse!"

They wheeled the patient down the hall. Barney's pulse was rapid, with excitement or terror, he didn't know which. By the time they got Di Silva into the OR, the second pupil was enlarging.

"Hey, Dr. Lukacs," the anesthetist said. "The breathing's gone into Cheyne-Stokes."

"Right pupil?" asked Barney.

"Dilating."

"We won't scrub. Give him a local," Barney said to the anesthetist, and to the nurse, "Get me a hand drill. Two millimeters." He held out his hands for the gloves.

The knife was in his hand. The lights moved into place, reflecting for a moment off something. And then the skin of the temple leapt at him. The blood pulsed just underneath. Fragile. He saw FRAGILE written across it in red block letters, as though it were full of glass or electronic equipment. Every instinct warned him to get out of there. He looked up and met Erskine's eyes.

They were kind; they understood; they said, go, man, go, and Barney made a swift incision, about three inches long, from above the hairline to the cheekbone just in front of the ear. The zygoma. Blood squirted out.

"Retractor," Barney said to Erskine, and he began to cauterize. "Get that artery. Hemostat." Erskine clipped it on.

"Periosteal elevator," he said to the nurse. She already had it in her hand, and his concentration was perfect. One minute altogether, before the burr hole was made. The sucker was in there, snuffling out the blood, the bright liquid, the gobs of currant jelly. The procedure was familiar, thorough, rapid. His hands moved by themselves with perfect accomplishment.

"Pulse coming up," the anesthetist said. "Sixty-two. His right arm is moving."

It took less than an hour. Erskine put his arm around Barney's shoulder as they walked out of the operating room.

"That was beautiful," he said. "It's nice to see things done really right."

Barney caught his breath. It was nice to do something right for a change. He said, "I couldn't have done it without you. Thanks."

He changed his clothes and went out. It was late afternoon on a splendid Fourth. The sun enriched the grimy buildings, throwing deep shadows over the crates and garbage of Chinatown, and gilding pagoda shapes and restaurant signs. Lights were strung across the street, already turned on. Rackety bursts of firecrackers, small boys running around, people from uptown window-shopping and looking for a place to eat. On a rooftop farther up the street, someone who couldn't wait for dark was setting off illegal Roman candles.

Barney decided to walk home. He was living in a

small apartment on Spring Street. Everybody was out on the streets or sitting on fire escapes. He felt odd, like a molecule churning around inside matter, bumping off other molecules, following his own course. If he were to look down, there would be nothing but blackness, bottomlessness. A firecracker went off right under his feet. He jumped, and then he felt the terror draining away out of his fingertips and his arms, leaving a tingling. It was a frequent sensation these days.

He stopped at a food place. It was full of bare wood and rubber plants and mirrors. And artists. He had a drink and ordered. He wanted a cigarette, but it was a no smoking establishment, and there was sawdust on the floor.

A small TV set stood on a shelf over the bar; the news was on. Barney picked up his drink and went over to see the President on the campaign trail.

"Way to go, Prez," someone shouted. "Talk 'em up."

There was laughter, and then a groan when the President pinched a baby's cheek.

"I don't believe it," said a voice.

"Neither does he." More laughter.

Then it was Ben Curry, the roving reporter, his slow just-plain-folks voice reaching through the after-image of the President's smile.

"Nothing ever happens here, in the town of Little Bend. There's a carnival three days in the summer. The annual Heart Fund barbecue. Church suppers, covered dish, usually on Thursday nights. The bar down by Cutty's Creek is pretty full, even on weekday nights. Today things are different: There's a real event. People are dressing and getting their children ready, and making sure the old truck is running. To a man, the whole town is going over to the Holiday

Inn, out at Interstate 91, where Brother Luke and Brother Abe are preaching and healing for the Bread of Heaven ministry. Mrs. Coles, you going to get your rheumatics healed?"

"If that's what the Lord intends for me." A perky wizened old woman grinned at the camera. "If he don't, he don't. I'm goin' to see Sister Glory; that's where I'm goin'."

The camera closed in on three boys sitting on the wooden porch in front of the General Store, sharing a big Hershey bar.

"You boys going to the Holiday Inn tonight?"

The boys were shy. They nodded and then looked down at the pavement.

"You going to get saved?"

One of them said, his eyes still on the pavement, "No sir. We going to hear Sister Glory sing."

"The Bread of Heaven ministry is on the road," said Curry. "Campaigning all through the South and Kansas, Nebraska, the Dakotas, and everywhere they go people are turning out by the thousands for Sister Glory. Sister Glory, you were an actress, I believe?"

"I was indeed," said Zoe, in tones of delight. "I was an actress and I was lost in the desert, in a dry place where there was no drink and no bread for the soul, and the soul cried out in hunger and pain, and the Lord spoke out to that poor creature, saying Come, come, come, come."

The camera blinked, and three hours had passed. There was a large paneled double conference room, with doors that opened on to a terrace crowded with people. A white tile floor had been laid on a platform at one end. A battery of stainless steel lights hung from the ceiling on a circular pipe, bearing down on the preachers and their helpers and the band, and lighting up a long white banner which read: THE

WHOLE WORLD IS GROANING FOR SALVATION. Rom. 8:22.

The crowd parted and Zoe, dressed in white gauzy stuff, like a toga, wheeled down a ramp in her bright wheelchair. She came to rest in the center of the platform, her arms upraised, her palms open. She looked transcendent; she beamed love.

"My darlings, He is calling you. Can't you hear Him calling? I don't know what you came to do, but I came to praise the Lord." She spoke the words of the song, and the crowd shouted back at her, surging forward, stopped by a little motion of her hands. She spoke the words again, and looked around, and then she gathered herself and sang, her contralto voice reaching out, and the people joining in the song, rising, dancing, sobbing. "I don't know what you came to do, but I came to praise the Lord."

Even before she'd finished there was a movement toward her, a quick instinctive rush, and the stage was stippled with dark heads and upraised arms. Zoe was blotted out. People surged in from the terrace. As the song came to an end, it too was blotted out with other cries and noises, and the sound of electric guitars joining in. The camera's eye moved to the banner as Curry made his closing comments, so that the screen was filled with the legend, *The Whole World Is Groaning for Salvation*.

The people around the bar were silent, moved, but then a bearded joker wearing silver half-glasses and a dark pinstriped suit said, "She's a lulu," and everyone started to laugh with a relieved air, and talk rapidly, and there was a long wolf whistle from down at the other end. Barney took his drink and turned to go back to his table. He bumped into a youngish cheerful-looking man with a great thatch of white hair who said, sorry, and then, looking at Barney, added, "Almost makes you want to believe, doesn't it?"

"No. It goddamn well doesn't," Barney answered. It didn't make him want to believe; it made him want to weep for shame. Zoe, the famous cripple, Zoe, bathed in light and tears: grotesque. He ground his teeth. Singing about joy and humility while behind everyone's back, behind her own back, she was yapping with the legal jackals in a malpractice suit. Refusing to let her right hand see what her left was doing. Stupid, venal, hypocritical. And passionate, intelligent, gifted, frightened. Halfway between the brutes and the angels.

He sat down at his table, under the succulent leaves of a rubber plant. People in the room were still excited. He hated her; he hated himself. How could he ever have cared for such a person? And yet, he remembered, aside from her moments of sudden and bleak reserve, between them there had been an extraordinary harmony—times of such closeness that they had almost been painful. He could feel, even as the waitress brought his dinner, the silver quickness of Zoe's body in his arms, giving way, gradually, to her luscious, slow response, her absolute and utter gift of self. The waitress drifted off.

The veal was odd. There were crunchy bits of fresh spring onion in it, and healthy grains of undecipherable origin, bulgur wheat maybe, or rye. It tasted like nuts. Barney asked himself if he'd actually been in love with this incredible woman who was destroying his life: impossible. He was not a masochist. He liked life. He had no desire to be eaten up, flattened, sucked dry. When he thought of Zoe, as she'd been, he didn't see a vampire or an opportunist or even much of an egotist—he saw her in blue jeans and a faded brown sweatshirt that said CAMP ROARING FIRE. She was learning to walk again, coming toward him with her arms spread wide for balance and her eyes flushed with tenderness. That had been the moment, perhaps. There'd been none other like it in his life. His sense of loss was overwhelming.

He put down his fork and put some money on the table and went out into the night. It was cooler now, and there was a breeze that played around the streets, wrapped itself around the lamp posts and the people on their front stoops and the lovers strolling. Sweet. A rocket burst at the end of the street, releasing a thousand brief stars. People turned and exclaimed, "Oh, isn't it lovely!"

Barney looked at the cafe he'd just left. The windows shone, and the striped awning, and the dark plants inside. Late diners at the tables on the sidewalk. I'm a mule, he thought, a survivor. I'll win this lawsuit. Or, if I lose it, I'll find some other way to live. But I'm damned if I'll leave her in that fool's paradise.

He tucked his head down and turned for home, three grimy rooms with assorted vermin, at five hundred dollars a month. He'd get a week off and see if he couldn't get at her while she was on the road. Perhaps she'd be less protected. He'd put Ross to work, digging out the Bread of Heaven's soul-saving itinerary.

3

Barney had an appointment in early August with his lawyer and Ross MacGill. He had faith in MacGill. The man was clearly honest, and though he was young, he gave the impression of great competence. Ross handed Barney a list of towns where Zoe would appear with the Bread of Heaven ministry.

"Is Cohen back from Israel yet?" Barney asked him eagerly.

Ross took his pipe out of his mouth. "I have bad news for you there. He's postponed his return. He won't be back until the end of the year."

It was a blow. For months Barney had been waiting impatiently for Cohen's return. "Can we send Ross to Israel?" he asked Sperling, but Sperling shook his head.

"It's not worth it. We're all pushing the case, even the plaintiff. I guess everyone wants to get it over with. But it can't possibly come to trial before next year, and that would be about three years earlier than usual. Cohen will be back. Did you get anything from his secretary?"

"Just enough to whet your whistle," Ross said. "It's tantalizing. I saw Zoe's file. The damn-fool secretary—she's his niece, actually—had it in her hands. I pulled a subpoena on her. No dice. But she did identify the case. She said, 'Adolescent trauma with regressive tendencies.' "

"That's it!" Barney said jubilantly. "Sperling, that's it."

Sperling smiled at him. "That's what?" he asked.

"Proof. Proof that she's been there before."

"Yes, well—it's a beginning. She's had *some* mental disturbance. But it's not going to do us much good in court unless we have something in hand. Besides, what does it mean, regressive tendencies!"

"Unresolved dependency needs, severe anxiety, back to the womb syndrome—in general, the desire not to grow up."

"Okay, so she's neurotic. That doesn't mean she hasn't got arachnoiditis."

Barney sat back. "No, I don't suppose it does. But it's more than a lead: It tells us that she has a formal record, at least of neurotic disturbance. We've got to get hold of Cohen."

"We will. Meanwhile, here's more encouragement." He passed Barney a typed report. "Jim Harvey's diagnosis."

Barney read it quickly, skipping over the immediate findings. Here, this was what he was looking for.

Following Dr. Lukacs's suggestion of hysteria, I made the Hoover test, which suggested that the condition may be psychogenic in origin. Further tests, specified below, encourage that diagnosis . . . I am of the opinion that Dr. Evans misinterpreted exaggerated residual findings as confirmation of arachnoiditis, and having fixed it in the patient's mind, is helping to create the condition, which I believe to be iatrogenic as well as psychogenic.

*   *   *

"Thank God," Barney said. "That should put us out of the woods. But," he added, catching Sperling's eye, "I don't suppose it does. It's his word against Evans's."

"Right," said Sperling. "And they'll have other expert testimony to back up Evans. So will we. Medically, it will be fifty-fifty. Legally, the outcome is up for grabs. Actually, it depends on the credibility of the witnesses."

"A popularity contest?" asked Barney.

"Absolutely. It's a battle to win the jury. It's a medical controversy which the jury is not qualified to judge. So it will hang on how the material is presented."

"My future usefulness as a doctor and, I might add, as a human being, depends on which side has a better sense of theater?"

Sperling nodded. "But a lot of unforeseen things can happen in the course of a trial. Meanwhile, the EBT—Examination Before Trial—is scheduled for the twenty-second. You'll have to take some time off for that."

"Sounds frightening. What is it exactly?"

"Depositions. I have yours here." Sperling held up a typed manuscript of about sixty pages. "Take this copy and check it over before then. Make sure that it says exactly what you want it to say. You might go over the section that describes your reasons for operating in spite of Foote's reluctance: that will be crucial. Depositions and pretrial testimony form the factual basis for the trial. They'll be referred to constantly."

"Shall I bring in some literature on the hysterical conversion reaction?"

"No. We'll save that until we have evidence."

"They might reexamine her in the light of my testimony."

"No. They'll simply prepare a terrific case against it. Zoe's deposition, unless I miss my guess, will contain no hint of any significant medical history. That will be in our favor later on. Meanwhile, our case is simply this: The doctor did everything correctly; he used his best judgment in accordance with standard medical practice. He is not responsible for any bad results. As you may know, there is no judge present at the EBT—it's just the attorneys and the parties involved. The attorneys question the parties, jockey for position, line up their cases. In this case the defendants consist of three doctors plus St. Mark's—there'll be a lot of attorneys, each one trying to flesh out his scenario. Max Ward will go for you—he won't be too concerned about the others."

"And after the EBT? What's the next step?"

"We get on the trial calendar. Ward is hustling this case. I think he'll have us on the calendar by March or April, maybe even sooner. Once that's set, there is the malpractice panel. You're familiar with that."

"Then the trial?"

"Then the pretrial settlement conference. Your insurance company will want you to settle, so will the other defendants, at least Dr. Foote and the hospital. I don't know about Rubin. I've talked with the other defending attorneys: they think the case is a disaster and they don't want to be too near the fan. They'll push to settle out of court, but they can't make you do it. However, it's a long road, and by then you yourself may want to settle."

"Not on your life," said Barney. "I'm going all the way. They can't force me, can they?"

"No. That clause in your contract with the insurance company requires your consent to settle."

"Good. It's out of the question. Do you know what iatrogenic means?"

Sperling nodded, but Ross said, "No, what is it?"

"It means that an illness is created by the physician. His diagnosis confirms a condition which does not exist or which is only partial. If I were to settle, I'd be taking part in an iatrogenic conspiracy to keep Zoe crippled. There's no chance I'll do that. Ross, I'm depending on you. We've got to get Cohen. Your evidence, my profound conviction that that's the way it is, and Harvey's diagnosis are all part of a radical therapy intended to separate that girl from her wheelchair."

"Piece of cake," said Ross, grinning.

On a Sunday morning Barney parked his hired car in front of the post office in Gunnison, Colorado. The wide clean streets were empty in the sunlight; the shops were closed, the tourist season was finished. Barney traversed the town on foot. He wanted to get the feel of it. The streets leading right and left were straight; they ended in bright level land. Beyond that, in the distance, was the solemn ring of mountains which surrounded the town. Signs were posted everywhere: BREAD OF HEAVEN and a picture of Zoe. At the end of one of the streets there was activity: a grove of cottonwood, a lot of vehicles, posts silhouetted against the sky. Barney walked toward them.

Tents and wagons and campers were parked under the trees. There was a smell of bacon mixed here and there with the smell of urine. Families sat around makeshift tables eating breakfast. Smiles and good mornings welcomed him, followed him. Several tents were placed on the edge of the grove, yellow, with awnings, offering breakfast. Barney stopped at one of them. He ordered some bacon and eggs. Children milled around; people sat at wooden tables eating. It must take a lot of money and organization to put a campaign of this size on the road.

"Here you are, my friend." The fresh, sloe-eyed young man behind the counter passed him a paper plate. "Ketchup, silver, over there. Praise the Lord."

"Thanks," Barney said. He leaned against the counter to eat. "Can you tell me where I'd find Brother Luke? Or Sister Glory?"

"They're staying in town somewhere. I don't know."

Barney took his plate and went over to one of the tables. About ten people were sitting around it, talking about the meeting the night before.

". . . And there were added that day three thousand souls," a man quoted.

"Well, two hundred anyway. Praise the Lord."

"A-men."

"Hallelujah."

"D'ja see that old man carried up on a stretcher?"

"He got up and walked away. Praise the Lord. Were you there, brother?" The man turned to Barney in a friendly way. Barney felt like an imposter.

"No."

"Well, you're surely welcome today. Would you like some home fries? Coffee?" He pronounced it *cawffee*.

"Thanks. I'd like some coffee."

"Pass the coffee thisaway," the man said in a loud voice. "And a cup. Are you saved, brother?"

"No." Barney thought the man would turn away from him then, but he put his arm around Barney's shoulder. He was dark and heated-looking, with a heavy growth of early-morning beard.

"You will be. Wait till tonight. Wait till you hear Sister Glory; she'd save Hitler himself, if he was to come. You ever down? I mean, you know, really *down*? I am. When I'm down, I say the joy of the Lord is my strength."

"A-men." Everybody at the table was listening.

"Then I'm surprised, like. And I say, hey, man, it *is*. It really is. The joy of the Lord *is* my strength. You know, people had witnessed to me, but I didn't pay no mind. What did Jesus ever do for me, I thought. I was busted out on the road, walking to Chicago, and I said, you know, Lord, give me a break. Y'know? What happened? Someone stole my shoes while I was sleeping. In a field. I woke up. It was raining, cold rain, and my string had run itself out. No food, no money, no shoes. My guitar ruined. So prove it to me, I said. Prove it, Lord. You know what? I walked across this field, through some trees, and right in front of me, on a platform, like, was this Sister Glory. Singing her heart out in the rain. He heard me. He showed me. You *promised* me, Lord, I said, and there she was. He keeps his promises, you know. He promised Abraham. It took him ninety years—*ninety years*," he bellowed. Everybody vocalized. "But then Abraham had this son. That's what he was promised, and that's what he got. Ninety years. Look at Nebuchadnezzar. You'll get your promises."

There was something childishly sincere about the man, about all of them, which Barney found moving. But it was all so unreal that he couldn't think of any way to respond. He felt like a tourist. "Where can I find Sister Glory?" he asked.

"She's staying in town. With the minister, what's his name."

"Mullins," someone said.

"Yeah, Mullins. Baptist Church." He laughed. "She's even got the regular churches with her. But you can't see her now. Wait till tonight."

Barney thanked him and stood up.

"It's nothing. You need a place to stay, we got room."

"Come back later," said his wife, a diminutive woman, flat-chested, innocent-looking and serious.

"Thank you," Barney said again. "Good-bye."

The house was neat, Western-Victorian, with a lot of bushes in front and a wrought-iron fence. Barney opened the gate, and a young man wearing a T-shirt and a ten-gallon hat got up from a bench and came over.

"Good morning," Barney said. He wondered how he should ask for her. "I'd like to see Zoe Carter."

The man looked him over. His face was pale and his eyelids were swollen.

"You an' a thousand others," he said. "I'm sorry."

"I've come all the way from New York," said Barney. "Give her my name at least. She'll see me."

The man nodded and walked up the path to the front door. A girl was sitting on the porch in a wooden chair, rocking a toddler. She said something; he shrugged and went inside. She looked about sixteen. She put her hand on the back of the baby's curly head where it hung on her shoulder, and went on rocking her body. The man came out and ambled back down the path. He shook his head.

"You gotta understand, everybody wants to see her. She's resting. She has to have it quiet."

"Did you tell her I'm here, or was it somebody else?"

"I told her father." The man grinned. "You don't want to know what he said. But come to the meeting tonight. She'll be there. You a Christian?"

"No." Barney took a hundred-dollar bill from his shirt pocket, where he had it ready. Eyes reacted, but the long pale face stiffened.

"I'm sorry, fella. We don't do things for money. It's like we're all members of the same family. You come to the meeting tonight."

"I'll double that," Barney said. The girl rocked and rocked, watching them.

"No way, brother. I'd like to help, but I can't do it."

Later, when Zoe sang, it was almost night. The distant line of foothills was dark beneath an emblematic sky, orange, mounted with great stripes of purple streaming cloud. Overhead it was black. Thousands of people sat hushed in the semidarkness around the lighted square of the stage where Zoe, quite alone, spoke in a low confiding voice about the love God has for each one, each infinitesimal, broken, scarred, misshapen one of the members of his family, gathered here tonight, gathered elsewhere, drifting alone and aimless, waiting for the Word.

She went on to talk about the word. When Moses asked God His name, she said, it was Jahweh: *I am.* He said I am what I am. God is pure being, and the Word is the expression of being. In the beginning was the Word. God spoke, and these things happened—that was creation. Genesis, out of blackness, nothingness. And the first Gospel of John repeats the beginning of Genesis. When God spoke again that was the Word, and the Word was Jesus. The Word is the Creation and the re-Creation. Jesus is the paradox: the Word made flesh. A man who is born again recapitulates the Bible, the Creation, and then the Gospel; the Old Testament and then the New.

The crowd stirred restlessly, with longing, with incipient joy, and Barney made his way silently toward the front, near the stage. He wanted to watch where she went, so that he could try to see her after the show. The *meeting,* he corrected himself. He still felt like a tourist. It was darker now, and the lights had become stronger with the darkness. They lit up the faces in the first rows. Some people had gotten to their feet, and Barney raised his arms to look like a believer.

"The Word is Jahweh, I am, I am; the Word is Jesus, risen from the living waters; the Word is your self and my self and the Word is the world, all drawn into one, waiting to be uttered by your mouth. Say it with me. Say it with your mouth.

"I'm going down to the river, my Lord . . ."

I'm going down to the river, the thousand voices said.

"I'm going to be buried alive."

> *I'm going to be buried alive.*
> *I want to show my heavenly Father*
> *The man I used to be has finally died.*

Zoe's bittersweet voice rose out of the chant. Most people joined in the song, except for those who had abandoned themselves to tongues. They had all risen now, swaying, and as the song finished they moved forward. Barney was carried to the edge of the stage. The lights blazed on Zoe's white face, full of conviction and sorrow. Zoe saw him at that moment, suddenly radiant. She raised her arms and cried out, "Thank you, Jesus! Thank you for bringing Barney to us, for bringing him to you." She fixed her eyes, shining but somehow distant, on his face.

"Barney, give up your self. Confess! Confess! Jesus is waiting." Her arms reached toward him, and he held his out. He thought, It's all so simple, and then again, It's all a lie. People were pressing around him, pushing him up to the stage, following him, touching him. He put his hand on Zoe's arm and leaned close.

"I want to talk to you," he said clearly.

The otherworldly shine went out of her eyes, and she looked at him more personally.

"When can I see you?"

She stared at him. Abner Carter came over, and Zoe's agent, Sidney Greene, and the pale man who'd been guarding the house that morning, and two other men, one of them in uniform.

Abner said, "Take off, Doctor." When Barney stood still, looking at Zoe, he said, "Get your ass in gear." He pulled Zoe's wheelchair back. The others closed around it, leaving Barney behind, and marched on each side of the chair as Abner wheeled her off and down a ramp.

There was a hostile silence as Barney turned and walked back through the crowd. It was very dark, but he could see the lights of Gunnison.

4

When the time came in March for the pretrial settlement conference, Dr. Cohen had still not returned from Israel. However, his secretary-niece assured Ross that he would be back on the twenty-sixth of that month, in plenty of time for the trial. It was definite this time. The air ticket had been purchased.

Barney, his hopes invested in Cohen's return, was still working in the emergency room at Williamsburg. He went to the conference in good spirits. All the parties were represented, and Zoe was present. Barney couldn't stop watching her. At last after sixteen months, he was face to face with this astonishing enigma. If only he could talk to her. Absorbed in his thoughts, Barney missed some of the preliminaries. But then Max Ward named his figure: four million.

Nobody spoke at first. His claims against St. Mark's, and Doctors Foote and Rubin, had been modest. Zoe made an odd disarming gesture, as though she were saying count me out; it's nothing to do with me. Then the judge, the Honorable J. J. Matlock, hitched his robes and sat forward in his leather chair.

"Mr. Ward, you must be serious."

"It's by no means too much, sir," Max answered. "Miss Carter is a fantastic actress. There's no one on the horizon with anything like her kind of talent. And the play, *Sister Glory,* has been running now for eight months. She would have played the lead. It's a resounding success. It's been signed by Universal, and Miss Carter would have been in a position to make her fortune from the movie."

Then I imagine it would be fair to say that you don't want to arrive at a settlement here?"

"No, I don't," Max said. "I think Miss Carter should pursue her claim into trial."

"Mr. Fairchild?"

The attorney for the hospital had been conferring with the administrator. He looked at the judge.

"The hospital is in a difficult position, your Honor. It is our position that there was no negligence involved. However, there has been publicity. As a community service we feel that it's time we resolved the problem. If we can arrive at a settlement figure . . ."

The judge nodded. "Mr. Long?"

Austin Foote's attorney made a suitable speech to the effect that his client would be willing to settle out of court.

"Rats leave a sinking ship," Barney muttered behind his hand to Sperling. "Can I speak?"

Sperling nodded.

Barney surveyed the table. They were down to the wire: settlement, or the case goes to court. He wanted the others with him.

"Gentlemen," he said. "This case can be fought, and there are reasons why it should be. It is a good case. We are in the right. At no point in the medical procedure was anything done which was unacceptable by current standards. Controversial perhaps, but not unacceptable. The results, for Miss Carter, have not been good, but that's not the question here. The question, as I understand it, is whether or not the hospital or the doctors are responsible for the outcome. I don't believe for a minute that we are. There are other elements which enter into Ms. Carter's condition—" He caught Sperling's warning look, and nodded. "Other possible causes for her relapse. There are urgent reasons for not settling out of court at this point. It encourages further negligence suits. It compounds an already profiteering situation. If we settle on this matter, instead of fighting it, we are tacitly agreeing to the principle that a doctor's judgment in a crucial situation *must be confirmed by good results*. We all know that's not possible. All our best efforts cannot avoid some tragic results. But none of us are legally or medically at fault. It's up to us to prove that, instead of copping out. If we settle, it implies guilt. I beg you to reconsider."

There was a pause in the proceedings, and a buzz of private conversation. The judge called a ten-minute recess, which stretched into twenty. When the table reconvened, the judge called on the defendants' attorneys again. St. Mark's and Austin Foote were firm: They wanted to reach a settlement figure. Gerry Rubin's lawyer announced that Rubin would prefer to settle, in order to avoid the complications of a trial, but that he agreed with Barney. He would fight the case.

"Mr. Sperling?"

"Yes, Judge. Dr. Lukacs's policy requires his consent in order to settle. You have heard his position, and I must say I'm thoroughly in agreement with him. However, if you wish to recommend a settlement..."

Matlock shook his head. "Gentlemen, forget it. We have here, clearly, a profound opposition. This case will have to be tried."

A little over a year ago, Barney thought, he'd been a big frog in a little puddle. Now he was a very small tadpole in the city system and the water was getting

very cold. He was still in the emergency room at
Williamsburg, doing routine work. He was insured
only to a limit of two million. He would be personally responsible for anything beyond that. He looked
at Zoe. She smiled at him as though nothing eventful
were going on. Just simple and friendly. *What a
nutty broad*, he thought, liking her nonetheless.

"I'll see you outside," he said to Sperling. The
other attorneys were collecting their papers; they
would be meeting with the judge to negotiate a settlement.

Barney picked up his coat and walked over to Zoe.
"Long time no see," he said pleasantly.

"That's right, Barney." She held up her face for a
kiss. He remembered that they did that, in her world,
and kissed her cheek. It was cool and friendly, all at
once, as though they were acting a scene on stage.
But his lips burned, and he wished he could get her
alone.

"You'll see," she said. "It will all work out for the
best."

Max Ward's eyes flickered in their direction. He
stood up.

"For the best?" Barney said. "Good God, Zoe,
you're losing your marbles. You're killing me, did you
know that?"

"The Lord chastiseth the ones he loves," she said in
a stern voice. "Recognize him."

"Let's talk about it. How about a cup of coffee?"

Max was standing behind Zoe's shoulder. "That
would be highly unsuitable," he said. "Besides, Zoe is
required here."

"Am I really, Max? I thought you didn't need me
for the rest."

"I need you," Max said.

"Later on, then?" Barney asked Zoe.

She turned to Max. "When will I be done here?"

"Not until after the trial," he said firmly. "You're suing the man, Zoe. You can't go having cups of coffee with him."

"Because she might drop the case?" asked Barney.

"Zoe wouldn't drop the case. I've invested a year's hard work in it, free of charge."

"Ah, the donkey and the carrot. There must be something in it for you."

"But Max," Zoe said charmingly. "We're not talking about dropping the case. Just about a cup of coffee."

"I'm sorry," said Max, looking ruffled but pompous. "I'm your lawyer. You have to accept my guidance about something like this. It's out of the question."

Zoe looked ruefully at Barney. "We're caught in legalities," she said, as though she were refusing an invitation to tea. "I wanted to talk to you about why . . . all this. I want to bring you to Jesus," she added, after a pause, in a low voice.

Barney laughed. "Christ, Zoe. All right, I'm willing."

She hesitated, but Max said sharply, "No, Zoe," and Zoe said, "No, Barney. After the trial." She smiled, an insulated, fragile smile, and held her hands out to him, but Barney felt suddenly brutal; he turned quickly and left. It was hopeless. She was hopeless. She wasn't—how did they put it?—she wasn't playing with a full deck.

The trial was scheduled in April, three weeks away. Ross MacGill checked into a big ramshackle structure called the Captain's Inn, just outside of Gloucester. He was conscious of a rising blood-lust. The kill was near. Cohen was back from Israel, an old man come home to wind up his affairs before his final retire-

ment. Ross hadn't made an appointment to see him.
A feral instinct told him not to announce himself. He
deposited his bags in his room and went out for a
walk.

A flag in the center of the lawn snapped in the
March wind. The grass gave way to rough turf,
sloping down to slabs of whale-back granite rocks,
gray and brown and yellow, massed here on the Atlantic coast, worn and eroded by millennia of abrasive
waves. Everything was damp, with spray, with the
dampness of March. Gray clouds streamed across a
gray sky. Breakers rode in, arched, smashed themselves against the rocks with a breathless thud.

Ross sighed. It reminded him of Maine, but the
landscape was softer. He wanted to live here. The
rocks and waves and wind seemed to shout at him,
here, here, here; here is where you belong, and a bell
buoy yawing mournfully offshore echoed, *belong, belong*. He sighed again.

He thought of Piri. He put his hand on his heart
and then held it out questioningly to an imaginary
her. She was in New York now. She had wanted to be
with her father, at least until after the trial, so she
had moved in with him and was going to NYU. Over
the winter Ross had seen a lot of her, and he could
see her now, in this wind, striding across the turf,
calm and red-cheeked, scarves and coat flapping, a
couple of dogs romping around her. But—he
shrugged—perhaps she had other things in mind. He
sketched a description of the rocks with his hands.

The next morning was bright, with something of
yesterday's wetness still on the shingles and turf, and
on the bark of the trees. Ross walked through the old
part of town, down by the wharves, and then up the
hill. Fishermen's houses, leaning and weathered, and

then rich fishermen's houses, fresh-painted white, set back from the street. Cohen's house was modest, a saltbox behind a white picket fence, surrounded by bushes. The office was in the wing, but there was no answer there. Ross went up to the front door and knocked. It was answered by the niece secretary, who was middle-aged, a widow. Tight, pale-blue pants suit, a pale sharp face under a poof of salt-and-pepper hair. She smiled.

"It's Mr. MacGill," she said. "Come in."

"You've a wonderful memory. It's been months."

"I don't forget anything," she said, pleased. "I suppose you want to see my uncle."

"Well, I had thought of it."

"You're out of luck this morning. He's gone fishing. He's mostly retired anyway, since before his trip."

Ross hid his impatience. "Can you tell me where he's gone?"

"No. Usually he fishes with Tom Branch. Tom's an ambulance driver down at the hospital. But he couldn't go today. You could ask him, I guess."

"Where would I find him, at the hospital?"

"What's the big rush, Mr. MacGill? You've waited a year to see my uncle. He'll be home by supper-time."

Ross laughed. "I can't tell you. Compulsive, I guess."

"Well, you'll find Tom at home. Emerson Street, first house on the right. It's painted pale green."

Tom Branch was in his fifties, lean and bony, bald-ing, a man's man. He came out on the front porch.

"Yeah, I know where he is, but I'm damned if I can tell you how to get there. You know the area?"

"No."

"You a friend? It's not business?"

Ross eyed him, wondering what tack to take. He decided that Branch's cooperation would more likely be gained by the truth.

"I'm a private investigator—a detective—and I just want to get a couple of facts from Dr. Cohen. Nothing to do with him."

He was right. Branch's eyebrows shot up.

"And you're in a hurry?"

"That's right," said Ross, wondering again, why. He wasn't in that much of a rush. But Branch caught fire.

"Tell you what. Hop in the wagon, and I'll take you up. It's not far, and I've got a little time before I'm on. I'll make a couple of casts, while you two are talking." He called to his wife inside, vaulted over the porch railing, and disappeared around the side of the house. Ross walked down the steps. A motor started, a door slammed, and the ambulance braked in front of him, grinding over the pebbles. Ross walked around it and got in the other side: all of a sudden he was the easygoing one. Branch was a nervous guy. He slammed into gear and out onto the street. The town of Gloucester flung past them, docks, masts, fish factory, small streets, heads turning, the siren screaming.

When they got out of town, Branch turned it off. The silence was terrific. They were speeding through the interior of Cape Ann, meadows and woodland.

"Slow down a little, will you?" Ross said. "I'd like to see what the place looks like."

"Not much to see, this neck of the woods. We're coming into Rockport, though—you've heard of Rockport. Every artist in the country's painted it a hundred times."

He drove through a fishing town on the water, done up for the tourist trade.

"You get a lot of work around here?" Ross asked.

"And how. Times have changed, since they built Route 128. Lot of traffic, commuters even. I was born right here in Pigeon Cove. When I was a boy, I used to walk to Gloucester." He waved his hand nervously. "Piece of gum?"

"No, thanks."

Branch put a couple of sticks in his mouth. There were few houses around now. He picked up speed. Ross braced himself, one hand on the dashboard.

They veered off the macadam onto a dirt road, bouncing off potholes and ruts. Branch didn't slow down. They came over the top of a rise, where a field led down to coastal rocks. "Irv'll be down there," Branch said. "There's a cove, deep water rocks. Great for blackfish." He pulled up at the edge of the rocks.

A squat figure was down there, stolidly braced on a square rock which dropped straight down into the water. A lovely crescent of beach curved toward them.

"Hey, Irv," Branch yelled. The man saw them and waved, watching as they clambered down and walked across the beach. He reeled in and fixed his hook. Then he started to meet them.

Irving Cohen was a detached sort of person. He'd grown up in New York, in a dark apartment on West End Avenue, with a grand piano and a lot of stuffed armchairs, barely discernible in the light which struggled past dark velvet drapes and patterned lace. He'd been a very clean boy, brushing his teeth regularly and parting his hair with water several times a day. He always did his schoolwork, not brilliantly but well, and he'd rarely been absent at *cheder*. When he grew up he went to medical school; thereafter, he specialized in psychiatry. Life, in its odd way, had taken him to Atlanta, his wife's hometown, and he'd set up his practice there. It was a good practice and he'd done well. His wife had been happy enough, his children had grown up and become the kind of people they ought to become, and Irving had watched the whole development with surprise. Everything happened so properly. Everything was all right! And yet he himself felt that it had all happened without him, that he was not associated with it. It was just life. He could not get himself to feel connected, and yet he did everything in the right way.

Then Zoe had become his patient. She was so cocky. She behaved in such monstrous ways. She was the most vivid thing that had ever happened to him. He was fifty-one; she was sixteen. Her skin, so white that at times it seemed almost blue, her hair, still slightly reddish then, her whole being, fragile and explosive, touched him in some profound way, made that connection which had been so clearly absent in his life.

He realized that he should transfer her to a different analyst; he was far from objective in his treatment. He loved her. Distractedly, foolishly, without reserve. When she had left for New York, he became an old man. He had had his life. The rest was mechanics. Nothing else ever happened to him, really, except going to Israel. In Israel he had found a home, even though it was alien. He'd loved the dry, harsh land, the sudden softnesses; he'd loved the sense of purpose. His plan was to sell his place here so that he could go back there and spend his final years as someone who belonged somewhere.

Ross held out his hand. Dr. Cohen had an old man's walk, sturdy but sluggish. He was paunchy. There was something firm and contented about him, like a fat old fishing boat that's come in to harbor.

Perhaps it was in his eyes, which were deeply an-
chored in the loose flesh of his face.

"How do you do, sir. I'm Ross MacGill; I've waited
a long time to see you." They shook hands. Branch
took the rod and went off to fish. Ross looked around.
He picked out a low flat rock and nodded at it. They
sat, looking out across a rocky headland to the open
ocean. Ross lit his pipe.

"I think you treated a girl named Zoe Carter some
years back. Do you remember her?"

Cohen nodded. It took him awhile to answer.

"I remember Zoe. Why do you want to know?"

Ross explained.

"She is suing your client? Zoe, paralyzed? How incredible. I'd like to see her. What do you want from
me?"

Ross described Barney's diagnosis of Zoe's condition.

"You must know I can't reveal that kind of information. It would be a betrayal of the whole doctor-patient relationship," Cohen said.

"I can subpoena you, of course."

"Subpoena, subpoena. I'm not interested in your
subpoenas. I'm not even interested in the outcome—
what does it matter who wins a million dollars? Or
loses it?" He watched the water. "What is Zoe doing
now, aside from fooling around with lawyers?"

"She's a born-again. She sings. She saves souls.
Look, Dr. Cohen, I know you have a problem with
confidentiality. But other things are going on here.
Lukacs is a good doctor, and a good man. He's been
ruined. Then there's the other side of it: Zoe. She's in
a religious trance, hiding, terrified of life. I'm not religious, you understand—someone else might think
she'd found reality. Barney and I don't think so. We
think she's an escape artist. It will take a terrific jolt

to bring her back. If she loses the trial, perhaps, or if the truth comes out at the trial. Dr. Cohen, could you say that Zoe displayed hysterical tendencies? In the technical sense of the word? Regressive tendencies? Could you say she somatizes?"

Cohen was visibly suffering. He crossed his short arms. "Confidentiality, Mr. MacGill. I'm not prepared to answer these questions."

"I'm not just a private eye, here on a job, Dr. Cohen," Ross said seriously." I'm involved. I agree with Dr. Lukacs. We believe there's hope for Miss Carter, if she faces things. Gets help. The legal issue is another matter. A gross injustice is taking place, a woman is deluding herself to the point of idiocy, and by God, I want the truth." Ross thumped his thigh with his fist, and then looked surprised.

"I'm sorry," he said. "I get carried away. You're probably our only hope, since the medical data is iffy. We can bring up the episodes, the fainting, the rebelliousness, numbness—I can get all that from the school records: but you're the one who knows what it all means. If your files on Zoe confirm our diagnosis, it would be . . . helpful. If they don't, well, then, perhaps we're wrong."

Cohen was quiet. Ross stopped talking. Small waves lapped at the protected beach. It was cold. Finally Cohen said, "It's not the kind of decision I want to make. I don't want to get drawn into it: I've made my plans." Ross didn't say anything. He watched Branch, who was reeling in rapidly. "But I'll think about it."

"The trial begins in three weeks."

Cohen nodded. Branch, out on the rock, played his fish. Both men watched him. Then Cohen got up, grunting, from the rock. He looked sad.

"Anyone with adolescent trauma is going to have

ramifications," he said, "if it's not worked through successfully. I hoped . . ." He shook Ross's hand. "I don't know."

He turned and trudged across the beach toward Branch, who had his boot on the flopping body of a fish and was tearing the hook from its mouth.

PART IV

1 ---

The trial took place at the old county courthouse in
Riverhead, a sprawling agricultural center for
Eastern Long Island. The jury was mostly men. Max
Ward had spent a lot of time on the selection, rejecting anyone connected with medicine, anyone who
seemed too intelligent, rejecting women, blacks, poor
people. He ended up with the jury he wanted—white,
male, middle class, devout.

"It's obvious," Sperling said to Barney. "He's looking for a fairly affluent jury that won't be afraid of a
big settlement. And he wants people on it who'll respond to Zoe. But don't worry. The same group will
be sympathetic to you. I wish we could have gotten
more women on it." He grinned. "You're not bad, for
an older man."

Barney laughed politely. It was all about to begin.
Max Ward was shuffling papers at the other table
next to Zoe, who was in her wheelchair. The jury
filed in: a contractor, the owner of a jewelry store, a
graphic artist, a car salesman, a flight engineer, and
the sole woman, an administrative secretary. She was
Baptist, Barney remembered. Both the alternates were
men. He wondered if he would be able to speak to
these people, or if they disliked doctors as much as everyone else seemed to these days. Don't be paranoid,
he said to himself. You're here for a purpose. Invol-

untarily, he looked at Zoe. She must have felt it, because she turned and looked back at him, and smiled.
She seemed to be wishing him luck. Impossible
woman!

The wheelchair didn't take away from Zoe's beauty.
She looked better than ever, and the signs of her maturing were clearly to be seen. They were there in the
long line of her flanks and the luxurious carriage of
her chest; in her wide cheekbones and ivory skin; in
the breadth of her face and in her clear eyes, the
color of sea water at the very edge of the strand, one
slightly larger than the other and speckled with gold;
in her lovely mouth, slightly puckered with its short
upper lip. She was still thin but she had filled out in
the course of her spiritual marriage, and she sat in
her steel chair as though it were a throne, as inevitably the focus of all eyes as a topaz in a field of
pebbles.

Everyone was aware of her. The seats at the back
of the courtroom, which provided space for ninety
spectators, were already full. The early publicity had
brought in a lot of curiosity-seekers, but Krupp was
there among other reporters, and Culpepper was en-
sconced dead center, flanked by Abner, Ngiep, and
Brother Luke. Barney identified a group of born
again Christians and he saw some staffers from St.
Mark's. The crowd chattered and pointed, and as he
looked at them, Barney wondered what they thought
of him. For a moment he felt guilty as sin itself. A
butcher, as one newspaper had described him.

He straightened his shoulders. That was the trouble with a trial—it made anyone feel guilty. Are there
human beings so whole, he wondered, that they don't
conceal within themselves a reservoir of guilt bred in
childhood? Hidden by layers of adult activity and
self-justification and complacency, guilt lies there,

ugly as a cesspool, waiting to be tapped by the accusations of one's fellows. The trial, perhaps, was just the crystallization of a permanent condition. A human rendition of Judgment Day.

He looked at Zoe again. It occurred to him that possibly her reservoir of guilt was larger than most, and that she took refuge in acting or religion or paralysis even, to cover it up. Maybe the trial itself was a cover-up for her feeling of guilt. It allowed her to be the accuser. It seemed unbearably sad that she should go to so much trouble.

Piri came in with Ross, his arm around her shoulders. Ross gave Barney a thumbs up signal and then looked around for seats. Maggie was right behind them, strolling through the double doors as though she owned the place. She stopped inside the door and looked for Barney, and when she saw him she waved. Barney only nodded, but he felt inexpressibly cheered by their arrival.

The clerk called out the *All rise, please,* and the Honorable J. J. Matlock swept in from his chambers with all the dignity of his office. Max put his papers together, and got up to make his opening statement. He took off his horn-rimmed glasses and held them in his hand, leaning on the polished oak railing of the jury box.

"Ladies and gentlemen, you are here today to sit in judgment on a case with extraordinary repercussions. Some of you may have read recent articles and books describing the number of unnecessary operations that take place in this country. A lot of them are written by doctors. The situation is severe. It is documented by reliable sources. It leaves behind a legacy of maimed and crippled patients, the result of a rampant pattern of unwarranted surgery. It must be stopped. Here. Now."

Max paused, as though the whole thing were too much for him. He looked through the window behind the jury while he collected himself; then he spoke quietly again. "That is the broad view of this case. The immediate view is no better. I don't know about you, but it seems to me that it's bad enough to be crippled and in pain, without having your livelihood taken away from you. Here we have a woman, an actress on the verge of stardom, caught in the full flood of her career and forced to give up the work which makes life meaningful to her."

He moved to the side, to give the jury a full view of Zoe. She looked at them gravely. Max raised his voice. "Miss Carter was committed to the care of a neurosurgeon—Dr. Barney Lukacs—as the result of a waterskiing accident that damaged her back. How severely her back was damaged we do not know, can never know, as the only X rays that were made of the site of trauma were blurred and virtually unreadable. Dr. Lukacs failed to repeat the X rays, which you will see here in this courtroom, and failed to make further diagnostic tests. You will hear the consulting neurologist testify to that. As a result of the surgery, the plaintiff suffered from a massive development of scar tissue in the spinal canal. It grew to the point where it exerted pressure on the spinal cord. Miss Carter had been making a good recovery, but the condition, known as arachnoiditis, caused her to be confined once again to the wheelchair, a helpless invalid for the rest of her life. We will present witnesses, experts in their field, who will testify to the irremediable condition of the plaintiff, and others who will testify to the inadvisability of the operation. Still others will describe the bloody and uncontrolled nature of the surgery, leading to that postoperative bleeding that caused the scar tissue to form.

"Ladies and gentlemen, money cannot make up to Miss Carter the loss of her life's work. She will have to go forward in whatever ways are open to her. But money is pressure. If, in your judgment, a large verdict can be brought against Dr. Lukacs, other doctors may begin to think twice before they plunge into surgery, and our country may be rid of a social evil that begins to take on the proportions of an epidemic."

Max nodded to the jurors and sat down, whispering something to Zoe. Dave Sperling rose to make his statement for the defense. He expressed his sympathy for Zoe in a natural, easy voice, and went on to say that the plaintiff's attorney had made some rather large claims. "Let's get down to brass tacks," he said. "This is a court of law. We try here to set aside our natural sympathies and determine each case on the basis of evidence. You'll hear a lot of it. At this moment we're not interested in social causes. We're interested in finding the answers to two basic questions. Did Dr. Lukacs actually cause any injury? Second, was it malpractice to cause that injury? If Miss Carter is suffering from a partial paralysis, that doesn't mean that the doctor is at fault. It's my opinion that he's not at fault. There are many reasons for paralysis. There are many possible causes for the development of scar tissue, not the least of which is the accident itself. A doctor may be superbly competent and still have a bad result. The witnesses I will call are well qualified, and they'll tell you bluntly that the steps taken by Dr. Lukacs were acceptable and even desirable in the light of standard medical practice. The question before us is not whether Miss Carter has become an invalid, although a tragedy like that is bound to affect you; it is whether Dr. Lukacs is morally and legally responsible for her condition. I think that when you hear the evidence, you'll agree with me that he is not."

The opening salvos fired, Max proceeded to flesh out his case. The radiologist testified on the accuracy of his original report. Yes, the films that were made immediately after the accident were of poor quality. Definitely substandard. The posterior-anterior view was inadequate and the lateral, probably due to a cough, had some blurring. There was a fracture of the posterior arch of D-10, and possibly of D-9, where there was an indication of lines in the spinous process and the lamina. A three-millimeter dislocation at D-9. Yes, he had offered to repeat the X rays. A neuroradiological expert confirmed his conclusions. A set of clear X rays, taken of someone else's back, were passed around to the judge and jury, so that they could evaluate the difference.

Barney was called to the stand. As a hostile witness, his testimony was confined to pure fact. He described the condition of the patient after the accident. Both he and Max Ward referred to his deposition.

"Doctor, can you explain the precise nature of a partial Brown-Sequard?" Max asked.

"It is the damage of a lateral half of the spinal cord, causing motor and sensory disturbances below the level of the lesion. That is, you get motor paralysis and loss of position sense and vibration sense on one side of the body—the same side as the damage to the cord; on the opposite side there is loss of pain and temperature sensation. That is due to the crossing of nerve pathways. Partial refers to a partial lesion; the symptoms are somewhat less well-defined."

A large chart clipped to an easel showed the structure of the vertebrae superimposed by a map of neural patterns shown in red. Barney used it to show the jury precisely what happened in the Brown-Sequard. Max paced savagely.

"Doctor Lukacs. Assuming a severe blow of the spine, what are the possible causes of the symptoms you describe?"

"Penetration of the cord. Contusion. Edema. I think—"

"Am I right, Doctor, in saying that not all of these require surgery?"

"Yes."

"It's dangerous, is it not, to open up the spinal canal?"

"All surgery has repercussions."

"Is it dangerous, Doctor?"

"Certainly."

"Not a thing, in good neurosurgical practice, that you would do without a firm diagnosis?"

"No."

"What would be the treatments if you had diagnosed, for instance, contusion?"

"Steroids. Bed."

"But your diagnosis in this case, Doctor, was not contusion. What exactly was your diagnosis?"

"Neither contusion nor the small vertebral dislocation accounted for the severity of the symptoms. There was bony penetration. A spicule of bone had penetrated the spinal cord. As it turned out—"

"Just answer the question, please. Now, Doctor, may I direct your attention to the original X ray?" A blowup of Zoe's spinal column hung near the witness box like a long silvery streamer. "Will you show the jury where the fracture is located?" The negative was grainy. It looked even more blurred than the normal small one. Barney located the visible fracture at D-10 and then pointed out the vague gray tracery that indicated a compound fracture at D-9. The lines were slightly darker than the bone smudge.

"Could you positively state those are break lines?" asked Max.

"Yes, considering the symptoms."

"But if you had not examined the patient, you wouldn't be sure of the fracture?"

"Fairly sure."

"Now, Doctor, please show the jury where the penetration occurs."

"It doesn't show on the X ray."

"Does not show on the X ray?" Max asked, with an air of intense surprise. "Well, imagine that. Dr. Lukacs, I believe you told us that a fracture of the spinous process, or the lamina, does not necessarily require surgery?"

"I did."

"And that contusion, edema, etcetera, do not require surgery?"

"Yes."

"And that all surgery is potentially dangerous to the patient?"

"Yes."

"And yet, looking at this blurred negative, at a set of lines which may or may not indicate fracture, you diagnosed a bony penetration that does not show in the picture, and took the patient in for surgery?"

"There were other—"

"Yes or no, Doctor?"

"The condition of the—"

"Doctor, will you kindly address yourself to the question? Yes or no?"

"It's not a yes-or-no question," Barney shouted.

"Objection," said Sperling. There was the usual flurry and explanations from counsel, and the judge advised Barney to answer the question. "You'll have ample opportunity to explain yourself later," he said. Max asked the stenographer to read out the question again.

"Yes," Barney said.

Max paced in front of the jury box, giving them time to absorb the implications. When he spoke, it was very softly.

"Did the radiologist tell you that the film was substandard?"

"It was obvious."

"Did he tell you that it was—"

"Yes."

"And did he ask if you wanted another one done?"

"Yes."

"But you refused, Doctor?"

"Yes. This one is sufficiently—"

"Just answer my question, please. You refused?"

"Yes."

"And did your consulting neurologist, Dr. Foote, ask for a myelogram?"

"Yes."

"But, Doctor, you refused. Why?"

"It would have taken too much time."

"Too much time, Doctor? Compared to the patient's whole life?"

"It's not a question of—"

"Doctor!" Max roared. "Yes or no?"

"Objection!" Sperling was on his feet.

"Sustained."

Barney closed his lips firmly. He must not explain himself. He responded to Max's questions automatically, defining, describing, answering monosyllabically whenever it was possible. Max had altogether dropped the political tone of his opening talk to the jury. Tall, wearing a dark beautifully tailored business suit, he gave the effect of a fearless crusader interested only in the truth. Gerry Rubin took the stand after Barney, his honest, rather doughy face shining with sweat. His testimony, like Barney's, was limited to fact, and Max took him through the operation step by step.

"Now, Dr. Rubin, let's see if we can determine where everyone was standing." He went to the chart. "Dr. Raines is back here, somewhat out of the picture. Miss Auerbach, the head nurse, is in this position, relative to the operative area. Dr. Lukacs is here." Max marked it on the chart. "Where are you standing?"

"Right next to him on his right."

"So you had a clear view of the field?"

"Well, you understand that—"

"Did you have a clear view of the field?"

"Usually, yes."

"Only usually? You're standing right next to him, but you can't see the field?"

"Usually."

"Tell me, Doctor, how far was your head, your eyes that is, from the field of operation?"

"Two feet. Eighteen inches maybe."

Max referred to his papers. He leaned forward on the lectern and stared at Rubin intently. His voice was almost a whisper, but it was quite clear. "You were standing right next to Dr. Lukacs. Your eyes were eighteen inches from the actual site. Did you see the spicule of bone, where Dr. Lukacs says he pulled it out of the spinal cord?"

"No. There was too much blood."

"Ah, I see. Too much blood. More than is usual?"

"Possibly. But—"

"Thank you, Doctor," Max said sharply. "Now, the penetration of the cord would show, would it not, after the spicule was removed? There would be a slit in the dura?"

"Yes."

"And when Dr. Lukacs had removed the spicule, Doctor, did you see the slit?"

"No. I was—"

"That will be all, Doctor. Thank you."

On cross-examination, Sperling asked how Dr. Lukacs had found the spicule, if it wasn't visible. Rubin drew a diagram on the blackboard to show a cross section of the cord, and where the blood had collected. Dr. Lukacs had found the spicule only by feeling for it with the forceps. And where was Rubin when Dr. Lukacs was putting the stitches in? Well, unfortunately, he was looking at the spicule. Yes, that's right. The head nurse had it, still in the forceps. It was about three-eighths of an inch long and sharp as the devil. They were laughing about it. You could use it—they were saying—for a poison dart. He hadn't watched while Barney put the stitches in.

"So you didn't see the slit in the dura?"

"No."

"Thank you, Doctor." Rubin stepped down from the stand. Max asked Zoe something, in a low voice, but her eyes were wide and fixed on someone who had just come in the door. She looked bemused and didn't even notice Max. Barney, who had been watching them, looked quickly at the door. He saw a short man in his late sixties with a discolored face and remote but kindly eyes. He was wrapped in a heavy tweed jacket and a scarf. He glanced at Zoe, dropped his eyes, and took a seat near the door. After he'd settled himself, he paid absolute attention to everything that happened.

*　　*　　*

"Now, Miss Auerbach, you are operating room supervisor at St. Mark's Hospital?"

"Yes."

"You were in charge on the twenty-third of August, when Dr. Lukacs operated on the plaintiff's back?"

"Yes."

"Would you kindly describe for the jury what happened after Dr. Lukacs had removed the lamina at D-9 and D-10?"

She did so, elaborating on the extreme flow of blood. "It was difficult," she said, "but Dr. Lukacs kept at it. He was brilliant. Then he found the spicule of bone and pulled it out."

"Did you actually see the spicule?"

"Oh, yes. I sent it down for a specimen."

Max leaned forward. "Did you see *where it was lodged*?" he hissed.

"No. It was way to the left. I was standing on the opposite side of the patient."

"Thank you."

When Zoe took the stand it was already three o'clock. She was obviously tired—dazed, even. Max questioned her about her life, then led her to talk about her role as Sister Glory. She answered his questions, but it was clearly an effort. Max, who had evidently hoped to wind up the day in good style, pointed out that she was exhausted and asked for an adjournment until morning. It was granted. Barney wondered briefly if it had been intentional, a play for sympathy, but he didn't think so. He thought that the late-entering spectator must be the elusive Dr. Cohen and that Zoe was shaken. She couldn't have known, until now, that anybody was aware of Cohen's existence. Would it trouble her? Or would she simply rise above it all, with that invincible faith in her own specially protected good fortune.

* * *

The morning was fresh and beautiful—one of those April mornings when the world is everybody's oyster. Even in the courtroom there was a noticeable liveliness, a sort of natural vigor that came from the elements outside.

Zoe was April itself. As soon as she took the stand, she began to establish a rapport with her audience. Max picked up the questioning where he'd left off. Zoe described the accident, her green eyes gazing out the windows as though she were recreating the total experience. Briefly, everyone was there—judge, jury, spectators—on that planked beach between the sea and the sky. Everyone shared her controlled anguish en route to the hospital and shared her absolute confidence in the doctor who would do the surgery. She described the postoperative treatment, and the excitement as she got better. Then the relapse: the increasing pain, the fall on the stairs, and one morning, the return of paralysis. Her voice was full and sweet, but there was a tremor, the tiniest disturbance in the clear course of her narrative, which suggested the suffering that she must be withholding from her audience. There was a universal sigh. Ah, poor lady. The sparkling sun swept in through the windows above the jury box and illuminated her as she went on to tell of the further treatment she had received: new doctors, further diagnostic tests, and the final therapies. Only a barely visible trembling in her generous lips betrayed her feelings. She did not touch on her personal grief; Max left that to the imagination. But he did lead her into a short description of her new career as Sister Glory. He'd coached her, and she was good.

* * *

"She's marvelous," Culpepper said. "They'd believe her if she said it was midnight and raining."

"That's my girl," said Abner. "She's doing good."

Barney looked ruefully at Sperling. "You see what I mean?" he whispered, and Sperling made a face.

"Absolutely. The perfect witness," he answered. "Don't worry. We'll get our innings." When he got up to cross-examine, he was gentle with her. He had his own kind of authority: a quiet manner, a stubborn mouth. His flyaway white hair gave him a look of wisdom and innocence, all at once. He asked Zoe to be more precise about her relapse. How severe was the pain beforehand?

"Only moderate."

"I realize that these things are difficult to measure. But can you tell me exactly when the pain began to increase?"

"No, I don't believe I can."

"Was it a week before?"

"I don't think so."

"Three days before?"

"I don't remember. Does it matter?" She smiled. The point seemed inexpressibly trivial.

"But you hadn't informed Dr. Lukacs that you weren't feeling well?"

"I was sure it would pass."

"The morning of the relapse, Miss Carter. Did you wake up feeling ill?"

"Yes."

"How ill? Were you able to get up?"

"Yes."

"Will you tell us what you were doing that morning?"

"I was having breakfast in bed."

"But you'd been up already? To brush your teeth? You'd walked?"

"Yes."

"What was your state of mind, Miss Carter?"

She looked at him in astonishment. "My state of mind?" She looked at Max.

"Objection," Max said. "I don't see what possible relevance—"

"Your Honor, I am trying to arrive at an overall appraisal of the patient's condition at that time," Sperling said.

"Proceed," said the judge.

"What was your state of mind, while you had your breakfast? Were you content?"

"In a way."

"Were you reading?"

"Yes, you're right! I was reading the paper."

"Were you in pain?"

"Yes."

"What paper were you reading, Miss Carter?"

"I don't remember. I think it was the *Island News.*"

"Ah, the *Island News.* Then it was this paper, Miss Carter, dated December 4, 1979, the date of your relapse?" Sperling walked to the witness box and handed her a copy of the paper. She looked at it. He passed another copy to the jury and one to the judge.

"I suppose it was," Zoe said. "Yes, this is the one."

"And will you tell the jury what you see on the front page?"

"You mean the picture of myself?"

"Is there a caption as well? What does it say?"

Zoe read the headline. "SISTER GLORY REGAINS HEALTH. Do you want me to read the whole thing?"

"No. Just tell the jury, if you would, what it says about rehearsals starting."

"It says that rehearsals for the play were to begin in January."

"And that you would be well enough to take part?"

"Yes."

"About a month from that day then. The day of your relapse. You must have been excited, Miss Carter, at the prospect of getting back to work?"

"Yes." She passed a hand over her eyes.

"What happened after that?"

"Happened? Nothing happened."

"You mean that's the last thing that you did before your relapse? You read the paper?"

"I suppose so. I don't see—"

"You read the article about yourself, and then you began to feel ill?"

"Yes. The pain was severe, in my back, and I felt numb below that. I couldn't move my left leg. It was just like after the accident."

"Thank you, Miss Carter. I'm sorry to dwell on these things. Now, when you suffered this terrible relapse, why didn't you call in the doctor who had taken such good care of you up to that time? Why didn't you call in Dr. Lukacs?"

Zoe looked at Barney with a serious air and then back to Sperling.

"I had lost faith in him," she said firmly.

"Yet you had seen him just the day before. Had you lost faith in him then?"

"No."

"You let him examine you at that time?"

"Yes. But that was before the relapse."

"You lost faith in him because you had the relapse?"

"Yes."

"And you wouldn't let him see you?"

"No."

"But he saw you in the hospital anyway?"

"Yes."

"Miss Carter, will you tell the jury what he said to you then, when he made a quick examination of your condition."

"He said—I'm not sure, you understand. I was—" She put her hands to her temples in a delicate gesture. "He said it was up to me. That I could recover."

"But you still wouldn't call him in or let him see you? Why was that, Miss Carter?"

"I no longer believed in him; he'd failed me. I didn't want him to touch me. I see things differently now. I know that these things are in God's hands. But at that time I felt it was Dr. Lukacs's fault." A shadow seemed to pass over the wonderful repose of her face, and she burst out childishly, "Why do you make me say these things?"

"Let me get this quite clear. Dr. Lukacs said your condition was curable. And Dr. Foote told you that the damage was irremediable?"

"Yes."

"And you continued in the care of the doctor who said your condition was permanent—Dr. Foote, that is, and you rejected the doctor who said you might recover?"

She frowned. "Yes."

"You know, Miss Carter, that there are people to whom illness is a necessity. Is it possible that you preferred not to recover?"

Max jumped to his feet. "Objection. I object to this whole line of questioning. Your Honor, may I approach the bench?"

The judge nodded, and Max and Sperling had a low-voiced consultation with him. When Sperling took up the cross-examination again, it was on a different subject.

"Miss Carter, have you been ill before?"

She thought for a moment. "Yes. I had the chicken pox." There was a ripple of laughter from the spectators.

"Seriously ill. Have you had any illness of a serious nature?"

"No. I'm never ill." Barney glanced over at Dr. Cohen on the spectator's bench. Cohen, absorbed in Zoe's testimony, raised his eyebrows. Barney wondered whether it was a deliberate lie, or whether Zoe had really forgotten. Perhaps she didn't think of Cohen as a real doctor.

"Then you have no serious medical history? You've never had to consult a doctor over a sustained period of time?"

"No."

"Thank you, Miss Carter."

Max called Dr. John Evans, the neurologist who had examined Zoe after her relapse. He led him through his professional history and established his qualifications.

"Now, Doctor, you examined the plaintiff on the sixth of December, 1979. Will you tell the jury what you found?"

Evans described his examination of the patient, after her relapse. Left leg paralyzed. Increased deep tendon reflexes on the left. Increased tone. A little spasticity. Some impairment of position sense, also on the left. A Babinski sign on the left, not total, but very distinct. Sensation on the right impaired. His diagnosis? Arachnoiditis. Adhesions due to bleeding caused by surgery. No, the condition was inoperable.

Miss Carter had made the optimum improvement possible, under the circumstances. Regrettable.

Sperling got up to cross-examine.

"Your position then, is that connective tissue was damaged during surgery, giving rise to scar tissue?"

"Yes."

"Correct me if I'm wrong, but is it not true that connective tissue is always damaged during surgery?"

"Of course."

"So that to describe a surgeon as incompetent simply because he has damaged tissue would be absurd."

"Yes, of course. It depends on the extent of it."

"Good. Now, would you tell us whether or not arachnoiditis could develop from the initial trauma alone? In other words, could scarring arise from the original blow to the spine?"

"It could develop, yes."

"And assuming the surgery was justified, arachnoiditis could follow from surgery without reflecting on the doctor's competence?"

"Yes."

"Have there been similar cases where surgery was effective?"

"Of course."

"And if there is a spicule of bone sticking into the spinal cord, will Decadron remove it?"

"Of course not. Decadron is a steroid. It reduces swelling and thus reduces pressure."

"So if there is a spicule, the sooner it is out, the better?"

"Yes."

"And your findings, Dr. Evans. The paralysis, the Babinski sign, the slight sensory impairment. Could these symptoms represent normal residual deficit? The normal deficiency that one would expect after trauma and surgery? Exaggerated perhaps by unavoidable scarring or by the patient's own state of mind?"

"No, sir," said Evans in clipped and final tones. "Look at the outcome." He gestured toward Zoe. "It is a question of degree. These are absolutely objective signs of an abnormal degree of impairment. There is no sign of an abscess in the myelogram, and there is considerable blockage. No *state* of *mind* will produce an unmistakable, though partial, Babinski."

"Please describe the Babinski sign, Doctor. For the benefit of the jury."

"Okay. The Babinski indicates a neural abnormality. If you administer a painful stimulus to the sole of the foot, the normal reaction is for the toes to go down, clenching themselves—so to speak—against the pain. In an abnormal situation, the big toe goes up, extends, and the small toes fan. That's a full-fledged Babinski. In this case the patient has only the big toe sign: a partial Babinski. Nevertheless, along with the increased reflexes, it's a clear objective indication of organic malfunction."

"Thank you. By the way, Doctor, did you administer the Hoover test?"

"No, sir. I saw no reason to."

At the lunch break, Barney hurried out of the courtroom. Ross was waiting outside in the hall with Maggie and Piri.

"I want to catch up with Cohen," Barney said. "I'll see you after the afternoon session."

Ross nodded, and Maggie said, "Good luck." Barney made his way through the crowd. As he turned the corner, he could see Cohen's square figure just outside the double doors. He was pulling his scarf around his throat. Barney caught up to him, and together they went down the desolate stone steps outside the courthouse. Even on a sunny April afternoon, Riverhead looked dreary.

"You're Dr. Cohen, aren't you?"

"Yes," Cohen said. He stopped and held out his hand. "I am pleased to meet you." He had the subtle remains of a German accent.

"Would you like a drink? Or a bite to eat? I'd like to talk to you."

They walked over to the Chinese restaurant. Cohen was slow and deliberate. He asked Barney where he'd trained. Barney smiled. The feeling of urgency left him. The old man wanted to get to know him.

"You mean my residency?" he asked. "University of Pennsylvania." Barney wanted to get to the point, but he allowed himself to be drawn out. Before long he and Cohen had gotten into a discussion of where psychiatry stops and neurosurgery begins—the fine line between psychological and physical disorders of the mind. It was a subject that always interested Barney, and Cohen was intelligent, but time was short.

"We represent opposite views," Barney said. "I think it's temperamental. I like action, rather than reflection. I love to get things done. Your job is to empathize, to understand, to observe—you have to reflect on the object in front of you until you understand it totally."

"Perhaps. But I too go into action, even while I'm trying to understand the nature of the problem."

"True. Not as directly, perhaps. And your job is so lengthy. It would drive me nuts. Physical things—you know, pathology, chemistry, structure—are stubborn. But they don't defeat one the way the human emotions do."

"No," said Cohen. "However. There may not be that much difference. Emotions, in the final analysis, are chemistry too."

"At any rate," Barney said, closing the discussion, "in this case we may not be so far apart. Do you think it's possible that Zoe's condition is hysterical?"

Cohen didn't answer right away. He finished off his tea and settled back, nodding thoughtfully. The top of his head shone. "I have not decided yet what to do. I am—as you said—reflecting. I do not desire to testify. It's against my whole belief. I will let you know."

"You heard that she lied yesterday?"

"I heard."

"You know that we could subpoena you?"

"Of course. And I would testify to a little adolescent disturbance, long since repaired. The woman is matured."

Barney raised his eyebrows. "Mature? Zoe?"

"It would be unwise to coerce me, Dr. Lukacs. I am watching."

Barney nodded. "A great deal hangs on your decision."

"I know."

"Dr. Foote, I understand that the patient was packed in ice before she was brought to the hospital. What was the point of that?"

"Pure nonsense," said Austin Foote. "How are you going to cool the spinal cord, through four inches of skin, muscle, fascia, bone? It's the kind of thing you try on animals. With human beings it's nothing short of theatrical."

"Thank you," Max said. "Now, when you saw that the X rays were poor, did you ask for a repeat?"

"I don't remember. I asked Dr. Lukacs to do a myelogram."

"But he refused?"

"Yes. He was in too much of a hurry."

"Am I correct, Doctor, in saying that good medical practice is directed toward a careful evaluation of spinal fractures?"

"Yes, indeed."

"And that a fracture of the spinous process does not necessarily require surgery?"

"That's right."

"How would such an injury be treated, Doctor?"

"A good hard mattress and steroids to reduce the swelling. Unless further tests indicated a blockage in the spinal cord. A myelogram, for instance."

"Even if the patient has a partial Brown-Sequard?"

"Even then. Such symptoms might be caused by contusion."

Foote made an excellent witness. He was stocky and uncompromising. His manner was irritable; his face was red; his hair stood up in iron-gray spikes; he obviously didn't want to be there, testifying against a fellow doctor. But his evidence was honest and muscular. The jury liked him. Max asked him what his diagnosis had been at the time.

"Hard to tell, given the lack of diagnostic tests."

"What did you *think* was the trouble?"

"Contusion of the cord."

"And the treatment for contusion?"

"Decadron. Immobilize the patient."

"No surgery?"

"No surgery."

"But how about the spicule?" Max asked him, looking innocent. "The alleged spicule? The piece of bone which Dr. Lukacs says he pulled out?"

Foote got even redder. He blew out his cheeks and exhaled, sputtering. "I didn't see any spicule," he said cantankerously.

"Then you believe—correct me if I'm wrong—that there was contusion but no spicule?"

"That's what I believe."

"That the patient was subjected to superfluous surgery?"

"Well, look at the results."

"You think the surgery was unnecessary?"

"I do."

"Why would you think, Dr. Foote, that Dr. Lukacs would claim there was a spicule, if there wasn't one?"

"He had to justify the operation."

"In your opinion, Doctor, is the surgery a contributory cause of the plaintiff's condition?"

"Quite possibly. The surgery was prolonged."

Max went on to establish, through Foote, the comparatively heavy bleeding throughout the operation. Now that Foote had committed himself publicly, he was easier with the accusations he was making. He described the surgery and went on to explain the manner in which postoperative bleeding may give rise to arachnoiditis.

"If Dr. Lukacs had not operated, the arachnoiditis would not have developed?"

"That's it," Foote said curtly. "First surgery, then bleeding, then arachnoiditis."

Max turned to the blowup of the myelogram that had been done after the relapse. He dealt with it briefly. It was not a conclusive picture. It showed an attenuated section of the back, the ghostly vertebrae on a black field, and the column of bright contrast fluid only partially blocked by scarring at D-9 on the left. Foote explained the myelogram to the jury, showing them the places where the dye did not flow freely through the spinal canal.

"Adhesions of this nature are a secondary effect of surgery. They press on the spinal cord and gradually they exert pressure on some of the blood vessels or on the nerve roots." He turned to Max. "If we had one of these before the operation, then we'd know where we are. It's asinine to work in the dark when we have the equipment."

"Your witness," said Max. Sperling rose to cross-examine.

"Dr. Foote," he said. "Modern diagnostic tests are a great aid to the physician. But do they form the sole basis for your diagnosis?"

"Of course not."

"What other factors do you consider?"

"Well, the patient's condition for one thing. The whole picture. That includes the tests, symptoms, the patient's history, and the doctor's knowledge of how complex factors in the body work together."

"What you might call smell? Or instinct?"

"Not at all. Pure hard fact, and knowledge."

"Dr. Foote, is there enough pure hard fact in this myelogram to explain the severity of the patient's condition?"

"I believe there is."

"Look at the amount of contrast that gets through. Don't you find it surprising that *this* amount of blockage," Sperling tapped it with the pointer, "should cause *that* amount of immobilization?" He waved at Zoe. She folded her hands calmly.

"No," said Foote. "It's not always easy to tell. There is sufficient indication here of potential compression to explain her condition."

"Could it also be read this way? The filling defect here, which blocks the passage of some of the contrast, is situated exactly where Dr. Lukacs pulled out the spicule. It represents scar tissue at the site of trauma, a normal consequence of such an operation?"

"Her condition isn't normal."

"We are talking about the myelogram, Doctor, not the plaintiff's condition. Does this picture state, as a

matter of cold hard fact, that the patient suffers from
severe arachnoiditis causing the Brown-Sequard syndrome, or is it liable to other interpretation?"

"All X rays must be interpreted."

"In the light of all the factors involved? One's
knowledge, one's experience, one's sense of the patient, a sort of amalgam of all these things? Doesn't it
happen almost unconsciously, Doctor? A flash of understanding? An instinct?"

"No. It's hard work. Logic. Judgment."

"And in your judgment, this myelogram provides
absolute evidence of the presence of massive scar tissue compressing the spinal cord in such a way that
the Brown-Sequard symptoms are an inevitable consequence?"

Foote sighed. "It's not that conclusive," he said.
"But look at the patient. A functioning woman, well
on her way to recovery, becomes paralyzed, displays
hyperactive reflexes and a Babinski sign on the same
side as the scarring. The myelogram shows the scarring. A child of two could see the connection."

"Ah. Then you do believe, at least, in judgment,
when it comes to diagnostic technique?"

"Of course."

"You argue that because the symptoms are such
and such, then so and so must be the cause?"

"That's right."

"Isn't that exactly what Dr. Lukacs did in diagnos-
ing the patient in the first place? Isn't that what you
call judgment? Isn't he on trial for using his judgment?"

"Yes. But—"

"Thank you, Dr. Foote." Sperling walked slowly
over to the jury box and turned to face the witness.
"Dr. Foote, when you examined Miss Carter after her
relapse, did you do the Hoover test?"

"No. Why should I?"
"Thank you, Doctor."

Irving Cohen wandered aimlessly along Main
Street, looking in the shop windows. His mind didn't
register where he was but was filled with Zoe, with her
calculated magic, her beauty, her enforced calm, her
repression. He didn't want to do anything that would
be harmful to her. There was a window full of Whit-
man's chocolate boxes and, looking up, he saw that it
was a soda fountain. He went in and ordered a cup of
coffee. There was the undeniable basic principle of
his schooling: repression causes personality disorders.
When you find out what it is that is being repressed,
and bring it into the light, you have started the cure.
The process of psychiatry is that of making the hidden visible. But publicly? At the trial? Zoe was over-
controlled, tight. It bothered him. Would she snap
under pressure? Become worse?

He took a paper out of his pocket. Barney had sent
him a Xerox copy of an article in the *Psychiatric
Journal.* It was called "The Pentecostal Experience."
Cohen drank his coffee while he looked through it
again.

The central idea was that Pentecostalism was a hysterical manifestation, a reaction to social stress. The
article compared the born-again phenomenon to
medieval religious manias, which were described in
terms of mass hysteria.

Barney had attached a note. "What do you think of
this?" he wrote. "Does it fit the pattern of Zoe's character? You may be the only person who knows
whether or not Zoe had any need to *retreat from life.*
If so, her religion and her paralysis may be connected. Have you come to any decision?"

The girl behind the counter refilled his cup. Cohen

looked at his watch. He should be getting back for the afternoon session. The witness today was a retired neurosurgeon with a respectable background. He had called Lukacs "alarmingly incompetent," and the courtroom had reacted first with a gasp and then an outbreak of whispers. Lukacs had sat there, sturdy, uncompromising, slightly flushed, his blue eyes bravely fixed on the witness.

If I speak up, Cohen thought, it would all turn around. Zoe would be the one who was on trial, thrown back into the inner drama of her whole life. Guilty again. It seemed to him, as he watched her, that her incredible poise was something that merely created her existence in other people's eyes, that she herself was hardly there, anymore, and that even as she projected that indelible image of herself around the courtroom, she was slipping, slipping away, toward an irrevocable detachment from reality. What would happen if she snapped? He sympathized with Lukacs, but he was afraid for Zoe. His heart was pounding. He was too old for coffee. He pushed it roughly away and watched it slop into the saucer.

2

"Doctor, let's assume," Max said to his witness, "that the X ray is not blurred. Let's say it shows a clear compound fracture at D-9. Would you go in, Dr. Geddes? Would you operate on the patient?"

"No, I would not."

"Will you tell the jury why?"

"It's simple. There wouldn't be much I could do for the fracture. Unless, of course, I had other diagnostic tests that gave me further information. First of all, I'd give it twenty-four hours. Give her Decadron. Reduce the swelling. See if she improved. If there's nothing for the surgeon to do, there's no reason to operate. First, it's traumatic to the patient. Second, it damages tissue around the spinal cord, which may be on the borderline, but which is potentially viable. Probing, exploring—every tenth of a millimeter is packed with ascending and descending neural tracts that may be essential to regaining function. No, indeed. I wouldn't have gone in there."

"Poor lamb," one of the spectators said to the woman next to her, letting her knitting drop for a moment. "She's so brave."

"Isn't she. And you know, she's never said anything against him. Never. Well, praise God, it brought her to Jesus."

"Amen."

*   *   *

"Arrogant bastard, isn't he?" said an orderly from St. Mark's.

"Who, Lukacs?" asked his friend. It was a day off for both of them.

"Yeah. Just look at him. I don't think it was the money he was after—he just had to be right. Like Foote said, Lukacs had an itch to use the knife, and he used it, and then he had to come up with the goods."

"I don't know, Jack. I don't think he'd lie. He's not like that. Cocky, you know? Sure of himself. Impatient—everything's got to be for the patient. I've seen him down in emergency chewing out everyone but the janitor because some little thing wasn't done to his liking. But I don't see him lying."

Maggie looked over at Piri. "Don't worry yet," she said. "It sounds bad now, but the defense will show it in a different light."

Ross glanced at Dr. Cohen. "I hope he comes in with us," he said. "How can the jury decide between these opposing medical opinions?" Maggie nodded.

On cross-examination, Sperling asked Dr. Geddes if he was still a practicing neurosurgeon.

"No. I'm retired."

"Oh? And do you testify frequently as an expert witness, in this kind of lawsuit?"

"From time to time."

"From time to time? Once a year perhaps?"

"More often than that."

"Once a month?"

"I testify when a case comes up which lies within my specialty."

"You testified, I believe, on Monday of this week, in the case of *Hutchins* v. *Fabiola*?"

"I did."

"And once last week?"

"Yes."

"Doctor Geddes, what is your fee for appearing here today?"

"Fifteen hundred dollars."

"So you've made three thousand dollars this week?"

"Yes."

"How old are you, Doctor?"

"Fifty-four."

"You're retired, you're fifty-four years of age, and you've earned more than two thousand a week for the last two weeks. Would you say, Dr. Geddes, that you make your living as an expert medical witness testifying to malpractice?"

"It's not always so frequent."

"No? How would you estimate your yearly earnings, derived from giving evidence?"

"About seventy thousand."

"Ah." Sperling let that sink in.

"Dr. Geddes, have you considered the possible influence that Miss Carter's medical history might have on this case?"

"She has no medical history to my knowledge."

"No? Are you familiar with her school records?"

"No."

"You haven't seen them?" Sperling asked in a voice full of surprise. He picked up a sheaf of papers. "You, an expert witness to Miss Carter's condition?"

"Objection!" shouted Max. "Nothing of that nature has been entered as evidence."

"Sustained."

"Dr. Geddes," said Sperling. "Are you aware of the

fact that Miss Carter was subject to hysterical lapses during her high school career?"

Max was on his feet. "Objection! Judge, nothing—"

"Sustained." The judge ordered the question struck from the record and cautioned the jury to disregard it.

"Let me put it this way, Doctor," said Sperling. "You are giving expert testimony in regard to the plaintiff's illness. Are you sure that you are sufficiently informed about her general medical background to be positive about her present condition?"

"As far as I know."

"Thank you. Now tell me, Dr. Geddes: Isn't it unusual for a slow-growing adhesion such as we see in this case to make its appearance so suddenly? I mean, one day the plaintiff is a functioning woman, walking, going up and down stairs, and the next day she is a helpless invalid. One morning she is up and about; an hour later she can't move her left leg. Is that the way these things happen?"

"It's not usual. But the spinal cord is highly complex. Thousands of bundled nerves run through it— the roots, you might say, of the brain—and disperse in thousands of little branches to different parts of the body. These things can happen like that. A little pressure, and then a little more pressure, and bingo: You have compression."

"But usually the onset of dysfunction is more gradual? Attended by severe pain?"

"Yes."

"Doctor, have you dealt much with hysterical patients? I mean, specifically, patients whose illness is functional rather than organic?"

"Every doctor has patients who somatize—especially a neurosurgeon."

"Is there any general personality trait which you find such patients have in common?"

"There certainly is. They're passive dependent." He smiled. The jury looked at Zoe. She raised her chin. Her serenity was absolute. She seemed separate from the courtroom, as though she existed in a pool of light, resolute, self-sufficient, and immobile. She looked at Sperling with a touch of severity and turned calmly back toward the witness. She was crocheting something out of bright green yarn.

"Is that aspect of character always obvious?" asked Sperling.

"I can usually tell."

"Doctor, have you ever had a case where paralysis was hysterical?"

"Yes."

"Objection," Max Ward said sharply. "I'd like to know, and I'm sure the jury would too, what all this nonsense is leading up to." The judge looked at Sperling.

"I will make the connection very soon, Judge."

"Your Honor, there's no foundation for a psychiatric line of questioning. There's no hospital record to establish psychiatric reaction."

The judge looked at Sperling again. "What are you asking these questions for, Mr. Sperling? You have a connection to prove in the defendant's case?"

There was a recess for a ruling of law. The jury filed out. Sperling submitted his brief to the judge. Max spoke angrily. The spectator's benches were full; people shifted in their seats and whispered. Barney sat tensely. It seemed to him a turning point in the case. Only Zoe was untouched. She crocheted quietly, as though she were entirely unaware of her circumstances. An aura of peace spread out from where she sat, subduing the rustling and whispers and the nervous coughs. Finally, everything was quiet. There were only the low voices of the judge and the two attorneys, like flies humming on a summer's day.

"Thank you," said Sperling. Max went back to the plaintiff's table. The jury filed back in, and Sperling resumed his questioning.

"Can the Brown-Sequard symptoms be hysterical in origin?"

"Partially. But not in this case."

"No? Why not, Doctor?"

"These findings are absolute. I don't believe for a minute that the Babinski sign, even the partial Babinski, can be reproduced. Or the reflexes."

"Even if the patient is following known patterns? Is familiar with all the organic symptoms of the illness? Knows how she should react?"

"The patterns are unconscious."

"Is hysteria unconscious?"

"Of course. But in this case everything, *everything*, points to the same conclusion. Besides, she's not the type."

"Ah. Doctor, when you examined the plaintiff, did you look for the Hoover sign?"

"No, sir, I did not."

"Thank you, Doctor."

"Zoe, what's all this about school records?" Max asked. "What are they getting at?"

"School records?"

"Yes. Whatever it was that Sperling was waving around today. He'll establish them later, you know."

"Yes, I suppose he will."

"Well, what's in them?"

"I don't know. Grades, I imagine." Max looked at Culpepper. They were en route to Easthampton in the old Packard, after the day's proceedings. Zoe looked peacefully out the window. "It's very beautiful today," she said.

"Zoe," Culpepper said. "Tune in. Is there evidence in your school career to support Barney's case?"

"There must be, Willie, or he wouldn't bring it up."

"For God's sake, Zoe. Don't be so—oh, *immune* to everything. This is *your* case." Max calmed himself. "You've been wonderful all through this. Nobody could fail to believe in you. But if there's anything in your school records that I ought to know you'd better tell me, so I can prepare for it. Damn, I wish your father was here today."

"Of course, Max. It seems like forever since then." She laughed. Her wheelchair was folded up and wedged in front of the jump seats.

"Barney mentioned hysteria. Were you—hysterical?"

"Never. I was a little crazy for a while, though. I smoked joints and climbed the flagpole, and I—well, you know, hung out with boys. They sent me to Atlanta to live with my grandmother. It's all rather hazy. I was very unhappy."

"See if you can remember more precisely. Why were you sent to your grandmother?"

A shadow crossed Zoe's face. "I don't really know."

"Didn't your mother object?"

"My mother was dead."

"Oh. That's why you were so unhappy?"

"I was unhappy because I was alone, separated from God."

"Yes. And did you go on being 'a little crazy' when you got to Atlanta?"

"Max! Why are you so concerned about this? No. The doctor said I was fine."

Max sent Culpepper a look of despair. "Doctor? What doctor?"

"The therapist. That's enough, Max. I don't want

to talk about it." Zoe picked up her crocheting. The old Packard swayed as it turned south. Ball fringe swung heavily on the plush curtains. Out of season roses drooped in the chromium vases attached to each side.

"Lord, lord, how this world is given to lying," quoted Culpepper. "Zoe, did you or did you not tell Barney's lawyer that you'd never seen a doctor?"

"Cohen wasn't a doctor. He was a shrink."

"Good grief," said Max. "Zoe, this is all going to come out."

"Let it," she said. "There's nothing wrong with it. Max, you think I'm being stupid. I'm not, you know. The fact is we're not directing this production, you and I. We're only the actors. What comes out will come out. Who wins will win. What happens will happen. It's in His hands."

"You are John Herman Randolph, M.D., D.Sc.?"

"I am."

"You, sir, were chief of the neurosurgical service of the Meadowlands University Hospital from 1961 to 1975? And you held the appointment of Professor of Surgery at the Medical School?"

"I did."

"You are a diplomate of the American Board of Neurological Surgery?"

"I am."

"A fellow of the Royal Society of Medicine in England?"

"Yes." Max continued down the list of his witness's distinguished appointments and qualifications. Dr. Randolph was a handsome, self-satisfied individual in his early sixties.

"Now, Dr. Randolph, you have examined the evidence. You have studied the original X rays, the hospital charts, and the deposition of the defendant. Will you tell us, sir, whether or not, in your opinion, surgery in this case was justified in the light of good and accepted medical practice?"

"No. It would be difficult to justify it."

"I see. Would you have operated on the basis of that X ray?"

"No, sir. I would have wanted a second X ray, tomogram, myelogram. I would have made sure there was a block, a genuine indication of necessity, before I operated. But I am a cautious man."

"Cautious? Or, perhaps, deliberate? Careful? Responsible?"

"Well, I hope I am those things."

"Doctor, you have examined the plaintiff. What is your diagnosis of her condition?"

"Arachnoiditis. The myelogram shows it. The scarring is horrendous. It would not have occurred in that form if Dr. Lukacs hadn't operated."

It went on and on. Barney wondered why Randolph was doing it. He gave it up: A man had to make a living, didn't he?

"Dr. Randolph," Max said. "I'll ask you this before defendant's counsel does. How much are you being paid to appear here?"

"Two thousand dollars."

"Have you testified before in cases of malpractice?"

"No."

"In that case, why did you agree to testify here?"

"A situation exists, which is getting out of hand: unnecessary surgery. Surgery for this, surgery for that! I am a surgeon myself, sir; I'm concerned."

"Did you write a book on the subject, called *The Risks of Surgery?*"

"I did."

"And did you agree to testify because in your mind this case is an example of unnecessary surgery?"

"That's right."

"Your witness, Mr. Sperling."

Sperling got up. He pointed out that the blockage which showed on the myelogram appeared to be far less severe than the plaintiff's symptoms.

"Is there any possibility in your mind, Dr. Randolph, that the patient might be malingering?"

"No sign of it. No sign at all."

"Hysterical? Is it possible, do you think, that the residual deficit from the trauma provided patterns for the patient's unconscious mind to work on? That the severity of her symptoms indicates a hysterical overlay on legitimate organic deficiency?"

"That's a lot of questions. But the answer to all of them is no. The personality is wrong."

"But it would be correct to say that hysteric can mimic organic disease?"

"Absolutely. But not here. It simply doesn't apply."

"Tell me, Dr. Randolph, did you do the Hoover test? Or any of the neurological tests which might give you the same information?"

"No. There was no need."

"That will be all. Thank you, Dr. Randolph."

"She's a cool one," Ross said. "I hate to say it, Barney, but how can anyone believe you?"

"Cohen does," said Barney. "I know he does."

"Can we do anything to move him toward a decision?"

"Only what we're doing. We have to bring out the issue, repeat it, emphasize it. Each time it happens, Zoe becomes more trancelike. Everybody else is stunned by her, but Cohen will see it for what it is:

An increasing and dangerous withdrawal from reality. I think, I *think* he'll speak up."

"Can't we talk to him again?" Piri signaled.

"I don't think so. He's got a conflict. How can he reveal, in public, what a patient said to him once in the privacy of his confessional? On the other hand, how can he let her destroy me, and put herself in a sort of other-worldly purgatory for the rest of her life? He's between a rock and a hard place, poor fellow, and there's nothing we can do except keep putting it to him throughout the trial. He'll decide, and until he does, we'll wait."

"How about Culpepper?" asked Maggie. "Do you think he knows?"

"I think he does. But he and Zoe form a kind of perfect mutual admiration society. It's not exactly love; it's more that they form an artistic enclave, separate from life and protected from it by each other. They're special," Barney said bitterly. "He's got his art, and she's got God, and either way it justifies whatever they do. Besides, the accident was Culpepper's fault. It was his boat. He had no business letting that idiot drive it, stoned out of his mind. He's only too glad to shift the burden of responsibility. Let's go have a drink."

"In a minute," Ross said. "Listen, Barney. Do you honestly think she'll crack, even if Cohen testifies?"

"I don't know, damn it," Barney said, slapping the palm of his hand on the table. "I just don't know."

Max had interpreted the defense correctly and moved to forestall it. He produced a psychiatrist—Dr. Gordon—a youngish thoughtful man with a high forehead and a luxuriant mustache.

"Did you talk to the plaintiff, Dr. Gordon, on a professional basis?"

"Yes, I did, for a total of three and a half hours on two different occasions."

"Did you find her to be a normal, stable individual?"

"Yes, on the whole. She shows no signs of psychotic or unduly neurotic patterns. She has sufficient strength of ego to deal with reality, to sustain trauma and adjust to traumatic situations. I found no indication of extreme anxiety; in fact, Miss Carter has shown a rather remarkable ability to adapt to difficult circumstances."

"Then you would conclude, Doctor, that a hysterical conversion reaction is unlikely in this case?"

The witness hesitated. "I've only seen her twice," he said. "But she does not fit into the classic patterns of the hysterical personality. Of course, conversion symptoms are often deeply entwined with those of actual physical illness. But I cannot discover any true indication that these *are* conversion symptoms." He paused. Max waited. "Hysterical conversion can be defined simply, for our purposes here, as the involuntary physical effect of emotional disturbance. No. Miss Carter is emotional, but she is not disturbed."

Sperling got up to cross-examine. "Dr. Gordon. Freud said, I believe, that hysteria arises from psychic trauma?"

"Yes."

"Usually occurring in early childhood, and resulting in a state of mental conflict which is too painful to face consciously?"

Gordon nodded.

"The individual represses the conflict, which, thereafter, according to Freud, expresses itself in physical pain or disability?"

"That's correct."

"So, in hysteria we are dealing with a disorder of

infinite variety, whose motives derive from the funda-
mental experiences of childhood?"

"That's right."

"Are you familiar, Dr. Gordon, with the experiences of Miss Carter's childhood?"

"No, as I explained."

"Are you aware, for instance, that Zoe Carter's
mother put her head in an oven when the child was
nine?"

"Objection," shouted Max.

"Sustained," said Judge Matlock. "This is not a
theater, Mr. Sperling; it is a court of law. If there's
any more of this I will direct a mistrial."

"I'm sorry, Judge. I'm trying to evaluate the credibility of the witness."

"Strike that question from the record," said the
judge. "Rephrase your question, Mr. Sperling."

"Dr. Gordon, don't you think you are insufficiently
informed about Miss Carter's formative years to give
evidence as to her present condition?"

"Objection."

"Sustained."

"No more questions," said Sperling shortly. Max
got up again.

"You have made it clear, Dr. Gordon, that you
weren't able to spend much time with Miss Carter.
Nobody could expect you to know her life history.
Am I right in believing, however, that it is legitimate
for you to assess her condition as it is *now,* in the
present, guided by your professional experience and
your knowledge of mental disturbance?"

"Of course."

"And she is, in your experienced judgment, free
from profound personality disorders?"

"Yes."

*   *   *

A sharp-looking fellow wearing yellow pointed shoes and a sharkskin suit answered Max's questions about the economics of the theater. Yes, anyone who starred in one of Culpepper's plays was—damn near—automatically famous. Home free. Yes, successful.

"Would she be likely to get other offers, Mr. Sigal?"

"Take her pick," Sigal said, displaying his teeth.

"The play, *Sister Glory,* was still running, wasn't it? What kind of salary would Miss Carter have been able to command if she had played that part? What kind of salary might she expect from the film? Fringe benefits? T-shirts? Advertising?"

"Yes. Of course, there's always the possibility that she wouldn't catch on. But assuming she made even a moderate success in the film, you wouldn't set her yearly income at less than three hundred grand. Besides, I hear she was terrific."

There was a buzz of excitement among the spectators. The benches were always full these days. Zoe paid no attention to them. She raised her head and looked at Sigal as though she were looking through him. As though he represented ten thousand years of human triviality.

"Your Honor, the plaintiff rests."

3

The first witness for the defense was Barney himself. He got to court early. There was a pinkish hard rubber model of a backbone on his table, and another one of the spinal cord itself, resting in the vertebral groove. Barney sighed. He was tired. It was the seventh day of the trial.

Sperling put a hand on his shoulder. "Ready for the big day, Barney? I hope you got a good night's sleep."

Barney looked up. "I'm fine," he said. "Scared shitless, but just fine." They both laughed. Zoe wheeled herself through the gate in the railing which separated the court from the spectators. She looked tired too. There were dark circles under her eyes. Max Ward arrived, tall and restless, carrying several books and an attaché case. The jury filed in, and then the judge. Everyone, by now, was familiar with the routines and with each other; it was like being in the same platoon in a war, or shipwrecked together on a desert island. There was an intimacy. When Barney took the witness stand, he looked over at Zoe, and a faint color washed over her pale face. What did she want? Forgiveness? There was nothing in her look but love, amazing love, and this curious questioning. He felt close to her. Comrades-in-arms.

The first part was easy, since it was Sperling who

questioned him, going back over the same ground, letting him talk freely and enlarge on his actions. It was the cross-examination that worried him, when Max would go for him. He would have to keep cool and answer sensibly, no matter what Max said.

". . . And the ice pack treatment, Dr. Lukacs?" Sperling asked him, giving him a chance to explain it. "I believe you've done some laboratory work in hypothermia?"

"Yes. On animals, of course. Let me give you an example. I've done hypothermia on dogs. You can drop a weight on a dog's spinal cord, and the dog will become paraplegic. You can drop the same weight on another dog, and if you immediately bathe the cord in ice water, paraplegia won't follow."

"That's an exposed cord?"

"Yes."

"Earlier, Dr. Foote ridiculed your attempt to cool the patient's spinal cord. He said, I think, that it was nonsensical?"

"Possibly," said Barney calmly. "In an emergency, especially when you haven't gotten there yet, it's reasonable to work for a good result. It couldn't harm her."

"And it may have helped?"

"Yes. I've always thought that hypothermia should be used more in cord injuries. By lowering the body temperature, it may have helped to keep the cord cool. The point is to prevent any permanent changes in the cord from taking place."

"Is that why your aim was to do everything as fast as possible, while the cord—presumably—was still cool, once you got her into the hospital?"

"Of course. I hoped no permanent damage had taken place. I wanted to get that bone fragment out immediately."

"You didn't want a clearer X ray picture?"

"Of course I did. But weighing the advantage of a better X ray against the time we'd lose getting it, I decided to go for the spicule. Same goes for the myelogram. You see, you've got a pointed weapon, in a case like this, lodged right in the cord. That's a mass of vital nerve tissue. The longer it stays, the more harm it can do."

"Now, Dr. Lukacs," said Sperling, going to the blowup of the myelogram. "This was done after the relapse. Will you describe what you see there?"

"A lot of extradural scar tissue," Barney said promptly. "I see exactly what I would expect to see. Whenever you have injured tissue, you have scarring. Technically speaking, this is not really a picture of arachnoiditis of the chronic adhesive type, which forms *inside* the dura. This is normal scar formation outside of the dura. Surgery can cause scar. Injury can cause scar. The spicule can cause scar."

"She would have had the same result, whether or not you operated?"

"Probably."

"Right. Now, Dr. Lukacs, after the operation did you keep track of the patient's progress?"

"Yes."

"Was that usual?"

"No. It was an interesting case." Again he met Zoe's blazing glance. It was as though they were alone in the courtroom.

"She was recovering nicely?"

"What? Oh, very."

"But after, say, eight weeks, she still had some residual deficit. That is, some of the original symptoms in a diminished form?"

"Yes."

"Please describe them for the jury."

"Yes. She was walking, you understand, with a barely noticeable limp. But there were still signs. An increased knee jerk on the weak side—the left, that is, and a small partial Babinski. On the right side, there was some residual diminution of sensation."

"But you didn't make a record of these signs?"

"I was no longer officially her physician."

"All right, Dr. Lukacs. You are telling us, then, that these objective signs, which have been so much discussed in this courtroom, existed *prior to the patient's relapse?*"

"Yes."

"They were residual, from the initial trauma? Did you expect them to disappear?"

"I expected further improvement, yes."

"But you were not surprised to hear that these same signs are still a part of the plaintiff's condition?"

"Not at all."

"So you do not think, Dr. Lukacs, that they constitute 'objective' and 'absolute' signs which confirm the presence of arachnoiditis?"

"I do not. They show the same residual deficit which I observed in Miss Carter before her relapse."

Max attacked like a tiger. He paced twice up and down the length of the jury box, looking straight ahead and slapping his hand against his thigh as though he were wrestling with iniquity. Then he turned suddenly to Barney.

"When you have animals in your laboratory, Doctor, you can do whatever you want with them, can't you?"

"More or less."

"It doesn't matter what happens to them, right? As long as the interests of science are served."

"Yes."

"So you'll try anything?"

"It's not quite like that. But yes."

"Do you ever get them confused, Doctor?"

"What?"

"Animals. And human beings."

"Objection," Sperling said.

"Sustained."

"Do you find, Doctor, that what works on animals often works on human beings?"

"There's a difference—"

"Oh, so what works on animals often doesn't work on human beings?"

Barney shrugged. "No."

"Do you find, Doctor, that in experimentation you often get carried away by an idea? That you want to prove your hypothesis?"

"One looks for the truth."

"And that in your excitement you bend the truth?"

"Not at all," Barney said, and Sperling lodged an objection. Max paced again, thinking.

"Doctor," he rapped out savagely. "Do you have an opinion as to whether inexpert operating techniques can lead to postoperative bleeding?"

"It's possible," Barney said.

"And would you agree with me, *sir,* that a skilled neurosurgeon could have operated on Zoe Carter without causing massive hemorrhage leading to arachnoiditis?"

"Objection," Sperling called out.

The judge said, "Sustained," and Max stopped in front of the jury. He shrugged and cast his eyes to heaven.

"Doctor, am I correct, sir, that excessive probing can mutilate the tissue surrounding this highly delicate area?"

"Objection. There's a lot of innuendo going on here, Judge."

"Sustained."

"And Doctor, would it be considered a departure from good medical practice for a doctor to cut excessively in the area surrounding the spinal cord?"

"Naturally," Barney said.

"And would you agree with me that scar tissue is caused by inexpert cauterization?"

"That is one of the possibilities."

Max strode to the table and picked up the model of the spinal canal. "And that excessive bleeding *here* and *here*," he pointed out the spots, "could lead to arachnoiditis?"

"Objection. Your Honor, no connection between the relapse and arachnoiditis has yet been established."

"Sustained."

"Doctor Lukacs," Max said in a whisper, "don't tell me that you think you are completely blameless?"

"I can't hear you."

Max repeated the question, still very *sotto voce*.

"Mr. Ward," the judge said, "will you please raise your voice?"

Max spread his arms, with his palms raised. "Dr. Lukacs," he said loudly, "are you saying that you think you are completely blameless?"

There was another objection from Sperling.

"Doctor, medicine is not an exact science, is it? I mean, doctors do make mistakes?"

"Undoubtedly."

"And when you took on Miss Carter, Doctor, you did not acquire any state of infallibility, is that correct?"

"Objection."

"Sustained."

"I have nothing further to say," Max said, and he turned abruptly on his heel and walked rapidly back to his table.

"How'd I do?" asked Barney.

"You were great," Sperling said. "He was just needling you."

"Let's go get some lunch."

Zoe was talking to some reporters in the hall, so Cohen waited. When she was free he approached her. She looked pleased to see him.

"Dr. Cohen! I noticed you were here. How are you?"

Culpepper detached himself from Max and walked hurriedly over to them.

"Willie, this is Dr. Cohen."

"Glad to meet you. I've heard about you, of course." They shook hands.

"Zoe," said Cohen. "I'd like to talk to you. What would be a good time?"

Zoe looked at Culpepper.

"Perhaps you would come to my house," Culpepper said. "For drinks? We could make it today, if you'd like, when the afternoon session is finished."

"Good," Cohen said, with a slight bow. "I will see you then."

Sperling called the first of his expert witnesses—Dr. Sanderson, a well-known neurosurgeon from Massachusetts General. He was tall and bearded, about forty-five, and he responded to Sperling's list of his impressive qualifications in an impatient tone.

"Given the patient's condition, and the X ray which you see here," Sperling asked him, "would you have operated?"

"Yes, I might well have. It's a marginal case; you have to go on your own judgment."

"You would not find further diagnostic tests essential?"

"Well, I'd like to have them, but I can understand his haste. If the spicule is in there, you see, you're sitting on a bomb. Any movement can lead to further damage. If there is a severe lesion, there may be permanent loss of function."

"Good. Now, can you say that the development of arachnoiditis reflects on the competence of the surgeon?"

"Not necessarily. It may be unavoidable. Unfortunate of course, but it follows, often enough, without any negligence on the part of the surgeon."

"Have you ever operated and had scar tissue develop?"

"Yes."

"Was it because your surgery was at fault?"

"No. You always have some scar tissue."

"Then arachnoiditis can result from expert surgery?"

"Yes."

"Could arachnoiditis result from the original trauma? A shattering blow to the spinal column, fracture, bleeding?"

"Yes."

"So that even if Dr. Lukacs had not operated, the scar tissue might well have formed as a result of the accident?"

"Yes."

Sperling turned to the myelogram. "Dr. Sanderson, is this a picture of arachnoiditis?"

"Technically, no. The myelogram shows heavy epidural scarring, outside, not inside, the dura."

"Of the kind you would expect, given the circumstances?"

"Yes. The scarring is extensive. I would call it a secondary effect of the trauma and/or the surgery."

"Thank you. Now, sir, you have said the scarring is a natural consequence of trauma. Would you also expect that nine weeks after the accident and the surgery, before she had her relapse, the patient would still exhibit unmistakable signs of that trauma? The increased knee jerk, for instance, and the partial Babinski?"

"It's likely."

"So that when the doctors examined her after her relapse—Dr. Foote and Dr. Evans—they might have mistaken those signs, which indicated a normal residual deficit, as a firm indication of arachnoiditis?"

"That's entirely possible."

"So that what remains as objective evidence of arachnoiditis is the paralysis on the left side?"

"Yes."

"Have you ever had cases of hysterical paralysis, Doctor?"

"Yes."

"Is there any cure for it?"

"The outlook is almost always good in such cases, if it is treated early enough. It's not my field, of course. The diagnosis of hysteria is the province of the neurologist; the cure is up to a psychiatrist."

Max rose to cross-examine.

"Doctor, you referred in a casual way to the *secondary effects of trauma*. Don't you in fact mean *scarring*?"

"Yes."

"Well, that's what arachnoiditis is, is it not? Scarring? Fibrosis? Adhesions due to fibrosis?"

"Yes."

"You mean, any operation of this nature may lead to scarring fibroses and adhesional scarring due to fibrosis"—Max jabbed his finger at the witness—"in short, *arachnoiditis*? Is that what you mean?"

"When you get that kind of—"

"Answer yes or no."

"I can't. Well, yes. It can, but it doesn't always."

"But *this* operation led to fibrosis, scarring, adhesional scarring due to fibrosis. Do you call that normal?"

"Yes. No. It depends how extensive—"

"Thank you, Doctor. Now. Did you examine the patient before her relapse?"

"No, of course not."

"Then you cannot know, can you, what residual deficit may or may not have existed?"

"No, but—"

"No more questions."

A cheerful fire was burning in Culpepper's great living room while outside a cold spring wind whipped the beach, driving spurts of foam across the water. Cohen removed several layers of clothing, but retained a scarf, tucking it firmly under his lapels even as he settled himself before the fire. He thought of Israel, the burning sands and harsh configurations of rock, the softness of the olive trees misting in the bright sun. That landscape shrieked of truth, and he longed to be there, instead of picking his way through the gross complexities of the American ego, over cocktails.

He accepted a glass of wine from Culpepper, who then moved behind Zoe's chair, putting his hands on her shoulders. Culpepper had grown heavier. The half-moons under his protruding eyes were deeply incised, and the flesh on his cheeks hung in flabby pouches over his tight collar. There was an uncomfortable pause. Max Ward leaned against the mantel and Cohen, looking up at him, was startled by the animosity in his eyes. He waited for someone else to speak and it was Zoe, finally, languorous and a little shy, who broke the silence.

"It seems forever since those days in your office, Dr. Cohen. Those fifty-minute days." She laughed softly. "I'm surprised you remember me."

"How could I forget you? You were a rare individual. How are you, Zoe?"

"Wonderful. I never thought I could be so happy. I must have been awful when you knew me. I was a nut."

Cohen nodded. "A very charming nut. I am not so sure I accomplished with you what I should have," he said. "You are happy, even—?"

"Life isn't all walking," Zoe said. "Marching up and down, getting things done. How are you, after all this time?"

"Don't you want to walk again, Zoe?"

"Of course I do," she said placidly. "And I will. But *how* shall I walk, Dr. Cohen? Spirit-filled? Worthy of the vocation? Or just stumbling along, blind, in an ordinary way?"

"You don't even mind being an invalid?"

Her eyes filled with light. "It is a purification. It has made—other things—available to me. You know about that?"

"Yes. Why are you pursuing this lawsuit, Zoe?"

"The Lord opens many doors," she said. "This is one of them. I do not question His ways."

Max had been fidgeting with an enameled box on the mantel. Cohen could feel his impatience, and now he snapped it shut and sat on the arm of the sofa.

"Let's get to the point of all this, Dr. Cohen. Are you going to take part in this action?"

Cohen looked at him mildly. "I don't know," he said. "I'd like to talk to Zoe privately for a time."

"I'm her lawyer. This is a crucial time. I'm sorry, but I want to be present while you interview her."

"Zoe's been under a lot of strain," added Culpepper. He sat down on the sofa. "Max is only saying that she needs her friends."

"You are afraid to let her talk with me?"

"Not in the least. But I won't have her badgered by anyone."

"Zoe?" asked Cohen.

"Why should we talk in private, Dr. Cohen. I have no private life anymore. Anything you want to say can be said here quite openly." She smiled pleasantly, firmly even, but even as Cohen thought, *Well, that's that, then,* it seemed to him that there was something else, a question, an appeal, a sudden grief, that shivered the luminous curtain of her gaze. He leaned forward. It was as though she'd shouted, *Help me,* but by the time he reached for her hand, it was gone. "Are you quite sure, Zoe?" he asked.

"We're all quite sure, Dr. Cohen," said Culpepper. "It was extremely nice of you to stop by today."

Cohen finished his glass and got himself laboriously out of the deep armchair. "You have been through this kind of experience before, Zoe. Don't you remember it? I want you to drop the lawsuit."

"I knew that's what you were after," Max said. "Why should she? She's got a very good case, and the medical evidence is largely on her side. Every time the defense speaks, they're hanging themselves with the jury—all this airy-fairy stuff about states of mind and childhood experience. Pie in the sky. Did you ever see anyone sounder, more composed, more idealistic than Zoe? She's not even bitter. My summation will tear them to shreds."

"I'm not concerned with who gets the verdict, Mr. Ward. My concern is Zoe. I want her to drop the suit. I want her to see a psychiatrist. I want her to recover, her mind as well as her body. Yes, I've seen people sounder than Zoe. If she does not take these steps, I will testify for the defense."

"What will you have to say?"

"I will say that she has suffered from hysterical illnesses earlier in her life." He looked at Zoe. "I will have to enter my files in evidence. Will you mind, Zoe?"

"I don't know. I am doing the right thing, the thing which has to be done. I have talked to God; I've listened; I've prayed; I've heard Him speak. Everything else is unimportant. I am unimportant. I am only a vehicle for the Lord's intention." Her eyes widened as she looked at him, and she appeared to be looking at a distant, inward view. She lifted one hand, with its palm turned softly upwards.

"This is not a crusade, Zoe," Cohen said. "It's a rather sordid legal action, and it does you no credit. My dear—" But it was no good; she had removed herself. She didn't seem to hear him. Cohen walked toward the hallway, and Max followed him.

"I wouldn't testify, if I were you," Max said. "A million adolescents go through that kind of thing. It won't amount to a hill of beans."

Cohen found his woolly vest hanging on a coat tree in the hall. He started to put it on. "And furthermore," Max said in low cutting tones, "Zoe said you were in love with her. I'll take you apart, up there on the stand. She was only fifteen, for God's sake, and you were already an old man."

Cohen shrugged into his overcoat and reached for

his other scarf. He wrapped it around his head and stood blinking up at Max in the dimness.

"Your testimony will be worthless, old man, and everyone will see you for what you are. A piece of filth."

Cohen opened the door. "It's not true," he said.

"Close enough. By the time I finish with you, it'll be true."

"I hate to leave right now," Maggie said. "Just when things are coming to a head."

"I'll bet you do," said Barney. "Like putting down a good book on the next to the last page. Maggie, I can't tell you how grateful I am that you could come at all."

Maggie was on her annual poetry-reading tour. She had canceled two of her appearances to come back for the trial, but it was dragging on longer than anyone had expected. She had a reading on the next day in Bloomington, Indiana, and so she'd come out with Barney for a farewell Chinese dinner.

"I wouldn't have missed it for anything," she said.

"Sensationalist."

"Well, there's that. It *is* interesting. How do you feel, Barney? Do you think you're going to win?"

"I have to. It's necessary that I win. That's how I feel." The waiter brought lime sherbet for dessert and two fortune cookies in a saucer.

"Do you feel ground down by fate?" Maggie asked.

"No. We live in times when expediency is the name of the game. One has to fight it."

"Really. Look at Dr. Geddes. What an astonishing creature! Malpractice is a whole damn industry."

"Geddes is what's called, in the trade, a legal whore."

"Open your cookie, Barney. Let's see what's in

store for you. Wait." Maggie reached across the table, touched his hand. "I'll tell you first. You'll win," she said with conviction. "Not because there's any justice in the world—I don't believe that for a minute. You'll win because it's your nature to win, because you're honest, because you've got heart. There's something exotic about this case, something dark and obscure, and everybody in the courtroom is confused and frustrated by it. It has nothing to do with medicine, it's the personalities. I think that whatever is simple and natural will carry the day."

Barney smiled at her. "Thanks, Maggie. Thanks for everything."

"Now open your cookie." She waited while he broke it open and took out the slip of paper. He held it close to the light, a candle in a pink globe, and squinted at it.

"That which you think can't happen, can," Barney read. "What the hell does that mean? It's a double-edged sword."

"It all depends on what you think can't happen."

"Like Murphy's Law, you mean? Anything that can go wrong, will?"

"Well that's the pessimist's view," Maggie said. "I prefer to take it optimistically. Nothing is impossible, never give up hope, and all that."

"Daniel in the lion's den?"

"It's not as bad as all that."

"What have the fates got in store for you, Maggie? Open your cookie." Maggie broke hers open and read the message to herself. She laughed.

"What is it?"

"May your house be safe from tigers."

They stared at each other for a moment, as if confronted with the riddle of the sphinx, and then burst into laughter.

*   *   *

Sperling had kept Jim Harvey for the windup. A neurologist at Columbia Presbyterian, with twenty initials after his name, Harvey had dual certification and practiced both neurology and psychology. He could testify in both fields. He was a vague-looking man, with a bony face and large steel glasses which he put on and took off nervously. He confirmed Sanderson's statements. Yes, he might well have recommended surgery. No, the myelogram did not provide conclusive evidence of arachnoiditis. Yes, at the time of the relapse, the patient would have been likely to exhibit a certain residual deficit. Yes, the partial Babinski, the increased knee jerk. Yes, a physician might well mistake those residual signs as proof of chronic adhesive arachnoiditis.

Sperling questioned him, slowly, giving the jury plenty of time to absorb his answers.

"Doctor, would you describe for the jury the concept of hysterical overlay?"

"Yes. It happens quite often. The patient has been ill and recovered. Or partially recovered. He meets a stressful situation in his emotions and becomes hysterically ill in order to avoid facing it. Unconsciously he models his hysterical symptoms on the illness which he has already experienced—something he's familiar with. This is particularly true where there is some organic deficit for him to work with."

"In other words, the patient tends to build on known patterns or existing organic defects?"

"Yes."

"Involuntarily, of course? It's not a matter of will?"

"No. It's a psychogenic pattern of reaction to mental or emotional stress. If you were fanciful, you might almost call it a psychological reflex."

"Dr. Harvey, you have examined Miss Carter?"

"I have."

"Did you find that her symptoms were psychogenic?"

"Partially. As I explained, a hysterical conversion reaction is frequently intertwined with some organic defect. The Babinski sign, the hyperactive reflexes, I believe, are initially organic. The paralysis is functional."

"Hysterical?"

"That's right. Functional means that there is an abnormal change in the way an organ functions, but there is no structural change in the tissues involved. Organic means that there is structural impairment."

"Thank you, Doctor. Will you explain how you arrived at your diagnosis? Did you, for instance, do the Hoover test?"

"I did."

"What is the Hoover test, Dr. Harvey?"

"It's one of many neurological tests that help the doctor identify a real paralysis as against one which is psychogenic."

"Will you describe it, please?"

"I'll try. It's very simple and ordinary, like most such tests. You've got the patient on her back on the examining table. You put your hand on the paralyzed leg. 'Raise that leg,' you say. She can't. Put your hand under the heel and say, 'Press down as hard as you can.' The patient can't. Hand still under heel, you raise the leg. There's no resistance of course. You keep your hand there. You put your other hand on top of the good leg and say, 'Raise this leg.' She raises it, working hard, while you press against it. Then you try at the same time to raise the paralyzed leg with your hand still under the heel, and you can't raise it. The pressure downwards is automatic. The leg is not paralyzed. The muscles are still working. It's a classic differentiation. Miss Carter's paralysis is functional."

"Did you do any other tests of that nature?"

"I did. This one is just as primitive as the Hoover, and it gave me the same information."

"Will you describe it?"

"Well, as you know, the patient had recovered sensation in her good leg, with some impairment. After the relapse, she lost sensation again. You touch her with the pin. 'Do you feel this?' you ask. 'Nothing,' she says. 'Nothing at all.' Later in the examination you go back to it. You tell her this time to close her eyes. You tell her, when you feel the pin say yes, if you don't, say no. Then, when you touch the paralyzed side she says yes, when you touch the sensory-impaired side she says no. That's impossible, organically. Her eyes are closed and she can't feel anything: How can she say no? She shouldn't be able to answer at all, if the impairment was organic, because she wouldn't be aware of the touch."

"So this second test confirmed your initial conclusion. The illness is hysterical?"

"Yes. Hysterical overlay on organic deficit."

"How can all these eminent doctors disagree, if the diagnostic tests are so simple?"

"Well, it's my opinion that the doctors who examined her after the relapse never even entertained the idea of psychogenesis, because of the sensory impairment, the Babinski, and the increased reflexes. These are objective abnormal findings, and the paralysis was consistent with them. In short, they misinterpreted residual findings for a confirmation of the relapse."

Max rose. "Are you trying to tell us, Dr. Harvey, that the patient is making all this up?"

"No."

"That after years of hard work and discipline, on

the verge of playing a role that she longed for, the door open to success and prestige, she said to herself, 'I'd rather be nobody and sit in a wheelchair?'"

"No."

"Neurological examinations are confusing to the patient, are they not? It's difficult for her to tell, is it not, whether she feels something a little or not at all or a lot? Do you have patients, for instance, who are trying to do a good job? To pass the test, so to speak?"

"Of course. It's a tricky business."

"One such test might be explained by involuntary reflexes. Another by confusion. How can you make distinctions between those things?"

"Objection. Counsel is leading the witness."

Max rephrased his question. "How can you make the distinction between her conscious and her unconscious confusion?"

"As I said, it's very tricky. It's hard to tell how much *organic* impairment is really underneath. But as you work with a patient, you get a certain sense of these things. Sometimes it's hard to pin down."

"Dr. Harvey. Sir. We have here a wheelchair case, a clear case of a woman with all the technical objective signs of a Brown-Sequard dysfunction. A woman whose sensory impairment, Babinski, reflexes all bear out the terrible paralysis that has struck not only her leg but her life. A star eclipsed. A woman who could have no possible motive for lying—and you ask us to believe that this is a *tricky business,* and that you get a *certain sense* of these things?"

"Certain of those symptoms are residual from the accident. It's a question of severity only."

"Yes?" said Max, his eyes flashing. He seemed to tower over the jury. "How severe do you call severe?

Look—" he flung his arm toward the plaintiff, who sat humbly in her steel chair. *"Look* at the outcome."

"Why didn't you redirect after that?" Barney asked Sperling.

"What's the use?" Sperling said. "It was all dramatics. We have to assume that the jury has some intelligence."

It was eleven thirty, almost lunchtime. The judge looked at the clock. "Do you have another witness, Mr. Sperling?" he asked.

"Yes, your honor. I have one that will be brief. After that I think—I hope—I have one who will be more lengthy."

Cohen blinked. He wanted badly to pick up his overcoat, neatly folded on the seat beside him, and go out the frosted glass door just across the aisle from him and shake the dust of Long Island from his feet forever. His ulcer hurt. He was so tense that his teeth ached and felt loose in their sockets. He blinked again. It was time; he couldn't be an observer any longer.

Sperling looked at his watch and involuntarily Cohen extended his arm and regarded his own. Eleven thirty-two. He had to come to a decision.

"All right," Judge Matlock said. "Call your next witness, and then we'll take a break for lunch." Sperling called Robert Emmett, the principal of the Pittsville Junior High School in Georgia. He established Emmett's position and his connection with Zoe during the time she was there.

"Mr. Emmett, do you recognize these records?"

"Yes, indeed, those are our school records. Zoe Carter's records." Sperling passed copies of them to Max, the judge, and the jury.

"Mr. Emmett, was Zoe an emotional girl?"

"Very."

"Did she perform in school plays?"

"Yes."

"And did she get nervous when she was to perform?"

"Yes, I remember one occasion when she fainted."

"Now, Mr. Emmett, would you read the comments made by the school nurse at the bottom of page two?"

"Fainted at baseball practice. Fainted in class. Fainted in the locker room. Fainted at lunch. Very anxious. Severe loss appetite. Weight one hundred and three."

"And again, on page four?"

"Fainted at Christmas concert. Complains of numbness in hands, legs, feet. Has not menstruated for over a year."

"And the school doctor's comment?"

"Phobic. Adolescent turmoil. Physically sound, except for weight loss."

"What does phobic mean, do you know?"

"It means she suffered from irrational fears or aversions."

"Now, Mr. Emmett, did you, or anyone at the school, discuss Zoe's difficulties with her parents?"

"We tried. Her mother was deceased. We tried to talk to her father. We suggested that Zoe needed counseling."

"But Mr. Carter was not amenable?"

"He ran me off the premises."

"So the school referred the matter to social agencies?"

"Yes. It finally came up in Family Court. Zoe was removed to her grandmother's house in Atlanta."

"Thank you, Mr. Emmett. Your witness, Mr. Ward."

"Tell me, Mr. Emmett," Max asked, getting up

from his seat at the plaintiff's table, "You have had considerable experience dealing with adolescents?"

"Yes. A lot."

"And do you find them, on the whole, to be stable, content, and well-regulated human beings?"

Emmett smiled, and there was laughter from the benches. "Not in the least. It's a chaotic time in anyone's life."

"Would you agree with me, sir, that many of them suffer from irrational fears?"

"Yes, sir."

"And do they faint sometimes?"

"Yes. But not often."

"But would you say that fainting was in the normal range of adolescent disturbance?"

"Oh, yes."

"Thank you. You can get down now."

Sperling reorganized his paperwork while everyone left the courtroom—the judge, then the jury, and then, in a burst of speculation, the spectators. Max wheeled Zoe out.

"How do you think it's going?" Barney asked.

Sperling tapped a sheaf of papers to make it square, and then arranged all of them in two neat piles. He put his briefcase under the table, and then he raised his eyes to Barney's. "Fifty-fifty," he said. "Almost precisely."

"Nothing seems to shake her, does it?" Barney said.

Sperling smiled. "She's a tough cookie."

"A frightened cookie," Barney said. "She's working on a survival level. That's the whole pattern."

"C'mon. Lunchtime."

The hall was empty by the time they got there, dim and dirty. Cigarette butts were all over the floor. A square figure peered at them from one of the benches and came toward them. Barney held out his hand.

"Hi," he said. He and Cohen shook hands, and he introduced Cohen to Sperling. "Glad to meet you," Sperling said. "And that's an understatement."

"I will do it," said Cohen. "With a few limitations."

"Good. Let's go map it out over lunch." They went out the double doors to the street.

It was afternoon. Cohen was on the stand, homely, determined, and deeply ill at ease.

"Right, Dr. Cohen," said Sperling. "You saw the patient twice a week over a period of two years. Who referred her to you?"

"The doctor at Pittsville Junior High School."

"And how old was she then?"

"Fifteen. She started with me when she started high school."

"And what was the technical category of her illness?"

"It was a case of regression with hysterical features. That was some years ago; of course, I believe that now the case would belong to a general syndrome called Borderline."

"What does that mean?"

"Borderline varies. But all Borderline patients have in common, I believe, a severe abandonment depression. It can arise even in the most unremarkable circumstances. Between eighteen months and three years of age, the infant must undergo a separation process from the mother, or else turn his back on his own unfolding individuality. The same process repeats itself in early adolescence. Both times it is painful. It gives rise to severe feelings of abandonment and despair. If the maturing is imperfect, these painful feelings are repressed, held down by a variety of defense mechanisms. The patient clings to the mother, but denies her. There is conflict."

"You are describing what is popularly known as a back-to-the-womb complex?"

"Perhaps. There are oedipal complications, of course. The sexual relation with the father in the case of a girl, and the concomitant guilt in her relations with her mother. All this is within the normal range. But, depending on the severity of the conflict, this is the ground that nourishes so many adolescent character disorders and problems, shall we say, phobias, obsessions, conversion reactions, dissociation, and hypochondriasis."

"What were the plaintiff's symptoms when she came to you?"

"First of all, there was her school performance. The patient was brilliant, but she was close to failing all year. When this happens, it indicates that there is a need to fail, one which is as strong as her need to succeed. She needs to fail in order to maintain her dependency needs, that stance of helplessness which is her appeal. She needs to succeed in order to prove to herself that she is independent. Often, on the verge of success, the patient will hang back. This patient, subconsciously, didn't want to graduate from junior high school. It would present her with a new stage of growing up, self-sufficiency, responsibility. She would lose her child status. When she came to me, I took it as an indication of unresolved dependency needs."

"There were other symptoms?"

"As it shows in the records and as still true when we began our therapy. There was much of what we call 'acting out.' Rebellious behavior, or complete withdrawal. Loss of appetite. Failure of menstrual cycle. Fainting spells. When she came to me, she suffered from severe anxiety, as though daily life had taken on the quality of a bad dream. She felt as though everything around her were receding. Inter-

mittently, you understand, but frequently, in precipi-
tal situations. At times when she had a date, an
examination, a school play, she would get the sensation that her hands were paralyzed, so she couldn't do
this or that. A feeling of numbness in her legs and
feet, or in her hands. A feeling that the room was getting narrower, closing in on her, that she was falling
off the bed. There was what is called depersonaliza-
tion—a superawareness, accompanied by the emotional effect of not being connected."

"Was it severe?"

"No. A soft type of regression. Plastic: she moved
in and out of regressive states, rather like an actress
taking curtain calls."

"Doctor, is there such a thing as a hysterical type?"

"No. You might say that certain types incline
toward hysteria, but it is impossible to say that people
with hysterical reactions fit a definite type. As Kret-
schmer said, a predisposition toward hysterical reactions is widespread, deeply rooted in an instinctive
defense mechanism. There is a certain theatricality,
perhaps, that all hysterics have in common. A manip-
ulative quality."

Cohen kept his eyes steadily on Sperling. Most of
the courtroom watched Zoe. Barney was profoundly
embarrassed; he was disgusted. It should never have
happened, this public exposure; it should simply not
take place. Krupp was scribbling furiously. Barney
was tempted to leap up and call the whole thing off,
settle for whatever they wanted, pay the damn money.
Anything, anything which would stop this terrible
process, the prurient sideways gaze with which the
jury regarded her, the frank curiosity of the spectators, and most of all, the careless distant intensity
with which Zoe kept her eyes on Cohen, as though it
wasn't her at all that they were talking about. Abner

was leaning forward. He wet his lower lip with his tongue.

"Did the mother's death precipitate the condition?"

"Among other things. I do not wish to go into the diagnostic formulation here. But in an oedipal situation there is always the unconscious wish that the mother should die, and then, if she does, there is always a feeling of guilt. It's normal. This case, of course, is complicated by the mother's suicide; the patient was the one who found her. The patient felt she had contributed to the suicide, as might any child. There were other factors."

"Tell me, Dr. Cohen, did the symptoms continue?"

"During the first year of our therapy, yes. Then she improved."

"And after the second year, your relationship was terminated?"

"Yes, except for one occasion."

"And that was?"

"She was to play Blanche in *A Streetcar Named Desire*. Zoe became sick, and the opening had to be postponed."

"Sick?"

"She suffered a return of some of her earlier symptoms. Numbness, fainting, disconnection, and terror."

"You treated her?"

"Yes. The play opened two weeks later. Zoe had a tremendous personal success."

"You are saying, Dr. Cohen, that *the opening date for the play* precipitated an hysterical attack?"

"Yes."

"Do you believe, Dr. Cohen, that this same patient, having sustained an acute medical emergency, three quarters on the way to a full recovery, walking and responding with only the slightest apparent deficit, might read in the paper that rehearsals were due to start shortly, and suffer a psychiatric relapse similar to the one she had before *Streetcar Named Desire?*"

"I do, indeed. There is something about organic weakness that encourages regressive tendencies."

"Dr. Cohen, the plaintiff, as her attorney has been quick to point out, seems to have made a mature adjustment to an extremely difficult reality. She is crippled. She has adjusted to her condition and seems to be not only resigned to it, but cheerful. She has found a second career. How does that square with the notion that her illness is hysterical?"

"One aspect of hysterical patients," Dr. Cohen said, "which has long been accepted, is that they show a lack of concern with their symptoms. They display an acceptance of hardship and pain that would be surprising, actually, in someone who has suddenly developed a significant disability. There is a compulsive, dreamy attitude toward the whole experience. It is called *la belle indifférence*—literally, the beautiful indifference. Of course, in actual fact, the symptoms have solved her conflict. If the patient is happy to be ill, in order to escape from a more difficult problem, then *la belle indifférence* is readily understood. In this case, the patient had the opportunity to succeed, but because of her relapse, she did not have to shoulder the responsibility for following it through. It is the best of both worlds."

Max rose to his feet. "Doctor, the plaintiff doesn't look hysterical to me. Her condition must be a strain on her; the courtroom itself must be a strain. Does she look to you like someone who can't sustain a difficult time?"

"No. I've explained that."

"Does she look like someone with—what was it?—a defective ego?"

"No."

"Like someone who cannot adjust to reality, inside herself, or without?"

"How she—"

"Would you agree with me, Doctor, if I said that a person suffering from dependency needs would be unlikely to leave her family at the age of nineteen, and, living alone, work hard at her chosen art for a period of ten years with almost no close personal relations during that time?"

"No. But—"

"Now this *belle indifférence,* Doctor. You are saying that because a person doesn't exhibit his suffering for all the world to see, he is actually not suffering?"

"Possibly. In some cases the systolic blood pressure actually drops."

"That sounds good. Are you saying it's bad? You mean to tell me that when a person's acting most normal, he's least normal?"

A wave of laughter rose from the spectators' bench. The judge used his gavel.

Max put his hands in his pockets and rocked thoughtfully on the balls of his feet. "Dr. Cohen, do you specialize in adolescent psychology?"

"No."

"Have you dealt with many adolescents?"

"No."

"Are you familiar, Doctor, with the work of Cumberland and Weiss in this area?" Max selected a book from a stack of impressive volumes on his table.

"I am familiar with their work in general."

"Would you recognize as authoritative their book entitled *Anxiety, Ego, and the Psychosomatic Disorder*?"

"I haven't read it, but their work is, in general, solid."

"I would like to have your opinion on a paragraph

from the chapter called 'Adjustment Reaction of Adolescence.' Max opened the book to one of several markers. He put on his horn-rimmed glasses and began to read. 'Adolescence is a time of such marked emotional turbulence that in a given patient it is sometimes difficult to decide whether he suffers from a psychiatric illness that requires treatment or from what we may call *normal adolescent turmoil,* which will subside with further growth.' " Max looked pointedly at the jury over his glasses, and went on to read some details of the study. "Now, Doctor, would you agree with me if I said that the implications of this paragraph are that most adolescents simply grow out of it?"

"Yes. When was the book published?"

"I ask the questions, Doctor. You answer them. Now this paragraph would suggest that adolescents recover from emotional disturbances which become resolved and do not set a pattern for their adult lives?"

"Perhaps."

"Does it or does it not?"

"The excerpt says in most cases."

"Good. Doctor, were you fond of your patient?"

"Yes."

"Did you sit on the couch with her during treatment?"

"I may have, from time to time."

"And you were at the time, let me see, fifty-two years of age?"

"I suppose so."

"And you held her hand, did you, caressed her, kissed her perhaps?" Dr. Cohen flushed horribly, the red rising on his throat and spreading outwards and upwards, until even his ears were crimson. "Would you say, Doctor, that you are in a position to be objective about this patient?"

"It's not true," said Cohen. "At least in the way you—"

"Not true?" thundered Max. "Not true that you were in love with her? That you molested her? That she rejected you?"

Zoe watched, with the same bright, uncaring look.

"Not true," said Cohen quietly, his flush receding. "If you want the truth, here in this courtroom—and I am under oath—it was her father who—"

"That will be all, Dr. Cohen," shouted Max. There was a burst of excitement from the benches, and the judge pounded his gavel. "If there is any more racket in this room, I will clear the court." Max sat down.

Sperling went to the lectern. "It was her father who—? What, Dr. Cohen?"

Cohen spoke quietly. "The patient was deeply disturbed. Her childhood was shot with brutality and family dissension. Her mother killed herself, when Zoe was a child. In early adolescence her father molested her." Barney glanced at the place where Abner had been sitting. The seat was empty. "He was drunk. He beat her, and then he felt sorry. He laid her back on the kitchen table and tried to make it up to her in the only way he knew. He is an animal. The attack was sexual, and in all probability included sexual intercourse. But the technicality of penetration is not what is in question here. What matters is that the child was traumatized and that it had an effect on her behavior.

"When she came to me, she had 'forgotten' it, repressed it, that is. She didn't know what was troubling her, but she had the symptoms we have talked about—the numbness, the disorientation, the fainting."

"Were you able to treat her?" asked Sperling.

"Yes, I was able to bring it to the surface. She needed therapy; I worked with her. She needed kindness, love. I tried to help her. That is all."

"Did she recover through your treatment?"

"Her behavior became normal. But no, the therapy was not complete. She needed more time. But she was young; she thought she was fine. She stopped coming."

"Do you think it is possible, Dr. Cohen, that her present illness is hysterical?"

"Entirely possible. It would be in keeping with her former patterns of behavior. I have been here every day, heard the evidence, watched Zoe. I have talked with her briefly. My opinion is that the relapse was hysterical."

"Thank you, Doctor. Your Honor, the defense rests."

The judge glanced at the clock. "The court will convene again on Monday morning. The court is adjourned."

4

"Well, it's all over but the shooting," said Sperling. "But that's not to say it's all over. The shooting will be rough."

"How is that?" asked Cohen.

"The summation," Sperling said. "I can tell you what it will be already." He stood up and threw his head back in a fair imitation of Max." 'Gentlemen, ladies of the jury. We have here a classic example of the red herring. You have seen for yourselves, gentlemen, the rare honesty and composure of the plaintiff. And yet the defense—' he drops his voice here, 'says she is hysterical.' Louder now: 'You have seen for yourselves the courageous adjustment that the plaintiff has made, and yet the defense says she has—er—*ego defects.*'" Sperling screwed up his mouth as Max might, in an expression of distaste. "'You have seen for yourselves . . .' And so on. He'll say, for instance, something like this. 'And the defense's own highly expert witness, Dr. James Harvey, describes the diagnosis as *a very tricky business . . . you get a certain sense of these things. A certain sense,* gentlemen? Is this patient crippled, or is she not crippled? We don't deal in *certain senses* here; we deal in life, real life, a life full of pain and restraints, a life that is half a life . . .'" Sperling thumped his fist on the table. "Need I go on?" he asked.

They were sitting around a circular table in a bar called the Left Bank. Barney felt light-headed. Piri and Ross were there.

"You make too good a case," Ross said. "What do you think our chances are?"

"I don't think," Sperling said. "We'll do our summation, and we'll pray that the jury has followed all this. It's hard for them, you know. But I think there's a good chance they won't fall for Ward's histrionics. He comes on too strong. He acts as though it's a personal vendetta."

The waiter came up. "You want another round?"

"Yes," Barney said.

"Not for me," said Sperling. "I want to go over my summation for Monday, while I've still got everything fresh in my mind. See you later." He collected his things.

Barney stood up and shook hands with him. "Thank you, Dave," he said.

"Take it easy. See you Monday."

No one spoke for a while. The waiter brought them another round of drinks.

"She didn't turn a hair," Barney said to Cohen. "I thought something would happen when everything came out."

"No."

"You know, the whole thing is meaningless, whether we win or lose, if Zoe doesn't recognize what's happened. Say she loses. She'll shrug her lovely shoulders and say, 'Well, it was meant.' It won't change anything for her. She'll still be crippled. She'll still be the Lord's messenger. She'll still be beautifully indifferent—my God, insanely deaf."

"It may be different if she wins," Ross said. "She'll feel badly for you, I think."

"No. She's praying for me to get saved. She thinks

if I hit bottom, I'll come to Jesus. Also, if she wins, she'll never dare walk again."

"There's always faith healing."

"If I could only get her alone for a few hours," Cohen said. "I think I could crack through. But she's too well-protected. In every sense. Her defenses are just too good. She's too trancelike, too able to simplify, too able to ignore reality. For a moment there, at the house, I thought I was getting a response, but it passed."

"This *belle indifférence* is a condition of false complacency?" Barney asked.

"Yes," Cohen said. "A dreamy, stubborn self-protective device. The patient is sick in order to avoid certain real-world problems. She is literally indifferent to her condition. It suits her. She holds on to it stubbornly. The same goes for her sporadic amnesia. She forgot things which were too painful—the actual incidents with her father for example. I suspect she had forgotten them again. It's a way of escaping, a never-never land. But it's not truly forgotten. It's in there, an unidentified presence, creating terrors and denials which are beyond her control."

"I was watching her, when that came out," Barney said. "If anything, her serenity increased."

"Yes," said Cohen. "Gentlemen, shock treatment has failed." He spread his chunky, old man's hands. "It is too bad. Now, while the verdict is still to come in, is a time of vulnerability. Of great intensity. Now. I would give a lot to have two hours, an hour even, alone with her."

Piri had been following the talk. She was nineteen now, and she'd lost her puppy-fat, although she was still ample. In spite of the tensions of the trial, she was happy. It showed in every look and gesture, in the sparkle of her eyes and the confident curve of her smile, and in the charming way she turned to Ross. They were openly, joyfully, in love, and Piri's warmth was almost tangible. She touched Ross's arm, and turned to Cohen. "Could Dad get through to her, do you think?" she asked with her hands. Ross translated.

Cohen looked at her fondly. She reminded him of a kibbutznik, with the bandana over her head, her ruddy cheeks and her clarity of soul. "I see no reason why he should."

"She's conscious of him. I've watched her all through the trial." Piri's hands flew. Ross translated. "It's as though the whole show were for Dad—I agree with him. I don't think she wants to win; I think she wants him to lose. I think she's forcing him to his knees, so he'll be desperate. So he'll be born again, and they can have some ghastly spiritual marriage in the love of Jesus. He's what it's all about. I think he could reach her."

Cohen pursed his lips. "There was something between you?" he asked Barney.

Barney nodded. "But it went wrong. I thought there was a lot of understanding. I blundered, and she took it wrong. She—fled."

"One tends to think you're lucky," said Ross, but Cohen spoke at the same time: "That makes everything much clearer. I do not wish to say any more about my work with Zoe, but you will understand that she was confused by her past. She feared rejection. Did this misunderstanding take place at the time of her relapse?"

"Yes."

"So she had two—very strong—reasons to retreat from the world."

Piri touched her father's hand. "You have to see her again," she said.

"It's not as though I haven't tried," he answered with his hands. "They've got terrific security. It's like trying to break into a jail."

"I do not know," Cohen said. "It is possible that you could do something. On the other hand, if you are what she is fleeing from, it might just crystallize the whole stance. Besides, I don't see how you can get to her."

"Neither do I." There was an unhappy silence.

Finally Ross said, "We better get going, Piri." They were going into the city for the weekend.

Piri looked at her father. "Shall I stay?" she asked.

"No. Thanks anyway, Piroshka. Go. Enjoy yourselves. It's nice to know that some nice, normal living is going on, somewhere. I'd like to be alone for a while."

Barney was to be sorry he'd said that. He'd stayed in Riverhead for the fishing, but it poured on Saturday. Two long solitary days loomed before him.

He walked around in the rain. Riverhead, an old-fashioned rural center, supplied the farmlands and villages around the eastern end of the county. There wasn't a lot to do. He went back to the motel and sat in his room for a while, watching the rain on the windowpanes. It was claustrophobic. He should have gone back to the city. He got out a little music box that Zoe had given him a year and a half ago, when she was recuperating. It had been her mother's. He wound it up, and listened while the silvery notes spilled out in the empty room. It played "Rock of Ages," *Cleft for me, let me hide myself in thee.* Hide. Zoe trying to hide. Barney's body recoiled. Zoe, young and quicksilver, alone with her father. Abner's pale blue eyes and coarse eyelashes, his thick neck. Where could she hide? Behind her little brother? Under her

bed? Abner's footfalls, heavy and inevitable, his voice calling drunkenly, "Zoe, *where are you? Come to Daddy.*" Then the beating. With what? His fists? A cane? In the kitchen. Compulsively, Barney visualized the scene: a table, a stove, an overhead light. Zoe trying to escape, to hide. And then—it didn't bear thinking about. No place to hide. *La belle indifférence. La belle endormie*: Sleeping Beauty. Barney found the brass knob on the base of the music box and pushed it to *off*. He stared at the rain.

Several martinis later it was still pouring, the wetness flowing at him in windy gusts. Walking, walking. The bank, with its huge clock printing out the time and the temperature. The smoke shop, exotica, T-shirts, enameled boxes, splendid water pipes, and inlaid roach clips. A strobe light. The optometrist, empty frames hanging out there in the weather. Bleak eyes, blank eyes: *let me hide*. The railroad tracks and Polish town. Pulaski, Dzenkowski, Kowalski—square little houses side by side, corner groceries. Rain running down inside his collar. The county road, the hospital, Dunkin' Donuts, Harrow Swimming Pools, a great black parking lot seamed with ruts and random curbings, a landscape in itself. Lake country, dirty rivulets, and a car parked here and there, or in lonesome clumps, rain running down and off and carrying the filth of many highways into the floods. OTB, the Parlor. A gray pocket dank with nicotine. The sign on the wall: COMPULSIVE GAMBLERS CALL 516-398-5210 FOR HELP. My dear, my dearest girl. *Let me hide*. The nearest bar. "Very dry, please. With an onion."

Piri came back early on Sunday afternoon, uneasy and compelled. She walked from the station. How could she have left her father here, alone, on this sus-

penseful weekend? She walked faster. The day was fine. A gusty wind blew old papers around the streets, and the gutters ran with yesterday's waters. She strode around the traffic circle, her hands in her pockets and her scarf fluttering behind her, past Howard Johnson's and into the motel. Her father's door was unlocked. The curtains were drawn; the room was dark; her father sat blankly in the only chair, his face reflecting the electronics of the tube. He was bleary, pale, unshaven. With an effort, he withdrew his gaze from the TV and looked at Piri without comment. She walked over and, sliding on to the arm of the chair, she drew him forward with both arms. She rested her head on his and rocked him gently. He was defenseless—her father—his piercing blue eyes, his good-natured laugh, his deliberate sweetness. She embraced him; she let her strength flow into him. She didn't move. Gradually she was aware that he was taking shape again, warming, filling out, *firming*, while the tube flickered and the darkness thickened in the corners of the room.

He took a deep breath and got up. He turned off the TV and disappeared into the bathroom. Piri opened the curtains. She made the bed. She picked up his socks. The music box was sitting on the bedside table. She picked it up and let it play a couple of bars, smiling at the sound she couldn't hear and watching the small drum, stippled with golden teeth, turn in its casing. When Barney came out he had shaved and washed and put on his jacket. He smiled at her—better now—and without anything having to be said, they left the room.

Howard Johnson's, that great emporium, had excellent coffee. The waitress put a thermos pot on their table and bustled off. Dishes clattered. A child's voice, from the booth behind them, piped, "Anything I

want, Oompah?" Barney smiled. *Thank you,* he said
with his hands.

Piri watched him make his way through a large
platter of scrambled eggs and sausage while she put
her thoughts together. Her father had a lot of that
curious masculine kindness, half ego and all heart,
that made butterflies fly again and little children
swell with pride. He was a mender of things. She felt
herself to be very young in the face of his unhappi-
ness. It was effrontery to think that she might offer
anything useful in the complexity of legal and medical and human relationships that presented itself at
this moment, and that, like some vaporous Northern
bog, now claimed her father.

But her hands began to move, almost without volition, and she found herself saying whatever it was
that she had not been able to clarify beforehand, in
her own mind.

"You'll have to find some way to see her," she began. "Cohen is not the one who can reach her; you
are. You did it for me. She feels like a cripple. You
can't quite know what that's like. It feels like being
scarred, disfigured—awkward and misformed and unfit
among other people. It's as though one had to hide
all the time. That's how she is; I can feel it. As
though she were dirty." She drew one hand across her
face. "Smeared. If she is crippled now, it's only that
she's made that the visible sign of how she feels inside. You remember when I wouldn't say anything for
a year? I was hiding. You pulled me out. You made
me feel I could do anything. You showed me things.
We walked. Sun. Wind. Anthills. That cedar tree, do
you remember it? Blotch, you called it. *Let's walk by
the blotch today.* Fishing. The neat way things work
in the world, how to weight the line, and knot the
leader. Eating apples. MacIntosh, McKoun, Russets,

Granny Smiths—Empire. You remember those Empire apples? They were the best."

Barney wiped his mouth and poured himself another coffee. "I like McKouns," he said.

"You don't know what that year was for me. Everything blank, withheld—threatening—became approachable. It began to be unimportant whether I could talk or not. I ceased to be a cripple. You have the magic touch. Go. Get in there, somehow. Talk to her. The house isn't made of stone, is it?"

"No." Barney's smile was weak. It was a hangover smile. "How is it that I can talk to you, who can't talk, and I can't talk to her, who can?"

"Nothing is this way or that, but thinking makes it so. You must have quoted that at me a hundred times." She grinned childishly, her eyes full of tears. "Let's get out of here."

It was eight o'clock. Barney paced mindlessly up and down the room. He was wearing two sweaters under his dark blue sweatsuit. He put on sneakers. Silence crowded the room as the brain does the skull. He seemed to be inside it, as in some organic mechanism, without volition. He looked at his watch. Looked around the room. Neat to a fault. He put a pack of cigarettes in his pocket, some matches, and stuffed his gloves in on top. Then he went out. He'd borrowed Ross's car. He'd sold his own.

It was about forty-five minutes to Easthampton. There was the tiniest moon. The night smelled fresh and dank, permeated with the raw chill of April. He parked on Lily Pond Lane. He took a flashlight out of the glove compartment, but he didn't use it. He felt his way quietly up the dark driveway, past his former cottage and the tennis court, avoiding the puddles where he could. The garage was open.

Bumper chrome gleamed from the old Packard. He hesitated. He didn't know what he was going to do. It was, as Zoe would say, in God's hands. But he would see her. He knew it as he knew that the ground was under his feet, or that the temperature was 47.3 degrees on an April night in the Western Hemisphere. It was cold fact.

There would be a ladder in the garage. But whatever it was that directed his movements caused him to pass up the garage. He continued up the drive and across the lawn and past the house. The Atlantic glimmered in the faint light. The broad sweep of glass doors that fronted on the beach were lit, a luminous bar intersected by uprights.

He'd been here before, in what seemed to him now like a childish move to storm the citadel. Then it had been reckless, hopeful. Now there was no question of hope; there was only necessity. He walked up onto the deck and stood there, bathed in light from the living room. He didn't care. He was immune. He'd bottomed out; nothing could touch him. Certainly not Zoe's incredible God.

Zoe was not in the living room. Culpepper was there. Max Ward. Abner. They were shouting at each other. Behind them, sitting in the hallway, Barney made out the dim figure of a uniformed man. Was that all of them? Ngiep must be somewhere. The kitchen was on the other side of the house, facing inland, under Zoe's room. That ruled out the ladder. Barney moved out of the light and sat on the railing to watch. Abner was on the defensive, appealing to some remote figure of justice. It was a dumb show, but so clear that Barney could almost hear the words: . . . *As God's my witness.* Ngiep came in with a tray. He put it down, and addressed a question to Culpepper. Culpepper shook his head. Ngiep with-

drew, not to the kitchen, but to his room on the other side of the hall. Good. He would draw his blinds. The time, like a piece of huge hanging fruit, was ripe. Ripe. And soon would fall from the branch and be gone.

Barney slid off the railing and padded back to the garage. He skirted the Packard and, moving into the large empty space beside it, he switched on his flashlight. The place had been a carriage house once, and there were still some remnants of the posts and plaster and wrought iron that once had formed the stalls. There was a long workbench at the far end, saws and tools and a vise, cans of paint, some cartons. The stalls to the side were empty. Where was the ladder? He shone his flashlight around the walls. Old studs and weathered sheathing, hooks with shovels hanging, water skis, rakes leaning against the wall, a lawnmower, an old coat, a barrel, some posts. No ladder. He knew they had one; he'd seen it leaning up against the house. In the cellar?

He turned out the flashlight and went back across the lawn. There was a light in Zoe's windows. So close. If he reached up—no, it was miles away. Around to the side. He lifted the old-fashioned slanting cellar door and went down the steps into the musty darkness. His flashlight picked out the ladder straight off, an easy-to-handle aluminum affair, about ten feet high. It would do. He carried it out, careful not to bang or rattle it, and took it round to the front of the house. It reached to the overhang of the porch. Setting it firmly in the damp earth, Barney had barely started to climb when the front door opened over to his right, and he froze.

Abner appeared in the square of light and Max behind him, holding the door. Abner was shouting, ". . . The last you'll see of me. Bunch of shitass

old women." The door banged shut and Barney couldn't see him in the darkness, but Abner was muttering curses. Heavy feet descended the porch steps, crunched on the gravel. Then silence, but apparently Abner was standing on the grass, because his voice came out of the silence, furious and quiet and precise. "Motherfuckers," he said, and then he made off across the lawn.

Barney followed. He wanted to see him off the grounds, but near the garage the noises stopped. Barney went softly closer. There was a fumbling ahead of him, and then the sibilant murmur of water on metal. "Piss on you," Abner said in the same furious voice, and he kicked the bumper of the old Packard. "Fags." He zipped himself up and there was the flare of a match shining off the chrome and lighting Abner's heavy jaw. He made a couple of passes at the cigarette in his mouth, and finally struck a second match and got it lit.

Then Abner walked into the empty part of the garage, lighting matches and looking around, talking to himself. He stumbled into a box, swore, lit another match, and then he began to laugh. It was a carton of painting gear, rags and scrapers and brushes standing in a tin of turpentine. He kicked it against the wall. Barney could smell the turpentine. The brushes splayed out in a puddle of turpentine and rags. Abner lit another match and, holding it between his thick thumb and his forefinger, he lowered it so that it glimmered on the wetness and the rough wooden sheathing of the wall. Then, with a finicky deliberate gesture, he dropped it. It eclipsed, but then a small blue flame leapt up. It shot across the puddle and ran over the box and at once the whole thing was a bonfire and Abner was roaring with laughter and stumbling toward the open door.

Barney pulled back as Abner, silhouetted by the blaze, emerged from the garage and stopped, looking across the lawn at the house. He giggled. "Time to skedaddle, Abner honey," he said to himself, and he turned down the driveway. This time he kept going.

Barney ran to the house to call the fire department. He went up the steps of the porch and stopped. He looked back toward the garage. Nothing yet. He hesitated. The fire was nothing. Culpepper's garage didn't interest him. He was here to find out the truth, and that's what he would do. He went back down the steps and went around the house to the deck, where he hiked himself up on the railing and composed himself to wait. Culpepper and Max were still talking. Culpepper asked a question. Max spread his hands disgustedly. Then he took Culpepper's glass and fixed him another drink. The wind freshened. Barney could feel it between his shoulder blades. It gusted past him and rattled the windows, raised sand from the dunes beyond the deck. The dune grass whistled. Indoors, the phone rang. Culpepper finished his sentence with a gesture of his hand, as though in a flourish of lace, and picked up the phone with his other hand. He spoke. He did a double take. His enormous eyes stared and his wide thin mouth opened. He hung up, spoke briefly to Max, looked up a number and dialed it. He spoke again, hung up, and shouted. The security guard had joined them, and Ngiep ran in, wearing a bathrobe. There was a moment of confusion and talk and then Culpepper ran, in his fat childish way, to open the front door on the far side of the hall. Barney caught a glimpse of rosy air, and sparks, and then the door closed. The living room was empty.

Barney ran to the sliding doors and pushed one open, closing it behind him. He crossed the room to

the hallway, bounded up the stairs, and found himself—his blood humming—in front of Zoe's door.
Without a thought he opened it and suddenly he was
inside, with his back to the door, still holding on to
the knob by which he had closed it, and looking
down at Zoe, who sat peacefully by her fireplace with
a Bible in her lap. She was facing him. Her eyes
blazed for a moment and then were eclipsed, half-
lidded, by the somnolent chastity that was now her
usual expression. Behind her a row of long casement
windows gave on to the night sky, now orange with
fire and blooming with sulphurous clouds of smoke.
The windows were closed.

Well, here I am, he thought. It had taken him
more than eighteen months to arrange this interview.
The door was solid behind him and he leaned against
it, searching the guarded face in front of him for a
sign, a clue, some fault in its smooth facade. Nothing
was evident; she was tranquil, amiable, seemingly
quiescent, but distant as the peaks of Everest. He
stayed where he was, his gaze traveling down the
creamy satin of her dressing gown to the swell of her
hips and the long line of her thighs, one visibly smaller than the other. Then back to the shuttered eyes.

What could he offer her that she didn't already
have? Food and shelter? Culpepper took care of that.
Sex? Sublimated already, in the divine orgasms of the
Fellowship. Love? What kind of love could he offer,
after the beating he had taken at her hands, after his
many dismissals, after the disturbing emergence of the
real Zoe, demanding and terrified and obstinate as a
mule in clover? What was his poor love, next to the
all-giving love of her personal Daddy-Jesus? She
touched her dressing gown lightly, drawing it more
securely over her breasts. He had nothing to offer her

but life—raw, exacting, and uncontrollable life. Awesome to her, and threatening.

He heard sirens in the distance. He didn't have too much time, and he was no Prince Charming to awaken with a single kiss the lovely lady asleep in the center of the forest, surrounded by thickets of briar thorns. He was only a man. He didn't have any kingdoms, only life. But he loved her; he knew that now, and he knew that it filled the air between them, warm and tangible, and that she was aware of it, and that the stiffened posture, the even more resistless look that he now saw in her face, were signs of her awareness. Half of her swam to meet him; the other half drowned itself still deeper in her own blurred and intricate consciousness.

The sirens were closer now, screaming up the lane. Headlights brightened the windows and turned away, and an intermittent reddish light began to flash outside. A bell was clanging. The fire was burning higher now. Barney could see it through the window. Culpepper's studio, above the garage, must have gone up.

Zoe was white, unchanged. "Don't you wonder what's going on?" asked Barney.

"What is it?"

"The garage is on fire."

"Oh. Oh, Willie's study?"

"Yes."

He felt with his hands the molding on the door. It was solid ground, but he left it, and walked across the room to Zoe. He leaned down and took the Bible out of her lap. He put it on the table beside her and took her limp hands in his. They seemed small.

"I have strength enough for both of us, Zoe. There's a whole world out there, fire and water and earth and sky. Come out of your hiding place. Get

out of that wheelchair, out of this house, out of that
excruciating courtroom where you are being pillo-
ried. We could be walking—you could be walking—
running, flying, charging down city streets, making
love." He laughed. "Make love—not war, that's what
the kids say. Your lawsuit is war. We could live, instead. We could be free, instead of locked in an
endless battle of wills. You can do it. Your life isn't
over. You're not a cripple. You don't need what you
get from your Christian family. You don't even need
the fairy-tale Jesus you've created. It's so simple. It's
all there inside of you. You are unbelievably strong.
You don't even need to be a good girl, because you
are a good girl. I know you."

She kept her eyes on his, but they didn't reveal
much, only the golden brown flecks that danced on
the surface. The palest color washed over her face.
"You're not deformed," he went on. "You're not a
child. You're beautiful, inside and out. What kind of
apples do you like best? Courtland? Winesap? Deli-
cious?"

Zoe laughed.

"That's it. Movies. What do you like? You want to
forget the dishes and go to the movies? Take a bike
ride? Go to bed?" There was a real glow in her eyes,
deeper now. "Come on, love," he rested one hand on
her thigh. "Let's see you move this leg."

The fire had really caught hold. The wind, blowing
from the west, fanned the flames against the back
wall of the carriage house, and they had spread out to
both sides and upwards. The place was a firetrap,
huge, drafty, gabled and shingled. The wood had
been drying out for a hundred years, and when the
flames had reached the floor of the apartment above
they had exploded into the windy spaces there. Fire-

men pushed the crowd back, and diverted those who were still walking up the lane. The newcomers huddled by the tennis court watching as the fire ballooned out through the gables of the roof, lit by the pivoting red light on the roof of the Chief's car.

The double doors were still closed on the empty side, downstairs, keeping the wind out. The fire was more vigorous upstairs than down. Culpepper stood transfixed, his short arms hanging helplessly. "My play," he moaned. "My play." Ngiep put his arms around him. Max and a neighbor were helping a fireman to roll the old Packard out before it caught, or exploded from the heat. Once they had it clear, some neighbors pushed it around the driveway, chromium gleaming and the ball fringe bobbing heavily in the wind. Someone must have left the windows open. They parked it in front of the house at a safe distance from the fire.

Zoe froze. Too soon, damn it. This mustn't be a struggle between his will and hers, it should be a seduction—an imaginative portrait of life that she would be unable to resist. Barney removed his hand from her leg.

"I'm in trouble too, you know. You can help me. Not with that—" he put his hand on the Bible. "Only with your whole self. You can help me live; you can free me to work. You know that I can't practice anymore?"

She was praying. Damn it, she was praying. How vicious, he thought, that he should be standing here, talking his heart out, reaching, reaching, and she was praying. Patience, he said to himself, but the sky was streaming with red, like the soul's blood, and jets of water streaked across it. How long did he have? What was she made of—iron? He seemed to see the red of

the sky behind his eyeballs. He rushed to the door
and turned the key in the lock, and just the action,
somehow, released his rage. "Damn you, Zoe. Walk,"
he said. He pulled her upright, hands under her arm-
pits, and she swayed. Her whole weight was on his
arms. "Walk!" He took a step backward. She fell
toward him, dragging her paralyzed limb. "Walk!"
His eyes bored into hers, and he took another step.
She let her weight carry her forward. He was inarticu-
late. He was doing everything he'd promised himself
not to do. He picked her up and put her back in the
chair and turned to the window, clapping his hands
in frustration. How? What now? He paced. The fire
was lower now. The water had soaked the wood.
There was more smoke, clouds of it, rising torpidly
above the blackened roof and the small flames, reflecting the fire in thick vaporous puffs.

The Packard, stately and cumbersome, rested in
front of the porch steps. Inside, on the embossed
plush of the upholstered seats, a few sparks had
caught and were smoldering. The horsehair padding
caught and burned, stifled for a time beneath the
heavy upholstery. Then it ignited. The seats blazed
up, and the fire leapt to the ball fringe. The ancient
curtains caught, and the whole plush interior of the
automobile went up, flames blasting out the windows.
A fireman was moving the crowd from the driveway;
another turned his hose on the Packard, concentrating on the back windows where the fire was nearest
the gas tank.

"It's almost out now," Barney said. The Packard
was hidden from him by the steep gabled roof of the
front porch. "Abner lit it, you know. Your father. I
let him." She raised her eyes, and something happened in there, a response, an event, deep down in

the green pools. "It's almost out. This is my last effort."

He spread his arms. The sky behind him was still filled with orange smoke and dying sparks. "I wanted to spring you from your own trap," he said. There were tears in his eyes and running down his face.

Zoe's mouth trembled, and she pushed her wheel-chair forward. There was a sudden tremendous explosive impact. The windows blew in, and the glass shattered and spun in a million brilliant fragments. Barney was blasted forward, as though he'd received a staggering blow in the back, and then he fell on his side on the floor in the middle of the debris. A piece of glass two inches long stuck out of his neck and blood welled out around it. Zoe stared at him. His eyes opened, a deep blue, and the color seemed to penetrate the furthest parts of her being, piercing tissue and bone, labyrinths and caverns, shedding its cold light on ancient facts and artifacts, drenching the whole interior seascape in a limitless truthful blue.

What had she done? What was she doing, immobilized here in canvas and steel, while his blood poured out? She grasped the arms of her chair and pushed herself forward, planting her feet on the floor. The chair skidded out behind her and she wobbled, caught her balance, and in five wild uneven steps she covered the space between them before she fell. He smiled at her. She covered her hand with the hem of her dressing gown, grasped the shaft of glass and pulled. It came out cleanly. She pressed her fingers firmly on the wound.

"Press below it," Barney said. The blood began to subside. "I love you," he said. "I knew you could do it."

She met his eyes like a newborn babe, and without

any reserve or self-consciousness, without any clever inflections, with no paltering or gestures or movements of the face, with no fear, with deep feeling, with pride, with dignity, with honesty, she said, "I love you too."

The unforgettable saga of a
magnificent family

IN JOY AND IN SORROW

by

JOAN JOSEPH

They were the wealthiest Jewish family in Portugal, masters of
Europe's largest shipping empire. Forced to flee the scourge of
the Inquisition that reduced their proud heritage to ashes, they
crossed the ocean in a perilous voyage. Led by a courageous,
beautiful woman, they would defy fate to seize a forbidden
dream of love.

A Dell Book   **$3.50**   **(14367-5)**

At your local bookstore or use this handy coupon for ordering:

 DELL BOOKS   IN JOY AND IN SORROW $3.50   (14367-5)
P.O. BOX 1000, PINE BROOK, N.J. 07058-1000

Please send me the books I have checked above. I am enclosing $ _____ (please add 75c per copy to
cover postage and handling). Send check or money order—no cash or C.O.D.'s. Please allow up to 8 weeks for
shipment.

Mr./Mrs./Miss _____

Address _____

City _____ State/Zip _____

The controversial novel of the world's most fearsome secret!

GENESIS

by W.A. Harbinson

First came the sightings, sighted by nine million Americans. Then came the encounters. Then came the discovery of an awesome plot dedicated to dominate and change the world.

An explosive combination of indisputable fact woven into spellbinding fiction, *Genesis* will change the way you look at the world—and the universe—forever.

A Dell Book $3.50   (12832-3)